"You're emba
the attraction
after watching

He sounded amu
with self-consciousness. Could her ~~~~~~ ~~~~~ ~~~~~
hotter?

"This releasing of compromising photos is very shrewd," he said in an abrupt shift.

His tone suggested it was an item of political news, not a gross defilement of her personal self. His finger rested across his lips in contemplation.

"Jensen has very cleverly made himself appear a victim," he said. "Whatever story he comes up with, it will point all the scandal back to you and the bank."

"I'm aware that my life is over, thanks," she bit out.

"Nothing is over," he said with a cold-blooded smile. "Jensen has landed a punch, but I will hit back. Hard. You must want to set things straight? If so, you'll help me make it clear you have zero romantic interest in Jensen."

"*How?*" she choked, wondering what was in his drink that he thought he could accomplish that.

"By going public with our *own* affair."

Canadian **Dani Collins** knew in high school that she wanted to write romance for a living. Twenty-five years later, after marrying her high school sweetheart, having two kids with him, working several generic office jobs and submitting countless manuscripts, she got 'The Call'. Her first Modern Romance novel won the Reviewers' Choice Award for Best First in Series from *RT Book Reviews*. She now works in her own office, writing romance.

Books by Dani Collins

Mills & Boon Modern Romance

Vows of Revenge
Seduced into the Greek's World
The Russian's Acquisition
An Heir to Bind Them
A Debt Paid in Passion
More than a Convenient Marriage?
No Longer Forbidden?

The Wrong Heirs

The Marriage He Must Keep
The Consequence He Must Claim

Seven Sexy Sins

The Sheikh's Sinful Seduction

The 21st Century Gentleman's Club

The Ultimate Seduction

One Night With Consequences

Proof of Their Sin

Visit the Author Profile page at
millsandboon.co.uk for more titles.

BOUGHT BY HER ITALIAN BOSS

BY

DANI COLLINS

First Published in Great Britain 2016
By Mills & Boon, an imprint of HarperCollins*Publishers*
1 London Bridge Street, London, SE1 9GF

ISBN: 978-0-263-92122-9

Our policy is to use papers that are natural, renewable and recyclable products and made from wood grown in sustainable forests. The logging and manufacturing processes conform to the legal environmental regulations of the country of origin.

Printed and bound in Spain
by CPI, Barcelona

BOUGHT BY HER ITALIAN BOSS

For my editor, Kathryn,
because she 'loved, loved, loved' it.

CHAPTER ONE

GWYN ELLIS LOOKED from the screen to Nadine Billaud, the public relations manager for Donatelli International, then back to the screen.

"This is you, *oui*?" Nadine prodded.

Gwyn couldn't speak. Her heart had begun slamming inside her rib cage the moment she had recognized herself. Cold sweat coated her skin. Air wouldn't squeeze past her locked throat, let alone words.

That *was* her. *Naked.* Right there on that computer, the line of her bare bottom clear as the crack of dawn, neatly framed by her hot pink thong. Everyone had a backside that looked more or less like that, but she was extremely selective about showing hers to *anyone*. She certainly didn't email shots like this to men she barely knew. Or post them online.

Her whole body felt like a frozen electrical current was vibrating through her, paralyzing her.

The photo changed and that bare torso with the sheet rumpled across her upper thighs was all her, too. The way her breasts lifted as she arched her back and ran fingers through her hair bordered on deliberately erotic, coupled with that blissful, upturned expression. She looked like she'd been making love all day—as if she even knew what that felt like!

Then the final one came up again. She was adjusting the band of her hot pink undies across her cocked hip, looking like she was teasingly deciding whether to keep them on or remove them, eyes still lazily drooped and soft satisfaction painted across her lips.

The lighting was golden and her skin faintly gleamed—with oil, she realized as her brain began to function past the shock. These had been taken at the spa where she'd had a massage, trying to fix the ache between her shoulder blades that had been torturing her for weeks. She was sitting up and dressing after her appointment, relaxed and comfortable in what she had perceived as complete privacy.

The massage table had been cropped from the images, leaving muted sage-green walls and indistinct, blurred flowers in the background. It could have been a hotel room, a bedroom—whatever the viewer wanted to imagine.

Her stomach roiled. She thought she might be hyperventilating because she could hear a distant hiss. She wanted to throw up, pass out, *die. Please God, take me now.*

"Mademoiselle?" Nadine badgered.

"Yes," she stammered. "It's me." Then, as the sheer mortification of the whole thing struck, she added a strident, *"Can you close that, please?"*

She glanced at Signor Fabrizio, her supervisor. He sat next to her with a supercilious expression on his middle-aged face.

"Why are you showing those like that? With him

in here?" Gwyn asked. "Couldn't we have done this privately?"

"They're available to anyone with an online connection. I've seen them," Fabrizio said pithily. "I brought them to Nadine's attention."

He'd already taken a long look? *Gross.*

Tears hit her eyes like the cut of a hard, biting wind. An equally brutal blow seemed to land in her stomach, pushing nausea higher into the back of her throat.

"Surely you knew this could happen when you took those photos and sent them to Mr. Jensen?" Nadine said.

Nadine had kept her snooty nose high in the air from the moment Gwyn had followed Fabrizio into her office. Fabrizio kept giving her darkly smug looks, like he was staring right through her perfectly respectable blue pencil skirt and matching jacket.

He made her skin crawl.

And worry for her job. Her palms were sweating.

"I didn't take those photos," she said as strongly as her tight throat would allow. "And you think I would send something like that to a client? They're—oh, for the love of God." She heard the door opening behind her and shot to her feet, reaching to push the lid of Nadine's laptop down herself, wishing the images could be quashed that easily.

Deep in the back of her psyche, she knew she was going to cry. Soon. Pressure was building behind her collarbone, compressing her lungs, pushing behind her eyes. But for the moment she was in a type of shock. Like she'd been shot and still had the strength to run before the true depth of her injuries debilitated her.

"Signor Donatelli." Nadine rose. "Thank you for coming."

"You notified him?" Signor Fabrizio jerked to his feet, sounding dismayed.

Whatever remained of Gwyn's composure went into free fall. The *owner* of the bank was here? She tried to gather herself to face yet another denigrating expression.

"It's protocol with something this dangerous to the bank's reputation," Nadine said stiffly, adding to the weight on Gwyn's heart.

"She's being dismissed," Fabrizio hurried to assure Signor Donatelli. "I was about to tell her to collect her things."

Time stopped as Gwyn processed that she was being fired. Stupid her, she had thought she was being called in to talk about a client's possible misappropriation of funds, not to be disgraced in front of the entire world.

Literally the entire world. This was what online bullying felt like. This was persecution. A witch hunt. Stoning. She couldn't take in how monumentally unjust this was.

The only experience she could liken it to was when her mother had been diagnosed. Words were being said, facts stated that couldn't be denied, but she had no real grasp of how the next minute or week or the rest of her life would play out from this moment forward.

She didn't want to face it, but she had no choice.

And the silence around her told her they were all waiting for her to do so.

Very slowly, she turned to the man who'd just entered, but it wasn't Paolo Donatelli, president and head of the family that owned Donatelli International. No, it was far worse.

Vittorio Donatelli. Paolo's cousin, second-in-command as VP of operations. A man of, arguably, even more stunningly good looks, at least in her estimation. His features were as refined and handsome as his Italian heritage demanded. He was clean-shaven, excruciatingly well dressed in a tailored suit and wore an air of arrogance that came as much from his lean height as his aloof expression. His ability to dominate any situation was obvious in the way they all stood in silence, waiting for him to speak.

He didn't know her from Adam, she knew that. She'd smiled brightly at him not long after arriving here in Milan, forgetting that secret crushes didn't know they were the object of such yearnings. He'd looked right through her and it had stung. Quite badly, illogically.

"Nadine. Oscar," Vittorio said with a brief flick of his gaze to the other occupants of the room before coming back to give Gwyn a piercing stare from his bronze eyes.

Her heart gave a skip between pounds, reacting to him even when she was verging on hysteria. Her mouth was so dry she couldn't make it stretch into a smile. She doubted she would ever smile again. The strange buzz inside her intensified.

"Miss Ellis," he said with a hostile nod of acknowledgment.

He knew her name from Nadine's report, she supposed. The furious accusation in his eyes told her he'd seen the photos. Of course he'd seen them. That's why he had stooped from the lofty heights of the top floor to the midlevel of the Donatelli Tower.

Gwyn's shallow breaths halted and her knees quivered. She was weirdly shocked by how defenseless the idea of his seeing her naked made her feel, but the ef-

fect this very perfect stranger had had on her from the
start was unprecedented. She'd seen him stride through
the offices in Charleston once and that simple glimpse
of an incredibly handsome and dynamic man had made
her view the postings at the head office in Milan that
much more favorably than any other branch in the organization. She had wanted to advance, would have taken
whatever promotions she could land, but this was her
dream location.

Because it gave her the chance to see him.

Be careful what you wish for. She mashed her lips together into a hard, steady line, heart scored, then turned
her face away, trying to recover.

He was, quite obviously, nothing like the man she'd
constructed in her mind. Italian men were warm and
gregarious and adored women, she had thought, expecting he'd flirt with her if they ever actually spoke. She
had expected him to give her a chance to intrigue him,
despite the fact that she worked for him.

But the man she had been obsessing over had not
only glimpsed her naked, he was completely unmoved
by what he'd seen. He was repelled. Blamed her. Was
privately calling her a whore and worse—

She stopped herself from spiraling. The pieces of
her shattered world were being kicked around enough.
She had to keep a grip.

But she wasn't used to being rejected out of hand,
seeing no interest whatsoever from a man. The reaction
was usually the opposite. Her body had always pulled a
certain amount of male attention. She didn't encourage
it and was pretty boring personality-wise. She worked
in *banking*, for heaven's sake. Her hair was the most
common brown you could find and she wasn't terribly

pretty. Her face was only elevated from plain to pleasant by her mother's exceptionally good skin and a cheery nature that usually kept a smile on her mouth. So she shouldn't be that surprised when a man who could have his pick of women showed no interest in her.

It made her ache all the same.

Think, she ordered herself, but it was hard when she was stuck in this swamp of feeling so thoroughly scorned by a man who enthralled her.

"I want a lawyer," she managed to say.

"Why would you need one?" Vittorio asked with a wrathful lift of his brows, so godlike.

"This is wrongful dismissal. You're treating me like a criminal when those photos are illegal. They were taken at a spa without my knowledge. They're not selfies, so how could I have sent them to Kevin Jensen? Or anyone? His wife is the one who recommended I go there for my shoulder!"

Vito flicked his gaze to the laptop, mentally reviewing images that would have been very titillating if they were a private communication between lovers. For long seconds as he'd reviewed the photos, he'd been captivated against his will, having to force himself to move past his transfixion with her sensual figure to the fact that this was a hydrogen bomb aimed directly at the bank that was his livelihood and the foundation that supported his entire extended family.

But the photos weren't selfies. That was true. He had thought Jensen must have taken them.

Nadine seemed to think his shift of attention was a prompt for her to bring them up for another look. She started to open her laptop.

"Would you stop showing those to people, you freak?" Gwyn cried.

"Let's keep this professional," Nadine snapped.

"How would you react if you were me?" Gwyn shot back.

Gwyn Ellis was not what he had expected. There was an American wholesomeness to her that neutralized some of the femme fatale that had come across on-screen. He had expected, and received, an impact of female sexuality when he had entered the room. He'd felt the same thing the day she'd smiled at him in the lobby.

She'd already been under suspicion, so he'd pretended not to notice her, but nothing could downplay her allure. That body of hers didn't stop, with her firm, well-rounded breasts that sat high beneath her neatly cut jacket and her waistline that begged for a man's hands to clasp before sliding down to the flare of her hips and her gorgeously plump ass that he dreamed of kneading. Knees were not something he'd normally catalogue, but she had cute ones.

An image of cupping them as he held them apart drifted through his brain.

She was a very potent woman. Her shoulders were stiff, her frame tense and defensive, but her slight stature and smooth curves announced to the animal kingdom that she was undeniably a female of the species, of fertile age and irresistibly ripe.

She called to the male in him, quickening the blood of the beast that he suppressed at all costs.

Visceral reactions like lust were something he indulged in very controlled quantities. This was not the time and, judging by his reaction to her, Gwyn was not the woman. High-octane risk-taking was his cousin's bailiwick. Vito controlled his bloodlust ruthlessly— even though there was a part of him that beat with excitement for the challenge of throwing himself into this perfect storm of chemistry to see if he could survive it.

What they could do to one another...

He turned his mind from speculating, hearing Nadine aim a very pointed barb at Gwyn. "I wouldn't sleep with a married man. This wouldn't happen to me."

"Who said I slept with Kevin Jensen?" Gwyn challenged hotly. "*Who?* I want a name."

So indignant. This was not the reaction of a woman who had posed for a lover, running the risk of exposure. She ought to be furious with Jensen or his wife, perhaps tossing her hair in defiance of judgment over her decision to pose naked for her paramour. Instead, she was a woman on the edge of her control, reacting to a catastrophe with barely contained hysteria.

"His wife said you slept with him. Or want to. Obviously," Oscar Fabrizio interjected, "since she posted these filthy photos when she discovered them on his phone. You've been having lunches and dinners with him."

Vito found that attack interesting. He had brought certain suspicions about their nonprofit accounts manager to Paolo's attention a few weeks ago. The assumption had easily been made that the New Girl was in on the arrangement, facilitating.

"Kevin wanted to do things—have our meetings, I mean," Gwyn quickly clarified, "away from the office." She was visibly distraught, looking to Vito in entreaty. "He's a client. I didn't have a choice but to go to him if that's what he requested."

Vito had to accept that. Excellence of customer service was a cornerstone at Donatelli International. If a client of Jensen's caliber wanted a house call, employees were expected to make them.

"You didn't take those photos?" he pressed her.

"No!"

"So they're not on that phone?" He nodded at where she clutched her device in a death grip.

Gwyn had forgotten she was holding it, but she always grabbed it out of habit when she left her desk, and had switched it to silent as she came into this meeting. Now she stared at it, surprised to see it there. At least she could say with confidence, "No. They're not."

"You'll let me confirm that?" He held out his hand.

On the surface it was a very reasonable request, but, oh, dear Lord, *no*. She had something on here that was beyond embarrassing. It would make this situation so much worse... *So much worse.*

She knew her face was falling into lines of panicked guilt, but couldn't help it.

His nostrils flared and his jaw hardened. The death rays coming out of his eyes told her she'd be lucky to merely lose her job.

"This phone is mine," she stammered, trying not to let him intimidate her. If she hadn't already been violated, she might not have been so vehement, but he was going to have to knock her out cold to pry this thing out of her hand if he wanted access. "I get an allowance to offset my using it for company business, but it's mine. You don't have any right to look at it."

"Can it clear you of suspicion or not?" His gaze delved into her culpable one.

She couldn't hide the turmoil and resentment coursing through her at being put on the spot. "My privacy has been invaded enough."

She was naked. On the internet. She supposed everyone in the building was staring at her image right now. Men saying filthy, suggestive things. Women judging whether her stomach was flat enough, saying she had cellulite, calling her too bony or too tall or too something so they could feel better about their own body issues.

Gwyn wanted to hang her head and sob.

All she could think was how hard she'd worked not to be pushed around by life the way her mother had been. At every stage, she'd tried to be self-reliant, autonomous, control her future.

Breathe, she commanded herself. *Don't think about it.* She would fall apart. She really would.

"I think we have our answer," Fabrizio said pitilessly.

She was starting to hate that man. Gwyn wasn't the type to hate. She did her best to get along with everyone. She was a happy person, always believing that life was too short for drama and conflict. Being the first to apologize made her the bigger person, she had always thought, but she doubted she would ever forgive these people for how they were treating her right now.

A muted buzz sounded and Nadine looked at her own phone. "The press is gathering. We need to make a statement."

The press? Gwyn circled around Fabrizio to the window and looked down.

Nadine's office was midway up the tower, but the crowd at the entrance, and the cameras they held, were like ants pouring out of a disturbed hill. It was as bad as a royal birth down there.

She swallowed, stomach turning again.

Kevin Jensen was an icon, a modern day, international superhero who flew into disaster aftermath to offer "feet on the ground" assistance. Anyone with half a brain saw that he exploited heart-wrenching situations on camera to increase donations and boost his own profile, but the bottom line was he showed up to terrible tragedies and brought aid. He did real, necessary work for the devastated.

But lately Gwyn had been questioning how he spent some of those abundant donations.

Had this been his answer? A massive discrediting that would get her fired?

She hugged herself. This sort of thing didn't happen to real people. Did it?

Her gaze searched below for an escape route. She couldn't even leave the building to get to her rented flat here in Milan. How would she get back to America? Even if she got that far, then what? Look to her stepfather to shelter her? Who was going to hire her with this sort of notoriety? Ever?

She'd be exactly what she'd tried so hard to avoid being: a burden. A leach.

Oh, God...oh, God. The walls were beginning to creak and buckle around her composure. The pressure behind her cheekbones built along with weight on her shoulders and upper arms.

Nadine was talking as she typed, "...say that the bank was unaware of this personal relationship and the employee has been terminated—"

"Our client has stated that the photos were *not* invited," Fabrizio interjected.

Gwyn spun around. "And your employee states that

she's been targeted by a peeping tom and an online porn peddler and a vengeful wife."

Nadine paused only long enough to send her a stern look. "I strongly advise you not to speak to the press."

"I strongly advise you that I will be speaking to a lawyer." It was an empty threat. Her savings were very modest. *Very.* Much as she would love to believe her stepbrother would help her, she couldn't count on it. He had his own corporate image to maintain.

The way Vittorio Donatelli continued to emanate hostility made her want to crawl into a hole and die.

"How long have you been with the company?" Nadine asked.

"Two years in Charleston, four months here," Gwyn said, trying to recall how much room her credit card balance had for plane fare and setting up house back in Charleston. Not enough.

"Two years," Nadine snorted, adding an askance. "How did you earn a promotion like this after only that short a time?" Her gaze skimmed down Gwyn's figure, clearly implying that Gwyn had slept her way into the position. Night school and language classes and putting in overtime counted for nothing, apparently.

Fabrizio didn't defend her, despite signing off on her transfer and giving her a glowing review after her first three months.

Vittorio's expression was an inscrutable mask. Was he thinking the same thing?

A disbelieving sob escaped her and she hugged herself, trying to stay this side of manic.

While Vittorio brought his own phone from his pants pocket and with a sweep and tap connected to someone. "Bruno? Vito. I need you in Nadine Billaud's office. Bring some of your men."

"For my walk of shame?" Gwyn presumed. Here came the tears, welling up like a tsunami with a mile of volume behind it. Her voice cracked. "Don't worry. I plan to leave quickly and quietly. I can't *wait* to not work here anymore."

"You'll stay right here until I tell you to leave." His tone was implacable, making her heart sink in her hollow chest while another part of her rose in defiance, wanting to fight and rail and physically tear at him to get out of here. She was the quintessential wounded animal that needed to bolt from danger to its cave.

To Nadine, he added, "Confirm the photos belong to one of our employees. For privacy and legal reasons we have no other comment. Ask the reporters to disperse and enlist the lobby guards to help. Issue a similar statement to all employees. Add a warning that they risk termination if they speak to the press or are observed viewing the photos on corporate equipment or company grounds. Oscar, I need a full report on how these photos came to your attention."

"Signor Jensen contacted me this morning—"

"Not here." Vittorio moved to the door as a knock sounded. "In your office. Wait here," he said over his shoulder to Gwyn, like she was a dog to be left at home while he went to work. He urged the other two from the room and pulled the door closed behind the three of them.

"Yeah, right," Gwyn rasped into the silence of Nadine's empty office, hugging herself so tightly she was suffocating.

A twisting, writhing pain moved in her like a snake,

coiling around her organs to squeeze her heart and lungs, tightening her stomach and closing her throat. She covered her face, trying to hide from the terrible reality that everyone—everyone in the world—was not only staring at her naked body, but believing that she had had sex with a married man.

She could live with people staring at her body. Almost. They did it, anyway. But she was a good person. She didn't lie or steal or come on to men, especially married ones! She was conservative in the way she lived her life, saving her craziest impulses for things like her career where she did wildly ambitious things like sign up for Mastering Spreadsheets tutorials in hopes of moving up the ladder.

The pressure in her cheekbones and nose and under her eyes became unbearable. She tried to press it back with the flats of her hands, but a moan of anguish was building from the middle of her chest. A sob bounced like a hard pinball, bashing against her inner walls, moving up from her breastbone into her throat.

She couldn't break down, she reminded herself. Not here. Not yet. She had to get out of this place and the sooner the better. It was going to be awful. A nightmare, but she would do it, head high and under her own steam.

Gritting her teeth, she reached for the door and started to open it.

A burly man wearing a suit and a short, neat haircut was standing with his back to the door. Guarding her? He grabbed the doorknob, keeping her from pulling it open. His body angled enough she could see he also wore some kind of clear plastic earpiece. His glance at her was both indifferent and implacable.

"Attendere qui, per favore." Wait here, please.

She was so shocked, she let him pull the door from her lax grip and close her into Nadine's office again.

Actually, it slipped freely from her clammy hand. The room began to feel very claustrophobic. She moved to the window again, seeing the crowd of reporters had grown. She couldn't tell if Nadine was addressing them. She could hardly see. Her vision was blurring. She sniffed, feeling the weight of all that had happened so deeply she had to move to the nearest chair and sink into it.

Her breath hitched and no amount of pressure from her hands would push back the burn behind her eyes.

The door opened again, startling her heart into lurching and her head into jerking up.

He was back.

CHAPTER TWO

GWYN ELLIS LOOKED like hell had moved in where her soul used to be, eyes pits of despair, mouth soft and bracketed by lines of disillusion. Her brow was a crooked line of suffering, but she immediately sat taller, blinking and visibly fighting back her tears to face him without cowering.

"I want to leave," she asserted.

The rasp in her voice scraped at his nerves while he studied her. Vixens knew how to use their sexuality on a man. If she was a victim, he would expect her to appeal to the protector in him. Either way, he wouldn't expect her to be so confrontational.

Gwyn was a fighter. He didn't want to find that dig-deep-and-stay-strong streak in her admirable. It softened him when he was in crisis control mode, trying to remember that she had, quite possibly, colluded to bilk the bank and a completely legitimate nonprofit organization of millions of euros in donations.

"We have more to talk about," he told her. He had made the executive decision to question her himself, like this, privately. And he wasn't prepared to ask himself why.

"An exit interview? I have two short words," she said tightly.

That open hostility was noteworthy. Oscar Fabrizio had been full of placating statements until Paolo had been patched through on speakerphone. Then Oscar had seemed to realize he was under suspicion. He'd asked for a lawyer. Sweat had broken across his brow and upper lip when Vito had ordered his computer and phone to be analyzed. Both were company issued and it had been obvious Oscar was dying to contact someone—Kevin Jensen perhaps? A plainclothes investigator was on the way. A full criminal inquiry was being launched down the hall.

While here… Vito was sure she was an accomplice, except…

"You say you had no knowledge of those photos," he challenged.

"No. I didn't." Her chin came up and her lashes screened her eyes, but there was no hiding the quiver of her mouth. She was deeply upset about their being made public. That was not up for dispute. "They were taken after a massage. I didn't know there was a camera in the room."

The images were imprinted on his brain. The photos would have made a splash without Jensen's name attached, he thought distantly. She was built like Venus.

But he saw how they could have been taken during a private moment and manipulated to appear like shots between lovers. He had made certain presumptions on sight: that she was not only having an affair with a client, but was engaged in criminal activity with him. If Jensen was prepared to steal from charity donations, would it be such a stretch to photograph a banking underling in an attempt to cover it up?

Powerful men exploited young, vulnerable women. He knew that. It was quite literally in his DNA.

"Are you picturing me naked?" she challenged bitterly, but her chin crinkled and she fought for her composure a moment, then bravely firmed her mouth and controlled her expression, meeting his gaze with loathing shadowing the depths of her brown eyes.

Such a contrary woman with her wounded expression and quiet, forest-creature coloring of dark eyes and hair, then that devastatingly powerful figure of generous curves and lissome limbs.

"Wondering if you are having an affair with Jensen," he replied.

"I'm not!" There was a catch in her voice before her tone strengthened. "And I wasn't trying to start one, either. I barely know him." She crossed her arms. "I actually think he's been skimming funds from his foundation for himself."

"He is." He steadily returned the shocked brown stare she flashed at him. Her irises had a near-black rim around the dark chocolate brown, he noted, liking the directness it added to her subtly tough demeanor.

Her pupils expanded with surprise, further intriguing him.

"You know that for a fact?" Her brows were like distant bird wings against the sky, long and elegant with a perfect little crook above her eyes. She was truly beautiful.

He wanted her. Badly.

He ignored the need pulling at him, stating, "We also know someone in the bank is colluding with him. We've been conducting an extremely delicate investigation that blew up today, thanks to your photos."

Vito was angry with himself. He was a numbers man, calculating all the odds, all the possible moves an opponent might try, but he hadn't seen this one coming.

"I'm not colluding with anyone!" Her expression was earnest and very convincing. But he was a mistrustful man at heart, too aware of the secrets and lies he lived under himself to take for granted that other people weren't self-protecting or withholding certain facts to better their own position.

"And yet you won't let me look at your phone," he said pointedly.

Her jaw set and she turned the device over in her hands. With a shaky little sigh that smacked of defeat, she tapped in her access code, surprising him with her sudden willingness.

"Look at my emails," she urged. "You'll see I was counseling him that certain requests could be interpreted as shady." She offered him the phone.

Gwyn didn't know much about climbing out of a hole, but she knew you had to bounce off rock bottom, so she went there. At least this humiliation was her choice and only between the two of them, now that the room was empty. At least she was getting a chance to speak her side. Maybe he'd see that she didn't have anything to hide except a stupid attraction. Hopefully he'd read between the lines and also see that she wasn't the least bit interested in stupid Kevin Jensen.

Still, it was hard to sit here with the anticipation of further shame washing over her. He would see that her handful of texts and emails with friends back home were innocuous and seldom. She was friendly with many, but actual friends with very few. It was a symptom of moving so much through her childhood, as her mother had tried to find better positions for herself. Gwyn kept in touch with people she liked, mostly through social media, but she didn't bond very often. She had learned early that it hurt too much when she had to move on. The person she was closest to, her stepfather, didn't "do" computers. They talked the old-fashioned way, over the phone or face-to-face.

If Vittorio glanced through her social media accounts, he'd see she followed liberal pundits and quirky celebrities. If he looked at her apps, he'd discover she kept her checking account in the black, played Sudoku when she was bored, read mostly romance and had finished her period three days ago.

And if he looked at her photos, he'd see that she had been taking in the sights of Milan on lunches and weekends. Sights that included his extremely handsome head shot hanging in the main foyer of the Donatelli International building.

Her cheeks stung as she waited out his discovery of the incriminating photo. She'd taken it in a fit of infatuation the other day. After passing the fountain in the lobby a million times since her arrival, she'd noticed someone taking a selfie with the burbling water in the background. It had made her realize she could *pretend* to take a selfie and capture the image of her obsession on the wall.

Why? Why had she followed through on such a silly impulse? It had been as mature as pinning up a poster of a movie star in her bedroom and talking to it.

Especially when he'd been so dismissive the one time she'd smiled at him, like he couldn't imagine why she, a lowly minion, would send such a dazzling welcome his direction. He worked at such a high level in the bank, he barely showed up to the offices at all. He didn't consort with peasants like her.

How many times had she even seen him since arriving here? Four?

She mentally snorted at herself. Like she hadn't counted each glimpse as if they were days until Christmas. She looked for him all the time. It was a bit of a sickness, really. Why? What on earth had convinced her that she had anything in common with a man like him?

Her heightened awareness of him picked up on the subtle stillness that overcame him.

She refused to look at him, certain he was staring at his own image. He must be thinking she was a weird, stalker type now. By any small miracle, was he also noticing that she didn't have those stupid nudes on there?

"Today is full of surprises." Vittorio clicked off her phone and tucked it into his shirt pocket, drawing her startled glance. His hammered-gold eyes held an extra glitter of male speculation, something dark and predatory, like he'd just noticed the plump bird that had landed nearby.

Her stomach swooped.

"Did you read the emails?" she asked shakily.

"I glanced over them."

"And?"

"They appear to support your claim that you weren't involved."

"*Appear* to support," she repeated. "Like I wrote those emails as some kind of premeditated attempt to cover my butt?" Her translucent skin was growing pink with temper. "Look, you have to know it's tricky to tell a client an outright 'no.' I've been trying to do it nicely while Mr. Jensen and Signor Fabrizio—"

Her face blanked. She touched between her furrowed brow.

"They've been setting me up this whole time, haven't they? That's why I got this promotion. They thought I was too inexperienced to see what they were up to. As soon as I proved I wasn't, they turned me into their fall guy. They just pushed me off the roof!"

She was very convincing, right down to the way her trembling hand moved to cover her mouth and her eyes glassed with anxious outrage.

He tried to hang on to his cynicism, but he was entertaining similar thoughts. The very idea ignited a strange fury in him. He knew better than most what happened when a corrupt man took advantage of an ingenuous woman. His father had done it to his mother and she had wound up dead.

His phone vibrated. He glanced at the text from his cousin. *Fabrizio claims it was all her. Any progress on your end?*

Vito glanced at Gwyn, at the way her shaking fingers smoothed her hair behind her ear while her concubine mouth pouted with very credible fear.

He wasn't without concern himself. Even if Paolo managed to build a case against Fabrizio, Kevin Jensen had positioned himself very well to walk away along the high ground, leaving the bank wearing a cloak of muddied employees. An institution that staked its success on a reputation of trustworthiness would cease to appear so.

Vito refused to let that happen. He protected his family at all costs. They would, and had, done the same for him.

And this *would* cost him. Gwyn was dangerous. The

fact that he was drawn to her, looking to see her as an innocent despite the very real fact she might be involved in crimes against the bank, was unnerving. Being close to her would be a serious test of his mettle.

But his glimpse into her phone had revealed a move to him that even a master chess player like Kevin Jensen wouldn't see coming, even though it was one of the basic rules of the game: if a pawn was pushed far enough into the field of play, she could be promoted to a formidable queen.

CHAPTER THREE

VITTORIO PLUCKED HIS handkerchief from his jacket pocket and moved to dampen it under the tap of the water cooler.

Gwyn watched him, wondering what he was doing, then noticed her purse was over his shoulder, looking incongruous against his tailored charcoal suit.

"Did you get my stuff from my desk?"

Fabrizio seeing her naked was creepy. Vittorio touching her possessions was...*intimate*. Disturbing.

"I did." He came back to tilt up her chin and started to run a blessedly cool, damp, linen-wrapped fingertip beneath her eye.

His touch sent an array of sensation outward through her jawline and down her throat, warm tingles that unnerved her. She tried to jerk away, but he firmed his hold and finished tidying her makeup, telling her, "Hold your head high as we walk to the elevator."

His tone was commanding, his mouth a stern line, while he gave her a circumspect look and tucked a loose strand of her hair behind her ear.

She knocked his hand away, chest tightening again. "I just explained that they're using me. You won't even take a second to consider that might be true? You're just going to fire me and throw me to the wolves?"

"Your termination can't be helped, Gwyn. I have to think about the bank."

His detached tone sent a spike of ice right into her heart. "Thanks a lot."

They wound up in another stare down that pulled her already taut nerves to breaking point. She hated that he was standing while she was still seated. He seemed to have all the power, all the control and advantage.

She hated that, with their gazes locked like this, her mind turned to sexual awareness, refusing to let her stay in a state of fixed hatred. She wondered things like how his lips would feel against hers and grew hot as an allover body flush simmered against the underside of her skin.

She stood abruptly, forcing him to take a step back.

"Good girl," he said, moving to the door.

"I'm not *obeying* you. I—" She cut herself off. She wanted to leave, she did. She wanted to lock herself in her flat where she could lick her wounds and figure out what to do next.

"The reporters won't leave until you do," he said heartlessly. "People will be trying to go for lunch."

Don't inconvenience the staff with your petty disaster of a life, Gwyn. Think of others in the midst of your crisis.

"Everyone's going to stare," she mumbled, trying to find her guts, but her insides were nothing but water.

"They will," he agreed, still completely unmoved. "But it's only two minutes of your life. Look straight ahead. Come. Now."

Her heels wanted to root to the floor in protest. She

wanted to beg him to let her hide here until after closing, but he was right. Better to get it over with.

She knew then what it was like to walk toward exe-
cution. While her low heels took her closer to the door,
her heart began slamming in panic. Sweat cooled the
ardor she'd experienced a moment ago, leaving her in
something close to shock.

She sought refuge in her old yoga lessons, concen-
trating on breathing in through her nose, out through
her narrowly parted lips, holding reality at bay, picturing the crown of her head being pulled by an invisible
wire toward the ceiling.

"Good," Vittorio said as he opened the door, then
settled his arm around her, tucking her shoulder under
his armpit as his hand took possession of her waist.

She stiffened in surprise at the contact. A disconcerting rush of heat blanketed her, making her knees
weaken.

He supported her, forcing her forward and keeping her on her feet when she would have stumbled.
He matched their steps perfectly, as though they had
walked as a couple many times before.

Two minutes, she repeated to herself, leaning into
him despite how much she resented him. She'd never
realized how long a minute was until she had to bear
the rustle of heads turning and chairs squeaking, conversation stopping and keyboard tapping halting into a
blanket of silence.

Vittorio's aftershave, spicy and beguiling, enveloped
her. It was dizzying. An assault to already overloaded
senses. Were her legs going to hold her? Amazing how
being escorted like this made you feel like a criminal
as well as look like one.

Her eyes were seared blind. She couldn't tell who was looking, couldn't really see the rest of the open-plan office because Vittorio kept her on his side closest to the wall and stayed a quarter step ahead of her so his big shoulders blocked her vision of the rest of the floor.

Another man paced on his far side, broad and burly and carrying a file box that held a green travel cup that she thought might be hers. Had they also collected the snapshot of her with her mother and stepfather, she worried?

The elevator was being held open by another hitman type with a buzz cut. He couldn't care less about her silly scandal, his watchful indifference seemed to say. He was here to bust heads if anyone stepped out of line.

The elevator closed and she let out her breath, but rather than dropping as she expected, the elevator climbed, making her stagger and clutch instinctively at Vittorio's smooth jacket.

He cradled her closer, steadying her, fingers moving soothingly at her waist. Disturbing her with the intimacy of his touch.

"Why aren't we going down?" she asked shakily.

"The helicopter will avoid the scrum."

"Helicopter?" she choked out, mind scattering as she tried to make sense of this turn of events.

"Thirty seconds," he warned, tone gruff, and nudged her a step forward as the elevator leveled out with a *ding*.

His arm remained firm across her back, urging her through the opening doors.

She trembled, trying not to fold into him, but he was the only solid thing in her world right now. She had to remember that despite his seeming solicitude, he wasn't on her side. This was damage control. Nothing more.

The refinement at this height in the building was practically polished into the stillness of the air. Nevertheless, humans were humans. Heads came up. Eyes followed.

Vittorio addressed no one, only steered her down a hall in confident, unhurried steps, past a boardroom of men in suits and women with perfectly coiffed hair, past a lounge where a handful of people stood drinking coffee and into a glass receiving area beyond which a helicopter stood, rotors beginning to turn.

The security guard took her box of possessions ahead of them and tucked it into a bulkhead, then moved into the cockpit.

Wow. This wasn't a helicopter like she'd seen on television, where people were crammed into three seats across the back wall, shoulder to shoulder, and had to put on headphones and shout to be heard.

This was an executive lounge that belonged on a yacht. She didn't have to duck as she moved into it. The white leather seats were ten times plusher than the very expensive recliner she'd purchased for her stepfather two Christmases ago. The seats rotated, she realized, as Vittorio pointed her to one, then turned another so they would sit facing each other.

There was a door to the pilot's cockpit, like on an airplane. An air hostess smiled a greeting and nodded at Vittorio, taking a silent order from him that he gave with the simple raising of two fingers. She arrived seconds later with two drinks that looked suspiciously like scotch, neat.

Vittorio lowered a small table between them with indents to hold their glasses.

Gwyn took a deep drink of her scotch, shivering as the burn chased down her throat, then replaced her glass into its holder with a dull thud. "Where are you taking me?"

"This isn't a kidnapping," he said dryly. "We're going to Paolo's home on Lake Como. It's in his wife's name and not on the paparazzi's radar."

"What? No," she insisted, reaching to open her seat-belt. "My passport is in my apartment. I need it to get home."

"To America? The press there is more relentless than ours. Even if you managed to drop out of sight, I would still have an ugly smudge on the bank's reputation to erase."

"I care as much about the bank as it does about me," she informed him coldly.

"Please stay seated, Gwyn. We're lifting off." He pointed to where the horizon lowered beneath them. "Let's talk about your photo of *me*."

A fresh blush rose hotly from the middle of her chest into her neck. "Let's not," she said, squishing herself into her seat and fixing her gaze out the window.

"You're attracted to me, *si*?"

She sealed her lips, silently letting him know he couldn't make her talk.

Nevertheless, he had her trapped and demonstrated his patience with an unhurried sip of his own drink and a brief glance at the face of his phone.

"You smiled at me one day," he said absently. "The way a woman does when she is inviting a man to speak to her."

And he hadn't bothered to.

"I play a game with a friend back home," she muttered. "It's silly. Man Wars. We send each other photos of attractive men. That's all it was," she lied. "If it makes you feel objectified, well, you have a glimpse into how I feel right now."

Her insides were churning like a cement mixer.

"You're embarrassed by how strong the attraction is," he deduced after watching her a moment. He sounded amused.

Her stomach cramped with self-consciousness. Could her face get any hotter?

"This releasing of compromising photos is very shrewd," he said in an abrupt shift. His tone suggested it was an item in political news, not a gross defilement of her personal self. His finger rested across his lips in contemplation.

"Jensen has very cleverly made himself appear a victim," he said. "The moment we accuse him of wrongdoing, he'll claim he only took advice from you and Fabrizio. Fabrizio may eventually implicate him, trying to save his own skin, but Jensen has this excellent diversion. He can say you came on to him, maybe that you were working with Fabrizio, that you sent those photos to ruin his marriage. Perhaps they were cooked up by the two of you to blackmail him into skimming funds. Whatever story he comes up with, it will point all the scandal back to you and Fabrizio and the bank."

"I'm aware that my life is over, thanks," she bit out.

"Nothing is over," he said with a cold-blooded smile. "Jensen landed a punch, but I will hit back. Hard. If he and Fabrizio were in fact using you, you must also want to set things straight? You'll help me make it clear you had zero romantic interest in Jensen."

"How?" she choked out, wondering what was in his drink that he thought he could accomplish that.

"By going public with our own affair."

Gwyn pinched her wrist.

Vittorio noted the movement and his mouth twitched.

She shook her head, instinctively refusing his suggestion while searching for a fresh flash of anger. Outrage was giving her the strength to keep from crying, but his proposition came across as so offhanded and hurtful, so cavalier when she couldn't deny she was weirdly infatuated with him, it smashed through her defenses and smacked down her confidence.

"I don't *have* affairs," she insisted. She looked out the window at the rust-red rooftops below. The houses below were short, the high-rises in the center of the city gone, green spaces more abundant. They were over outlying areas, well out of Milan. *Damn it.*

She wanted to magically transport back to Charleston and the room where she had stayed during her mother's short marriage to Henry. She wanted to go back in time to when her mother was still alive.

"It's such a pathetically male and sexist response to say that sleeping together would solve anything. To suggest I do it to save my job—no, *your* job—" She was barely able to speak, stunned, ears ringing. Her eyes and throat burned. "It's so insulting I don't have words," she managed, voice thinning as the worst day of her life grew even uglier.

"Did I say we'd sleep together? You're projecting. No, I'm saying we must appear to."

Oh, wonderful. He *wasn't* coming on to her. Why did she care either way?

"It would still make it look like I'm sleeping my way to the top," she muttered, flashing him a glance, but quickly jerking her attention back to the window, not wanting him to see how deeply this jabbed at her deepest insecurities.

From the moment she'd developed earlier than her friends, she'd been struggling to be seen as brains, not breasts. A lot of her adolescent friends had been fair weather, pulling Gwyn into their social circles because she brought boys with her, but eventually becoming annoyed that she got all the male attention and cutting her loose. The workplace had been another trial, learning to cope with sexual harassment and jealousy from her female coworkers, realizing this was one reason why her mother had changed jobs so often.

Her mom had been a runner. Gwyn tried to stay and fight. It was the reason she had stuck it out in school despite the cost. Training for a real profession had seemed the best way to be taken seriously. Yet here she was, being pinned up as a sex object in the locker room of the internet, set up by men who believed she lacked the brains to see when people were committing crimes under her nose.

And the solution to this predicament was to sleep with her boss? Or appear to? What kind of world was this?

She looked around, but there was nowhere to go. She might as well have been trapped in a prison cell with Vittorio.

He swore under his breath and withdrew her phone from his shirt pocket, scowling at it. "This thing is exploding." His frown deepened as he looked at whatever notification was showing up against her Lock screen. "Who is Travis?"

His tone chilled to below freezing and his handsome features twisted with harsh judgment. She could practically see the derisive label in a bubble over his head.

"My stepbrother," she said haughtily, holding out her hand, not nearly as undaunted as she tried to appear. Her intestines knotted further as she saw that she'd missed four calls and several texts from Travis, along with some from old schoolmates and several from former coworkers in Charleston.

All the texts were along the lines of, *Is it really you? Call me. I just saw the news. They're saying...*

Nausea roiled in her. She clicked to darken the screen.

Travis had been vaguely amused with her concern over not having every skill listed in this job posting for Milan. *Do you know why men get promoted over women? Because they don't worry about meeting all the criteria. Fake it 'til you make it*, had been his advice.

Really great advice, considering what such a bold move had got her into, she thought dourly.

But his laconic opinion had been the most personable he'd ever been around her. He was never rude, just distant. He never reached out to her, only responded if she texted him first. He didn't know that she'd overheard him shortly before her mother's wedding to his father, when he'd cautioned Henry against tying himself to a woman without any assets. *There are social climbers and there are predators.*

Henry had defended them and Gwyn had walked away hating Travis, but not really blaming him. Had their situations been reversed, she would have cautioned her mother herself. It had still fueled her need to be self-reliant in every way.

She had been so proud to tell Travis she'd landed this job, believing she'd been recognized for her education, qualifications and grit. *Ha.*

"I guess we can assume the photos have crossed the Atlantic," she muttered, cringing anew.

It was afternoon here. Travis would be starting his day in Charleston, and the fact that he'd learned so quickly of the photos told her exactly how broadly these things were being distributed. Maybe reporters had tracked down the family connection and were harassing him and Henry?

Damn that Kevin Jensen. His headline name was turning her into a punch line.

She set her phone on the table, unable to think of anything to say except *I'm sorry*, and that was far too inadequate.

She swallowed back hopelessness, realizing a door had just closed on her. She could go back to America, but she couldn't take this mess to Henry's doorstep. He'd been too good to her to repay him like that. Travis might make her cut off ties for good.

"You're not going to call him?" Vittorio asked.

"I don't know what to say," she admitted.

"Tell him you're safe at least."

"Am I?" she scoffed, meeting his gaze long enough for his own to slice through her like a blade, as if he could see all the way inside her to where she squirmed.

And where she held a hot ember of yearning for his good opinion.

"He's not worried," she dismissed, feeling hollow as

she said it. "We're not close like that. He just wants to know what's going on." So he could perform damage control on his side.

She had worked so hard to keep Travis from seeing her as a hanger-on, so he wouldn't think she was only spending time with his elderly father in hopes of getting money out of him and possibly cut her off. She was vigilant about paying her own way, refusing to take money unless it was a little birthday cash which she invariably spent on groceries, cooking a big enough dinner to fill her stepfather's freezer with single-serve leftovers. She always invited Travis to join them if she was planning to see Henry, never wanting him to think she was going behind his back.

Now whatever progress she'd made in earning Travis's respect would be up in smoke. But what did that matter when apparently no one else would have any for her after this?

"Do you have other family you should contact?" Vittorio asked.

"No," she murmured. Her mother, a woman without any formal training of any kind, had married an American and wound up losing her husband two years into her emigration to his country. He'd been in the service, an only child with elderly parents already living in a retirement home. They had died before Gwyn had been old enough to ask about them.

With no home or family to go back to in Wales, her mother, Winnifred, had struggled along as a single mom, often working in retail or housekeeping at hotels, occasionally serving for catering companies. She'd taken anything to make ends meet, never deliberately making Gwyn feel like an encumbrance, but Gwyn was smart enough to know that she had been.

That's why Gwyn was so determined to prove to Travis her attachment to Henry was purely emotional. It was deeply emotional. Henry was the only family she had.

"You do make an easy target, don't you? A single woman of no resources or support," Vittorio commented. Perhaps even desperate, she could hear him speculating.

"You must think so, offering an affair when I'm at my lowest," she said. "You might as well hang around bus stations looking for teenaged runaways."

Something flashed in his gaze, ugly and hard and dangerous, but he leaned forward onto the table between them and smiled without humor.

"It's not an offer. Until I say otherwise, you're my lover. I'm a very powerful man, Gwyn. One who is livid on your behalf and willing to go on the offensive to reinstate your honor."

His words, the intense way he looked at her, snagged inside her heart and pulled, yanking her toward a desire to believe what he was saying.

"You mean the bank's behalf. To reinstate the bank's honor," she said, as much to remind herself as to mock him. Her prison-cell analogy had been wrong. This was the lion's cage she was trapped in with the king of beasts flicking his tail as he watched her.

"You understand me," he said with a nod of approval. "We've been very discreet about our relationship, given that you work for us," he continued in a casual tone, sitting back and taking his ease. "But I assure you, I'm intensely possessive. And very influential. This crime against you—" the *bank* "—won't go unpunished."

He was talking like it was real. Like they were actually going forward with this pretense. Like they were really having an affair.

She choked on a disbelieving laugh, pointing out, "That just switches out one scandal for another. It doesn't change anything. I still look like a slut."

She might have thought he didn't care, he remained so unmoving. But sparks flew in the hammered bronze of his irises, as if he waged a knife fight on the inside.

He still sounded infinitely patronizing when he spoke.

"Sex scandals have a very short lifespan in this country. A little one like a boss-employee thing, between two single adults?" He made a noise and dismissed it with a flick of his fingers. "Old news in a matter of days. I would rather weather that than have the bank suspected of corruption. The impact of something like that goes on indefinitely."

"Do you even care if I'm innocent? All you really want is to protect the bank, isn't it?" She looked at where she'd unconsciously torn off the whites of two fingernails, picking with agitation at them.

"Of course the bank is my priority. It's a *bank*. One that not only employs thousands, but influences the world economy. Our foundation is trust or we have nothing. So yes, I intend to protect it. The benefit to you could be exoneration—which I would think you would pursue whether you're guilty or not. We'll imply that Paolo knew of our affair and that's how he and I were made aware of Jensen's activities. We kept you in place to build the case."

"Will I keep my job?" she asked, as if she was bargaining when they both knew her position was so weak she was lucky she wasn't being questioned by the police right now. Or being hurled from this stupid helicopter.

"No," he said flatly. "Even if you prove to be innocent, putting you back on our payroll would muddy the waters."

"Let's pretend for a minute that I'm as innocent as I say I am," she said with deep sarcasm. "All I get out of this, out of being targeted by *your* client with naked photos that will exist in the public eye for the rest of my life, is a clean police record. I still lose my job and any chance of a career in the field I've been aiming at for years. *Thanks.*"

He didn't own the patent on derision. She found enough scorn to coat the walls of this floating lounge, then turned her dry, stinging eyes to the window.

After a long moment, he said, "If you are innocent, you won't be left with nothing. Let me put it another way. Cooperate with me and I'll personally ensure you're compensated as befits the end result."

"You're going to pay me to lie?" she challenged, her tone edging toward wild. "And what happens when that comes out? I still look like an opportunist."

He didn't flinch, only curled his lip as he asked, "Which lie is closer to the truth, Gwyn? That you want to sleep with Kevin Jensen? Or that you've been sleeping with me?"

Could he see inside her thoughts? Did he know what she fantasized about as she drifted into slumber every night? She sincerely hoped not. Talk about dirty images!

Blushing hotly all over, she crushed the fingers of one hand in the grip of the other, trying to keep herself from ruining any more of her manicure. Having him aware of her attraction made this worse, just as she had suspected. It was mortifying to be this transparent around him.

All she had to do was picture Nadine's disapproving face to know how far protesting with the truth would get her, though. If she had more time, she might have come up with a better solution, but the helicopter was much lower now, seeming to aim for a stretch of green lawn next to a lakeside villa.

On the table before her, her phone vibrated with yet another message.

It didn't matter who it was from. Everyone she knew was being told she had sent naked photos of herself to a married man. The existence of the photos was bad enough, but she was prepared to do just about anything, as the people in Nadine's line of work would say, to change the narrative. Vittorio said this would cut the scandal down to a few short days and she had to agree that it was a more palatable lie than the one Kevin Jensen had put forth.

"Fine," she muttered, swallowing misgivings. "I'll pretend we were having an affair. Pretend," she repeated. "I'm not sleeping with you."

He smiled like he knew better.

CHAPTER FOUR

HE LET HER into the house, then watched her wander it as he made a call, allowing her to listen as he greeted someone with a warm, *"Cara. Come stai?"*

Gwyn took it like a punch in the stomach, wondering how crazy she was to agree that he could call *her* his lover if he already had one.

The restored mansion was unbelievable, she noted as she clung to her own elbows and stared at the view of Lake Como that started just below the windows off the breakfast nook. The rest of the interior was warmly welcoming, with a spacious kitchen and May sunshine that poured through the tall windows and glanced off the gleaming floors with golden promise. Family snapshots of children and gray-haired relatives and the handsome owner and his wife adorned the walls, making this a very personal sanctuary.

This felt like a place where nothing bad ever happened. That's what home was supposed to be, wasn't it? A refuge?

Would she ever build such a thing for herself, she wondered?

Gwyn moved into the lounge and lowered into a wingback chair, listening to the richness of Vittorio's voice, but not bothering to translate his Italian, aching to let waves of self-pity erode her composure. She felt more abandoned today than even the day her mother had died. At least then she'd had Henry. And a life to carry on with. A career. Something to keep her moving forward. Now…

She stared at her empty hands. Vittorio had even stolen her phone again, scowling at its constant buzz before powering it down and pocketing it.

She hadn't argued, still in a kind of denial, but she was facing facts now. She had no one. Nothing.

In the other room, Vittorio concluded with, *"Ciao, bella,"* and his footsteps approached.

He checked briefly when he saw her, then came forward to offer the square of white linen that was still faintly damp and stained with her mascara.

So gallant. While she felt like some kind of sullied lowlife.

She rejected it and him by looking away.

"No tears? That doesn't speak of innocence, *mia bella*," he jeered softly.

She never cried in front of people. Even at the funeral, she'd been the stalwart organizer, waiting for privacy before allowing grief to overwhelm her.

"Is that all it would take to convince you?" she said with an equal mixture of gentle mockery. "Would you hold me if I did?" She lifted her chin to let him see her disdain.

"Of course," he said, making her heart leap in a mixture of alarm and yearning. "No man who calls himself a man allows a woman to cry alone."

"Some of us prefer it," she choked out, even though there was a huge, weak part of her that wanted to wallow in whatever consolation he might offer. She'd had boyfriends. She knew that a man's embrace could create a sense of harbor.

But it was temporary. And Vittorio was not extending real sanctuary. They were allied enemies at best.

He wasn't even attracted to her. He thought she was a criminal and a slut.

"Just show me where I can sleep." She was overdue for hugging a pillow and bellyaching into it.

His silence made her look up.

"Paolo is still tied up questioning Fabrizio. His wife has very kindly offered her wardrobe." He waved toward the stairs. "She has excellent taste. Let's find something appropriate."

"For?" She glanced down at her business suit, which was a bit creased, but in surprisingly good shape despite her colossal besmirching.

"Our first public appearance," he replied in an overly patient tone, like he was explaining things to a child.

"You said we just had to wait out the scandal for a few days." A strange new panic began creeping into her, coming from a source she couldn't identify.

"Oh, no, *cara*," he said with a patronizing shake of his head. "I said that the worst of the scandal should pass in a few days. We are locked into our lie for a few weeks at least. You don't get seasick, do you? The wind might come up this evening and the dinner cruise could get rocky."

Vito wondered sometimes, when his dispassionate, ruthless streak arose this strongly, whether his father's genes were poking through the Donatelli discipline he had so carefully nurtured to contain it.

The mafiosi were known for their loyalty to family, he reasoned. The ferocity of his allegiance to Paolo and the bank had its seeds in his DNA. Of course he would do everything and anything to protect both. Of course he would do whatever was necessary to neutralize the threat Jensen posed.

Vito was aware of something deeper going on inside him, though. A pitiless determination to *crush* Jensen. It was positively primeval and he wasn't comfortable with it.

He glanced across at the fuel for his suppressed rage and was impacted by intense carnal desire.

Why?

Oh, Gwyn was beautiful. He couldn't deny it, even though she was pale beneath a light layer of makeup. It had been expertly applied by Lauren's very trustworthy stylist from Como. Like anyone who worked for society's high-level players, the stylist knew any sort of indiscretion meant a loss of more than just one lucrative client. Lauren had sent the woman "to help a friend." The stylist kept her finger on the pulse of celebrity gossip. She had recognized Gwyn with a very subtle start, then grinned and put her at ease so Gwyn had been smiling as she emerged as a butterfly from the chrysalis of a guest bedroom an hour later.

Her smile had faded when she had found Vito waiting for her. That had bothered him, making him feel a small kick of guilt, like he was responsible for her unhappiness.

...targeted by your *client with naked photos that will exist in the public eye for the rest of my life...*

He had asked her for the name of the spa and had ordered a team to look into it, wondering if a connection to Jensen might turn up beyond his wife recommending Gwyn visit it for physiotherapy.

Gwyn could have used something to relax her in that moment, as she'd stood so stiffly, projecting hostility as she seemed to wait out his judgment on her appearance.

He could hardly breathe looking at her. She was a vision in a long, sparkling blue skirt with a high slit and a black, equally glittering halter top that clung lovingly to the swells of her ample breasts. Her midriff was bare and her hair loose so her face was squarely framed by the blunt cut across her brow and the straight fall of rich, mahogany brown. She wore silver hoop earrings and a dozen thin bangles supplied by the stylist. Lauren's shoes were a half size too big, but Gwyn's toes were freshly painted a passionate red.

"You're stunning," he had told her sincerely.

Her hands had grown white where she clutched a small black pocketbook. Averting her face, she'd said, "Not sure why I bothered when people are going to look through what I'm wearing."

"Do you need me to tell you you're beautiful either way?"

She flinched. "Took a long look, did you?"

So much resentment. It annoyed him to be lumped in with all the other voyeurs. He had spent the past hour taking stock of how thoroughly Jensen was arrowing those images back at the bank, how the world media was exploiting Gwyn's naked body for ratings. He had looked at everything *but* her photographs, deliberately sparing her one more pair of male eyes and himself the disturbing dual reaction of arousal and fury.

The thought that men around the world were licking

their lips in lascivious heat over her figure was making him grow murderously affronted.

So he didn't appreciate her goading him.

"They're imprinted on my mind," he said without apology, watching something tense and disturbed flash across her expression before she quelled it. "You have nothing to be ashamed of. I don't mean that from a physical standpoint, but that's true, as well."

She reacted with a startled stare of confused vulnerability.

"That sounds almost kind. Are you practicing? Because there's no one here to overhear you being nice to me." Her mouth pouted in consternation, lips possibly trembling a moment before she firmed them.

It struck him that she didn't know he was attracted to her.

He would have laughed if he hadn't been so stunned. Admiration of her figure was a given. Why did she think she'd been chosen for this particular form of exploitation?

But there was more. Tendrils of possessiveness had rooted in him during those first seconds of viewing her pale nudity. A prowling hunger was growing, urging him to make her aware that he ached to touch her. He wanted to see the knowledge, the catch of excitement in her gaze. The exponential increase of passion as it reflected back and forth between them like parallel mirrors.

He didn't know how he knew it would be like that, he just did.

"You'll have to get used to looking insipidly pleased by my compliments," he said to disguise his growing need, grasping at her remark about practicing. "And welcome my touch," he added, giving in to temptation and letting the backs of his fingers graze the softness of her bare arm.

Goose bumps immediately rose on her skin and her nipples tightened.

It was such a visceral reaction he experienced an answering pull in his groin, one that very nearly had him throwing in the towel on his precious discipline. He had wanted to scoop her up and head straight to the nearest bedroom. Hell, the floor.

She blushed. Hard. Hurt flashed across her expression. "I'm already a powerless game piece. Don't make it worse by taunting me with my own stupid reaction to you." Shame darkened her eyes, but she dared to threaten him. "Or we will have a very ugly public breakup."

"And a very hot and public reunion," he responded fiercely, catching at the taut tendons in her wrists where she clenched her hands into fists. Tucking them behind her back, he pulled her in close and slid his lips along her perfumed neck, eyes almost rolling back into his skull as male hunger slammed through him. He *wanted* her. "Because your reaction to me is exactly what will sell this story of ours. So get used to revealing it."

Then, because she strained her face away from him, he sucked a tiny love bite onto her neck where it met her shoulder. Her whole body shuddered and a sensual moan escaped her. Her hips bucked to press her mons against his straining erection and lingered to rock with muted need, teasing both of them.

In that second, they could have both lost it, but he had forced himself to release her, his grip on his control far too tenuous for his liking.

He was unsurprised by the hatred she flashed at him as she took a staggering step away from him. She looked stricken. Shocked by her own reaction. He was unnerved himself. They would tear the skin from each other's bones if they gave in to this thing between them.

That hatred was good, though. It armed him against making love to her. He was driven, not despicable.

She hadn't spoken to him again, moving to the car like an airman with jump orders, sitting stiffly, keeping her stoic expression averted.

Everything in him itched to knock through that wall of hostility with another sample of their amazing chemistry, but he needed time to get hold of himself first.

The driver slowed to a crawl behind the line releasing rock stars, socialites, minor royalty and major league players onto the red carpet.

Vito wasn't on the list, but he knew the American actor hosting the cruise, so he had seized the opportunity to "come out" with Gwyn here. It was a precursor to an international film festival. The guest list was not only small and exclusive, but worldly enough that leaked sex tapes and mug shots were dismissed as "publicity." Nude photos were barely worth mentioning, as common to a portfolio as head shots.

He heard Gwyn's breath switch to measured hisses as she tried to control an attack of nerves. As the car stopped, he took her limp, clammy hand in his—and experienced a thrill of excitement from the contact despite the terror in the gaze she flashed at him.

"Chin up," he reminded her with a patronizing smile, sensing that kindness in this moment would be her downfall. She seemed to find her strength in anger, so he provoked it.

She said something under her breath that wasn't very ladylike, making him want to smile, but that wouldn't do for their purposes.

"Let them know how much you hate them," he said as the door beside him opened. He stood, bringing Gwyn with him, not giving her a chance to chicken out. Then he paused, giving the paparazzi the moment they needed to realize who they had.

The girl from the photos.

With Vittorio Donatelli.

His hand possessively slid so he had his arm around her and drew her closer, dipping his chin to look into her withdrawn expression with just the right level of concern before he lifted a hostile, contemptuous glare to the wall of cameras, silently messaging Kevin Jensen that he had messed with the wrong man's woman.

A buzz of gasps went through the crowd and the bursts of light intensified into a wall of exploding lights. The shouts became a rabid din.

Gwyn swallowed and revealed the barest moment of anguish before she leveled her shoulders and sent a haughty, dismissive glance toward the cameras that was gloriously effective in its disparagement. Her upward glance at Vito was not only a cold, silent demand that he remove her from this place, but a wonderful expression of trust that he would and could save her from it. He doubted she realized how revealing it was, but he saw it, knew the cameras caught it and was deeply satisfied.

She kept her spine iron straight beneath his hand as he steered her through the blinding lights to where the purser stood at the top of the steps to the gated marina.

"I'm not on the list," Vittorio told the uniformed young man. "But I'm on the list."

The purser didn't even relay his name, only glanced at the wild reaction they'd provoked and recognized the value they added to the event. "Thank you, sir. Enjoy your evening."

Vittorio started toward the steps, then turned back. "If Kevin Jensen is on the list, he's not on the list. Understand?"

"Absolutely." The purser nodded and flipped a page, striking through a name.

This morning, life had been normal.

Somehow, in roughly twelve hours, Gwyn had gone from mousy banking representative to notorious internet sensation. Thanks to Vittorio secluding her today, the full reality of her situation hadn't hit her until that moment outside the limo. Then strangers had called her name, clamoring for her to turn, shouting disgustingly invasive questions in a dozen languages.

When did you pose for those nude photos?

How did Mrs. Jensen find out about your affair?

Is Vittorio Donatelli your lover?

She stepped onto the yacht and a murmur rippled through the crowd. Heads tipped together and a few people pointed.

She instinctively edged closer to her date and his fingertips dug into her hip, oddly reassuring.

The last thing she ought to count on Vittorio for was protection. He'd behaved like a bastard earlier, using her own reaction against her like that. She was sick with herself for rubbing into his groin like she ached for his penetration—which she did. She was even sicker that finding him hard had excited her to the point she would have let him have her right there at the top of the stairs if he'd wanted.

Men were simple creatures, she reminded herself. Comedians were always complaining about erections popping up like dandelions at inconvenient times. As much as it would soothe her ego to believe Vittorio was attracted to her, she knew he couldn't possibly feel the same lust that had cut into her like a knife. His reaction had been about as personal as shivering from the cold.

They were united in one thing: pretending they were in a sexual relationship to defuse Jensen's allegations.

So she slithered closer to him, ignoring the fact that she drew genuine comfort from his strength. If he stiffened in a kind of surprise before tightening his arm around her, well, she wasn't a masochist who wanted another mean-spirited lesson in how incapable she was of resisting him. She stood close; she didn't soften and invite.

"Vito!" A gorgeous blonde approached them, tugging a legendary, award-winning, big-screen star in her wake. They turned out to be the host and hostess.

Gwyn silently laughed at herself. If the crowd was goggling at her, she goggled right back. The yacht was full to the gunwales of faces she'd seen in movies and on TV. Hugely famous people. It added a fresh layer of surreal to her already bizarro day.

"Thank you for coming," the tall, stunning supermodel said in a New York accent, kissing Vittorio on the mouth. "We'll have so much more exposure for the premiere now. I didn't see the photos," she said to Gwyn with an offhand shrug. "But my agent represents five of the top underwear models in the world. Judging from your figure, he would love to be your first call if you want to make lemonade out of this. Don't put it off. Attention like this doesn't last. Vito has my number."

"Vito," Gwyn repeated a moment later, when they were alone.

"My friends and family call me that. You should, too."

"Should I call her agent, is the real question," Gwyn said, taking a deeper drink of her champagne than was probably wise, but the impulse to get legless drunk was very strong.

"I would prefer you didn't," he said in a tone that was oddly lethal.

"Call her agent? Why? What other kind of work can I get? Even Nadine thought I wasn't good enough at my job to earn *this* promotion without falling onto my back. Maybe it's time I gave in to what the world has told me all my life and allow myself to be objectified. Make money on God's gift." She waved down her front.

An arc of dangerous fire flashed in his gaze again. "Have you come up against a lot of sexism in your life?"

"Is there an amount that's reasonable and acceptable?"

They were approached by someone else, stealing her moment of possibly taking him aback. They spent the next hour mingling. It wasn't awful, but she was tongue-tied and Vito kept stealing her champagne, setting the flutes out of her reach and giving her sparkling water or fruit juice in exchange.

"If you don't let me drink," she said at one point, fake smile pinned to her face, "people are going to think I'm pregnant. Surely I've hit the redline on scandal for one day?"

"I'm letting you drink. I'm just not letting you get drunk. You'll thank me tomorrow."

"I highly doubt you'll ever hear those words out of these lips," she assured him.

"We'll see," he said, catching at the hand she reached to the passing tray and tugging her in the opposite direction. "Come."

"Where?"

He only drew her from the main deck where glass panels provided a windbreak, keeping the laughing, dancing crowd contained in a pool of colorful light off a rotating mirror ball. A musician who had risen to fame three decades ago was going strong, shredding the piano, playing with a band of indie rockers on guitars and drums.

Vito tugged her down a narrow flight of stairs to where a cool gust raced along the lower deck, making her cross her arms as the chill hit her in the face.

"It did get windy," she said, hanging back in the alcove at the bottom of the stairs.

He removed his taupe linen jacket and draped it over her shoulders, enveloping her in a scent that was both his and something else. His cousin's aftershave, maybe, because he'd also raided the closets in the master bedroom. "We have work to do, now that you've relaxed."

"What kind?"

He drew her toward the stern where foam kicked up in a widening trail behind the yacht. The rush of wind and churning water filled the air. Pinprick lights from distant houses danced against the black silhouettes of the mountain-backed shoreline.

And a handful of smaller boats paced this big one, bouncing on its wake, buzzing like mosquitos. Something flashed. A camera.

"Oh."

"Sì," he confirmed. "We are stealing a kiss, *mia bella.*"

"You can try," she said stiffly, turning her head to glare at him with antagonism, hands on the rail. "I've about had it with being robbed of things I'm not willing to give up. This cruise could get very rough indeed."

He leaned his back into the rail and set his feet wide, then indicated she should come into the space. "I'm offering a kiss," he cajoled, surprising her with his tender tone. "Would it be such a chore for you to accept it?"

A spasm of pain went through her, increasing when she saw another flash and suspected her moment of torment had just been caught and would be fed to the online trolls.

She found herself ducking her head, letting him draw her into his chest in an embrace that she knew he staged to look tender, but it *felt* tender. Like a place of shelter. She was on her very last nerve and desperately wanted to believe she was safe with him, but she couldn't. Not by a long shot.

"I don't kiss strangers," she muttered into his chest.

He smoothed her hair behind her ear and his breath warmed her cheek as he spoke. "We're lovers, *mia bella.*"

In her periphery, more flashes were sparking, but maybe that was the electric reaction he provoked in her.

"You don't even find me attractive. Can you imagine how it feels to kiss someone you know feels nothing for you? Actually it's worse than that. You feel contempt. This is not a nice place to be. I can't pretend to be okay with it."

His hands stilled on her. "Have you had many lovers, Gwyn? You keep surprising me with what sounds like naivety."

"How is it naive to know that all these seduction moves of yours are motivated by a desire to protect the bank, that you're actually overcoming disgust to touch me?" She lifted her face to glare at him, unable to read his face in the dark. "Are you going to tell me next that I'm being too cynical?" She nearly choked on her own words. She was growing weak just standing against his body heat, reacting to him even though she knew he felt nothing toward her. This was so unequal.

"You're a very beautiful woman. You must know that." He rested the heel of his hand on her shoulder, fingertips toying at her nape beneath the fall of her hair.

The caress was so beguiling, the words so throaty, her whole body responded. Her knees weakened, her skin tightened and her nipples prickled. Deep between her thighs, damp heat gathered. Her breath hitched.

At the same time she heard the levelness in his tone and understood that his body might be growing hard, but his mind was still not affected.

"I suppose this *is* an affair then," she said, feeling him give a small start of surprise.

"What do you mean?"

"Well, it's not a relationship with a future. It's going to serve a purpose then end with neither of us calling or texting. You're right. I haven't had a lot of lovers and they've mostly been hit and runs. That's why I don't date much. I hate the part when I'm left feeling used. That's why I don't want to kiss you right now. I'll just feel dirty after."

"Ah, *cara*, you are very naive," he said with a gentle

laugh. "You're in a position to use *me*. Stop being so nice and do it. You'll feel terrific."

She gave him her profile, staring into the dark, angry that he made being nice sound like a character flaw. Angry that her life had been destroyed. Angry that there was no substance to what was going on between them. She was an object. Nothing real or important. This was how her mother had felt all the time.

A self-destructive impulse rose and she tossed her hair as she looked up at him.

"Fine. We'll kiss."

It was too dark to tell whether his brief hesitation was surprise or something else, but his hand moved to cup her cheek and he bent, capturing her mouth in a firm, hungry possession without a lead-up. No delay.

Because they were lovers, she reminded herself as excitement tore through her veins. According to the illusion they were projecting, they were familiar enough with each other to throw themselves into a passionate kiss without preamble.

Heart pounding, she returned his kiss with all the emotions roiling in her. Fury, mostly. She let her hand go to the short hairs at the back of his neck and increased the pressure, drawing him down to her, hurting herself with the way she mashed her mouth against his, liable to leave both of them bruised as she scraped her teeth against his lips in punishment for all that he'd done to her. For all that the world was doing to her.

He grunted and his hand went low on her back, pressing into her bottom to pull her tighter into him, fingertips flagrantly tracing the line between her cheeks.

She didn't protest. She shuffled closer, shoving herself aggressively into his frame, like they were combatants. She moved her hand to take a fistful of his hair, hoping his scalp stung while she moved her lips under his, mouth burning with avid, angry friction.

With another gruff noise, he lifted his head, let her catch one breath, then closed his arms more tightly around her, swooping into a deep, dominant kiss, tongue spearing boldly into her mouth.

Her reaction might have been frightening to her if she wasn't so close to exploding. She needed this outlet, this contained space of banded arms keeping her from flying apart. She fought letting him take over as long as she could, flicking at his tongue with hers, trying to make him break, but he was too strong willed. Way stronger than her.

With a little sob, she finally capitulated, softening and letting him take control.

Her reward was a wash of delirious pleasure. Suddenly she felt what this kiss was doing to her. Her blood was hot, her erogenous zones sensitized and singing. His body seemed to envelop hers in sexual need. She was so steeped in desire, her knees folded.

She would have gone anywhere with him in that moment. Would have let him do anything. She wanted him to cover her and push inside her and take her to a place where nothing could touch her.

His assertiveness eased. His hand moved soothingly over her back. His damp lips tenderly caressed hers until they broke apart to gasp for air. He tucked her head under his jaw and held her ear against his pounding heart.

She rested there, trying to catch her breath, listening to his heart slam, feeling like she'd been running and now the ache of exertion was catching up to her.

He was hard, she realized, and she panged again with longing for this to be real, for them to make love so she could lose herself in mindless pleasure. She ought to find his desire threatening, she thought. Or offensive maybe. She didn't move away from pressing against him, though, liking that evidence of his reaction even if it was strictly physiological. She stayed in that little cave of safety his arms provided, face pressed to his shirt, body sheltered from the wind by his broader one.

And she started to cry.

There was no stopping it this time. It wasn't a grand storm, just a slow leak of tears that grew into a steady, unstoppable flow. Her control surrendered to exhaustion, like a drowning victim letting go and sinking beneath the surface. She clung with limp arms and leaned her weight into him as pulsing waves of suffering rocked her.

He didn't tell her to *shush*. He held her, rubbed her back and didn't say a word.

CHAPTER FIVE

VITO SAT IN the armchair of the hotel room, feet on the ottoman, wearing only his pants. He was pretending to read emails, but sat angled so he could watch Gwyn sleep.

A full-out rainstorm had manifested while she'd been fixing her face in the head, after their kiss. The yacht had raced to moor at the nearest marina and, while most of the guests scrambled through sheets of rain for taxis to take them to their hotels, he had walked into the yacht club and paid a fortune for a top-floor room. He hadn't been interested in leading the paparazzi back to the mansion and Gwyn had been at the end of her rope.

He could have taken a suite, he supposed, but he didn't want anyone counting how many beds had been slept in. He had shared this one with her—until he'd given up trying to sleep. She'd been emotionally drained and slightly drunk, looking disturbingly vulnerable and wary after she'd washed her face and put on his shirt to sleep in it. She had threaded her bare legs under the covers and kept firmly to her side of the bed.

He'd kept his pants on, since he never wore shorts, and tried not to touch her once he had put out the lights and crawled in beside her. At least until he'd realized she was curled into a ball, shivering from the chill of getting soaked by the rain. He could have risen to turn off the air-conditioning, but he'd spooned her instead.

When she had stiffened, he'd said, "Go to sleep," in the same quietly firm tone he would use on any of his abundant underage cousins, nieces and nephews who might creep down the stairs when they ought to be in bed. Molding Gwyn to him, he'd gone quietly out of his mind while she had relaxed into the hot curve of his chest and thighs.

She had dropped into a deep sleep, leaving him nursing an aching erection, blood burning like acid in his arteries. Every time he dozed, his mind took him back to kissing her on the deck, when she'd aggressively tested his control.

He didn't know how he'd kept from lifting her skirt. Possessiveness, perhaps, because in that moment he hadn't cared if anyone saw his naked ass, but the idea of the paparazzi catching another glimpse of her unclothed had been intolerable.

He'd tried to slow things down while he calculated whether to steal into a stateroom or ask for one to be assigned, so they wouldn't risk interruption.

She had started to cry.

This woman. He was trying very hard to vilify her, to help maintain some distance, but there was no question in him any longer as to whether she had posed for those photos. She was too devastated to be anything less than violated.

Which did things to him. Provoked something that could turn into a blind savagery if he dwelt too much on the injustice.

He sipped the coffee he'd made in the small pot, studying her timeless features, so well suited to her surroundings.

The building was classic Renaissance, imposing and symmetrical. The interior was equally ornate and gracefully proportioned, enriched with dark wood grains and gold accents upon fervent reds and royal blues. The setting made a beautiful foil for her pale skin, pink lips and long dark lashes.

He'd neglected to close the heavy curtains so sunlight poured across her cleanly-washed face. The collar of his white shirt was turned up against her cheek, the unbuttoned sleeve pushed far up her bare arm.

His Lover At Rest, he thought with a sardonic smile, toying with the idea of snapping her photo. His conscience stopped him. *If it makes you feel objectified, well, you have a glimpse into how I feel right now.*

He wasn't bothered by her taking a photo of his photo. He knew he was good-looking. Female attention had always been abundant in his life in the very best way. He wasn't surprised that she found him attractive and certainly wasn't offended by it. He liked it. Too much.

She wasn't as comfortable with their chemistry. She was feeling used and he was being a bastard, not letting her see that he was equally ensnared by lust, but wanting her was weakness enough. Letting her see it would be akin to handing over a weapon, something he was too innately self-protective to ever do.

His phone vibrated in his hand and he dragged his attention off her peaceful expression to see that his cousin was forwarding something.

Can you deal with this? Will talk more when I get there.
Leaving in a few hours.

Vito understood by Paolo's desire for a face-to-face
that he was being abundantly cautious with traceable,
hackable things like texts and emails, but it surprised
him that Paolo was coming to Como. He had been working from home, refusing to leave his wife's side as she
approached the end of her third pregnancy.

But his cousin was smart enough to see the implication behind Vito's appearance with Gwyn last night.
He would want more details, to be sure they had their
story straight, especially before he made further statements to the press.

The multitude of demands for more information from
all corners was threatening to break Vito's phone, coming from every direction from family to news contacts
to the bank's core investors. The story across the sea of
media had shifted from lurid curiosity about the woman
in the photos to deeper speculation as to who she was
and how she had ensnared not just one, but two powerful men into a nude photo scandal. Was she sleeping
with both of them?

He stroked his thumb along the edge of his screen,
deciding it was time to feed another tidbit to the press,
leading them away from Jensen's version of events toward his own.

Yesterday, he had ordered a team to look for a connection between the spa owner and Jensen, suspecting
it could be a laundry for some of the funds Jensen had
funneled. Even if the spa's only crime was the breach
of Gwyn's privacy, he didn't see any reason they should
remain open and making money while Gwyn suffered.

With enormous satisfaction, he touched the query from one of his former paramours who worked as an anchor for an Italian morning talk show. Quote me as stating that the photos were taken without her consent at a local spa, he messaged to her.

As the *whoosh* sounded to tell him the text was sent, he could practically hear her spiked heels racing down to her producer's office, intent on identifying said spa and surprising the owner with an early-morning interview. She would seize world coverage with her exclusive by noon.

With a smirk at how easily the press was played, he turned his attention to the email Paolo had forwarded.

It was from Travis Sanders, director of an architectural firm Vito had never heard of. A quick swipe to his browser revealed it was a growing global corporation based in Charleston. Henry Sanders had started in real estate and morphed into renovation and restoration. His son, Travis, had earned his degree then took over his father's firm, expanding into design and engineering. All of their projects were prestigious; the most current one was a cathedral in Brazil.

Vito read Travis's email to Paolo:

I haven't heard from my sister since the tenth of last month. If you're screening her calls, stop screening me. I want to hear from her.

Short and decidedly acrid.

Gwyn shifted on the bed, rolling onto her back and opening her eyes. Confusion quickly fell into a wince of memory. She glanced at the empty spot beside her, sat up, saw him and brought the edge of the sheet up to the buttons closed across her chest.

"I thought you said he was your stepbrother?" Vito said.

"Who? Travis?" She frowned in sleepy confusion. "He is. Why?"

"He wants to hear from you. He thinks we're preventing you from calling."

She sighed and looked at the landline beside the bed like it was a snake he'd asked her to pick up.

Since she'd left her own mobile back at the house, he rose and took his across to her. "Would you rather text?"

Her gaze flickered across his bare chest and wariness trembled in her eyelashes while sexual awareness brought a light pink glow to her skin. He would have smiled with satisfaction if his entire body hadn't tightened in response. Her scent was coming off those rumpled sheets in a way that tugged at his vitals.

She expertly sent off a quick message and handed back the phone, not looking at him.

Despite it being very early in Charleston, the phone vibrated immediately with a response.

Vito glanced at it and couldn't help a dry smirk. "He wants to know his father's birthday. To confirm that was actually you who just texted, I imagine."

"Seriously?" She took back the phone, tapped out a lengthy message and slapped it back into Vito's hand.

He glanced at the exchange, reading that she'd told her stepbrother she was fine, not being held hostage, didn't know what to say and hoped the press wasn't bothering Henry. She wanted Travis to apologize to him for her.

Vito frowned at her expression of misery, started to tell her what was in store for the spa, but another message came through.

"'This isn't like you,'" Vito read.

"How the hell does he know what I'm like?" she muttered, sliding her feet out the side of the bed. "He barely talks to me."

"You're to call him when you can talk freely," he read aloud as she headed toward the bathroom.

She made a noise and said, "I'm going to see if it's possible to drown in a shower."

"Don't take too long. I'm hungry and plan to order breakfast now that you're up."

Funny how something as simple as a shower became a saving grace in a time of crisis. Washing her hair, smoothing a soapy facecloth over her body... It was comfortingly normal. Routine. She took her time, thinking of nothing as water rained down upon her.

Until her mind drifted to hearing the shower in the night.

Why had Vito risen to shower at 2:00 a.m.? He'd been hard against her butt. She remembered that. If she hadn't been so drained, she might have turned and let him do something she would be regretting right now.

Had he touched himself in here? Pleasured himself? When he could have had her out there?

The thought struck like a blow, tightening her midsection, making her miserable all over again. She had to stop thinking there was any sort of potential between them. Maybe sex was an option. He'd told her to go ahead and use him, after all. But that's all it would be: empty sex. There was no room for romance. They weren't lovers. Despite appearances, they weren't dating. They weren't even friends.

This was all fake.

And her life was a complete disaster, she confronted anew as she stepped from the shower and faced a choice between last night's sparkling evening wear and his rumpled white shirt. She was not in a fit mental state to start any kind of relationship.

She pulled on the robe from the back of the door. It had an embroidered sailboat on the left lapel and was made of thick, comforting chenille. She knotted the belt and emerged to scents of ham and eggs, coffee and sweet pastries. Her stomach contracted. When had she last eaten, she wondered? Vito had forced a few morsels on her last night from the extravagant buffet, but she hadn't been interested.

He was closing the door behind someone as she came out and waved at a stack of clothing that had been delivered. "See if that fits."

She didn't know what to say and found herself fingering through the clothes. There was a clean shirt for him, a short-sleeved, collared one in cobalt blue along with clean socks.

For her, he'd ordered clean underpants, a camisole with a shelf bra in butter yellow, palazzo pants with a subtle floral print and a sheer top that picked up the colors in the pants with splashes of emerald and streaks of pink.

"We're going shopping so you won't have to wear it long if you don't like it," he said, making her realize she was frowning.

"No, it's fine. I thought I'd be wearing the robe back

to the house." She looked for price tags, didn't find any and started to worry. How would she pay for this?

"Let's eat," he said, indicating the set table before the now open window.

Their view looked onto the red umbrella tables six stories below, the marina of bobbing, million-dollar boats and the deceptively placid lake glinting in the cradle of mountain peaks.

"Is the shopping really necessary?" she asked, breaking the yoke of her poached egg with the tine of her fork.

He shrugged. "It's a parade for the cameras and you need clothes for all the circulating we'll be doing over the next few weeks, so, yes. I would say it is."

She watched her fork tremble as a fresh wave of helpless anger swamped her.

"I would like to remind you that I don't have a job. How am I supposed to pay for a new wardrobe?"

"You are so cute, Gwyn," he said, *so* patronizing. "I am indulging my *innamorata*. It's what besotted men do."

Her appetite died. She put down her fork, vainly wishing she wasn't sitting here naked under a robe he had funded. She wished she had a better choice than walking out of here in clothes that were borrowed or an outfit chosen and paid for by him. She wasn't used to being this powerless. Even when Travis had been unknowingly annihilating her sense of self-worth, she'd had a job and enough savings to get herself and her mother started over in a cheap room if Henry had called off the wedding.

"Women love shopping, Gwyn. Why are you so upset by the prospect?" Vito asked, tucking into his breakfast with gusto.

"Because this isn't like me," she said, tartly quoting her stepbrother. "My mother didn't have much. She made ends meet, but we lived very simply and I still do."

She typically ate scrambled eggs she cooked for herself, not delicately poached orbs on toasted ciabatta with garlic and a pesto hollandaise, garnished with shallots and plum tomatoes. She drank orange juice she mixed from concentrate, or instant coffee, not mimosas and rich, dark espresso that made her want to moan in ecstasy with the first taste.

She swallowed her tentative sip of the hot, bitter brew and set down her tiny cup, noting that Vito was watching her, like he was deciding whether to believe her. She hesitated to open up, but figured it was better to be honest about her background than to hide it.

"Mom met my stepfather while working as a janitor in his office. Travis was *not* impressed by his father's choice in second wives. He was at university and I moved into his old room for my last year of high school. I guess it was weird for him to suddenly have this geeky girl underfoot whenever he visited his dad. Strangers living in his house."

She had taken refuge in homework when Travis was around, only emerging to eat dinner where Henry had put her at ease and made her laugh.

"My mother genuinely loved his father," she said, silently willing Vito to believe her. "She never would have brought me into any man's home for any reason except to give me a father. I think of Henry that way." She had to drop her gaze as she admitted, "But the day before their wedding, I overheard Travis warning Henry that we might be gold diggers. I thought his mind would change over time, as he saw that we were just trying to be a family, but a year into their marriage my mother was diagnosed with cancer. I was supposed to move out, go to college, but instead I stayed to help Henry nurse her. I took some online courses, but Mom felt like such a burden on us. Travis didn't come around much. I know how it looked to him, like Henry was stuck with a pile of medical bills for someone he shouldn't have to support."

She stared into the harsh glare of sunlight on the water to sear back the tears gathering in her eyes.

"It was such a raw deal that she finally found a man who loved her, who wanted to take care of her, and she died before she could make a proper life with him. Make him happy."

"I'm sorry to hear that," Vito said, sounding sincere, covering her hand.

She removed her hand, forcing herself to shrug off the bleak sadness.

"I'm very conscious of the fact that Travis thinks I'm only maintaining a relationship with Henry because he has money and I don't. I never take any when he offers, so letting you swan me in and out of Italian boutiques is not exactly the picture I want to paint so my stepbrother will let me continue visiting the only father I've ever had."

She looked at him, blinking several times to bring her vision back from a wall of white to see his toughened yet brutally handsome expression.

"But I'm hardly in a position to demand the luxury of pride, am I?" she added caustically.

He was watching her with a gravity that made her feel naked all over again. "Would he really stop you from seeing him?" he asked.

She shrugged. "I don't know," she muttered. "He

loves his father as much as I do and wants to protect him. He wasn't trying to be cruel. I mean, you'd probably say the same thing to your own father in that situation, wouldn't you?"

Vito's stare was inscrutable. He held her gaze for a long time, like he had a million responses and was sifting for the best one. He settled on saying, "Eat," and lowered his attention to his plate.

Well, that settled that, didn't it, she thought facetiously, and forced herself to take a bite.

No matter how sincere Gwyn seemed, Vito couldn't afford to let himself be swayed emotionally. While she finished getting ready, he reviewed her background more thoroughly.

She interrupted, emerging from the bathroom with a more natural look that was infinitely more beautiful than last night's smoky eyes and sharp cheekbones and red, glossy lips painted by the stylist. Gwyn had frowned when he'd handed her the pots of color and paint, grumbling about not wanting to look like a ghost if she was going to be photographed. If not for that, she implied, she wouldn't have accepted the makeup at all.

"What do we do with last night's clothes?" She looked for them.

"I've made arrangements."

She stared at him.

He lifted his brow in inquiry.

"I borrowed something. I want to be sure it's returned in good condition," she said.

"It will be." He frowned, annoyed by what sounded like a lack of faith, but also seeing yet more evidence of the do-it-myself streak of independence she seemed to have. "I reviewed your file and some other details," he told her as they left the room.

She looked over her shoulder at him, dismayed, but not fearful. "Like?"

Her financial situation. Her debt level was low, but she had a little, and hadn't made any significant payments or purchases recently. There had been nothing to red flag her as possessing or spending a sum that might have been embezzled. Instead, he'd found more evidence that she was exactly as she portrayed herself.

"You've worked hard for the education and position you've attained," he acknowledged once they were in the privacy of the elevator. "But Fabrizio signed off on your transfer despite there being two candidates with more experience. It supports what you said yesterday, that you might have been recruited because you were green and possibly more likely to let things slide out of ignorance."

"So you're willing to believe it based on your own assessment of hard evidence, but nothing I say has any bearing. My word means nothing to you. Isn't that the story of every woman's life." She shrugged on the cloak of righteous anger she'd been wearing since he met her, but he could sense the hurt beneath.

He wasn't sure what kind of reaction he expected, but he hadn't expected that. His belief in her *meant* something to her. It made him realize exactly how much power he had over her and he wasn't sure he was comfortable with it.

Since when did he not embrace power? He loved it!

But he was suddenly confronted with how vulnerable she was. To all the men in her life, but especially to him, right now. It slapped at his conscience, made

him think again about her saying he would protect his
father. The joke was on her. His real mother had been
light-years ahead of his father in social status, belonging to the Donatelli banking clan. His father had been
on the bottom of society's spectrum. A criminal of the
vilest order.

He had cold-bloodedly seduced her with an eye to
his own gain.

What are you *doing, Vito?* he chided himself.

He was protecting the bank, he reminded himself.
And his blood was decidedly hot when Gwyn's hand
was in his own.

He strolled her through the late morning sun, ignoring the cameras, entering every boutique on the prom-
enade and refusing to leave without making a purchase.

But for a woman who only needed to act enamored
to get herself out of trouble, she did a lousy job of it.
She wasn't outright defiant. No, her resistance was subtle enough to give credence to what she had said earlier about not wanting to look like a gold digger. She
needed cajoling to enter a change room, pulled a face at
the prices and frowned at the growing number of bags
he was having sent back to the yacht club.

It was beyond his experience. Every woman he knew
enjoyed being spoiled this way, whether sisters, mother
or lovers. He had been raised to be chivalrous, and not
only owned a sizable number of shares in the bank, but
investing was his living. He made more money in a day
than he could spend in a week. This was pocket change.

He began taking special care, looking for items that
were particularly flattering to her, complimenting her,
trying to soften that spine and coax a smile of plea-

sure out of her. Why couldn't she relax and see the fun in this?

A motorcycle jacket with a faux fur collar and narrow sleeves that capped the tops of her hands to her knuckles looked genuinely delightful on her. He stood behind her as she eyed it in the mirror.

"It suits you. Makes you look as tough as you are," he said.

She met his gaze in the mirror. "You do this a lot, don't you? I honestly didn't see you as the kind of guy who had to buy his women."

She might as well have butted that hard head of hers back into his lip and nose. He tightened his hands on her shoulders to freeze her in place.

Her gaze met his again and she saw the danger there, stilling, hand on the zipper of the jacket.

"Be very careful what you say to me, *cara*."

"You want those vultures out there to believe this," she said with a small toss of her head to the front of the store, where music was blaring so loudly they could barely hear each other even back here. "I don't have to. Or does your ego demand that I fall for you for real?"

Once again she had him thinking about a powerful man exploiting a vulnerable young woman.

That wasn't what this was.

She moved the zipper an inch then shrugged his hands off her shoulders. "Buy it if you think I should have it. I don't care."

The hell of it was, he believed her.

Gwyn watched cute sundresses and silk scarves, two hats and a designer bag that cost the earth all go into colorful boutique bags. Vito told her they'd buy eve-

ning gowns in Milan—for what?—but insisted she get
trendy jeans, cocktail skirts and flirty tops, lingerie
that she flatly refused to let him watch her try on and
shoes. Dear Lord, the shoes.

Deep in her most covetous, most materialistic heart,
she adored Italian-made shoes. She'd been saving up for
a pair, browsing regularly as she debated whether to be
practical and buy something she might wear often or
ridiculously capricious and own something that would
sit in a box in her closet, to be worn on only a few special occasions.

Vito bought her six pairs of very chic, very expensive
day shoes and completely dismissed them as, "They'll
do for now." More, he assured her, would be purchased
with the gowns in the city.

She might have protested, but he was already angry
with her. That moment at the mirror had made her tremble inside, he'd looked so lethal. At the same time, she
knew he wouldn't hurt her physically. It was her heart,
her own ego and self-confidence that were in peril.

Especially because, despite her nastiness, he didn't
let up on his solicitude. They walked from store to
store and paparazzi swarmed around them, clicking
and flashing and capturing every murmur and expression. One called something particularly disgusting and
she flinched.

"Ignore them," Vito growled, drawing her closer to
the shelter of his big body, brushing his lips against the
tip of her ear as he spoke, then smoothed his fingers
through the tails of her loose hair, caressing her waist,
so attentive to her needs.

She imagined she looked deeply smitten every time
he touched her like this. That's why she'd had to insult

him and drive a wedge between them. Her response to his pretend seduction was dangerously real. Her nipples tightened when all he did was touch the small of her back. She flushed with desire when she inhaled the scent of his neck.

How was she so comfortable under his touch? That's what she wanted to know. Normally she was quite standoffish with men. If they so much as took her elbow while they walked her down the street, she found the presumptiveness of it annoying.

Not Vito. Her skin called out for each light graze of contact. She was in a perpetual state of readiness, skin sensitized and aching with anticipation, eager for his merest caress. She wanted him to smother her with his big body. Absorb her.

In some ways it was exhausting. She was incredibly relieved when he pointed to a car with a chauffeur in sunglasses leaning against it, reading his phone. "We'll take a drive to some viewpoints, see if we can lose these cameras before we head back to the house."

Their last two boutique bags went into the trunk where the myriad of other purchases were now arranged along with dry cleaner bags holding the clothing they'd worn last night. The man really was a demigod, taking care of the dreary details of life with what seemed like a magical snap of his finger and thumb. Forget the other conquests who fell for this routine. She was becoming one of them. How could any woman *not* find this level of provision seductive?

She settled with a sigh on the leather seat in the back, pretending she wasn't aware of the scooters that kept buzzing up beside them for the next ten minutes as they drove into the hills. The windows were blacked out, however, so the followers soon fell away, accepting that their opportunity was over and they might as well go file the photos they had and collect their payments.

The car climbed high above the lake, the twists in the road taking them into stretches of quiet thoroughfare, where she finally let out her breath in a sigh.

Vito leaned forward to close the privacy window and poured both of them a water from the bottle in the door.

"Was it so bad?" he asked. "Spending my money?"

"No," she said, adding a sarcastic, "How was it for you?"

She heard how suggestive that sounded and made a noise into her glass.

"Why does everything I say come out sounding dirty around you?" she muttered.

"Freudian slip?" he suggested.

She slid her thumb along the rim of her glass, blushing and saying nothing.

"Your silence speaks volumes," he taunted.

"Am I the first woman to find you attractive? I doubt it," she said caustically.

"You're the first to be so annoyed by it," he said with a hint of laughter in his voice. "Why? Because you're so tempted?"

"I've never been a drug user and that's what it would be," she muttered. "You're sitting there like a giant pain-killer promising to keep me from feeling the bus that's crushing me. So, yes, I'm tempted." She couldn't believe how honest she was being. It wasn't like her to be this blunt, but what shred of dignity was left to lose? "But I've never gone to bed with a man purely for physical release. It makes me feel cheap to consider it."

"You're incredibly insulting when you want to be,

aren't you? The problem, I think, is that you don't know how powerful this particular painkiller will be." He leaned across and set her glass in her door. His was gone and his hands went to her waist. "Come here."

"What—?"

He dragged her to straddle his thighs, making her stiffen in surprise at the sudden intimacy of having her legs open across him, her inner thighs lightly stretched by the press of his thick, hard ones.

She kept her arms stiff, holding herself off him, but she was intrigued despite her wariness. "There's no one to see this performance," she reminded tautly.

"Yes, I know," he said smokily, and stroked his hands up and down her thighs, massaging in a way that sent ripples of anticipation into her pelvis. With a little shift, he slouched and they were sex to sex, her tingling loins firmly seated against the very hard ridge of his erection.

"If only I still worked for you and could charge you with sexual harassment," she said, but her voice had thinned and her twitching thighs wouldn't cooperate enough to lift her away.

"I don't have to buy women, *cara*. They come to me for this." His hips came up just enough to press where too many nerve endings were centered. She bucked in an allover response, gasping.

"You're so full of yourself," she told him, shivering, not fighting the hands that pressed her hips so she felt that delicious grind again.

The corners of his mouth deepened in satisfied amusement. "Let's see which one of us wants to be full of me, hmm?" His hand slid up her side, across her shoulder to cup the side of her neck.

A trail of tingles followed his caress, sensitizing her,

making her go still when self-preservation instincts told her to get the hell off his lap.

As he exerted a tiny pressure, urging her forward, asking for her mouth against his, she gave in.

It's only a kiss. They'd done it before.

But this wasn't a kiss. It was a match to a flame.

As her mouth reached his, he captured her in a hungry kiss, like last night, only hotter. With a confident hand on her butt, he rocked her against his erection, making her shudder and take over the move herself, seeking the rhythm that would build the desire in the heated, dampening flesh between her legs.

Distantly she told herself to be cautious, remember this was about the bank. He was only doing this to prove a point, but her arms went around his neck in a kind of instinctive twine. She pressed to crush her breasts against his chest. Their tongues tangled and they both opened their mouths to deepen the kiss into something flagrant and wildly passionate.

Maybe there was something else she ought to have been thinking about, fretting over, but few thoughts of any clarity stuck after that. She became a being of pure sensation. All her awareness centered on the points where they touched, how he stroked her back and hips, how her body prickled and responded like firecrackers were exploding at different points.

His hand slid to cup her breast, weighing and gently massaging. She rubbed her nipple into his palm, never so free when it came to sex. Maybe if he'd seemed surprised by her lack of inhibition, she would have pulled back, but he groaned with appreciation, encouraging her, giving her all the pressure she needed as he shaped and squeezed her breast. She loved the way the light fabric of her top and silky cami made it easy for him to find and tantalize her nipple, pinching the peak and causing a stab of arousal straight between her legs.

She gasped and moaned approval. More heat rushed to pool in her loins, making her ache there and seek that hard ridge. She rubbed, trying to soothe the needy throb between her legs, unable to remember the last time she'd had any sex, let alone thrown herself into it like this. No man had ever aroused her this quickly and thoroughly with little more than a kiss and a few brazen caresses.

She arched as his other hand found its way beneath her top and pulled her cami askew, so he could pull back and look at her through the translucent film of her overtop. They both watched his thumb circle her nipple, flicking back and forth, stimulating the tight bead so she shuddered and panted, scalp tight, excited beyond what she could imagine could happen from such a simple bit of teasing.

"Come here," he said, urging her to lift on her knees and push her nipple toward his mouth.

She did, bracing her hands on his shoulders, vaguely aware they were in a moving car. Maybe the blur around them was empty of humans, but the darkened glass at her back wasn't. She ought to be showing more decorum, but his tongue moved the silk of her top against her nipple in delicate friction. The dampness of his mouth enclosed her in heat, sucking and inciting. She was lost, groaning with delight as he tortured her, licking and moving that damp fabric, squeezing the swell of her breast just enough to push more blood into the tip.

She was going to climax from this alone, she thought, working her nails with agitation against his shirt, thinking she should stop this, but she was compelled to keep going because it felt so damned good.

Her waistband released and his other hand slid in, confident and possessive, cupping soaked lace, saying something in Italian she didn't have the wherewithal to interpret, but he sounded pleased. Like he was complimenting her. She absolutely flowered when he sounded so appreciative and admiring.

He held his palm steady for her to grind herself into the heel of his hand. She moaned with pleasure as her arousal became acute. She tore at his collar and tried to stroke his skin, wanted to bend and kiss him, but as she pulled back, he stared at her chest.

"Give me the other one," he growled, eyeing her left breast, still tucked away.

With trembling hands, she lifted her top out of the way, pushed the cami down so her breasts were thrusting out the top of it, brazen in the extreme—

He opened his mouth wide on her bare nipple and she nearly screamed at the sensation of his teeth closing softly, dragging all the way to the tip before he sucked her into the deep, wet cavern of heat that was his greedy mouth.

A rush of need flooded into her sex. Into his palm.

He made an animalistic noise and his fingers pushed past silk, fingertips seeking, two penetrating, burying deep, thumb tracing and finding. Circling.

"Yes," she gasped, giving herself up to the stunning height of pleasure, welcoming the thrust of his fingers, clasping him hard to her breast as he nipped in a way that was just short of pain. The sensations he was offering were so sharp and intense it was almost too much to bear. She clenched, trying to hold back, realizing how close she was to losing it. This wasn't what she'd meant to happen.

His arm clamped around her waist and he kept lashing her with those twin sensations until she couldn't hold back. Orgasm crashed over her. Her body nearly buckled under the power of it. Her cries of abandon filled the backseat and she pressed her hands to the ceiling, all of herself offered to him as he pleasured her, nearly bursting into jagged tears at the intensity of her release. Dying. She was dying and would never breathe again.

The paroxysm held her for a long time, until she slowly became aware that his caress had become soothing.

His damp hand moved, sliding onto her hip then cupping her backside, urging her to nestle her tender, throbbing flesh against the aggressive ridge of his erection straining the front of his pants. He lifted his head and licked at her panting mouth, teasing her into kissing him back.

She was still shaking with reaction and kept her eyes closed as she kissed him with swollen, trembling lips, aware of his hardness everywhere: shoulders, arms, thighs. Even his lips were firm where hers were soft with spent pleasure. His heart was pounding while she was still trying to catch her breath, both of them damp with perspiration.

Finally she dragged her eyes open to see he had a very smug, satisfied light in his half-closed eyes. That arrogance was unnerving, making her realize he had completely taken her apart while losing none of his own control. Only his collar was slightly askew, his hair barely out of place.

He told her in a low growl what he wanted to do to her.

What was wrong with her that she responded with an internal clench of anticipation to his dirty talk?

She pushed off his lap and shakily tidied her clothes, avoiding his gaze, trying not to think of where his hand had been. How she'd sounded as she called out with release. Had the driver heard her? How did things just keep getting more mortifying?

She managed to rally, responding to what he'd said with a scathing, "The way you're looking so self-satisfied, I'd think we already did that."

He angled to look at her, reaching to smooth a wisp of her hair from its tangle on her eyelashes. Her pulse leaped with excitement, but his finger didn't even brush her skin.

"It was bothering me that other men had seen you naked. But no man has ever seen you like that, have they? I'm very satisfied."

What an egotistical—

"You're a jerk," she told him, thinking there were saltier words and she was tempted to find them.

"Are you losing the feel-good already? Because I'm right here, ready and willing to take you to your happy place all over again."

"Oh, shut up," she snapped, turning her face to the window. Pride. Who knew it was such an unaffordable luxury?

CHAPTER SIX

GWYN DIDN'T KNOW how close she'd just come to being taken in the backseat under the straying eye of his driver. Oh, Carlo would have known they were petting, would have turned up the music so he wouldn't hear anything indelicate, but neither he nor Gwyn knew that Vito had nearly lost control, so caught up in Gwyn's pleasure he'd almost found his own, fully clothed and completely at her service. He'd barely stopped himself from rolling her beneath him on the seat, stripping them bare and quite possibly planting a baby in her without a single thought for the consequences.

The thought disturbed him. Was that how he'd been conceived? In a fit of blind passion that completely disregarded the impact to the woman in question?

By the few accounts Vito had from his adoptive parents, his mother had been deeply infatuated, if far too young and naive for a thirtysomething gangster with a pitiless determination to get whatever he wanted. He had wanted Antoinietta Donatelli. He had seduced her. His family had always sworn up, down and sideways that Vito wasn't a product of rape. No, he was the product of a man taking advantage of a woman who didn't have nearly the worldliness needed to resist him.

Not unlike Gwyn, who didn't take lovers strictly for the pleasure of physical release.

Because, he suspected, no man had given her a release like that. He probably shouldn't have, but her animosity had been eating at him. That remark about buying women and her resistance toward him on every level had been grinding away at his control. When she had called herself "cheap" for wanting to sleep with him, something feral in him had snapped, demanding that he *show* her how good they would be together.

Cheap? It was unique and precious, beyond even what he had imagined it could be. Disconcertingly powerful.

And honest.

Her reaction now, so taken aback by her own abandonment, told him how thoroughly he had owned her in those moments. He thrilled to it, but it caused a shift inside him. Something he wasn't fully prepared to examine, fearing he was making a rationalization to justify getting what he wanted: her.

But the way she'd ignited in his arms made thinking of anything except possessing her impossible.

They seemed to have left the paparazzi far behind and circled back toward the house. As soon as they were inside, Gwyn went straight through to the small patio outside the back door, where the cool afternoon breeze off the water gave her the first proper breath she'd taken since coming apart at Vito's touch.

She went down the steps to the pool deck where she stared out over the lake, blood cooling, hands curled around the rail to ground her back into harsh reality. Why had she let that happen? And what did it mean for the rest of this pantomime they were acting? Would they become lovers in every way, not just a one-sided grope that only proved his superiority over her?

That was the part that devastated her. She could give herself orgasms if she wanted them. But despite all the ways he'd turned out to be different from the urbane Italian gentleman she'd fantasized about, she was even more in thrall than ever. Would she become his lover?

She couldn't imagine finding the will to say, *No.*

Vito came outside with two wineglasses and a corked bottle. He wordlessly poured and offered her one, not speaking until she took hers.

"Salute," he said, gaze trying to catch hers.

She couldn't do it, too aware of how intimate things had been between them. Too vulnerable to him.

"I keep making you angry because it seems the only way to keep you from falling into despair," he said, as though explaining the answer to a riddle.

"Something else for my own good?" She snapped her gaze up to his.

He smiled faintly. "Whatever works."

She released a shaken sigh, finding his statement not exactly comforting, but oddly bolstering. He wasn't toying with her for fun, but trying to help her in his backhanded way.

She couldn't deny that his lovemaking had, for a few minutes, completely wiped away her anxiety over her nightmare of a life. Now everything was flooding back and she would be very thankful if he did something annoying. Despair hovered like a rain cloud looking to move in and burst over her.

He set his glass on a table and shrugged out of his new jacket, a vintage cut in light wool with leather patches at the shoulders. It was gorgeous on him, very debonair, but the dove-colored shirt beneath was equally smart, clinging to his muscled shoulders, buttons open in a V that showed his throat and collarbone and a few dark chest hairs.

He slung the jacket negligently over the back of the nearest chair, attention shifting to his phone. With a flick of his thumb across the screen, he paraphrased from something he was reading. "The spa is claiming they had no knowledge of the photos, but the press has found the same connection my team discovered this morning. Your masseuse is related to one of Jensen's employees. I'll take you to lodge a formal complaint with the police when we return to Milan so they can look at pressing charges for invasion of privacy."

"Charging the masseuse doesn't put the blame on Kevin, though, does it?"

"He has worked very hard to keep his hands clean, but we'll get there. It's early days yet." He picked up his glass and sipped, continuing to read his emails.

Days. It hadn't even been two full ones, but she'd already gone further with him than most of the men she'd dated for months. She was in so much trouble if that was a precursor of what was to come.

Pensively sipping the pale gold of the wine, she wound up exclaiming a very sincere, "Oh, that's very good!"

Not that she was any sort of connoisseur, but Travis always brought wine when she cooked and he didn't punish anyone with cheap stuff. She'd been enjoying trying bottles here in Italy and hadn't found a bad one, but this surpassed anything in her price range.

Vito glanced up, offering what looked like a very

genuine smile for a change. "It's the private reserve from my great-grandparents' vineyard. One of my cousins runs it and doles the bottles out to family every year. We could make a fortune, but it's too good to sell."

"Do you—" Gwyn forgot what she was going to ask as a flash of movement caught her eye.

Was that a little boy? He touched his lips to signal her to keep quiet as he climbed the rail that bordered the pool terrace then darted behind an oversize terracotta planter.

Vito followed her gaze and glanced backward at the empty landscape, then brought his alert frown back to her. "What's wrong?"

She started to say, "I saw a little boy—"

Before she could get the words out, the boy was barreling straight for Vito's legs.

In the same moment, Vito's expression hardened. He plunked his glass down and spun in a fluid motion, like he knew exactly what was coming. He crouched, grabbed, then threw the boy high into the air as he straightened, then caught him firmly and held him nose to nose.

"You little gremlin. I ought to throw *you* into the pool."

"Do it!" The boy's laughing eyes brightened with excitement. He splayed out his arms and legs, ready to fly through the air into the still, blue water despite being fully dressed.

"I won't," Vito told him, hitching the boy's wiry figure onto his arm so they were eye to eye. "That's your punishment for trying to push me in. No swimming at all. Say hello to Miss Ellis," he said, indicating her with a nod. "This is Roberto. He has all of his mother's sass and twice his father's disregard for danger."

"I was going to come in with you," the boy excused, curling his arm around Vito's neck and pressing his cheek to Vito's with open trust and affection. He was speaking perfect English but could have been Vito's son, his looks were so patently Italian. He turned his attention to Gwyn and pronounced what sounded like a coached speech. "It's nice to meet you. Welcome to our home." He offered his small hand for a shake, making it a firm one.

"It's a beautiful home," Gwyn said, ridiculously charmed, even though he couldn't have been more than five. "I'm very pleased to meet you, too."

Roberto gave her a stare reminiscent of Vito's most delving look.

"Are you American? Mama is Canadian and sometimes people think she's American, but your accent is different. You sound like our housekeeper in Charleston."

"Good ear," Gwyn said with a bemused smile. Honestly, he had more sophistication than some thirty-year-old executives she had met.

"Did you drive here yourself? Where is your father?" Vito asked, giving the boy a little bounce.

"He won't let me drive," Roberto said with a disgruntled scowl, then pointed to the top floor. "He's putting Bianca in her bed. She fell asleep in the car. She has a cold."

"He brought both of you? How is your mother?"

"So pregnant," a woman said, coming out the back door of the house.

Lauren Donatelli was very pregnant, but carried it

beautifully on her tall frame, glowing and graceful as she came down the short flight of steps onto the pool terrace, nary a waddle in her step.

Gwyn recognized her from photos she'd seen in the Charleston news several years ago, along with the odd image published in the company newsletter where Lauren invariably stood next to Paolo looking warm and approachable despite how aloof and distant her husband always seemed.

"Hi, I'm Lauren," she said, offering her hand.

"Gwyn," she murmured, and tried to thank her for the loan of clothes, but was waved off.

"Anything for Vito. Hello, *caro*," she said to him. He stooped a little so she could kiss both his cheeks.

"Should you be anywhere but a maternity ward?" he asked her.

"I offered to check myself into a clinic, but the doctor said there was no point since it will be at least two weeks. Paolo wouldn't let me stay in the city without him, of course. His mother is at the house, but you know what he's like. Won't let me out of his sight." She shook her head in exasperation.

"Roberto was born inside their front door. Bianca delivered in a car," Vito informed Gwyn.

"It was easier to lose the paparazzi waiting at the gate if we made it look like we were going for a simple family outing," Paolo said, arriving with a baby monitor that he set on the table next to Vito's wineglass. "Miss Ellis," he greeted with a cool nod.

"Signor Donatelli," she murmured, intimidated to the soles of her feet.

Thankfully his son pleaded, "May I swim, Papa. *Per favore?*"

"Vito and I must talk about work, but if you put on your trunks you can come to the shore with us and wade."

"Yes!" Roberto dropped out of Vito's arms and started to run toward the house.

"Quietly," Lauren warned, slowing his step. "Don't wake your sister. I'll start dinner," Lauren said with a well-practiced hostess smile.

"You will not," Paolo told her. "I'll cook when I come in. Stay off your feet."

A man willing to cook. Gwyn was so astonished it took her a moment to blurt out the sensible solution that broke the challenging stare between the married couple.

"I can make dinner."

Everyone looked at her. These two men really were too much masculinity in one impactful wall for any woman to handle.

"Unless you need me to be there while you talk?" She had no doubt she would be the topic of their discussion. Frankly, she was hoping to avoid listening to her humiliation being kicked over like something a dog owner had failed to dispose of properly.

"I would appreciate your cooking, if it's something you don't mind doing," Paolo said, then turned to his wife. "You may sit and chop tomatoes if you promise not to put your weight behind it."

She made a face at him.

"If our daughter wakes, would you call me?" he added to Gwyn. "She's under the weather and will want to be held, but Lauren needs to take it easy. At this stage the hiccups will start her labor. I have my hands full enough without catching a baby today."

"It's twenty minutes out of your life," Lauren murmured, looking at her fingernails. "I don't know what you're complaining about."

He caught her hand and brought her curled knuckles to his lips. "I can barely think of anything else as it is. You know that. Try to buy us a few more days while we settle this work crisis? Please?"

The looks they were giving each other were such a mix of open emotion, tender and teasing and loving, Gwyn knew she ought to look away. It was a private couple's moment, but it was so beautiful, she was transfixed. She wanted that. The cajole and silent communication and connection that bound in a thousand ways. The secretive smile. The way they looked like they wanted to kiss, but were in no hurry because Paolo was stroking her bent knuckle against his upper lip and they had an abundance of time and opportunities for loving affection.

"Maybe this one will have my patience instead of your lack of impulse control," Lauren teased. "We could get lucky."

"Do not blame me!" Paolo scoffed. "They wind up with your sense of humor and think it's funny—stop laughing. I'm serious. No laughing. You'll put yourself into labor."

Lauren disobeyed, releasing a hearty chuckle that made Gwyn smile along with her.

Their son came outside in his trunks and Gwyn turned her expression of amusement into a greeting for the boy, giving the couple their privacy to exchange a kiss.

When she glanced at Vito, she saw he was watching her, his expression unreadable.

* * *

A few minutes later, Gwyn was moving around Lauren's kitchen, chatting with her with surprising ease. Perhaps Lauren wasn't resting with her feet up as her husband had demanded, but since she wasn't holding anything heavier than a paring knife, Gwyn didn't say anything. Besides, every birth story she'd ever heard was a lengthy process, happening in the midnight hours. Lauren wasn't complaining of a backache or any of those other things women talked about as precursors to labor. She was relaxed and pleasant and ever so nice!

Feeling as vilified as she did, Gwyn was deeply relieved to be treated like a normal person.

"Did you get that top at the boutique on the far end of the lake?" Lauren asked. "I bought the red-and-gold one two months ago. They have amazing stuff, don't they?"

Gwyn agreed, then, as she set a pot of water to boil and the conversation lulled, she screwed up her courage and said, "I, um, lived in Charleston before I came here. I'm not trying to pry," she hurried to add. "I just thought I should tell you that I couldn't help but be aware of all the coverage about your husband. Um, first husband, I mean."

Lauren's expression smoothed to something very grave, gaze sliding away to hide her thoughts. "It was a heartbreaking time."

"I'm very sorry for your loss," Gwyn said quickly, feeling it was the decent thing to say to the widow of a war hero, but it wasn't why she'd brought it up. She wasn't asking the big question that had been on everyone else's mind at the time: had Lauren slept with her husband's best friend the night she had learned her husband was dead? The answer to that was outside throwing rocks into the lake, as far as Gwyn could tell.

"I wouldn't have mentioned it except… Is it bad taste to ask how you handled all the attention?" Gwyn asked.

Lauren smiled with empathy. "It's exhausting, isn't it? People so love to judge." She opened a cupboard and drew out a box of linguine noodles. "I guess you make peace with whatever you've done to get yourself into that situation and accept that you can't control what others think or say. It's what you think of yourself that matters."

"I'm obsessed with what other people think," Gwyn admitted glumly. She had a childhood full of starting new schools, being teased for being first to wear a bra, then constantly being underestimated because she was smarter than anyone expected from a girl with good looks.

Her mother had nursed the same sort of angst, having quite an inferiority complex due to an orphan's upbringing. Sometimes Gwyn wondered if that had been her mother's reason for moving so often—part habit, but also a continuous attempt to reinvent herself in hopes of ever-elusive acceptance.

For Gwyn, landing this job in Milan had been her first step in believing she really was good enough and smart enough to earn respect on her own merit, but she was seriously struggling to believe in herself now.

And while she could dismiss the dim views of strangers and comfort herself with the knowledge she hadn't done anything to deserve the humiliation she was suffering, she was acutely sensitive to what Vito might be thinking of her.

Why? Why couldn't she shrug off his judgment of her?

Because he affected her on every level, she acknowledged. Because he had literally controlled how she felt in the car today, working ecstasy through her. If he had the power to make her feel good, he also had the power to devastate her.

She started to blush, feeling the heat rise from deep spaces to become a hot glow on her cheeks. *Such* power. She wished she could get him out from under her skin!

"My turn to pry," Lauren said, handing Gwyn a bag of mushrooms, scanning Gwyn's guilty pink cheeks with interest. "This thing with you and Vito. Have you really been seeing him? Or is it just for show?"

"What?" Gwyn said dumbly, nerveless fingers nearly losing the featherweight of the bag.

"You don't have to tell me," Lauren said with a teasing twinkle in her eye. "I'm being nosy because he's one of my favorite people, but I realize there are things at the bank that can't be discussed. Believe me, I know." She made a face of long suffering. "But…" She sent Gwyn a cagey look as she moved to the sink. "I have a feeling that if he'd been seeing you before this story broke, I would have known."

"What do you mean?" Gwyn asked, knocked off balance by something she couldn't identify. Was she suggesting Vito acted differently around her? Lauren had only seen them together for a minute and a half before they'd come inside and the men had gone to the beach.

"I don't know. There's something in the way he looked at you—" Lauren shrugged, starting to wash her hands, then cut herself off as she gave the soap dispenser next to the sink a shake. "I think there's a new one in the upstairs bathroom," she said, turning off the tap.

"I'll get it," Gwyn said, setting down the mushroom she was stemming.

"I'll peek in on Bianca while I'm up there," Lauren said with a wave.

Seconds later, Lauren's voice was considerably less relaxed as she swore loud enough for Gwyn to hear her all the way down in the kitchen.

"Are you all right?" Gwyn called, making a panicked start up the stairs.

Lauren came to the open door of the main bathroom, bracing herself against it with a white-knuckled grip, expression somewhere between exasperated and remorseful.

"He's going to kill me. Tell Paolo my water just broke."

Vito was not a romantic, but he had seen the longing in Gwyn's expression and felt a kick of commiseration. Paolo and Lauren made anyone covetous of their happiness. He envied his cousin himself, not just for finding his soul mate, but for his freedom to pursue a life with her. Even if Vito did find the right woman…

He was adept at not letting himself dwell on such things and cut off the thoughts as he and Paolo took Roberto down to the water and exchanged reports.

Paolo expanded on what he'd already messaged, saying Fabrizio was a tough nut, but cracks were showing in his story. The board of Jensen's foundation was not yet moved to worry about any of this, let alone meeting to discuss Jensen's possible removal. Jensen himself was leaving the country for a minor quake that was more photo op than actual disaster relief, but would bolster his image.

"You haven't frozen the foundation's assets?" Vito asked.

"I don't have grounds. I'll be pushing for a forensic audit once Fabrizio breaks or we're able to prove Jensen was behind the instructions to move funds, but he is definitely playing a rough PR game right now. This—" He chucked his chin back toward the house and Gwyn. "I see where you're going and it would work if it was true, but I can't go on record saying that you've been having an affair with her all along. We all may have to testify at some point."

"Sì," Vito agreed. "But you can state that unnamed sources—me—" he shrugged "—made you aware some time ago that there were worrisome transactions within the account. We put it on a watch list and saw no reason to remove Miss Ellis because she was not only conducting herself with sound ethics, but has since proven to be an excellent source of knowledge with regards to the foundation's legitimate activities."

"You're convinced she has been conducting herself ethically?"

It was the judgment Vito had been avoiding making, aware that Gwyn was already a weakness to him. He wanted her and therefore he wanted to believe her, because how could he have an affair with a woman who was committing crimes against the bank? He couldn't gamble his family's future on his own selfish desires.

But at every stage, if she was the type to manipulate a man like Jensen, her actions would have been different, right up to this afternoon in the car. *He* would have been the one losing control to her hand or mouth, he was sure, if she was the type to lie and steal and wish him to believe otherwise.

At no time since he'd met her had Gwyn acted dishonorably, though. In fact, she was trying to protect the little family she had from the fallout of dishonor that, if she was innocent, wasn't hers to bear.

The problem was, if she *was* blameless, he was going to have to kill the man who had done this to her.

"I believe she is Jensen's victim, yes," Vito said, and heard the cruel edge on his tone. "They gambled on her lack of experience and when she showed her intelligence, they threw her to the wolves."

He understood the expression *bloodthirsty* as he said it. His tongue tingled and his throat tried a dry swallow, but he didn't long for water. He craved the tang of suffering for Jensen and Fabrizio and whoever had helped them by taking those photos.

He felt the quick slash of Paolo's glance before he returned his watchful gaze to his son, but his cousin obviously read his mood.

"So we imply you two have been having an affair all along and she's been feeding us information. What happens when I'm asked point-blank if I condone my VP of operations sleeping with a customer service rep?" Paolo folded his arms, eyes on his son, but his tone added, *Because I don't*.

"You never comment on the private lives of your family or your employees," Vito said, which was true. "But as a rule, you expect to be notified of such relationships in a timely manner and you have no quarrel with when and how your VP of operations has advised you of this connection."

Paolo shook his head, mouth pulled into a half smirk.

"People call me competitive, but strategy plays are your drug of choice, aren't they?"

"Live the lie and it becomes the truth," he said blithely.

Paolo sobered. "The photos certainly look convincing," he said with another pointed look, before returning his alert attention to his son in the water.

Vito had seen the photos online from today's shopping trip with Gwyn and last night's kiss. The passionate embrace on the stern of the yacht still made his pulse pound just thinking of it. His mind went to the car, the wet heat clenching his fingers as she shuddered and cried out with fulfillment.

There were a million reasons why he should merely *act* like they were an item, rather than make the affair real, but they would make it real. He knew it in the same way that adversaries knew a physical confrontation was coming. They could put it off, because they both knew in their gut that neither of them would come away unscathed, but their making love was inevitable.

"No comment?" Paolo prodded. "Because if she's a victim, don't make her more of one."

That stung. Vito hid it, countering lightly, "What do you want me to say? I like women. I can't help that they like me back."

It was the laissez-faire attitude he always affected when discussing paramours. Paolo was the head of the family. He couldn't escape marriage and the duty of producing progeny. Vito didn't have the same pressure to procreate. He was at liberty to play the field the rest of his life if he wanted to.

Paolo sent him a dour look, the one that told him Vito could show the rest of the world, pretend his entire life was one long, lighthearted affair, but he knew better.

Paolo knew him better than anyone. They had been adversaries themselves in childhood, scrapping constantly. Two strong-willed, alpha-natured boys of similar ages would. It had culminated in a fistfight of epic proportions when they were twelve, not far from here, on the property Vito's family still owned, high in the hills overlooking the lake. They had been beating each other with serious intent, their superficial argument transitioning into a far more serious drive for dominance over the other. Neither was the type to give up. Ever.

Paolo's father had stopped them. He'd been a man of strength and drive and purpose, the conservative head of the bank that had been the family's livelihood for generations. He was a loving man, a devoted uncle, a pillar of strength for all of them.

And he'd nearly cried when he'd pulled the boys apart.

You can't do this, his uncle had said. *No more. You're family.*

Vito didn't like upsetting his favorite uncle, but he had had nameless frustrations swirling inside him. He was claimed to be part of their clan, but he wasn't. Something was off and he knew it. He loved his parents. His mother doted on him. His father showed great pride in every one of Vito's accomplishments, but he didn't feel close to them. He was different. Not quite like them, not the same in temperament or looks as his sisters. He felt more kinship toward Paolo's father than his own. When they all came together for these sorts of big, family occasions, he caught watchful looks from some of the older aunts and uncles. It made him tense. Meanwhile, Paolo was so very confident in his own position, Vito was compelled to knock his cousin out of it.

So the angry accusation had come out. *Am I? Family?*

The way Paolo had looked to his father for that same answer, as if he too suspected Vito was not quite one of them, had been the most devastating blow of all.

Paolo's father had stood there with his hand on his hair, like he'd come across a bomb blast and was suffering a kind of shell shock himself, unable to make sense of the broken landscape.

Then, very decisively, he had nodded. *Fine. I'll tell you. Both of you.*

Vito had never questioned such huge news coming from his uncle, rather than his father. It was a Donatelli matter, after all. *He* was a Donatelli. Legally he was a Donatelli-Gallo. Women kept their maiden name when they married in Italy. He and his sisters used a hyphenated version of their parents' names, but he had always felt more drawn to the Donatelli side of his family and used that name to this day.

Because he had no Gallo in him, he had learned, sitting on a retaining wall overlooking the lake, hearing his uncle explain to him that his mother, his *real* mother, was the youngest Donatelli sibling, Zia Antoinietta. The aunt who had died and was rarely mentioned because her loss made everyone so sad. Vito would later look at her photographs and see more of himself in her than in her older sister, the woman who had called herself his mother all his life.

Your father was a dangerous man, Vito. Danger-

ous to us as a family, to the bank and very dangerous to your mother. I pulled her away from him so many times, but she kept going back. She was pregnant. She thought she loved him. I'll never forgive myself for not finding a way... She finally realized what was in store for both of you when he knocked her around and put her into labor. She called me to come to her where she was hiding from him. She died having you. I held her, waiting for the damned ambulance, and she begged me to keep you away from him, to keep you from turning into a mafioso like him. He wanted an heir to his empire, but it's a kingdom built on blood and suffering. We would have called you Paolo's brother, but well, you know the story we tell instead.

Vito did. His adoptive mother, the middle sister, often told the story of how she had thought she had miscarried, but Vito had miraculously survived. In reality, she and her husband had spirited her sister's newborn to the family home at the lake and waited out a suitable time before presenting Vito as their son. His birthday was off by four months.

I paid a fortune to the doctors to write out a certificate that you had died with her. And threatened your father with murder charges if the affair ever came out. I'm certain he would come for you if he knew you survived, Paolo's father had warned.

Vito could only imagine the fortune Paolo's father had paid to keep the liaison from becoming public knowledge and destroying the bank as it was. If online scandal rags had existed then, the affair wouldn't have suppressed as easily, he was sure.

Your mother was too precious to me, you are too

precious to me, for me to watch you two beating each other senseless. Turning to Paolo, he had lifted his shirt, showing a long scar that had always been blamed on surgery, but not today. *Did I take this knife trying to bring home my sister so my own son could kill hers? Save your strength for the fights that matter, then fight them together. Understand?*

He hadn't had to warn them to keep the secret. That was a given. He had risen and urged Paolo to come with him, to give Vito time alone.

No, Paolo had said. *I'll stay.*

They had sat in silence a long time, the space Paolo's father had taken up a wide gap between them. Finally Paolo had said, *Do you want to punch me?*

Yes, Vito had seethed. But he hadn't. They'd never fought again. They rarely mentioned it. Eventually Vito had learned the name of his biological father and the man's predilection for violence had sickened him. Then there was the second son's equally conscienceless disposition.

Vito wanted to believe he was different, but how could he claim to be a better man than what he'd come from when just the thought of those men and their actions put him into a state of mind willing to crush and kill? Vigilante justice was still brute force and only proved he was more like his biological father than he wanted to admit.

So he couldn't in good conscience make children with a woman without telling her what kind of blood he carried and he couldn't reveal the truth without endangering his family and the bank.

Therefore, he was a confirmed bachelor, destined to have affairs with women who didn't expect a future and to commiserate with the struggles of child-rearing from the sidelines.

"Your lips are blue. Come out," Paolo ordered his son.

"Three more," Roberto said, holding up three quivering fingers, teeth chattering, narrow shoulders shaking as he prepared to dive for yet another colored rock.

"One," Paolo said firmly.

"Two," Roberto responded.

"Everything is a negotiation," Paolo muttered, making Vito set his teeth because Paolo was complaining about a privilege not every man had. "Two. Then—"

"Paolo!" Gwyn came to the rail above them, at the edge of the pool deck. Her eyes were wide, her face pale. "Lauren says her water broke!"

Paolo went white and grim, swearing tightly. "Out, Roberto. Now. Stay with Vito," he ordered his son, locking gazes with Vito long enough to cement the command that Vito keep his son from drowning, but also sharing a moment of genuine fear.

It struck Vito that Paolo had never told Lauren why he didn't find these home births of hers as much of a joke as she did. He knew women could die.

It also told him how volatile his secret still was, if Paolo hadn't shared it with the woman who was his other half.

"I'll call the ambulance," he said to Paolo's back, pulling out his phone as his cousin took the stone stairs in great leaps, already pushing back his sleeves.

CHAPTER SEVEN

"THAT WAS THE most remarkable experience of my life," Gwyn said forty minutes later, as the ambulance carried off a grumbling Lauren and an infant boy who had squawked once, latched perfectly, then fallen asleep snuggled against her.

"They're just going to tell me that everything is fine and I can go home if I want to. I wish you hadn't called them," Lauren scolded Vito on her way out the door.

"Humor us, *mia bella*," Paolo said with equanimity, buttoning his clean shirt with hands that might have tremored a little, but he'd barely broken a sweat while carrying his wife to their bed and catching their son minutes later.

He'd been very coolheaded, calling Gwyn to bring him the bag he'd prepared with clean towels and receiving blankets, speaking to his wife in a calm, tender tone, using sterilized clips and scissors from the bag to cut the cord himself, as if he'd been a midwife all his life.

Their daughter slept through most of it, waking in time to glimpse her new brother, but quite content to cuddle with Vito amidst all the activity. Roberto called the little girl Bambi, which was adorable, and both children stayed with Gwyn and Vito while Paolo went in the ambulance with his wife. A car pulled out from the house across the street where the drivers and other ancillary staff were staying, following to bring them back once Lauren and the baby had been examined.

Vito didn't say anything as he closed the door. In fact, his color was down and he took a measured breath as if he'd just dodged a train.

"You're green around the gills, Vittorio," Gwyn chided, amused. "Were you worried?" She hadn't had time to panic and was riding a high of amazement.

"Lauren makes it look easy," he said in a tone that suggested he was well aware labor and delivery didn't always go so smoothly.

"I'll say," Gwyn responded. "I didn't even get the water boiled!" She moved into the kitchen where she had managed to snap off the gas on her way to fetch Paolo. "Shall I finish making dinner?"

"We'll help," Vito said, sliding Bianca onto a stool while Roberto climbed into the one his mother had been using. Vito was very good with the children and they openly adored him, grinning at his teasing, behaving angelically as he gently kept them on task.

Vito exchanged several texts with Paolo, who mentioned that everything was fine but there was a small delay in seeing the doctor.

"Paolo will be taking some family time now that the baby is here," Vito said to Gwyn. "We had planned for this, but we'll have a proper meeting when he gets back to review a few things before I assume his duties. You and I will spend the night here and head back to the city in the morning."

Gwyn nodded absently, too caught up in watching him cut up a little girl's food, steady Roberto's hand as he shook out red pepper flakes then smoothly reached to top up Gwyn's wineglass with a practiced flair. Throw in his ability give a woman orgasms and get the laundry done and he was the perfect man in every way.

He met her gaze.

Her thoughts must have reflected in her it. Building a career had been a dominating goal in her life, partly because she'd seen how hard her mother had struggled to support herself without a proper profession. Gwyn had focused on her degree and finding the right job and chasing opportunities for advancement. It had meant relegating a husband and children to a dreamy "some-day" that she hoped would find her when the time was right.

But she longed for a place to settle and call home. She wanted a family within it that wasn't a tenuous late-in-life connection, but a network of blood ties like this family had, where a woman could be nosy about a man simply because she cared about him. She could leave her children with him in utter confidence that he would keep them safe and give them the affectionate security that fed their souls.

"Be careful, Gwyn," Vittorio said with gentle gravity, holding her gaze.

She scanned for hazards the children might tip before meeting his gaze again, confused.

He wore the tough, circumspect look of the man who'd first stared her down in Nadine Billaud's office.

"This is not our life," he said in the same temperate tone. "Not yours. Not mine. So stop thinking it will happen."

She was far too transparent around him. It was ach-ingly painful to be this obvious, especially when he had touched her so intimately they were practically lovers, then shot down her dreams so dispassionately, leaving her nursing a giant ache that hollowed out her chest.

"Not with you, perhaps," she said, lifting her glass and her chin, holding his gaze even though the locked stare made her stomach cramp. "But there's no reason I can't have something like this, someday. Is there?" she challenged.

He might have flinched, but she wasn't sure.

And the silence went on long enough for her to remember her own notoriety. Would anyone want her after this? Ever?

A noise at the door told them the new parents had returned.

Gwyn rose to set two more places, grateful for a reason to turn away and hide that her eyes were welling up.

"Do you need the address for my flat?" Gwyn asked the driver as they slid into the car the next morning.

"I have it, thank you," the driver assured her as he closed her door for her.

The air was fresh, the sun shining and the children had both hugged her at the door. Nevertheless, Gwyn's good mood took a dip when Vittorio made no protest against her going home.

She wasn't about to ask him what *he* had planned for her, though. She had lain awake a long time last night considering her options. Her life wasn't over, she had concluded. It just needed to be re-envisioned.

As Vito flicked through messages on his tablet, she took a firm grip on the future she had outlined for herself. She opened her social media accounts and started removing objectionable posts. Dear Lord there were some nasty people out there. Some thought she was a harlot, others offered to do lewd things to her...

She didn't realize she was making noises like she was being roundly beaten in a boxing ring until Vito asked sharply, "What are you reading?"

"I want to connect with a headhunter to start searching out a position for when this is over." She winced as an invitation to hook up flashed into her eyes with a photo that couldn't be deleted fast enough. "I have to clean up my news feeds first, before potential employers look them over. It's a minefield."

"*You* don't," he growled, reaching across to click off her phone. "Plumbers exist to clean up sewage. I've already assigned you a PR assistant. She'll meet with you this afternoon and scrub all of this."

The last thing she wanted was to accept more generosity from him, but she was too grateful to refuse.

"And I'll see that you have a suitable position when the time comes so don't put out feelers for a job yet. It sends the wrong message."

"What does 'suitable' mean?"

"Something equivalent or better to the position you had, so you're not set back in your career. I've discussed it with Paolo and you'll receive a glowing recommendation, a severance package and a settlement for the damage caused by our leaving you in the position of working with Jensen despite having him under investigation. We've agreed that if we had removed you when we became suspicious, the photos wouldn't have happened, so we'll be accepting responsibility for that. We'll work out the exact details once we have Jensen on the ropes."

She blinked, stunned. Inside her chest, her heart rose like the sun from behind dark mountains, beaming light through her whole being. Lightness. The weight of being mistrusted lifted and something like hope dawned in her for the first time since she'd walked into Nadine's office and seen those photos.

"You believe me?" The words were very tentative. She could barely take it in.

"I do." His expression was grave, but there was a hard light in his eyes, not hostile, but daunting. It leaned even more impact to his words as he said, "These actions against you will not go unpunished."

She didn't fear him in that moment, but she recognized that he was a man to be feared.

And she was so relieved to have him on her side, so touched that he believed her, she grew teary and had to look away, unable to even voice a heartfelt, *Thank you*.

"But for now your occupation is 'mistress.'"

She flung her head around to confront him. "Did you say that to make me angry?"

He didn't glance up from flicking the screen on his tablet. "I said it because it's true."

"Oh, well, pray tell, what are the duties of that position? Does it come with benefits?" *Shut up, Gwyn.*

He took his time letting her regret that impulsive outburst, slowly lifting his attention to scan her expression while a faint smile played around his lips.

"Amusing me is your primary function," he said, adding a sardonic, "Check."

Then he had the audacity to let his gaze take a leisurely tour down her new top. It was a simple low-necked, peach-colored silk with a pleat at her cleavage. Not particularly sexy, but he seemed to look right through it, making her breasts feel heavy and her nipples tight. She found herself pressing her jeans-clad thighs together as a throb hit where he'd caressed her in this very backseat yesterday.

"We've covered the benefits," he added. "And that you may take advantage of them as often as you see fit."

"And this is supposed to fill up my nine-to-five?" she shot back, trying to cover her pulsing response, flicking her glance at the closed privacy screen while she willed her fierce blush to recede.

"I can't make love to you *all* day, *cara*. I have responsibilities."

She tried to send him a disgusted glare, but anticipation curled through her despite herself, melting her insides and turning her on. Yes, his low voice and sexy promise made her hot, curse him.

"Did you relive it last night?" he asked in a low tone of lusty pleasure. "I did. I wanted you to come to me, so I could feel you fall apart like that again. Under me this time."

Her stomach swooped and she turned her face to the window, trying to hide that she had toyed with the idea of going to him. She had ached with desire and had had to fight against the urge.

"I need to find healthier ways to deal with my situation than cheap sexual gratification," she said.

"Stop calling it cheap." His voice lashed with quick anger, making all the hairs rise on her body.

Now who was angry and who was laughing? She looked back at him and let him see her smug delight in getting a rise out of him.

"I'm sorry," she said with mock regret. "This is becoming quite expensive for you, isn't it? Because if you won't let me get a real job, you'll have to cover the lease on my flat." It was a childish jab and promptly fell flat.

"That's already in the works."

Her smarmy grin fell away.

He smiled at having drawn the wind from her sails. "I've had mistresses before," he added calmly, sobering a few degrees as he added, "Never one who has moved in with me, but we have a message to broadcast. I've assigned you an assistant. She'll send you our calendar shortly."

Moved in? *Our* calendar?

"I thought I was going back to my flat." She glanced toward the driver who had said he had her address.

"To get your passport and any other personal items you don't want to leave for the movers. Am I speaking English? Why are you staring at me like that?"

"When did I agree to move in with you? Do I get my own room?"

"Do you want one?" he asked, sounding oh-so-reasonable against her high pitch of disbelief, but the knowing slant to his half-closed lids made the question not just annoying, but far too rhetorical.

She didn't know how to be sophisticated and blasé about agreeing to be his lover. She was still fighting the longing to. Deep down, however, she knew she wanted to go to bed with him, and very likely would, which was the most aggravating part of it all.

Thankfully her phone buzzed. She glanced to see her new assistant was loading her calendar.

Gwyn scanned through, seeing that she had legal meetings, appointments with her PR assistant, stylists, boutiques—

"A *spa*?" she said sharply to Vito.

"All the women in my family frequent it. Don't worry. It's secure."

Luncheons, dinners—

"Berlin?"

"I have meetings." He shrugged.

London, Paris, back to Milan then three stops in Asia.

"What am I doing while you're working in all these places?" she asked, mind whirling.

"You'll have a security detail. Do whatever you want. Shop, visit the museums. You won't have as much time as you think. I'll need you at my side quite often."

She spent the rest of the drive answering questions for her assistant: Did she have any special dietary requirements or allergies? Any requests for products to have on hand at Vito's apartment or while she traveled? Was she due for any dental or medical appointments that should be scheduled? What about prescription refills?

More birth control pills? Was that what she was asking, Gwyn wondered with mild hysteria?

When they arrived in the city, they went straight to her building where a handful of photographers quickly snapped to attention from slouching on scooters and hovering on stoops. Vito's security guards kept them at a respectful distance and movers arrived shortly after Gwyn entered her flat.

The place was untouched, her plate with toast crumbs from a few days ago still sitting by the sink, but everything had changed. Not just her life, but there was something in *her* that was changing. She was a self-sufficient person, didn't want to look to Vito to rescue her like some kind of damsel needing a white knight, but as he gave instructions and spoke to her landlord to assure him the crowds at the entrance to the building would cease now that she was leaving, she felt grateful to have him on her side.

She hated feeling weak and managed and power-less, but if someone else was stealing control of her life, she was glad the rudder had wound up in his un-erring hands.

She trusted him, she realized. It was a weird sort of trust. He could and probably would hurt her, but he wasn't making any false promises not to. He wouldn't lie to her, even if the truth was harsh and unpalatable.

His governance over her world proved very advanta-geous when she made her statement to the police, too. Had she been merely a midlevel bank employee with no connections or legal team behind her, her complaint probably wouldn't have been such a priority, but she was assured charges against her masseuse would be forthcoming.

The rest of the day passed in a blur. There was a very short press conference announcing the birth of Paolo's son, Vito's assumption of his cousin's position for the next few weeks and he confirmed rumors that a formal internal investigation had been launched against an un-named, but high profile account.

"For privacy and legal reasons, we can't expound on that," Vito said.

Then he sent a look to Gwyn that said everything his mouth did not. His expression spoke of regret and guardianship and the suppressed anger of a warrior who must wait for the war. Which might have been a bit of overacting for the cameras, but she thought it had its seeds in what he had said earlier about Jensen not going unpunished.

And she was touched all over again.

The press conference had been held at a hotel where Vito was due to meet with various heads of the bank's branches before attending a mixer with those same people, their spouses and an exclusive list of their top-tier investors.

"It was scheduled a year ago, long before any of this hit the fan," he said, sending her to a penthouse suite with an entourage who coached her on everything from staying on message—*The investigation is ongoing. I can't comment.*—to how to lengthen her lashes most effectively.

She was mentally and emotionally exhausted when they all finally left her alone, seriously wishing she could go to bed instead of having to go out.

Then Vito materialized from the second bedroom like a freshly groomed panther, his black tuxedo a second skin, the white of his pleated shirt and bow tie a blaze that set off his swarthy skin tone, hollow cheeks and straight black brows. His hair, just a shade too long to be a conservative business cut, gave him the perfect balance between decadent playboy and powerful executive.

His silk pocket square exactly matched the reflective, lake blue of her gown.

She'd never worn anything so elegant or daring, with its strapless bodice and low back. The sweep of the skirt was gathered in loose edges, forming a slit over her left leg, and was ruched together with a sparkling broach on her hip, making her feel graceful and sexy at once.

She felt sensual. Beautiful. And, as she stood looking at the beautiful man before her, she felt for the first time like she was his match.

Vito was trying to make it to the end of a trying day. He understood the concerns of those around him, the questioning of his choice in female companionship, but he couldn't understand why he was so angered by all of it. He kept telling himself it was the bank he wanted to defend. To protect.

But it was Gwyn. He wanted to sweep a sword through the air to cut down all this resistance against his being with her.

And this was why.

She stood before him like a water deity, wearing that swirl of river blue and sapphires that gleamed like bubbles against her neck and ears. Her hair was caught in a low knot against the back of her neck, wisps framing her introspective expression, mysterious and enthralling.

She was a prize, a weapon, an illicit substance. She was something he wanted. Badly.

His libido was becoming a monster, first hooked by spending nearly every moment with her for the past forty-eight hours, then feeling her absence as he'd pushed her to the sidelines to weather attacks from close quarters.

It had left him keyed up, mood balanced on a knife's edge, the outlaw in him looking to ignore any sort of rules or propriety and simply take her, make her his. This wasn't the first time he'd chafed against the constraints he placed upon himself, but he always maintained this veneer of civility painted onto him by the family who had kept him alive, safe and living within the law.

She didn't want cheap gratification, he reminded himself, and heard Paolo again. *If she's a victim, don't make her more of one*. He kept remembering that look in her eye as they'd played house for an hour with Paolo's children. If only the world understood how laughable it was to think *she* was inferior to *him*.

"You look nice," he said gruffly, trying not to let the vision she made break the shackles controlling him. He moved to hold the door. "Let's get this over with."

She made a noise that might have been one of injury and muttered, "That's what she said," as she passed him into the hall.

"*What* did you just say?" he asked tightly.

Gwyn grappled her feelings back into their box, telling herself to quit taking his lack of real interest in her as a slight.

"It's just something people say. One of those online memes," she said, striding purposefully beside him toward the elevator. "Why are you so grouchy?"

The hotel was pure opulence, the carpets cushioning each step, the rail dripping leafy plants in terraced layers down to the lobby forty stories below.

He pressed the call button for the elevator and said, "I'm not."

She glanced around, saw they were alone and said, "You know, we may not have much, but I thought we had honesty. If you don't want to tell me, say it's none of my business. But don't lie."

His gaze widened at her audacity, making her swallow. But honestly. She was doing everything she was told, letting him treat her like a puppet after she'd already been misused. What else did he want from her?

The elevator arrived and an older couple stepped off, leaving them to enter the empty car alone, replacing what might have been an air of relaxed camaraderie with a charged energy that bounced off the refined walls.

At least it wasn't one of those glass boxes that made you feel airsick as you descended. It was red velvet and had mirrored panels split by a flat rectangle of gold for a handrail. A chipper, understated soft shoe drifted from the speakers, sounding incongruous.

"If you must have the truth, *cara*, I've been warned several times today that our relationship is ill-advised," he said, stabbing at a floor number, then thumbing hard into the door close button. "I know they're right, but I don't care. I want you, anyway. If we'd stayed in the room, I would have kept you there."

"Really?" she derided. "I thought I just asked you not to lie to me? Because you've never once acted like you wanted anything to do with me."

"Ha!" He punched the side of his fist into the red emergency button, stalling the elevator with a jar and a short buzz, making her stagger and reach for the rail. "The very fact that you can't read the signs tells me how ill-suited you are for an affair. But, just so we're crystal clear, *cara*, I don't care about that, either. *I want you.*"

She couldn't look away from him, fascinated by the way his gold-brown eyes shot glittering shards of bronze.

He stepped closer, setting one hand then the other on the wall next to her head, leaning in. "I wanted you when you smiled across the lobby and you were already under suspicion, so I couldn't do a damn thing about it. I wanted you when I looked at this…" His boiling metal gaze slid down her front, scalding her. "And I knew every other man in the world was looking at you, too." His gaze flashed up, bright and piercing. "I want to kill each and every one of them," he added tightly. "Especially Jensen."

Her knuckle bumped his side and she realized her hand had lifted of its own volition, moving to press against her chest and keep her heart inside its cage. It slammed hard and fast.

He looked at her splayed fingers. "Scared?"

"I honestly didn't think you…" Her voice trailed off as his expression hardened with accusation.

"How could you not know? You look at me constantly. I *feel* it. How could you not be aware that I'm watching you, too?" He picked up her hand and pressed it to his own chest, where his heart punched against her palm. "You felt this in the car, when just my touch made you scream with pleasure. How could you not know it's the same for me?"

Emotion pressed at the backs of her eyes and thickened her throat.

He watched her struggle to swallow and cupped his hand under her jaw, palm against her throbbing artery, thumb caressing the hollow below her ear.

"The only thing holding me back, *mia bella*, is your indecision. Have you made up your mind yet? Do you want cheap, physical gratification?" The bitterness in his tone scraped at something in her, making her squirm in a kind of guilt.

She had hurt him with that? She searched his eyes, the windows into his soul. "What else would it be?" she asked in a near whisper.

His lips hardened and his brow lowered in consternation. "I don't know. But it would be a hell of a lot more than that."

She lifted her hand to the side of his face, drew him in and pressed a kiss of apology onto his mouth. It was perfect and sweet and healing.

And a mistake.

With a moan from her and a tortured groan from him, they laced themselves together, mouths opening with instant passion, dragged together like magnets meeting its attractor. His fingers dug into her back, her bottom, crushing her close. She arched into his steely body, loving his strength and the smell of him and that firm evidence of arousal that was not purely incidental, but his reaction to *her*.

He pressed her into the wall with his body, stilling the rock of her hips with a hard pin of his own. "You want me," he said against her lips. It was a demand for confirmation.

"I do," she admitted with an ache of helpless need.

"Now?"

"Wh-what?" She opened her eyes to see a fiery passion in him that was barely controlled. This man who seemed to have command of the entire world was so affected by her, he was looking at her with a kind of desperation. She thought she could feel each pulse pound in him, rocking his entire being.

"Here?" she asked. She was achy and heavy and ready. The thought of waiting until they were upstairs— it was too far.

This was insanity. Complete insanity.

"No?" He shuffled closer, feet between hers, one hand going to the slit in her skirt, finding her bare thigh and stroking across her skin like magic. "If not here, say so now."

She might have hung on to a shred of decorum if

he hadn't found the front of her lace undies and traced lightly while his mouth found the side of her neck at the same time. Need flooded through her at that light caress. She gasped with longing, clinging to his shoulders, trying to keep her knees locked so she wouldn't wilt right to the floor.

"Open my pants," he said, breath hot on her skin while the nibble of his lips made her shiver with pleasure and that exploring touch worked past the edge of lace into wetness and need. She made a guttural sound of pure excitement as he circled and pressed the swollen bud he found. His other hand was gathering her skirt out of the way, lifting her bare thigh to his hip, opening her to his flagrant touch.

"We can't," she gasped, but her hands worked the button on his pants, the fly. She had never tunneled her hand into the heated front of a man's trousers, but there was his shape filling her palm, naked and hot and silky. He was commando, shockingly bare to her touch, smooth with a graze of rough hair at the base, so steely and thickly aroused she gasped and clenched in anticipation.

He bent his knees, urging her to line him up as he shifted her underwear to the side. He traced his thick tip along her seam, parted, sliding easily against her then probing. "Do I need a condom?"

Late for that, wasn't it? She was dying! Panting with excitement.

"I'm on the pill," she managed to say, moving in invitation. She wanted him so badly. *Now.*

Their breaths mingled. His nostrils flared as he found her opening and pressed with more purpose. Nerves made her stiffen slightly, but she was eager, anxious as she looked into his eyes, wanting him to like it, wanting this to be good.

"Oh," she whispered as he pushed the tip in, stretching her. Her gaze clouded and her breaths grew uneven. When she clenched on him, little shock waves of pleasure jolted through her. Her eyelids grew heavy and wanted to close.

He pressed farther in, his weight driving her against something that dug into her back. She wriggled, making a noise of discomfort. "The rail—"

He smoothly lifted her, one hand going under her bottom where he balanced her above that infernal rail and then he was firmly seated all the way in, eye to eye with her. It was incredibly intimate. Man and woman. Steel and silk. Their panting breaths humid against each other's lips.

"Hold on to me," he rasped.

She closed her legs around his waist, twined her arms over his shoulders.

He moved, watching her expression as he withdrew and returned, driving in deep, holding there a moment, then dragging out slow, tantalizing her to new heights, arousing her with each thrust. Then he built the tempo to swift thrusts that were exciting and delicious and sent her racing up the slopes of need.

She clung to him with every part of her. He was hard everywhere, tense and determined. Her lips ached to be kissed, but she needed air. She couldn't look away from his gaze, watchful, waiting, demanding. It was too wild, too erotic, too scorchingly fast. She was there, right there, shuddering and flying apart. Finally closing her eyes as the pleasure detonated into something otherworldly.

A deeply animalistic noise left him as he arched deep and pulsed inside her, holding her in that state of ecstasy.

She gloried in the moment, body electrified as they completely possessed each other, united in this moment of culmination.

CHAPTER EIGHT

GWYN COULDN'T BELIEVE she had let him do that to her. Her legs were still trembling as she joined him inside the ballroom, having slipped into the ladies' room the minute they left the elevator to recover herself.

"*Cara*, please meet some friends of mine," he said, settling his arm around her as he introduced her.

It was different. She was different and they were different. Her world had been upended all over again. The sexual awareness was still there, but instead of being a sharp, unmet need, it was a deep, perilous knowledge. She knew what her body was capable of. He did. They both knew what he could do to her, how he could strip her of willpower and blind her with desire. She wondered if she had really done the same to him because he didn't seem as affected.

His arm sat heavier on her, more possessive, but when his glance came into her eyes, his held the light of memory and male satisfaction, but none of her wariness.

She was suffering all the same crush and attraction and fascination, but it was even more painful now. Before, she had yearned for him to match this feeling. Now she knew it didn't matter if he did. She was lost regardless.

It made the stares and the curled lips and the dismissive way people treated her as he introduced her all the harder to bear.

She said nothing, still wondering how on earth she would survive Vito let alone the rest of all that had happened. It made her desperate for reassurance, but he was no help, standing here looking indifferent, letting one of his executives from New York talk his ear off about some policy Vito had assigned him to write.

To her, it sounded a lot like a guy trying to impress the boss by telling him how hard he was working, rather than actually doing the work.

Meanwhile, Gwyn realized she knew the woman from the Charleston branch who had just caught her eye. Here would come a gauntlet of questions. This was going to be the worst night of her life.

The moment she tried to excuse herself, however, Vito's arm hardened on her.

"I should say hello to Ms. Tamsin," Gwyn said, caught between homesickness and dread. She would love to hear the news on her former colleagues, but really didn't want to talk about herself.

"I'll come with you." Vito nodded at the man who'd been pontificating.

"But I want your advice!" the executive blurted.

Gwyn was so far into her own head, she completely misplaced where she was and who they were talking to. In that moment, a coworker was asking for guidance so she offered it. "Why don't you use the UK model as a template? Tailor it to US regulations and plug in that bit about interstate transfers. The section on overseas rates should work almost word for word."

The surprised pause and dumbfounded stares from

both men were almost laughable, except Gwyn realized how badly she'd overstepped and instantly wanted to die of embarrassment. She never would have spoken to Oscar Fabrizio or any other higher-up that way. No, she would have done that work for him, she thought privately, and let him take the credit. Such was the life of lower-level administrators.

The executive was taken aback and glanced between her and Vito, as if to say, *Are you going to let your porn star girlfriend talk to me like that?*

"Excellent suggestion," Vito said. "Why reinvent the wheel? I'll expect to see the draft tomorrow," he told his executive and walked her away.

"I'm sorry," she mumbled.

"For what?"

"Interjecting like that."

"Why? You were right. I would have thought of it myself eventually, but I wasn't really listening. Too busy thinking of something else," he said with a pointed look that shot sexual heat from her heart to her loins. "I've never gone without a condom before. That was exciting. *Grazie, mia bella.*"

Her hand tightened on his sleeve as her knees wobbled, making him smile like a shark.

The rest of the evening was a trial, but she got through it. And when they were leaving, he surprised her by taking her downstairs to a waiting car instead of back up to the penthouse he'd already paid for.

"What about the early morning meetings you have here tomorrow?" She tilted her head at the hotel. "I thought that's why we were staying here."

"I want you in my bed."

Her skin tightened in reaction. "Okay."

* * *

Vittorio was not a weak or needy man. He loved his family and would certainly be a lesser man without them, but he considered himself a supporter of *them*, not the other way around. He wasn't a dependent personality, either. He drank a glass of wine most days because it was a cultural habit, not because he was addicted.

Gwyn was another story.

As he tied his tie, he glanced at her sleeping form reflected beyond his shoulder, brunette hair spilled across his pillow where she'd rolled to hug it when he'd risen, murmuring a sleepy and satisfied, "Thank you," before falling back asleep.

Words she had promised him he would never hear, he thought edgily, still high on the powerful orgasm they'd shared from a very lazy missionary lock in the predawn hour, the paroxysm holding them gasping for long, exquisite moments.

It had been two weeks and, if anything, the chemistry between them was stronger. If he was in her presence, he wanted to touch her. If he touched her, he wanted to have sex with her.

His desire was becoming the sort of all-consuming hunger that he arranged the rest of his life around. If he had other thoughts, they tended to be of the reckoning kind: dark acts of retaliation against Jensen and his cohorts. He wanted justice for Gwyn, but not necessarily the legal kind that would put an end to their reason for being together.

"I'm jealous," Gwyn said in a soft morning voice that lifted the hairs all over his body.

"Of whom?" he asked, reaching for his suit jacket, shrugging it on like armor.

He'd had these sorts of conversations before, but he had to admit to shock that Gwyn would have any reason to feel possessive. Had he even looked at another woman since meeting her? If he had, it was a comparison that Gwyn always won. Not just in looks, either. If he heard a woman laugh, he thought the sound too sharp or coarse, not the perfect joyful huskiness of Gwyn's. None seemed to have her same intuitive ability with conversation either, steering seamlessly from business to small talk to current events. His lack of interest in other women might have worried him if his libido hadn't been showing such vigor and health in bed with this one.

"You," she answered ruefully, rolling onto her back and throwing her arm over her head. "Going to work." She touched the headboard, looking up to the pattern her finger found and traced.

Her remark didn't entirely surprise him. He might have had innumerable mistresses who expected to be supported, but his sisters and the bank's abundance of female employees told him that many women enjoyed their careers as much as men did. Gwyn was bright and confident and had had clear goals before Jensen had derailed her. A life of leisure was not something she had aspired to—which was yet another side of her character that set her apart and shone a favorable light upon her in his eyes.

It was also why he enjoyed supporting her. She didn't expect to be spoiled so her reaction was priceless when he collared her with precious stones and shackled her with gold bracelets. Her protests against his generosity were refreshing, her newness to belonging to a man endearing.

He moved to the bed and lowered to hitch his hip beside hers, splaying his hand over the rumpled sheet that covered her belly. "I thought you enjoyed the art exhibit yesterday?" He had liked watching her face light with enthusiasm as she had told him about it last night.

"I did. I'm not sure your bodyguards did, though." She covered his hand, traced her light touch over the backs of his fingers, sending a ripple of pleasure down his back, as if he was a wolf being petted by a maiden.

"Well-secured places like art galleries make their job easy. They're happy to follow you around one." That wasn't the real issue, he could tell, but he didn't know what else she needed to hear. Perhaps, "Rather than go back to Milan when I finish here, why don't we take a few days on the water?" he suggested. "I'll hire a yacht."

Her gaze met his. "I feel like I'm back in my childhood, moving around before I can establish myself, not even trying to make friends because there's no point."

He frowned, having supposed that she connected with her friends online when he wasn't around, but she never mentioned any conversations or told anecdotes, he realized. She'd already told him that the family she did have was a very loose tie. She was still too embarrassed to speak directly to her stepfather and was keeping to short texts with her stepbrother.

He couldn't imagine living in that sort of social desert. He had curtailed a lot of his nonbusiness dinners because of work pressures and was sidestepping family occasions to avoid awkward questions about his relationship with Gwyn, but he was Italian. An active social life was in his biological makeup.

"Why did you move so often?" he asked her.

She shrugged. "Every reason. Lost job, better job, good luck, bad luck, harassment, location…I think the biggest reason was that Mom had itchy feet. That's why she married my dad, to move to America. She and Henry were going to travel once I finished school." Her fingertips smoothed under his cuff, tracing the band of his watch. "I wanted to see the world, too, but by moving to a new city and settling in, so I could absorb the culture and become part of the community."

Whatever friendships she'd made in Milan had been blown apart by the photos and her termination. He hadn't forbidden her from contacting any of her co-workers or neighbors, but she had isolated herself and he'd been pleased to keep things simple. He wondered now if he should make more of an effort to draw her into his own circles, but to what end? This was a temporary affair, not a relationship.

And knowing their time together was finite, he found himself very unwilling to share her.

"No news from Paolo about how much longer the investigation will take?" she asked.

"No," he said so abruptly her eyes widened and a shadow of injury crept across the back of her gaze. He mentally kicked himself for revealing the brute that he was, but her question almost sounded as though she was anxious to end things and he wasn't ready.

"Living in limbo is hard," she said in stiff explanation, trying to sit up.

He gathered her tense form into his lap, looking at the pugnacious glare she tilted up at him. He pressed a kiss against her firmly closed mouth.

"I'm hearing you," he told her, thinking about those times when he caught a faraway, melancholy expression on her face. He had put those moments down to her distress over the photos, but there was more to it, he realized now. She was a woman longing to put down roots. "I'm not dismissing you. But there's nothing I can do right now."

"And nothing I can do either, apparently."

"Fold my socks?" he suggested, since she often nagged him to pick his up.

She snapped her teeth at him in playful retaliation.

He kissed her again and this time she softened and kissed him back.

But he was still thinking about her discontent when he broke from his meeting with the Hong Kong consortium and picked up a message from Paolo: *Fabrizio is asking for leniency in exchange for full disclosure. We could see charges against Jensen early next week.*

The tide was turning.

The need for their affair was almost over.

Gwyn was in a type of shock as they returned to Vito's penthouse less than a week later, mind still caught up in all that had just been said at the press conference and after it. *Be careful what you wish for*, she thought bleakly. She had been anxious to embark on her future and here it was.

"I wish to say a special thank-you to Miss Ellis for her patience and unwavering integrity during this entire process," Paolo had said. "Due to the sensitive nature of the investigation, we asked her not to make any public comments during a time that has obviously been very distressing for her."

The cameras' lenses had shifted to where she had stood next to Vito, trying to capture her reaction, which she had fought to keep noncommittal. Inside, she'd been screaming in agony and still was. This was it. *The End.*

Paolo's private words to her afterward were what had really done her in. Handlers had moved them into an anteroom and scattered. Vito had stepped away to call his assistant with some instructions.

"Grazie," Paolo had said to Gwyn, not showing any reaction when he shook her hand and found it clammy. "We will pursue defamation charges on your behalf and that could result in prison time for Jensen, but I realize that does nothing to compensate you for all you've lost. Vito promised you a settlement, *si*? Hire a good lawyer and begin those negotiations immediately. I want a number so I can add it to our list of damages when Jensen is tried."

"Of course," Gwyn had murmured, as if she had the first idea how to hire any kind of lawyer, let alone a "good" one. Her mind had started buzzing the minute Vito had called her to say he was sending a car and was bursting with a bigger swarm of bees over how abruptly this press conference ended the need for their affair.

She was devastated. Her very nascent and juvenile crush had become something real and deep and heart-wrenching.

She had started to think of his beautiful apartment as her home.

Vittorio had modern tastes and liked space around him. The penthouse had high white ceilings and three bedrooms, one that he used as an office, off a tiled upper hallway that he called a loft. It was nothing so modest as that. It was a second story. The main bathroom had His and Hers powder rooms on opposite ends of a tub that they easily, and frequently, shared. This flat was wall-to-wall understated luxury, from the designer furniture to the kitchen that sparkled with stainless steel functionality, positioned to allow the cook to visit with guests while stirring and chopping.

High-end art, lush plants and family photos rounded off the space into a haven of warmth and welcome. Her snapshot of her almost family, her own image with her arms around Henry and her mother, sat on the night table next to her side of the bed.

Gwyn swallowed, trying to hide her devastation at leaving all of this, along with the man who lived here, by kicking off her heels beside the front closet, then realized she would have to pack them. She couldn't wrap her brain around what that would entail so she moved to where she'd left her tablet on the sectional before the big screen TV, pretending she was checking email.

"Are you hungry?" Vito asked behind her, shrugging out of his suit jacket and tossing it across the back of the sofa. "I'm going to make coffee."

She wasn't, but she loved cooking with him, enjoying the foreplay of brushing bodies, senses stimulated by the aroma of fresh ingredients, the sizzle of a pan and the rich textures and flavors they seemed to create together.

The full scope of all that she was losing gripped her and she lifted her head to stare blindly through the bright windows.

"*Cara?*" He was right behind her, making her start. "What's wrong?"

"Nothing." *Everything.*

His gaze dropped to her tablet. "Something has upset you? Do not tell me you're reading reactions to today's press conference. Stop polluting your head that way."

"No, um—" She glanced at the tablet, saw Travis's latest message, started to gloss past it, then decided to confront it. Just pull the bandage off in one ruthless yank. She showed him what Travis had written.

I saw the press conference. Does this mean you're coming home?

Vito's gaze came up and slammed into hers. He was so handsome. Brutally, impossibly handsome with his white shirt and striped tie and tailored pants with their knifelike creases, then black leather shoes glossed to a mirror finish. She didn't know any other man who could wear a vest with the buttons offset at an angle like that, the edge piped in silver, and look so suave.

She longed to trace that piping, touch those buttons. She very much needed the connection that seemed to have been building between them with each physical encounter, but what did they really have? Sex. That was all.

"We haven't really talked about the next steps. I imagine I will be leaving?" she said, insides hollow. "Now that we don't have to pretend anymore?"

They weren't pretending. That's what his cocked brow said.

She licked her lips. "Because it would make it pretty obvious we got together just for show if I left right away, wouldn't it?" Tossing the tablet onto the sofa, she jerked a shoulder. "I could say I'm going to see family and we could let it die off from there."

"We could," he said carefully, so emotionless a scalding pain rose behind her breastbone.

For a moment she couldn't even breathe, let alone speak or move. Then she found a smile of false bravado and brought her hands to the sides of his head.

His hot palms settled on her hips, holding her off as he gave her a questioning look.

She didn't have a very strong grip on her emotions, and keeping anything from him these days was pretty much impossible, but she tried to affect nonchalance.

"Don't worry. I'm not staking a claim. I'll figure it out in a little while. But I'd like to leave you with something to remember."

Then, because she had spent a great deal of time devoting herself to learning what turned him on, she did everything she could to arouse him. She rarely instigated lovemaking unless they were in bed. It was shyness and lack of confidence, but today she left inhibition at the door and pressed herself against him suggestively.

She ran her hands over him with the proprietary touch she usually suppressed. His shoulders were a landscape of masculinity, appealing to the primal woman in her that sought protection and provision. His buttons opened to, first, the warm silk of his shirt, then the satin of his skin, with the fine hairs on his breastbone and a dark arrow to his navel that teased her lips as she kissed what she exposed. His nipples were sharp against her tongue and her teasing made him suck in a quick breath.

She kissed him, not just letting him know she was receptive, but taking the initiative, not hinting that she wanted to make love, but demanding it. It was exhilarating to be this assertive.

He let her bare his chest and open his pants, swiveling so he leaned his hips against the back of the sofa and stepped his feet apart, drawing her into the space. Then he cupped her face so he could kiss her, not taking control, but not passive. Never passive.

Her own clothes loosened, suit jacket falling away, bow at her neck tugging then falling into ribbons of blue polka dots on white. Vito drew back long enough to pull the sheer confection over her head then brought her against him again, skin to skin, both of them murmuring approving noises.

Vito had experienced the advances of women in the past. Often it was a power play or a quid pro quo of some kind. Sometimes he relaxed and enjoyed it, other times he set the pace that suited him.

Gwyn, guileless, sensual Gwyn, undid him. She was so very entrancing in her conservative exterior and her abandonment to lovemaking, especially today as she licked into his mouth, rubbing against him in a way that was not so much practiced as pure. She was trying to turn him on, but the way she grew bright-eyed and flushed with hectic color was even more arousing.

When she released his belt and opened his pants, he let her drag them down his thighs, watching her drop to her knees and loving the sight of her taking him in hand. The sensations of her wet worship, the encompassing heat and delicate suction, had him tempted to let her take him all the way. This *was* something he would remember for the rest of his life. He would never forget her. He had known that before she'd begun anointing him this way.

But if they were saying goodbye, he wanted to do the same to her. To make this last. To create the sort of memory that would sustain them both for the rest of their lives.

That knowledge was a sharp twist in his gut that allowed him to pull her to her feet, turning her so she faced the back of the sofa.

"Wait. I want—"

"Are you not doing what I want, *mia bella*?" He paused in bringing her skirt up, waiting. "Giving me something to remember you by?"

Her knuckles were white where she gripped the leather. "Yes," she whispered. "But I want to see you. Kiss you."

"You will," he promised her, kissing her bare shoulder, then drawing back to memorize the sight of plum wool bunched on the small of her back as he pressed her to bend forward. He stroked his hand over pale white cheeks wearing a line of amethyst lace. Those he dispatched to around her ankles in a moment, caressing her where she was plump and wet, hearing her whimper under his touch, back arching, shoulders shuddering with pleasure.

"We will always have this," he vowed, pressing into her. "Now come for me." He shifted his hand so he was giving her all the pleasure she could bear. "Surrender to me. It's what I love the most," he told her, opening his mouth on her nape, losing himself to the delight of thrusting into her, barely holding on as she suddenly gasped and clenched in strong pulses around him. Her gorgeous cries of fulfillment went through him like church bells.

He petted her as he carefully withdrew and kicked out of his pants. Then he scooped up her still-quivering body and carried her toward the stairs.

"You didn't—"

"I know exactly what I have and haven't done, *mia bella*." His ears were ringing with the pulse hammering upward from the damp, urgent flesh between his thighs. "If you think I'm going to let our last time be a one-sided dalliance in the front room, you haven't learned one damned thing about me or what I expect from my mistress."

It wasn't unusual for them to make love two or three times in a day. Sometimes it was a rush of passion, sometimes a slow, sultry buildup.

It had never been quite such a complete immersion. They ignored the phone when it rang, ignored the growl of their stomachs, barely even spoke except to encourage or compliment or groan incomprehensibly.

Finally, when it was well and truly dark beyond the windows, they landed weak and sated and aching with sensual exhaustion, limbs tangled, quiet and still at last.

The sense of closeness between them was so acute that Gwyn could barely comprehend that it was over, but it was. Those panting moments when their hearts had beat in unison had merely been physical compatibility. Nothing more.

Shifting her arm off her stinging eyes, she decided a trip to the ladies room might be in order to keep herself from revealing how hard this was for her.

"Stay," he said as she began to rise.

A helpless noise escaped her. "Honestly, Vito, I don't think I can. That was…a lot." Her loins were stinging and tender, her muscles quivering with overuse.

A gruff noise escaped him, part humor, part apology. He came up on an elbow and scooped her beneath him, heavy on her as he pinned her to the mattress. "That's quite a compliment if you think I have anything left in me," he growled, nose going into her neck and inhaling. "I mean stay in Milan. This doesn't have to end here and now."

She stilled. "You're asking me to stay as your mistress?"

"*Sì.*"

The room was dark shadows and rumpled blankets; her world narrowed to the warmth of his lips against her collarbone. He didn't see her wince of agony at the term. He might sometimes refer to her as his lover, but that was a euphemism for what she really was. She knew that and she had justified what she was letting herself become as necessary for their ruse.

But that was no longer necessary.

"Because it would look better for the press?" she asked.

"Because we're good together."

That surprised her, making her heart leap as though he'd admitted to deep, abiding affection even though she knew he only meant they knocked each other off the bed with the intensity of physical pleasure they gave each other.

If she stayed with him, wouldn't that allow time for him to develop deeper feelings toward her, though? It was the kind of treacherous, self-delusion all women were capable of, when they were half in love with a man who didn't love them back. She knew it, but she was still tempted to let him talk her into staying. To see.

She traced the line of his spine and lightly searched for proof that he might already be harboring feelings toward her.

"What if I don't want to?" she asked.

His turn to go completely still. He lifted his head and in the muted light she saw his hard mouth twist. "I'm not a man who begs, *cara*. Be careful about bluffing. I'll call you on it."

She ought to be happy he'd gone so far as to tell her he wanted her to stay, she supposed. It *was* quite an admission from such a self-sufficient man. One who could have his choice among women.

"It's not an ultimatum," she said, trying to hide her hurt behind a neutral tone. "I told you when we first met that I don't have affairs. Relying on you goes against everything I've tried to become. I ought to start salvaging my life, not leave it on hold."

His tense hand on her waist grew heavy. "I respect your independence. I do," he assured her. "But your life is already on hold, I carry some of the fault for that and I have the means to support you while you give real thought to your next steps. Let me do this for you, *cara*."

I respect you. Such a small phrase and it moved her so very deeply to hear it. How could she not stay and try to nurture that into something even more meaningful?

"I don't want to lose that respect," she said, hearing his breath catch and taking heart from it. It almost sounded like he was bracing himself. "But I do enjoy the sex."

If the noise he made sounded to her like relief, she knew that was wishful thinking. He was amused, which had been her goal. Keep it light. Don't let him know how emotionally dependent she really was.

"And I'm going to have to insist on more frequent feedings," she added, trying to rise. "I suppose I have to cook again?"

"Two words, *cara*," he growled, flattening her on her back and setting his teeth against her shoulder. "Bite me."

CHAPTER NINE

"GOOD JOB ON the lawyer," Paolo said dryly as he opened the door to his home to them a few nights later.

Gwyn was a bundle of nerves, not quite believing this was a mere social dinner, but Vito assured her it was. All she had done was ask casually how Lauren and the baby were getting on. Vito had called to ask and it had turned into a dinner invitation. Now, here they were.

"She's really nice, isn't she?" she said to Paolo, barely tracking the conversation as the old-world beauty of the house dazzled her. Vito had told her as they drove in that the house had been in the family for generations. It was set on a property that had to be worth millions of euros given its size and location. What charmed her more was the way the high ceilings and Renaissance architecture and formal furniture was peppered with colorful children's toys, a baby swing and the sleek lines of a laptop on an antique escritoire.

"Nice," Paolo repeated under his breath, saying to Vito, "Did you have anything to do with her choice?"

"I've stayed out of it. Why? Are we likely to lose these?" Vito plucked at his shirt.

"My stepbrother found her for me," Gwyn hurried

to say. "I didn't know who else to ask. Why? Is she awful?"

"Depends which side of the table you're on," Paolo said smoothly. "You're on the side where she is very nice. But she's already setting a high bar for our own legal team. It will be a good exercise for them in staying sharp."

Lauren came down the stairs at that point, newborn in her arm.

After a greeting of kisses all around, she brought them through the house to the back to greet the children who were playing outside under the eye of the nanny.

"Ignore the boxes," Lauren said as they came back in, waving at the dozens piled near the back stairs. "One of the aunts has embarked on a family history book. Paolo and I have been digging relics out of attics and pantries that haven't been opened in years. It's fascinating! So many old photos and diaries. *Love* letters."

Gwyn had just taken the baby from Lauren, gathering his warm body close and glancing at Vito like she was the first person to ever cuddle a baby. It was a vulnerable moment of wanting to share her excitement and joy, maybe see what he thought of the sight of her with an infant against her heart, but he wasn't looking at her.

He and Paolo had a lightning exchange that consisted of one look of inquiry and another of an infinitesimal shake of Paolo's head replying, *No.*

If Vito realized she had seen what had just transpired, he betrayed nothing. In fact, his direct gaze, so forceful as he met hers, was a silent declaration that he had nothing to hide.

But she'd seen something. She knew it.

"That's what brought me to Italy, you know," Lauren said, moving through to the lounge where she gathered toys. "Looking up family. My grandmother had a *scandalous* affair with a married man and went home pregnant."

"Here I thought you came to Italy for me," Paolo said, holding up a red plastic bin so Lauren could drop her collection of stuffed toys and books into it.

"You're why I stayed, *mio bello*," she said, offering her lips for a kiss.

The rest of the evening passed in entertaining conversation, excellent food and an invitation from the children to read bedtime stories. It was sweet, yet poignant, making Gwyn recall the way Vito had told her this would never be her life.

Later, as they were readying for bed, she asked him, "Did you ever live in that house?" She was still thinking about that odd moment when Lauren had mentioned love letters. Had he left some evidence of a lost crush?

"I stayed with Paolo's family at different times as a child, wherever they happened to be living. Both of our families traveled a lot, but my sisters and I were well matched in ages to Paolo and his sisters. We often had summer vacations together, that kind of thing. They were our favorite cousins and my uncle…" Vito shrugged. "I looked to him as much of a father figure as my own," he said with a hint of private irony.

"That must have been so idyllic," she said wistfully. "Did you and Paolo play with the girls? Or were you horrible sexists?"

"A little of both," he said dryly, unbuttoning his shirt. "We were never going to play with dolls without lighting their hair on fire, but if the girls wanted to play tag or hide-and-seek, we were up for it."

"And once you discovered real girls, the ones you weren't related to, I'm guessing you were never seen again?"

He didn't say anything, only left his shirt on a chair and bent to peel off his socks, leaving them on the floor. Where did he think those went? She always wound up putting them in the hamper because the housekeeper only came in every other day.

"You're not going to admit to having girlfriends back then?" she asked, brushing out her hair.

"I'm wondering why you need confirmation."

"Okay, I'll just admit that I saw you and Paolo have a silent conversation when Lauren mentioned finding letters. I wondered if you had some kind of scandalous affair in *your* past."

"I've always left it to Paolo to create the publicity stirs, keeping my own behavior to run-of-the-mill, pedestrian affairs that aren't very interesting." He held her gaze as he pulled his belt loose. "Current one being the exception."

She set her jaw, arms crossing. "Am I being too nosy? You're starting to sound hostile."

"Just bored, *cara*."

She set down her brush and worked her silver bangles over her hand, trying to hide how deeply his comment stung.

"Well, it's interesting to me," she said stiffly. "I can't imagine what a project that book will be for your aunt, having so much family history to sift through, so many people of note. I'm envious, if you want the truth. My tree is two people and I could write a single paragraph about each of them. Excuse me for being curious about yours when it has such depth."

She turned to set the bangles on the night stand and pulled off her earrings.

"A clean slate can be a good thing, *cara*. There are some family secrets better left out of the history books."

She shot him a look over her shoulder. "If that's supposed to make me less curious, you're going in the wrong direction."

"You told me you didn't want me to lie to you. Do you remember that?" He came up behind her and found the zip at the back of her cocktail dress. "It was the day we became lovers, in the elevator."

Her dress loosened and all of her tingled with memory and fresh anticipation. How did he do that? Steal the air from her body without really touching her, just opening her dress?

"I remember," she told him, standing very still, closing her eyes because he aroused her just by standing near enough to feel his own arousal emanating off his big body.

"You said if I didn't want to talk about something I should simply say so. I don't want to talk about this, *cara*."

"Okay," she whispered, transfixed by the way her bra tightened, then loosened as he released the clasp.

"I want to suck your nipples, then I want your heels in my back as I lick my way down and make you scream my name."

She swallowed. "Okay."

Vito watched Gwyn charm the head of their legal department. She was praising the man's country after their recent visit to Zurich, where Vito had stolen a day with her for scenic driving, a hike and a picnic, opera in the evening and a late-night dinner of fondue.

It had been a day like, well, he should just admit it— it had been like a honeymoon. She had basked under his attention and he had exalted in hers. He'd never had a woman in his life who was so compatible to him, not just in bed, but out of it. Laughing or silent, naked or clothed, he always felt comfortable around her. He was always proud to have her at his side, loved showing her off.

And was half jealous of that heavyset, middle-aged counselor now, as she poured all her charm and attention in that direction, her flushed pleasure utterly captivating.

At least he could take credit for that allure of hers. Not because he'd paid for the classic suit that was tailored to make the most of her million-dollar figure, or because the smooth chignon and subdued lip color and artistic platinum pendant and earrings were also billed to him. No, he liked to think he was responsible for giving her a place where she could blossom, not just privately in his bed, where she was developing an erotic command with regard to telling him what she liked and wanted, but in public arenas.

Gwyn wasn't a bold person by nature and her photo exposé had left her self-confidence seriously dented. Vito had reminded her again and again that she had no reason to feel shame or think she owed anyone explanations. Under his tutelage, she'd regained her confidence and an attitude of self-possession that was even more hypnotic than her exquisite outer shell. He adored seeing her personality shine through like this.

"She's staying after this?" Paolo asked in an under-tone, tucking away his phone.

"You disapprove?" Vito challenged lightly, but with very little actual lightness.

"I don't pass judgments on the private lives of family. You know that," Paolo said with a sardonic twist of his mouth. "If I saw impact to the bank I would comment, but I wouldn't have to, would I?"

No, he wouldn't, but Vito still wound up feeling defensive. He wasn't sure it would matter to him if this affair impacted the bank. He suspected he would carry on with Gwyn regardless.

He had intended to end things after the announcement of charges against Jensen. It would have been a tidy break without loose ends or deeply hurt feelings. Gwyn had been as prepared for it as he had. Even as she had suggested pretending a visit home to see family, he'd been thinking along the same lines.

Then she had touched him, kissed him, somehow stepped inside the shields he wore so easily against the rest of the world and imprinted herself on his very psyche. He had sought satiation that afternoon, certain that when his libido was exhausted, he'd be ready to release her.

But she'd only had to shift away from him in the bed and his entire being had been racked with agony. The single command for her to stay had slipped past his renowned self-discipline, left his lips and landed on her naked skin.

And he didn't regret it. Even though he knew she was falling in love with him. All the signs were there. She wanted to know about his childhood, wanted him to *share*. Aside from dining with Paolo and Lauren, he'd drawn a fine line between her and his personal life, but her yearning to feel connected to the broader landscape of his world, to make her place within it, was obvious.

He couldn't offer her the life she dreamed of when she held his cousin's son and scrambled his eggs in the morning and met him at the door with a kiss when he came home, though.

And cheating her of those things made him reprehensible. If Paolo didn't quite approve of the relationship, that was why. His cousin was an honorable man and knew that Vito was not behaving with complete honor. *If she's a victim, don't make her more of one.*

Vito was implying certain promises that he wouldn't keep, buying time with a woman who could be spending her affection more wisely elsewhere.

But Vito wanted her. His possessive desire was a kind of ferocious pulse beat inside him, territorial and unwavering. He was glad to get this settlement out of the way, glad to put another stage of the scandal behind them. Along with whatever arrangements he made for her when they eventually parted, she would have this very generous cushion for her future, but this was no more an end point to their liaison than the press conference had been.

She was his. He was keeping her. No one would stop him. If Paolo had tried, Vito might very well have shed his cousin's blood for the first time in twenty-odd years.

Gwyn only ever saw her stepbrother in casual clothes, usually wearing stubble and jeans. That's why it took her a full three pulse beats to realize the man who came in behind her lawyer, the man who was clean-shaven, wore a tailored suit as razor sharp as the Donatelli men's and said a grim, "About time," in a voice she knew was Travis.

"Oh, my God! What are you doing here?" She was taken aback, surprised by a light rush of excitement at seeing a familiar face. She almost stepped forward to hug him, but embarrassed realization hit at the same moment, along with the only reason she could imagine he would turn up so unexpectedly. "Is Henry okay?"

"He's fine. Worried sick about you," he said, sending a hostile glance around the conference room. "Why haven't you called him?"

"I…didn't know what to say. You told him I was okay, didn't you?"

"Are you? What is this?" He waved at the conference table where red folders had been set in front of a handful of chairs. "I told you not to sign anything without talking to me first."

"I texted you," she said.

"When I say talk, I mean talk, Gwyn."

Out of the corner of her eye, she saw Vito start forward with purpose, as if he took exception to Travis's patronizing attitude. Paolo stopped him with a hand on his chest and came forward with his own extended.

"Paolo Donatelli. And you are?"

"Travis Sanders. Gwyn's brother." He bit the words off.

Step, she almost clarified, but Travis was still talking.

"I'd like a word with her if you'll excuse us?" So dismissive to the men who owned the skyscraper.

Vito didn't move a muscle, stating implacably, "I'll stay."

Travis tried to stare Vito down. All the hairs on

Gwyn's body stood up, electrified by the open animosity pinging back and forth between the men.

"Look, um—" She glanced to Paolo for help.

"Take as much time as you need," he said, flashing a look at his cousin, but only waving the lawyers from the room and pulling the door closed behind them.

Gwyn looked to Vito, but saw immediately there was no point in asking him to leave. The hostility radiating off him was palpable.

Licking her lips, she turned back to Travis. "I'm *sorry*," she said with deep sincerity. "It's true, I was avoiding you and Henry. This whole thing has been very humiliating. I feel horrible for what Henry and you must be going through."

Vito made a noise that she knew was an admonishment against apologizing for something that wasn't her fault.

"Is that why you haven't come home? Because you were embarrassed?"

She shrugged, as disconcerted by his forcefulness as by the implication that what she considered "home" was her home in his eyes, too.

"Is it?" Vito demanded from his position on the far end of the table. His hot glare was equally unnerving because he looked so stunned.

Hurt, even?

He must know she'd stayed for him. She swallowed, sending him a reassuring look before she turned back to her stepbrother.

"I stayed here for a lot of reasons, but I knew you must be furious—" she began.

"I'm furious because I'm worried, Gwyn!" he cut in. His dark face reddened with deep emotion and his hand waved in the air. "None of this is like you except the part where you refused to pick up the phone and ask me for help! Instead, you're relying on…"

His gaze tracked Vito as he came down the side of the table to where Gwyn stood, closing in behind her in a silent message that might have been a warning to Travis to mind his tone. There was such an air of menace as he looked at the man.

"What the hell is going on here?" Travis asked, shifting his disbelieving gaze to hers. "I mean, I know what it was supposed to look like. Anyone with half a brain can see you were backing Jensen into an admission that he set up the photos, but why are you still here now that that's accepted fact? Why didn't you come home after he was charged?"

"I—" She didn't know what to say. Somehow she was in Vito's grasp, her back against his front, one of his heavy hands on her hip, the other curled around her upper arm.

"Why do you care?" Vito remarked in a dangerous tone.

Travis lifted his gaze to a point past her shoulder, his eyes so cold and deadly, Gwyn tensed and held her breath.

"We're family," Travis said through lips that barely moved. "Maybe we're not related by blood, but we're family. Do you get me? She's not without connections. So whatever the hell you think you're doing with my sister, it ends now."

Family?

Gwyn was dumbfounded by Travis's reaction.

The whole moment was so supercharged with emotion, she almost couldn't speak, thoughts scattered. But these two pitbulls were about to take each other apart, so she covered Vito's hand on her arm and tried to ground out his aggression.

"It's okay," she told him, then turned to Travis. "Your worrying about me is really nice, but it's not necessary. I've been in good hands this whole time."

In her head that had seemed like a sensible thing to say, but the hands upon her tightened and Travis choked out, taking on a thunderstruck expression.

"Have you? Have you really?"

"Yes," she insisted, shifting enough so she could see Vito's stony expression over her shoulder. She wasn't sure what she had expected to see there, but not that cast of iron. For some reason it undermined her confidence in what she was saying. "Paolo and Vito have had my back this whole time."

"That's odd," Travis said, tone dripping sarcasm. "Because what it looks like to me is that a man in a position of power took advantage of a woman who was already in trouble, used her to keep his bank from taking a kick to its reputation, hung on to her to influence the settlement that was being negotiated—" he nodded at the folders on the table "—and *if* he keeps you here, will be using you for reasons that have become far more basic."

"Travis," she gasped, stabbed by his cruel assessment.

"I'm sorry, did I miss a wedding announcement?" Travis asked, flicking his gaze to Vito's. "Are your intentions honorable?"

Vito's hands fell away from her body and stripped her of her skin at the same time. *No.* She wouldn't let Travis ruin this. Why wasn't Vito explaining this wasn't cheap, physical gratification but something so much more?

Public humiliation was a cakewalk compared to losing the regard of people you cared about, she realized, as one man looked at her with pity and the other didn't meet her gaze at all.

"You've always thought I was a gold digger, Travis. Why are you upset to find me exactly where you expected me to be?" she threw out.

"Gwyn," Vito growled in protest while Travis's head snapped back.

"When did I ever call you that?"

"The wedding day. You said Mom and I—"

"I barely knew you!" No apology or denial, she noted. He just railed on. "Now I do and you're as green and idealistic as they come. He's taking advantage of you, Gwyn." And he looked genuinely outraged by it. If she wasn't so furious with him for ruining a good thing, she'd be touched.

"I'm an adult," she asserted. "Perfectly capable of deciding when and with whom I want a relationship."

"Oh, tell yourself that, but this isn't a 'relationship.' It's an arrangement. The most rudimentary kind. He's miles ahead of you and it's all calculated for his best interests, not yours. You will come away with some very pretty material items that I know will mean nothing to you because you are a woman looking for love, not lucre. You're better than this, Gwyn. Don't let him turn you into something you're not."

"You don't know anything about what we have," she said hotly, half turning to snag Vito with her glance, urging him—*insisting*—he defend himself. *Them.*

His jaw pulsed and he stared at Travis, not with heat, not with guilt. Blank.

It hurt. His silence gutted her and his refusal to appear insulted and furious shook her to the core.

"If you have any decency at all, you'll send her home with me," Travis said flatly. "She's better than this."

No, I'm not, Gwyn wanted to say. Maybe she even said it aloud. She knew she argued, "That's a stupid ultimatum. He doesn't have to prove anything to you. *I* decide whether I stay with him or not," she declared.

"Sign the papers when you're satisfied, not before," Vito said, more to Travis than to her, reaching to square one of the folders against the edge of the table, then sending a second look, this one blistering, back to Travis again. "You're wrong about my interfering in this. It's all been negotiated at arm's length, but I'll leave so I'm not a distraction while you finalize it."

"Vito!" Panic edged into her voice as she watched him circle toward the interior door. This wasn't really happening was it? "You're— This isn't—" *Over.* Was it? She couldn't finish the question, afraid she already knew the answer.

He paused, but he didn't turn around. "This was always going to happen, *cara*," he said gently. "You knew that."

She thought of the day when she'd been prepared to leave and had likened it to tearing off a bandage. But genuinely facing The End was a kind of pain she couldn't describe, like her soul was wrenched from her body. Her heart beat outside her chest.

She did the only thing she could. She turned on Travis, the man who had marched in here talking like he cared about her and was destroying her life.

"Why would you do this to me? Do you resent me so much for taking some of your father's precious attention—"

"Gwyn," Vito said sharply, hand gripping the edge of the table with white knuckles, face grim. "*This was always going to happen.* Go home with your brother. Let him take care of you. I want to know you're safe there, not being harassed by the press or anyone else."

"Oh, do you?" she jeered. "What am I now? Not just a pawn, but a marble that gets picked up and taken home? *I* decide what happens to me!"

"Do whatever you want," he commanded. "But you're not coming home with me."

He might as well be throwing rocks at the dog that threatened to follow him. His words landed like sharp stones in her throat and her eyes and her glass heart, chipping and cracking it, leaving it in jagged broken pieces as he disappeared through the door and closed it with finality against her.

"Gwyn, I'm sorry," Travis said, touching her elbow.

She shook him off, distantly supposing she looked like someone had died in front of her because that's how she felt.

She had been miserable, absolutely devastated, when her nude photos had appeared. Vito had questioned her like a criminal and she had thought her life couldn't get any worse. Then he'd made everything better. He'd charmed and soothed and ignited her. He had made her fall in love with him. She had trusted him in ways she'd never let herself trust anyone, especially a man. She had offered her heart on a platter, let herself believe he cared for her at least a little…

But she meant nothing to him.

She hated him with everything in her. He was a bastard and she *hated* him.

At least, that's what she told herself.

The door he'd used to exit the conference room led into Paolo's office. His cousin stood up from his desk. "They're ready for us?"

"All I could see was your father," Vito told him numbly, trying to laugh it off, but ghosts were skimming across his skin, leaving it covered in gooseflesh. His chuckle came off his heart like a dry leaf. A kind of pain, the kind he would never let anyone, for any reason, inflict upon him, coursed like poison through his veins. "I can't be like mine, stealing something I'll end up destroying."

Incomprehension crystalized into understanding in Paolo's expression, maybe even something that might have been a protest, but Vito was already on the move again. If he didn't get out of here, he wouldn't be able to leave her.

"Finish without me. Give her whatever she wants."

CHAPTER TEN

NOT LONG AFTER her mother had married Henry, he had said to Gwyn, "Travis can teach you to drive."

Already far behind her age group in getting her license, Gwyn had declined, not wanting to look stupid in front of him, choosing instead to spend her hard-earned tip money on a couple of private lessons. She couldn't count the number of times Travis had offered to buy dinner over the years, but she'd always insisted on cooking. When she tried, she could think of four distinct times when he had asked whether she was looking for work because he'd heard about a particular position and was willing to recommend her. She'd always taken it as a criticism of the work she was doing or a favor that would make her indebted to him.

Not once had it ever occurred to her that he might give one solid damn about her.

He did. He might have blown up her relationship—*arrangement*—with Vito, but he was sorry. He was treating her like she was made of butterfly wings and soap bubbles, barely touching her, moving her with the gentle cadence of his voice. He told her that he shouldn't have waited for her to ask for help, but that he knew how important her independence was to her. He had wanted to respect her choices, but he couldn't watch her get hurt. He told her she could do better.

"I thought he cared about me," she finally broke her silence to say, as they flew first class back to Charleston.

"I know," he said after a surprised pause. She hadn't spoken since Vito had left the conference room, afraid her voice would crack and the rest of her control would follow. "And there are times when an affair like that is harmless. But you weren't coming into it as his equal. By that I mean the position you were in at the time, life experience, money, influence," he said with a glance from the corner of his eye. "You're a helluva better person."

"You don't know him," she mumbled into the drink he'd ordered her.

"I know him," Travis snorted. "It's like looking in a mirror."

For some reason that made her laugh, jaggedly and with fraught emotion, but as powerful and intimidating as she'd always found Travis, Vito was so much more. Everything she felt about him was massive and angsty and not the least bit brotherly.

Travis twisted his mouth and said, "Why is that funny? Shut up."

Which made her laugh more. Because the alternative was to cry and she'd wait to do that when she was alone.

He took her to Henry's and she really only meant to stay a week or so while she sorted out her life and got a job, but Henry practically begged her to stay. Then Travis walked her into an office a few blocks away and told her she was the comptroller for his friend's chain of high-end restaurants.

"Nepotism?" Her ego really needed to earn something on her own merit.

"Don't be like that. You're *over*qualified. But it's close, the money is good and no one will bother you. It's an excellent stepping stone," Travis urged. "It reestablishes you in the field which is something you need. He really needs someone who can upgrade his system and train the team to use it. You'll be doing him a favor."

"Right," she mumbled, but took the job.

It was awkward at first. Not so much at work. Everyone there was quite nice to her, but as she began moving around in public some people had the audacity to stare. Sometimes they asked outright if she was *that* woman. Usually if she replied, "Yes. Why?" it shut the interest down to a startled, "Just wondering."

Then there was the one day when she was feeling really thin-skinned and went off with the kind of fury that Vito had always warned her against.

It happened to be her mother's birthday. Her period had arrived that morning, severing any crazy illusions she had been nursing that she'd have a lifelong tie with Vito. Then a knock at the door had announced her things from Italy. Not just the boxes from her flat that had gone into storage. *All* her things. Gowns that had hung next to Vito's suits. Scarves and scent and sandals.

Her gaze had scanned the entire inventory list, from eyebrow tweezers to toe rings, seeing novels and anklets and flower vases, but no mention of "Vito's heart."

She had asked the men to stack the boxes in the den, closed the door on them, made a huge breakfast for Henry, ate none of it herself and had cried in the shower before forcing herself to leave for work, already thirty minutes late.

So when she parked her car outside her new job and saw the cameras running at her like laser-shooting weapons in a sci-fi movie, she was already on her last nerve. A million babbled questions washed over her, all of them prompted by some shred of news in the Jensen case that she no longer cared anything about. But when one of the voices said, "We deserve to know everything that happened between you and Vittorio Donatelli," she lost it.

"You *deserve* to know? I'm supposed to betray his confidence and my own right to privacy and tell strangers about our personal relationship? What is wrong with you people? Do you understand what a relationship is? You rely on the other person *not* to talk about you. That's why humans make connections, so we have a safe place to be ourselves. Vito Donatelli gave me that. That's what happened between us, okay? *Trust.* What a kinky, filthy concept, right? I'm sure it is to you!"

She used her elbows to get through the crowd, rather pleased when she heard grunts of startled pain and anxiety for their precious equipment.

"You don't deserve one damned thing."

Vito started to replay the moment where Gwyn gave the paparazzi a piece of her mind, but heard a squawk through the closed doors to Paolo's office.

He rose, not getting any work done anyway, and went through to find Lauren pacing in a light, bouncing step, patting the back of her fussing son.

"Hi," she said with a warm smile, coming across to kiss his cheeks. "Paolo's meeting me here with the other two, but I'm early. Sorry if we disturbed you. This one's fighting sleep even though he's overtired and grumpy."

She wrinkled her nose at her son, then kissed his crinkled little chin.

Vito took him and settled him into what he privately labeled The Sleeper Hold. He'd learned it from watching his many relatives comfort his many infant relations. If a baby didn't take to the shoulder or a cradle hold in the arm, they wanted to lie on their stomach across a forearm, head pillowed in the crook of his elbow, limbs dangling.

Arturo made a stalwart effort to keep up his complaints, but settled in short order with one discontented kick of his leg and a weary sigh. Vito kept rubbing his back, pacing laconically to the window and back. Moments later, he held a warm, limp, sleeping baby.

"You're such a natural," Lauren said, stroking her son's hair, stopping short of the words he'd heard from countless women in his family. *Don't you want children of your own?*

"Paolo was visiting the old bank today," Vito said. "He took Roberto and Bianca?"

Lauren nodded. "Your aunt was meeting them there with a photographer."

Erecting this modern building and moving the Donatelli fortune into it had been a massive decision into which the entire family had weighed. While no one could dispute the practicality of bigger rooms and proper air-conditioning, or the SMART Boards and Wi-Fi and improved security, there was something to be said of the old financial district. The community was a tight one there. It had relied for centuries on old-fashioned networking in the narrow, cobbled streets of the city center.

It was how a young, beautiful daughter of an Italian

banker had wound up catching the notice of a mafioso's son looking to launder his own father's ill-gotten gains.

"I've read there are hidden passageways under those old banks where secret deals were arranged back in the day. Paolo won't tell me if it's true."

"If he did, we would have to kill you," Vito said casually. It was a myth that all of Milan enjoyed perpetuating.

"You bankers," she said, with a teasing grin. "You pretend to be so boring, but you're walking secrets, aren't you?"

Vito glanced down at the sleeping baby to disguise his reaction. "Hardly. What you see is what you get, *cara*."

"So you won't tell me yours," Lauren said after a brief, decidedly significant pause.

"Secrets? I have none to tell," he said, lifting his head and looking her in the eye as he spoke his bold-faced lie.

She tilted her head, but her gaze was soft with affection. "I've always imagined you fell in love with someone you couldn't have. That's why you won't marry and have children when you would make such a wonderful husband and father—"

"Lauren," he said gently. "I adore you. Let's keep it that way. Stop now."

"But then I saw you with Gwyn." Here was the woman who was strong enough to be Paolo's match. She rarely had to show this sort of steel because her sweet nature inevitably paved smooth streets wherever she went. But Paolo was not as domesticated as he appeared. A weak woman would not have fared well as his wife.

"Take him," he said, rolling Arturo into her arms.

"We're not having this conversation." He started back to his office.

"I spent five years married to a man who didn't love me because I was afraid of what I felt for Paolo. Five years sleeping with the wrong man," she said to his back. "She'll find someone else you know."

He was at the door, feeling the latch like a knife hilt against this palm. A pain in his chest was the blade. He twisted it himself.

"She'll try to make babies with him," her voice continued in brutal purity behind him. "I did. Because she'll think that any man's baby is better than no baby at all…"

He almost had the door shut on her. Rude, but necessary.

Her voice elevated. "If you won't tell me, at least tell *her* why you're breaking her heart."

He pulled the door closed and turned the lock for good measure. Then he leaned his forehead upon it, blood moving like powdered glass in his arteries, the baby's body heat still imprinted on his aching arm.

CHAPTER ELEVEN

GWYN THOUGHT SHE was doing pretty well. It had been two months and most of the paparazzi vultures had learned that she lived a very boring life, going from Henry's to work to the grocery store to the dentist to the quickie oil change place. Even she was bored with her life.

Which is why she went on a date with a friend of her brother's. She told herself it was any number of things: getting back on the horse, research about a possible move to New York, interest in a career change to landscape architecture—hilarious. As if she had any interest in watching grass grow. But it was also an opportunity to eat in a restaurant where she didn't work, to see a jazz trio and wear one of the dresses she couldn't bring herself to discard.

She also told herself it was a test, to see if she could let any man other than Vito kiss her.

She was honest with him, told him up front that it was her first date since "it" had happened. He was good-natured, kept things casual and friendly, was a gentleman and a pleasant companion, making her laugh. He made her forget for moments at a time that she was pining and lost without the man she really loved.

But at the end of the night, when he moved to kiss her, she balked. It was instinctive. He wasn't Vito. It felt wrong.

He drew back, solemn and knowing, ruefully disappointed. "Not ready, huh?"

"I'm sorry."

"Don't be." He picked up her hand and kissed her bent knuckles. "I'll be back at the end of the year. We can go out again then. See if you feel differently."

"Thank you," she said, privately sighing. *But I won't.*

Then Henry turned on the porch light and they both chuckled.

Travis was at the breakfast table when she walked into the kitchen the next morning.

"Do not look at *anything*," he warned.

She knew the paparazzi had gone crazy. Cameras had been flashing around them all evening.

"He said we could go out again the next time he's in town." She poured a cup from the coffee he'd made. "But he doesn't realize how notorious I really am, does he?"

Travis said it wouldn't matter to his friend and as Gwyn went about her week, she wondered if anything mattered. It certainly hadn't mattered to Vito that she was dating other men.

Because deep in a sick corner of her soul, that was the real reason she had done it. She had hoped he would see one of those images that had been taken of her dining and dancing. She had hoped it would make him react.

Nothing.

Crickets.

Which was as painful and disheartening as the fact

that she'd felt nothing for a perfectly nice man when he'd acted like he liked her, not just her face or body or the bare skin he'd seen online, but her.

With a shaky sigh, she looked down at the payments she was approving and wondered how many times she'd written her initials without taking in what she was actually signing. She started again.

When she walked outside, summer was announcing its intentions with a heat just this side of uncomfortable and a memo that humidity intended to climb to unbearable.

She dug her keys from her purse, ignoring the sound of a car door opening because it was likely yet another paparazzo—

"Cara."

Cupid's arrow, right through the heart. Sweetly painful, painfully sweet.

She turned to regard him and wished she'd taken a moment to find a bored expression. Instead, she was sure he read all the mixed feelings of welcome and yearning and hurt and betrayal. Why would he show up now, as she was finding ways to live without him?

Why like that? So iconic in one of his banker suits, cut to precision on his leanly sculpted form. He wore a hint of late-day stubble on his cheeks and his eyes were the color of morning light on mountain glaciers.

He stepped to the side and indicated the interior of his limo.

She sputtered, arms folding, aware of footsteps running toward them as some lurking paparazzo realized who she was talking to.

"Have dinner with me," Vito said, paying no attention to the click and whiz of the camera.

"It's four-thirty. I have my own car." She showed him her keys.

He turned and leaned down to speak to his driver, then slammed the door, walking toward her to hold out his palm.

"Really," she said, letting the full scope of her disbelief infuse the word. "Just take up where we left off? No."

"I want to talk to you."

"Does it occur to you that I might not want to talk to you?"

"That is a bluff." He met her gaze and there was a myriad of emotions behind that brutally beautiful face and somber expression. Knowledge shone in his eyes, knowledge of her and what he did to her, his patented arrogance, a kind of desolation that stopped her heart. Heat that made it jump and race again.

He took her keys from her limp fingers.

"I said I wanted to talk. You only need to listen." He touched her elbow, turning her toward the parked cars. At the same time, he clicked the button so the lights on her hatchback flashed. Then he held the passenger door for her.

She hadn't sat on this side of her new car, which wasn't bottom of the line, but wasn't the kind of luxury Vito was used to. While he drove, she took out her phone long enough to punch in Henry's number, leaving a message that she wouldn't be home right away because she was going to dinner with Vittorio.

He glanced across as she dropped her phone into her purse.

"Things are well with your family? You're living with your stepfather. Is that because of the attention?"

He knew she hadn't moved into her own place? She hardly stalked him at all.

She shrugged. "He wants me there. I guess if there's a silver lining to the photos it's learning that I really do have a family. I know now exactly what other women mean when they say that older brothers are annoying. Your sisters must say that a lot."

His brow cocked at her cheeky remark, but he only said, "His protectiveness surprised me after the way you sounded so dismissive of him."

"Join the club," she snorted under her breath.

"He knows you went out with a man the other night?"

"I assume the whole world knows it, if you've heard about it." She reminded herself that it didn't matter that he was bringing it up—even if his voice had lowered to a tone that pretended to be casual, but was actually quite lethal. "He's a friend of Trav's so yes, he knows. He set it up." *Chew on that.*

"You had a nice time?" Again with the light tone, but his knuckles were white on the steering wheel.

"I don't talk about the men I date," she said flatly.

Silence for a full minute, until he stopped behind a line of traffic waiting for a light.

"No. You don't. I appreciate that, *cara,*" he said softly, and this time his voice was filled with gravity and sincerity. "I know you've had offers for tell-alls. They must have been generous. You wouldn't have to work again, I'm sure."

She only turned her face to her side window. If he thought she was the least bit tempted in profiting from what they had shared, he really didn't know her at all.

"How do you like your job?" he asked.

"It's a job, Vito. It's no pin-up gig as Kevin Jensen's

piece on the side. It's no mistress to a playboy banker. But it pays the bills."

"You're angry that I sent you away."

"I'm angry that you're here," she said, swinging her head around to glare at him. "My life was starting to look normal. Why stir it up again?"

Why? It was a fair question. One Vito couldn't answer. At least, not without admitting to himself that he was a very weak man.

"I want to explain why I sent you away," he said. Even though he had walked out on Lauren that day, telling himself she was wrong. Better to break ties cleanly, to let Gwyn move on with her life without knowing what kind of a near miss she'd had.

Why had he decided, after seeing her with another man, that he should let her know why she couldn't be with him? It was flawed logic.

He had wanted to see her again was the real answer. He could say that he wanted to talk and her to listen, but that was a lie. He wanted her to talk. He wanted her to relay every detail of the minutes she'd been away from him, the way she might have given him the highlights of her day visiting a museum, or conveyed a funny conversation she'd overheard on the street or simply traded views with him that might be more liberal than his own, but were always well thought out and left him with a broader view of the other side.

"I thought we were going to dinner," she said as he turned into the underground parking lot of the Donatelli International building.

"You said it was too early," he reminded, pulling into the spot reserved with his name, right next to the elevator. She scowled so mistrustfully at him, he had to chuckle. "I'm not going to kill you and eat you, *cara*."

No promises against licking and nibbling, of course.

It was all he could do not to pounce on her after he punched in the override code to get him to the floor he wanted. She had come out of her workplace with her jacket slung over her arm. Her black skirt was of a modest length, but narrow and stretchy, clinging to her hips and thighs. She wore a light green top that was so plain it was unremarkable, but the narrow belt at her waist gave it some traction across her bustline, emphasizing her hourglass figure. And those shoes with straps as narrow as her belt were positively erotic.

He hoped like hell he had paid for them, unsure why it mattered, just wanting to know she was still allowing him some place in her life.

She flicked her hair behind her shoulder, affecting cool composure, but her mouth was pulling at the corners as she said, "I know why you sent me away. It was an affair, nothing more. Like you said, it was always going to happen."

"*Sì,*" he agreed, and the word moved up from his chest like gravel. "But for different reasons than you think."

The elevator opened into the private residential floor, where he and Paolo had suites and guest accommodations were made available to other family members. There was a private gym and indoor pool here, a dining lounge with views to the ocean that was closed because he was the only one here. Paolo's suite, where he had taken Lauren the night he'd told her that her husband was dead, was on the far side of the oversize foyer. Vito's was here, to his left, but before opening his door, he paused in the foyer and indicated the portrait on the wall.

It was a print of the original that had first hung in the old bank in Milan and now occupied the main lobby of the new tower.

"My great-grandfather," he said, looking at the man who'd been painted in his middle-aged prime wearing a brown plaid suit and a bowler hat.

He felt Gwyn's gaze touch him, questioning why this might be important, but she gave the portrait a proper study.

"He had two sons and five daughters, but only his sons inherited." He nodded at the two brothers who had cemented the foundation for what Banco Donatelli would become. "This one is my grandfather. His brother only had daughters. We've become more progressive and all share in the dividends now, but my uncle, Paolo's father, was recognized as his successor."

He moved to the photo of his grandfather with his wife and five children. It was a formal color photograph with the family posed for posterity, the fashions laughably dated. His grandfather had long sideburns and his pointed collar jutted out like wings against his tan suit and gold tie. His grandmother wore a floral print dress and Paolo's father, nearing twenty, was dressed like a newsboy. The four teenage girls wore identical dresses in a truly horrid purple.

"You Donatelli men get stamped out with the same mold generation after generation, don't you?" She glanced from his great-grandfather, to his grandfather, then to his uncle and then to him. "The girls take after your grandmother. Except this one." She pointed at Antoinietta, barely twelve.

"Sì," he agreed, giving himself one last moment for reservations, but he had none. "That's why I look so much like a Donatelli. She is my actual mother."

Gwyn didn't know what to say, and Vito's profile gave nothing away as he moved to unlock a door and hold it for her.

She entered a private suite that was much smaller than his penthouse in Milan, but had such a similar decor, was stamped so indelibly as *his*, she felt as though she had come home.

"I don't understand," she told him, and the phrase covered many topics. Why had he told her that; why did it matter?

He moved to a photo on the wall in his lounge. The midnineties fashions weren't quite as painful as the seventies had been. A stout man wore a dark suit with a narrow tie that made his barrel chest seem more pronounced. His wife wore a black dress with a scoop neck. Young Vito actually pulled off the red suspenders over his white shirt, but his sisters' hairstyles, all wisped to look like a sitcom star's, were priceless.

She studied his image, realizing he looked…unlike the others.

Maybe she wouldn't have noticed it if he hadn't told her this was not his biological family, but he was taller, leaner, more intense as he gazed into the camera while the rest of them beamed warmly. They seemed relaxed the way a family should when they were together, but he had that smoldering personality that never stopped emanating danger.

"*Mia famiglia.* I love them. My parents taught me generosity and acceptance. They love me every bit as

much as they love their daughters. I would die for any
of them. But my sisters have never been told," he said,
making her swing her attention to him in surprise.
"Paolo knows, but he's likely the only one in our generation or lower who does. He hasn't even told Lauren.
I know some of my great-aunts and uncles have suspicions, but none has ever breathed a word…" He shook
his head and shrugged. "This is something that was put
in the vault and meant to be left there."

"Because your mother was young? Unmarried?"
she guessed. His grandfather might have progressed
to including his daughters in his will, but illegitimate
babies had still been a scandal for a man in such a lofty
position. It wasn't a big deal *now*, though. Was it? Why
continue to hide it?

"My mother was eighteen. I'm a bastard, yes. And I
won't tell you the name of my father, but that's for your
own protection as much as mine. He was mafioso, *cara*.
A truly dangerous and reprehensible man."

She blinked, shocked, and moved blindly to sit on
the edge of the sofa. "How—?"

"—does the daughter of a banker get mixed up with
a thug? He singled her out. I'm sure he had his moments
of charm. I've seen photos and I imagine any woman
would call him attractive. According to my uncle, my
mother might as well have been the youngest daughter
of a church minister, rebelling at her father's attempts
to keep her cloistered. My grandfather was ready to dis-
own her, but my uncle kept fighting to bring her home.
I mean that literally. He had scars. She went back, regardless. Again and again."

"Got pregnant."

"Indeed." He pushed his hands into his pockets,

rocked on his heels, scowl remote and dark. "Even though she came away bruised at different times. I will never understand—"

His profile was hard and sharp.

"She was late into her pregnancy when he bashed her around and she left for the last time. She called my uncle to come take her to the hospital, but she was far into labor when he got there. He caught me and held her as she died. She begged him to keep me from my father. If you could have seen his face when he told me these things…"

"Oh, Vito," she breathed, rising to go to him, hand reaching for his arm, but he was a statue, unmoved by her touch, barely seeming to breathe, face still and harsh as though carved into marble.

"This is what I am, *cara*. A mixture of impetuous Donatelli rebellion—have you met Paolo? I have that same cursed need to dominate and it is a monumental task to hold all of that back. Then I have this streak of brutality on top of it. My father killed people. And the dead ones are the victims who got off easy. His other son turned out as conscienceless, trafficking in women and drugs, winding up dead in the gutter outside his own home, like a rat. I even have a nephew. He's already been arrested for assault. There but for the grace of the Donatelli family go I."

"Vito," she chided. He didn't really think he would have turned out like that, did he? She frowned, hurting for him, feeling how tortured his soul was by a bloodline he didn't want and couldn't escape.

He ran his hand down his face. "I cannot perpetuate that sickness into another generation, not into the very family that took me in, kept me this side of the law and out of the hands of a man who would have turned me into himself. I *won't* risk it. Do you understand? Do you see now why I can't marry you and give you that dream I see in your eyes every time you rock a baby or hold a child's hand?"

She lowered her eyes, aching inside. He saw through her every single time.

"When your brother came to Milan that day," he said heavily, "all I could think was that it was better to let our separation happen then, before you were pregnant with an abomination—"

"Don't say that!"

He held up a hand. "But it tortures me, *cara*, that he made it sound like you were only a convenience to me. Our affair served many purposes, not all of them romantic, *sì*. That's true. But to let you think that was all it was is a lie. We are honest with one another if nothing else, are we not?"

"Are we?" she asked, mind reeling from all he'd told her, which made certain suspicions rise that were so sweet and fragile she barely let herself touch them. But why would he tell her all this, with that tortured look on his face, if he didn't care for her, trust her, not just a little, but a lot.

"Does some part of this sound made-up to you?" he asked, voice chilling and shoulders going back.

She made a noise. "Well, it is quite a story. But I do believe you. No, I'm questioning why you've told me."

She thought back to that day in the elevator when he'd been so angry at what she hadn't been able to see in him. All this time he'd presented her with the thick wall of the vault that fronted the man inside. Of course she'd had trouble seeing his true thoughts and feelings.

But now, now she thought she saw very clearly. It wasn't just wishful thinking, was it?

"I just explained," he said testily. "I didn't want you hurting unnecessarily."

"So I'm supposed to not hurt when you leave again? Secure in the knowledge that your rejection is for my own good? You know I love you, don't you?" There. She flung her own vault wide open, crashing it into the wall.

He flinched, dragging in air like he'd taken a knife to the lung. "I hoped that you didn't," he said through his teeth.

"Oh! Another lie!" she charged, stabbing a finger at his chest, hard enough to hurt her fingernail.

He grabbed her hand and glared, dark brows a fierce line. "I'm not lying!"

"You knew I was in love with you and you sent me away to get over it, but the minute you thought I might, you came back to see exactly how deep my feelings went. This—" she pulled free of his grip and pointed wildly to encompass all the photos he'd shown her "—is a test."

"Untrue. I'm explaining to you why I can't marry you and give you the family you've always wanted."

"Fine. I accept," she said, crossing her arms.

He grew cautious. "Accept what?"

"That we'll never marry and have children. Maybe we can talk about adopting someday, but that's not a condition. I'll accept simply living together without all those picket-fence trappings I always wanted."

"No!" he growled. "That's not what I'm saying. You deserve those things, Gwyn. Your brother is right. That's why—" He cut himself off with an impatient noise, palm scraping up his cheek, creating a raspy sound.

"So I should go marry another man and have his babies?" she confirmed.

"No! Damn you, no. I hated seeing you with that man. It made me sick. No. And damn you for forcing me to admit that." He stalked away a few steps, hand raking into his hair. "I'm trying to think of you, Gwyn, but I keep acting for myself. That is who I am. Greedy. Selfish." He pivoted. "Don't you see that's what I'm trying to protect you from? I want that deal you're offering. I want to take you into my home as my lover and shortchange you on all the things you have a right to. What does that make me? How could you love someone like that?"

"What kind of man are you really?" she cried. "One who blames himself for his mother's death?"

He jerked a little in surprise, said, "No," but without conviction. Then hitched a shoulder. "Perhaps. A little. Everyone, the aunts and uncles who knew, always looked at me as if… I used to fight with Paolo. A lot. But then my uncle told me about this and I knew I had to contain this part of myself. Stamp it out as much as possible."

"And you have," she told him. "Are you likely to hit me, Vito?"

"No," he said, his contempt for men who would do such a thing thick in the word.

"What if I provoke you? What if I push you?" she asked, coming across to give him a light shove in the middle of his chest.

He caught her hands and easily twisted her arms behind her back, hauling her close in such a swift move they both released a little, "Ha," as their bodies lightly slammed together.

She tested his hold. "Now what are you going to do to me?" she said, but softly. Knowingly. She was never frightened here, only eager with anticipation.

"Kiss you," he answered. "Make love to you."

"Love me?" she suggested. Begged.

He lowered his head with a groan, capturing her mouth in a way that instantly owned, but gave at the same time. Anointed. Worshipped. His kiss was almost chaste in its sweetness, but so carnal they couldn't help running their tongues together and opening to deepen the kiss until they were both breathless.

Then he released her arms and tucked her head against his chest where his heart slammed, his strong arms enfolding her to him.

She stroked his sides, soothing the beast.

"I could never hurt you, Gwyn. I wanted to carve out my own heart when I saw the way you looked at me that day you left Milan. The thought that I'd left you feeling anything but confident in how very lovable you are was intolerable. I do love you." He touched his lips to her ear. "I love you in ways I didn't know it was possible to love, with my body, with my breath. I ache with love for you every night and every day."

She closed her eyes, savoring the sting of joyous tears. Threading her arms around him, she held on to him and the moment. The strength that had sustained her and protected her and would be hers. Because she would fight for this.

Him.

"Vito, how did the Donatellis keep you this side of the law?"

"I don't know," he muttered, digging his fingers into her hair, petting her like he was comforting himself. "A million ways, I suppose. Redirection, distraction, love."

"I love you," she drew back to say.

His hold on her flexed and he swallowed. "She loved him. He didn't change."

"Look what she was starting with," she said wryly. "What makes you think a child of yours couldn't be molded the way you were? Especially if he or she started out loved, the way you did?"

"Cara—" It was both protest and longing.

"It's not a deal breaker, I swear. I'm just saying you shouldn't write off your genes as all bad. Either way, I'm yours. You're stuck with me, understand?"

"Your brother is never going to— Screw it," he muttered, ducking abruptly to scoop her legs out from under her and give her a toss, catching her in the cradle of his arms, high against his chest. "We're getting married. Maybe we will adopt, but I'm not having you walk around without my ring. No one will call you anything but my wife."

"Was that a proposal? Because I missed the part where I was asked," she said, but it was hard to sound tart when she was grinning and his neck smelled good and she wanted to crawl inside his clothes. Under his skin. "I missed you," she said against his Adam's apple, voice thready with need.

"I'm half a man without you," he said as he strode into the bedroom and placed her on his bed. "I'm only the worst parts of myself. Angry, jealous, miserable." He yanked his shirt open as he pulled it from his pants. "You understand what kind of possessive bastard you're consigning yourself to, don't you?"

"I'd like to say it's my choice, but I don't think I've ever had one." She lifted her hips to reach her zipper, then working her skirt down, enjoying the way his chest swelled at the sight of her bared legs. He hurried to finish undressing. "It has to be you or no one," she told him.

"Are you still on the pill?" he asked.

She nodded while she released the belt that she'd worn over her shirt, but she caught the little something that passed over his expression. It was a brief hesitation, words that rose but were second-guessed. One day, she knew from that tiny moment of betrayed thought, one day he would be ready to think about children. It was okay that today wasn't that day. She wanted him to herself for a little while, anyway.

He skimmed her undies away and settled his hot body over her, his hips between her legs. One arm reached to help her finish pushing off her top. "This is pretty," he said of her bra, tracing the edge of the blue-green lace. "It can stay for now."

He leaned to kiss her, but she drew back, needing to know.

"Does it bother you that so many men have seen me naked?"

"That will always bother me, *cara*. Not just because I am a jealous Neanderthal of a man, but because it hurt you so very badly. I would do *anything* to make that go away for you."

She traced her fingertips along his temple, down the side of his face, then cupped the side of his neck. "But we might not have found each other if that hadn't happened. And you wouldn't be here at all if your mother and father hadn't happened. Life is never going to be perfect and tidy, you know. Bad things can happen. We can only do our best with what we're given."

"Are you giving yourself to me?"

"I am," she said solemnly.

Excitement lit his eyes, but his kiss was tender. "Then I will do my best with you. That is a promise, *mia bella*." He settled his hips low and his hard, glorious length slid into her, slid home, making her groan in welcome. This was where they both belonged.

"Ti amo tanto," he groaned. *I love you so much.*

And later, when they were debating whether to rise and go out to eat, both completely lacking the will to move any more than a hand to caress a collarbone or turn their lips into each other's skin, her ringtone sounded from the other room.

Leaning off the bed for his pants, Vito pulled out his own phone and dialed, saying a moment later, "She's not coming home tonight. We'll come by your father's in the morning on the way to the jewelry store. I'll ask for her hand like a proper suitor. Good enough?"

It must have been because he hung up after one grumbled word from a voice she recognized as Trav's.

"I told you he's annoying," she said.

Vito set aside his phone and gathered her beneath him, bracing himself on his elbow above her, just looking at her in the half light of dusk coming through the uncovered windows.

"I like it, *tesoro*. I'm a competitive man. I will enjoy treating you so well he is forced to eat his words again and again."

She burst out laughing, not asking where his edges and superiority complex came from. At least he was using his naturally dominant nature for good instead of evil.

"I do love you, you know," she told him, gazing into his eyes. "I love you because you told me. You trust me. That means so much."

"I never imagined telling anyone." He frowned across the room, into the middle distance. "It's not about protecting me anymore, but protecting the bank. This could be a very big problem for the family."

"I'll never tell a soul, I promise."

"I know." His brows gave a little pull, like she was stating the obvious. "I knew when I came here that even if you were repelled, the secret would always be safe with you."

She petted his cheek, smoothing his rough stubble, chiding, "But I will take every opportunity to point out things like the fact that you have a crazy fierce capacity for loyalty. If your son or daughter had the same, we'd have nothing to worry about."

His beautiful mouth pursed. "One of the first things I admired about you was that fighting spirit of yours."

"Really?" She tussled with him and he let her win, so she had him on his back and she sat straddled over his thighs. But rather than crow with triumph as she pinned his big hands to the mattress, she leaned down to say against his lazy, satisfied grin, "You changed my world and I'm going to change yours."

"Vows to live by, *mia bella*. I do."

EPILOGUE

"DON'T YOU DARE, you little streaker!" Gwyn said, but her daughter had figured out that her mother was handicapped by a belly the size of Nebraska. She slithered away and left Gwyn on her knees holding a towel and a clean diaper.

"Vito!" Gwyn cried, and awkwardly clambered to her feet, waddling after her just-turned-two-year-old into the hall.

Antoinietta made her way down the stairs with determined little feet, hands gripping each of the uprights in turn, always tenacious about getting what she wanted, but willing to play by the rules once they were given to her.

Vito made no effort to come up to the girl, just stood at the bottom with his hands on his hips. "You really take after your mother, don't you?"

"Oh, you're funny," Gwyn told him, narrowing her eyes in a promise of retribution. "I told her who was coming for dinner. It was supposed to be an inducement to get her into her clothes, but…" She waved to indicate how well that had worked.

"Bea!" Toni called, trying to dodge her father as he made a grab for her at the bottom of the stairs. Then she said a very stern, "No, Papa," when he caught her and carried her up the stairs. The higher he went, the more she struggled and the louder she said, *"Down."*

"Yeah, that's all me," Gwyn said as he took the diaper from her. Their daughter was making a very serious effort to get out of his hold, squirming so hard her face was red, pudgy fists white and tiny brows screwed up with stubborn resolve.

"She's *two,*" Vito said.

"She's *yours,*" Gwyn said, chuckling when that actually made him close his arms even more tenderly around his adamant little girl.

"She is," he said proudly, and proceeded to speak in a calm voice, explaining that her cousins would be here soon, but she had to dress first.

He wrangled her into her clothes amid a great deal of negotiating and, *"Me do!"*

The bell rang as Vito carried her down the stairs a few minutes later and Toni's excitement soared as Bianca and the boys entered. She spared a moment to hug and kiss the adults, but her adulation was reserved for her true hero, Roberto, her partner in mischief, Arturo, and her dearest and most beloved Bianca.

"Bea." She hugged the girl who knelt to hug her back with every warm and sweet bone in her body.

Gwyn was almost as excited as her daughter when family came over. Henry now saw the advantage of a tablet and connected with them online when he wasn't actually staying at the apartment he'd bought nearby, so he could visit in person and watch his granddaughter grow up. He was flying in next week, anticipating the new baby would be with them. Even Travis had made a point of coming with his father for Christmas this year, since Gwyn had been too far along to travel.

Tonight it was Vito's turn for having family over. All of Vito's relations had made her feel welcome, Vito's parents especially, but Lauren was like a sister to Gwyn. Now that they were both pregnant, they were even closer than ever.

As for the man who was her boss again, after contracting her for a special project he'd offered to her a year ago? She didn't find him nearly as formidable.

"You're as much of a comedian as your cousin, aren't you?" she said to Paolo as he set a bag she recognized inside the door. It was the birthing kit he'd prepared when they had come to the house on Lake Como and Lauren had delivered Arturo. "I'm warning you right now, if your wife has her baby in my home, when I am already eleven months pregnant—" It was an exaggeration, but that was how she felt.

Paolo cut her off by kissing her cheek. "I brought it for Vito."

"Ha!"

"Bite your tongue," Vito muttered.

"The doctor said I'm at least two weeks away," Lauren assured them and they all groaned and rolled their eyes. "But honestly, Gwyn. The second one comes faster."

"So I can count on thirty-six hours reducing to thirty?" Gwyn joked.

"*Cara,*" Vito protested. He had been appalled, genuinely upset that all the pleasure they gave each other had resulted in so much pain for her, but Toni was such a gift Gwyn was more than willing to go through it again to meet the next addition to their family. In fact, she had a feeling it would be sooner than later. One of the reasons she had invited them for dinner was because she had that low, dull ache in her pelvis that had sat with her for two days before her labor had started for real with Toni.

Soon, she knew, she'd be tied up with a newborn and not entertaining for a while, so she wanted a proper visit with this family she enjoyed so much while she had the time.

Sure enough, a few hours later, as she and Lauren were drying dishes, the first pain hit, a nice strong one that took her breath.

"Vito," Lauren called as she took the plate from Gwyn's hand. "We're going to take Toni home with us. You and your wife have a date with a midwife."

They made that date, with no time to spare. Second babies did come faster and Vito almost had to eat his smug words to Paolo as they'd left, about how some men got their wives to the hospital before their children delivered. His son arrived as Gwyn was being admitted, caught by a startled ER nurse who barely had time to pull the curtain.

"Do you mind?" Gwyn asked Vito when she was settled in the maternity ward, pronounced healthy along with their son, but staying for overnight observation. "That he's a boy, I mean?"

"Why would I mind?" he asked, lifting a sharp gaze from studying the boy.

"You wanted a girl with Toni. I thought…" She had taken it to mean he believed girls were less likely to develop undesirable behaviors.

"Because I wanted to name her Antoinietta. I knew

my mother would be touched to have her sister remembered and she is."

"You're not worried your son will be like—"

"Me?" he cut in, mouth twisting into a wry smirk. "I'm counting on it."

She had to chuckle at that, and leaned forward to kiss him. "Me, too."

* * * * *

*If you enjoyed this story, check out these other
great reads from Dani Collins,*
THE CONSEQUENCE HE MUST CLAIM
THE MARRIAGE HE MUST KEEP
VOWS OF REVENGE
SEDUCED INTO THE GREEK'S WORLD
Available now!

Uncover the wealthy Di Sione family's sensational secrets in the brand new eight-book series
THE BILLIONAIRE'S LEGACY,
beginning with
DI SIONE'S INNOCENT CONQUEST
*by Carol Marinelli.
Also available this month.*

Luca bent toward her. She was diminutive to his own lean six-two. "What is it that suddenly interests you about me, Sophia? Have you finally decided you need another orgasm to sustain you for the next decade?"

Flames scorched her skin—that was how hot she felt. *Yes* floated to her lips, as if every cell inside her had conspired to form that word without her permission. This was easy for him—too easy—riling her up, sinking under her skin. Even knowing what he was, still she reacted like a moth to a flame.

"Not everything has to have a sexual connotation in life."

He made to speak, but before he could she covered his mouth with her hand. Long, elegant fingers traced the tender skin of her wrist, leaving brands on her sensitive flesh. The center of her palm burned with the heat of his mouth. Slowly, as if savoring every second of touching her, he pulled her hand from his mouth. Of course life itself was a big joke to be enjoyed for Luca Conti.

"What did you think I was going to say, Sophia?"

She pursed her mouth tight and took a deep breath. "I have a proposal I'd like to make to you—one that is mutually beneficial to us both."

"There is nothing you can offer me," he said, his gaze flicking over her, dismissal and insult all wrapped up in that few seconds, "that I won't get from another woman with a whisper, Sophia. Nothing remotely tempting."

"You haven't even heard it."

"Not interested—"

"I want to marry you."

The Legendary Conti Brothers

The Sinner and the Saint meet their match!

Known throughout the world as the Conti Sinner and
the Conti Saint, these legendary Italian brothers have
been the focused goal of many a gold-digger.

But hands off, ladies—that's now finally at an end!

For rumours are that Leandro, the Conti Saint,
has a seven-year-old secret…
and Luca, the Conti Sinner, is engaged!

Don't miss the chance to get your hands on
this fabulous new duet by Tara Pammi!

The Surprise Conti Child
June 2016

The Unwanted Conti Bride
July 2016

THE UNWANTED CONTI BRIDE

BY

TARA PAMMI

MILLS & BOON

First Published in Great Britain 2016
By Mills & Boon, an imprint of HarperCollins*Publishers*
1 London Bridge Street, London, SE1 9GF

© 2016 Tara Pammi

ISBN: 978-0-263-92122-9

Our policy is to use papers that are natural, renewable and recyclable
products and made from wood grown in sustainable forests. The logging
and manufacturing processes conform to the legal environmental
regulations of the country of origin.

Printed and bound in Spain
by CPI, Barcelona

Tara Pammi can't remember a moment when she wasn't lost in a book—especially a romance, which was much more exciting than a mathematics textbook at school. Years later, Tara's wild imagination and love for the written word revealed what she really wanted to do. Now she pairs alpha males who think they know everything with strong women who knock that theory *and* them off their feet!

Books by Tara Pammi

Mills & Boon Modern Romance

The Sheikh's Pregnant Prisoner
The Man to Be Reckoned With
A Deal with Demakis

The Legendary Conti Brothers

The Surpise Conti Child

Greek Tycoons Tamed

Claimed for His Duty
Bought for Her Innocence

Society Weddings

The Sicilian's Surprise Wife

A Dynasty of Sand and Scandal

The Last Prince of Dahaar
The True King of Dahaar

The Sensational Stanton Sisters

A Hint of Scandal
A Touch of Temptation

Visit the Author Profile page at
millsandboon.co.uk for more titles.

CHAPTER ONE

TONIGHT, SOPHIA ROSSI decided with mounting desperation, her spirit animal would be a skunk.

Because desperation had a particularly pungent stink. It probably clung to her pores, spraying whiffs of it over pitying and curious bystanders, betraying her panic.

She had never belonged in the uber-rich Milanese society that her stepfather and mother dwelled in, was only a Rossi because Salvatore had adopted her after marrying her mother when Sophia had been thirteen. Facts of her life she'd never been allowed to forget by the crowd around her.

She'd somehow weathered the end of her engagement to Leandro Conti.

But this latest rumor—her supposed affair with her one real friend, Kairos Constantinou, who was Leandro's sister's new husband—had made her an object of gossip and even malice. If she'd known what a spectacle it made of her, she'd have refused Leandro's invite to his brother Luca's birthday party, which had been extended weeks ago. The invite was only driven by his guilt at breaking their engagement.

Her fingers tightening over the fragile champagne flute, she made a casual, painted-smile-in-place round around the curving, wide balcony of the Villa de Conti.

Somehow they'd made her into this temperamental shrew, this marriage-wrecking wanton that had become a liability to her family rather than an asset.

How had she, despite all her hard work, jeopardized the most important goal of her life—to support her stepfather, Salvatore, and rebuild Rossi Leather until her half brothers were old enough to take over?

Antonio Conti, the patriarch of the Conti family, reached her just as Sophia deflected another barbed insult. Glassy and brittle it might be, but she didn't let the smile drop from her face.

Silver threaded abundantly through his black hair. Antonio reminded her of a wolf—cunning, wily and quick to gobble up unsuspecting prey.

"Tell me, Sophia," he said, neatly cornering her near a white pillar, "whose idea was it to propose a marriage between my grandson and you?"

Swallowing her shock, Sophia stared at him. No one should have even guessed. "Our engagement is irrelevant now that Leandro is married."

"Your stepfather is ambitious but not clever," Antonio continued as if Sophia hadn't even spoken. "Hardworking but no vision. Even knowing of my desperation to find a bride for my grandsons, Salvatore would have never thought to offer you.

"He has no use for women."

The words were curt, even cruel in their efficient summation. But true.

Sophia had been trying for a decade to get Sal to see the value she could provide for the company, with zero progress. He gave her small projects, refused to listen to her ideas for Rossi Leather.

All he cared about was leaving a legacy for her half brothers, Bruno and Carlo.

"It was mine," she admitted. What did she have to lose at this point? "There was advantage to your family and mine in that match."

Sal could hold grudges on Leandro Conti and the Conti family for breaking the engagement, but Sophia was nothing if not practical.

Rossi Leather couldn't tide over their latest financial setback by alienating the powerful Contis. Antonio still held much sway over the older generation in the leather industry and Leandro Conti, his eldest grandson and CEO of Conti Luxury Goods, held the younger, more heated generation.

Antonio's second grandson, Luca Conti, however... had no clout or morals. Probably no talent. Just oodles of charm, sexuality and utter self-indulgence.

Even thinking about him made her cross. And bitter. And her knees weak.

She'd spent nights pacing her bedroom, sleepless, panicky, when the idea of marrying Leandro had presented itself to her. She'd made herself sick. She'd had nightmares about her past and present morphing into a distasteful, torturous future.

But the welfare of her family had precedence over naive decade-old dreams.

Antonio didn't look surprised. But then he'd known to ask that question, hadn't he? His silvery brows rose. "You're a curiously resourceful young woman, Sophia."

Sophia's cheeks heated up. "Even for a half-Italian bastard girl with a broken engagement behind her, you mean?"

He continued looking at her.

If she hadn't lost her finer sensibilities a long time ago, if she hadn't developed elephant-thick skin, she'd have been insulted by the purely assessing look the old man cast her, from the top of her dark hair in an efficient knot to the soles of her black Conti pumps, her only nod to fashion, with leisurely stops at her face and several other areas of her body.

"I'm not a cow to be assessed," she added with a glare. The flash of something in his gaze gave her the creeps. "I'm not in the market for an alliance anymore, either." There was only so much she could stomach, apparently, even for her family. "Of any kind," she added for good measure.

Amusement shifted the rigid lines of his face. Flashes of a similar set of features sent a flutter down her spine. "You're not only dedicated to your family but you're also sharp and fearless. I like you, Sophia."

Rarely did the opposite sex, except for her ten-year old brothers, say something that wasn't condescending or insulting to her. "I wish I could say the same. But I've seen you use everyone's shortcomings to your own advantage, including Sal's."

His smile lingered. "Then why not advise your stepfather?"

She remained silent, frustration a quiet snarl inside her. Because Sal never listened to her. He loved her, but not enough to trust her judgment or intelligence when it came to Rossi Leather. All of which she was aware the cunning wolf knew.

"I can give you a way to help Salvatore, Sophia. Without throwing yourself at a married man."

Stinging anger burned Sophia's cheeks but she stayed still. He'd baited her well and he knew it. She was going to throttle whoever had started that distasteful rumor.

"I will pour capital into Salvatore's business," Antonio continued, "create new contracts for him, bring him back into the old class, so to speak. After his string of poor business decisions, he certainly needs the help."

"I'm not for sale," Sophia retorted, a slow panic building inside. She felt like a donkey with a carrot visible but just out of reach. "I suggested marriage to Leandro as a way to help Sal, but I'd have kept every vow I made to him. I would've been a good wife."

"You believe I did not realize that? You believe I would let Salvatore...*persuade* me into letting you marry my grandson without learning all about you? It is exactly why I make this proposal."

Her pulse sped up. "What is your proposal?" she forced herself to say.

"I do have another grandson, *si*? Bring Luca to the altar, marry him and I will take a firm handle on Rossi financial matters. Your mother, your brothers, their futures will never be in peril."

"No!" Her sharp reply turned heads toward them.

Marry Luca, the Conti Devil?

The very idea was like walking on shards of glass for the rest of her life. *Bare feet and with a lead weight over her head.* "I don't want to spend an evening with the Conti Devil, much less marry him."

As though invoked by their discussion, Luca Conti appeared in the midst of the perfectly manicured lawn before them, a tall, gorgeous blonde following him like a faithful puppy.

A woman on his arm, as always.

The rage in those languid, smoky eyes the night of her engagement to his brother had haunted her. But he'd avoided her as she'd done for a decade.

His dark, wavy hair was in that same stylish cut. Low on the sides and piled high on his head, making his angular face even narrower. Sophistication and grace oozed from his every stride. But any kind of austerity ended with his hair.

Because Luca Conti was the most beautiful man she'd ever seen.

His face, now visible only in flashes as he moved

through the crowd with that loose-limbed stride had such perfect lines that her breath caught even from this distance.

Broad shoulders lovingly hugged by gray silk, narrowing to a tapered waist and muscular thighs honed to pure steel by hours and hours of swimming. He moved sinuously through the crowd, the tall woman a beautiful accessory around his lean and wiry body, a little on the thin side.

But who could remember all that after one glance at his face?

Wide-set, jet-black eyes, with dark blue smudges underneath, always the shadows underneath his eyes as if the man never slept, a steel blade of a nose and a wide mouth made of plump, lush lips that invited one, two... oh, a hundred glances.

Collagen had nothing on this man's mouth...

A mouth that invited sin with one word... A mouth he knew how to use every which way...

Sharp cheekbones created planes and grooves, in concert with the high forehead, as if every inch of it had been painstakingly designed and carved to render him breathtaking.

Those features should have been effeminate, too beautiful, yet something in his gaze, in his will, immediately imposed his fierce masculinity on the onlooker, as if the space around him had to become an extension of him.

And the devil was aware of his exquisite beauty, and the effect it had on the female sex, whether they were seventeen or seventy.

It was clear, from even up there, that Luca was sloshed if not drunk and so was the disreputable beauty, who also happened to be the Italian Finance minister's *almost* ex-wife, Mariana.

Had she thrown away her powerful husband for Luca?

Did she know that Luca would dispose of her like a toddler did last week's toys?

Sophia could almost, *only almost*, feel pity for the woman.

The hiss of a curse falling from Antonio's mouth by her side punctured her obsessively greedy perusal.

Luca, as usual, was creating a ruckus. Heads turned toward him, including Kairos and Valentina. A stiff-lipped Leandro cast a hand on Luca to stop him but his younger brother pushed it away.

Whispers abounded, like the drone of insects.

As indulgent as his family and friends were of his usual escapades, it seemed an open lovers' spat—for Luca and the lady's argument was becoming clear now—with another man's wife was too scandalous for them to overlook.

"This is the man you want me to wed? The man who shamelessly shows off his affair with another man's wife with no thought to his family or hers? The man who thinks every woman is a challenge to be conquered, a bet to win?" The memory of her own humiliation at his hands was like acid in her throat. "One who tramples hearts like they were little pieces of glass? I wouldn't touch Luca if he were the last man on earth."

Antonio turned toward her slowly, as if that small movement cost him a great effort. One look into his eyes and Sophia knew he was going in for the kill. Now she was the deer caught in the wolf's sights.

"Are you aware, Sophia, that the bank is ready to call Salvatore's loan in? Or that he has no way to meet the next production per schedule?"

Her heart sank to her toes. "That's not true. He applied for an extension—"

"And was denied."

Sunken eyes peered at her with a cunning that sent chills down her spine. He'd done this, she knew.

Oh, Salvatore had paved the way to their financial ruin with his own faulty decisions but this latest setback—the bank's refusal for an extension—was Antonio's doing.

Apparently, Antonio was just as desperate as she was. "Even if I were to agree to your outrageous proposal—" her entire life tied to that reckless playboy who had made her so weak once "—how do you think I can accomplish this? Even I, desperate that I am, can't drag a man to the altar. And definitely not the Conti Devil, who cares for nothing except his own pursuits."

Drunk as he was, Luca had somehow managed to steer the clinging woman away from the crowd. But her husky laughter and frantic begging in Italian could be heard from where they were standing, behind and beneath the balcony.

Heat tightened Sophia's cheeks as she understood the gist of the woman's phrases in Italian. Instead of distaste and fury, she felt pity.

The woman was in love with Luca.

Antonio dragged his gaze away from Luca, his mouth a tight line. His frail body seemed to vibrate with distaste, rage and, Sophia sensed with mounting shock, grief. Antonio Conti was grief-stricken over his grandson Luca. *Why?*

The image of the manipulative old man shifted in her mind, even as he took a deep breath, as if to push away the emotion. "No, my grandson cares for nothing in this world. His parents are long dead and Leandro, too, has washed his hands of Luca now.

"But to protect Valentina and her happiness, Luca will do anything. He will make a bargain with anyone to keep her birth a secret from the world."

Sophia gasped, unable to believe what she was hearing. "Her birth? This is not right. I want no part of it—"

"Valentina is not my son's daughter. She is the product of an affair their mother had with her driver. And if this comes out, it will ruin Valentina's standing in society and even her marriage to your friend Kairos.

"So use it to bind Luca to you. He will bend for Valentina's happiness."

No words came to her as Sophia stared at Antonio.

The idea of blackmailing the Conti Devil didn't bother her so much as using Valentina's secret. Dear God, she didn't want to hurt anyone.

An acidic taste lingered in her mouth. "There are too many innocent people involved in this. I won't hurt one of them just because—"

"Just because Salvatore might lose the company? Just because your mother and brothers might have to leave their estate, give up their cars, their place in this society? And what will you do, Sophia? Take up the project manager job your Greek friend offers you to support them? Quietly stand by as Salvatore watches chunks of his company broken down and auctioned off?"

"Why me? Why can't you find a willing woman and force *him* to marry her? Why—"

"Because you're tough and you do what needs to be done. You don't have silly ideas of love in your head. Only you will do for the Conti Devil."

Only you...

Antonio Conti's words reverberated through Sophia.

Oh, how she wished she'd not come tonight... Now she had a possible way to dig their finances out of the ruin but it would only be achieved by selling her soul to the devil...

She wasn't considering it, Sophia told herself, as she walked through the unending corridor of Villa de Conti. The black-and-white-checkered floor gave the mounting nausea within a physical bent.

Surely Antonio deluded himself that his devil-may-care, womanizing grandson could care about his sister. But she had to try. She had to see if there was a chance of salvaging their finances, if there was even a small sliver of hope that her mother, Salvatore and the twins wouldn't be driven to the road.

She reached a wide, circular veranda at the back of the villa.

Jacket discarded, shirt open to reveal a dark olive chest, cuffs folded back, Luca stood leaning against the wall. A foot propped up against it, eyes closed, face turned to the sky. The curving shadows his long eyelashes cast on his cheekbones were like scythes.

Scythes and blades. Her usually nonviolent thoughts revolved around weapons when it came to Luca.

Moonlight caressed the planes of his face, shadows diluting the magnificent symmetry of his features. Rendering him a little less gorgeous.

A little less captivating.

A little less devilish.

Almost vulnerable and…strangely lonely.

Slowly, Sophia became aware of her own reaction. Damp palms. Skittering heartbeat. Pit in her stomach. Even after a decade, her body went into some kind of meltdown mode near him.

She must have made a sound because his eyes opened slowly. Only his eyes were visible in the silvery light. They fell on her, widened for an infinitesimal fraction of a second, searched her face and then assumed that laid-back, casual, infuriatingly annoying expression that she hated.

"Sophia Rossi, of steel balls and tough skin and icy heart." Whatever alcohol he'd imbibed, his speech didn't slur. Mocking and precise, it arrowed past her defenses. "Did you lose your way, *cara*?"

His sultry voice thickened the air around them so much

that Sophia wondered if she could breathe through it. "Stop calling me…" No, that was way too personal. If she was going to do this, Sophia had to enclose herself in steel, lock away even the slightest vulnerability she had, not that she had any. She'd do this for her family, but she wasn't going to be the Conti Devil's amusement. Not this time.

He pushed himself from the wall while she formed and disposed words. When she looked up again, he'd moved close enough for her to smell the crisply masculine scent of him. The light from the hall caressed his features.

Breath was lost. Nerves fluttered. A sigh built and ballooned inside her chest. That small scar under his chin. The sweeping arch of his eyebrows. The razor-sharp lines of his cheekbones. Darkly angelic features that masked a cruel devil.

Jet-black eyes glinted with sardonic amusement at her mute appraisal. He propped a bent hand on the wall she was leaning against, sticking his other hip out. A pose full of grace and languor. Of feigned interest and wretched playfulness. "Tell me, how did you end up in the farthest reaches of the house, away from all the wheelings and dealings of your business friends? Did Little Bo Peep lose track of her sheep and wander into big bad wolf's way?"

Sophia tried to command every cell in her body to keep it together, wrenched herself into a tight ball so that all that touched her was the man's whispery breath. "You're getting your fairy tales mixed up."

"But my point got through to you, *si*?" He ran the heel of his hand over his tired-looking eyes while Sophia stared hungrily, cataloging every gesture, every shift. "What do you want, Sophia?"

"Your…*situation* looked like it needed rescuing."

The slight tug of his mouth transformed into that full-blown grin that always seemed to be waiting for an invite.

Evenly set teeth gleamed in an altogether wicked face. "Ahh…and so Sophia Rossi, the righteous and the pure, decided to come to my aid."

"Where is your lover? I can have one of our chauffeurs drive her home."

His gaze held hers, a thousand whispers in it. "She's in my bed, thoroughly lost to the world." It dipped to her mouth. Snaky tendrils of heat erupted over her skin. "I believe I wore her out."

Nausea hit Sophia with the force of a gardening hose, the images of a sweaty and ravished Mariana burning her retinas as if she could see the leggy blonde amidst a cloud of soft, white sheets.

Luca's bedroom—pure white sheets, gleaming black marble, black-and-white portraits all around… It was like being transported into your worst nightmare and your darkest fantasy, all rolled into one. While being naked and blindfolded and without any defense.

She let all the disgust she felt seep to the surface and stepped back.

"Don't you think this is too far even for you? They are not even divorced yet. And you're advertising it for all and sundry to see."

"But that's the fun, *si*? Tangling with the dangerous? Riling up her husband into one of his awful tempers?"

"And then you walk away?" *Like you did from me.* "Her life will be in ruins in terms of the society, while you latch on to the next willing v—"

His mouth curved into a snarl and his hand covered her mouth. Opal fire burned in his eyes. "Is that what you tell yourself, *cara*? That you were a victim all those years ago? Have you convinced yourself that I forced you?"

She pushed away his hand and glared at him, all the while pretending that her lips still didn't tingle from the

heat of his touch. That she didn't burn at the memory…
"I didn't mean that you take them without their… Damn
it, Luca, you and I both know he will ruin her over this."

"Maybe ruin is exactly what Mariana wants. Maybe
to be utterly debauched by me is her only salvation." The
words were silky, casual, and yet…for the first time in her
life, Sophia saw more than the hauntingly beautiful face,
the wicked grin, even the seductive charm. "You would
not understand her, Sophia."

"I just don't think—"

Sophia watched that lazy face swallow away that fury,
saw the emotion blank out of his eyes as easily as if someone had taken an eraser and wiped it away. "I don't give a
damn about your opinions, so, *per carita*, stop expressing
them." He bent toward her, diminutive as she was to his
own lean six-two. "What is it that suddenly interests you
about me, Sophia? Have you finally decided you need another orgasm to sustain you for the next decade?"

Flames scorched her skin; that was how hot she felt. *Yes*
floated to her lips, as if every cell in her had conspired to
form that word without her permission.

This was easy for him, too easy—riling her up, sinking under her skin. Even knowing what he was, still she
reacted like a moth venturing to a flame. "Not everything
has to have a sexual connotation in life."

"Says the woman who needs to be utterly and thoroughly—"

This time her hand clamped his mouth. Sophia glared
at him. His breath kissed her sensitive palm.

Long, elegant fingers traced the tender skin of her
wrists, leaving brands on her sensitive flesh. Slowly, as if
savoring every second of touching her, he pulled her hand.
"What did you think I was going to say, Sophia?"

She pursed her mouth and took a deep breath. "I have

a proposal I'd like to make to you, one that is mutually beneficial."

"There is nothing that you can offer me—" his gaze flicked over her, dismissal and insult in that look "—that I won't get from another woman, Sophia."

"You haven't even heard it."

"Not interested—"

"I want to marry you."

CHAPTER TWO

Not "will you marry me, Luca?"

Not "I think it makes sense for me to marry you now even though I've hated you for a decade and chose your brother over you just a few months ago."

Not "I need you to save my stepfather from sure financial ruin, so, *please, oh, please*, won't you make me your wife?"

No, Sophia Rossi proposed marriage as she did everything else.

Like a charging bull and with the confidence that she could bend, twist or generally command him into doing her bidding. Probably with an adoring smile on his face, and the marble digging into his knees if she could manage it.

Dio, where did the woman's strength come from?

Luca Conti swallowed his astonishment. Her loyalty in considering this for her family's sake, when he knew how much she hated him—and with good reason—was admirable. He ignored the thudding slam of his heart against his rib cage—she was a weakness and a regret he'd never quite forgotten—and gave free rein to the riding emotion.

Amusement. Sheer hilarity.

It burst out of him like an engulfing wave of the ocean, like a rising crescendo of music, punching the air out of his throat with its force. There was a knot in his gut. Hand shaking, he wiped his wet cheeks.

What merciful God had granted him this wonderful moment?

For reasons all too Freudian, Luca hated his birthday. Loathed, despised with the hatred of a thousand exploding supernovas. But his self-loathing, as brightly as it flared from time to time, to his brother Leandro's eternal gratitude, had never overtaken his respect for life.

Over the years he had become better at handling his birthday. There was even a memorable threesome sprinkled through a couple of them. But not one of those miserable thirty birthdays had presented him with a gift like this one.

Just months ago Sophia had chosen Leandro over him to marry.

To see the one woman he had given up years ago—granted, after thoroughly breaking her heart—as his brother's wife every day would have been the straw that broke the camel's back. In other words, destination Hell on a direct flight.

He would have had to let the engagement go forward. The wedding itself, probably not.

He'd have seduced her, for sure. He'd have had to do it before the wedding, he remembered telling himself in a drunken haze. Luckily, his—now—sister-in-law Alex had shown up, turned Leandro's life inside out and spun Luca away from that necessary but destructive course.

And here Sophia was now…proposing marriage to *him* this time. The woman had balls. He loved her for that if nothing else. "I believe this is the best birthday present I've ever received, *bella*. How the mighty fall. Wait till I—"

He heard the outraged snarl before a filthy word fell from her stiff-lined mouth, and it was like a violin had joined the piano in his head. "If you tell anyone, I'll cut off—"

He burst out laughing again.

"Go to hell," she whispered, her petite frame radiating fury. Most of it self-directed, he knew, for Sophia hated betraying any emotion that made her weak.

He caught her wrist and pulled her inside the large, and thankfully empty, lounge behind them. Backing her into the wall, he pulled her arms above her.

The disdain in her eyes, the arrogant jut of her chin… It was like pouring petrol over a spark. Jerked at every primal instinct he had carefully banished from his life. Her breasts heaved as she fought him, as if they too fought against being confined.

"You thought you would propose marriage and walk away? You did not think I would find it entertaining?"

"You're a remorseless bastard." It was the first time she'd hinted at their past.

Regret was a faint pang in Luca's chest. Only faint.

Did he regret that he had hurt her ten years ago? *Si.*

So much that if given the chance he wouldn't do it again? *Non.*

He was far too selfish to willingly deny himself the true joy he'd found with her in those few weeks. "And you love playing the uptight shrew far too much."

Outrage, and most improbably, hurt, transformed her muddy brown eyes into a thousand hues of golds and bronzes.

Her stubborn, too-prominent nose flared. Incongruously wide mouth in a small face flushed a deep pink. The hourglass figure swathed in the most horrific black dress rubbed against him, bringing him to painful arousal.

In front of his eyes, she became something else.

She became the Sophia he'd known once and hadn't been able to resist, the Sophia he'd kissed with wonder, the Sophia she'd been before he had beat all the softness out of her.

She grunted and gave herself away, seconds before she raised her knee to his groin.

"How would this marriage of ours...*prosper and proliferate* if you turn me into a castrato, Sophia?"

Dancing his lower body away from her kick, he used the momentum to slam her harder into his hip. Her soft belly pressed and flushed into the lines of his body, his hip bone digging into it, as if it meant to make a groove for itself against her.

A softer gasp escaped her this time, throaty and wrenched away from the part of her she hid so well. So well that he had often wondered if he had known her so intimately once. That short huff for breath stroked Luca's nerves. Like strings of a violin...

Thick, wavy locks of hair fell from the ugly knot at the back of her head, touching the strong planes of her face with softness. The floral scent of her shampoo, something so incongruous with the woman she was, *or pretended to be*, fluttered under his nose. Luca pressed his nose into the thick, wavy mass. Kneaded the tense planes of her upper back as if he could calm himself by calming her.

He had never forgotten his amazement at the fire that had flared between them, how easily his plan had gone utterly wrong ten years ago. How, even for his jaded palate, Sophia had proved to be too much of a temptation.

Dio, suggesting marriage to him, of all men... Hadn't she learned her lesson? Why was she tempting the devil in him?

He *was* tempted. What man wouldn't want to muss up those ugly dresses and that shrewish facade and want to find the soft woman beneath? What man wouldn't want a claim on that kind of loyalty, on that steely core of her?

He set her away from him, none too gently. Lust riding him hard, he drew one rattling breath after another.

He controlled the pursuit of pleasure and the pleasure itself. Without shame or scruples, he used his charm, his looks, to draw women to him, amused himself for a time and then walked away.

He'd carefully built his life to be that and nothing more. He'd trampled her innocence even when he'd intended to do the right thing once. But in the end, he'd left. He would walk away again.

After having a small taste. She really expected it of him—to behave abominably, to torture her with his lascivious words and deeds. He couldn't disappoint her.

His humor restored, he eased his grip on her. Instantly she shoved at him. He didn't budge. "I can think of an infinitely more pleasurable *and* mature way to vent your frustration."

"It's hard to be mature when you laugh in my face like this."

"Your dignity is that fragile? The Sophia I keep hearing about in boardrooms and business mergers is apparently nothing short of Goddess Diana."

He curved his mouth into his trademark smile. Her glare didn't dim one bit. If anything, she stiffened even more.

Dio, when was the last time he had had such fun? And they hadn't even shed their clothes yet. "I was right, it is I that gets under your skin."

Her eyelids fell slowly. A second to restore her quaking defenses. Right on cue, she looked up, her fiery glare renewed. "I forgot that it's all a big joke to you."

"Being a debauched playboy who cares for nothing is hard work."

"I was stupid to think we could have a mature conversation. All you—"

"Then persuade me."

"What?"

Surprise in her gaze filled him with a strange satisfaction. Shocking, needling, generally startling Sophia out of that hard shell could become addictive. "Persuade me. Indulge me. Make me an irresistible offer."

Make herself irresistible to the most beautiful man on the face of the planet? A man who held nothing sacred?

"I have a better chance of finding treasure in my backyard," she said softly. Wistfulness snuck into her voice and she cringed.

"Kiss me, then."

"What?" She rubbed her temples, dismayed at how he reduced her to a mumbling idiot.

"Put your lips on mine and pucker them up. Your hands can go on my shoulders or my hips or if you're feeling bold, you can grab my ass—"

"What? Why?" Years of oratory at debate club evaporated, her brain only offering whats and whys.

"That should be the first step for a couple considering marriage, *si*? I could never marry a woman who didn't know how to kiss."

Don't. Look. At. His. Mouth. "It's obvious you're only torturing me and will never really consider it and you…" She looked and the contoured lushness of it made her lick her own lips, which made him grin and prompted her to raise her gaze. "Your lover is lying in your bed and you're—"

"If you'd been paying attention and not mooning over me—" Sophia fisted her hands, just fighting the urge to wipe that satisfied smile off his face, for he was right, damned devil "—then you would know that Mariana and I are over."

"You just said you wore her out!" Her brow cleared. "You said that just to rile me up, didn't you? There was hardly any time between when you left and I found you for you to...to—" She couldn't believe what her logic led her to say. If only she could stop blushing! "—*wear her out.*"

"I actually don't need that much time to get my lover off—"

"Where is she?" Sophia cut him off.

"She's a lightweight and I kept plying her with drinks. Her husband's divorcing her, which is what she wanted, but she's a little emotional about it. I couldn't just...throw her out of the party when she was in such a state."

"No, of course, not. They all adore you even when you're done with them."

Except her, Luca thought with something akin to a pang in his chest.

"You're free to adore me, too, *cara.* No one will have to know."

She snorted. That inelegant movement of that sharp, stubborn nose made him chuckle. "*God,* really, you don't need any more admirers, secret or otherwise. *And* I'm not kissing you."

Pink and wide, her mouth was like a long bow, the only feature in her face that was soft and vulnerable. A pillow of lushness. It betrayed that tough-as-nails, no-nonsense persona of hers.

He desperately wanted to feel it under his own, wanted to taste all that pent-up passion. One kiss wouldn't hurt. She was the one who'd cornered him, the one throwing outrageous ideas at him, the one looking all delectably confined and uptight in that dress. "How do you expect me to believe you're not playing a joke on me with this proposal? Maybe this is revenge? Maybe you intend to make me fall in love with you, and then leave me at the altar pining for you? Maybe…"

Brown eyes glittering, wide mouth mobile, she laughed. It was a full-throttled laugh, deep and husky. The kind that came all the way from your stomach, burned through your lungs, leaving you a little dizzy. Her body shook all over.

The sound stole into Luca, filling every hungry crevice inside him. It was one that could cut through the darkest space, filling it with light. "What is so funny?"

"You, falling in love. *With me.*"

He said it softly. "The whole world assumes Sophia Rossi is tough, brave, the conqueror of every challenge. Decimator of men. Only I know what a coward you are."

It fell in the space between them like a weapon, and he waited, breath balling up in his lungs. Anger and apprehension vied in her face until she covered the distance between them. He didn't know if she was going to slap him or kiss him or castrate him. No woman could create that mystery except Sophia. No woman had ever filled his veins with this heady anticipation.

Fingers on the lapels of his shirt, she jerked him close. "No one calls me a coward, *you manipulative bastard.*"

Throaty and tart, growly and yet with a deep vein of need pulsing beneath, it was Sophia to the end. Brave Sophia accepting facts and meeting them head-on. Dutiful Sophia kissing the man she hated just to hear him out.

Short and curvy, she barely came up to his chest. Hands on his shoulders, she pulled herself up, as if to elongate herself. Like a vine clinging to a cement wall.

That pressed every inch of her to him. Lush breasts, followed by such a thin waist that he wondered how it held up those glorious curves, then flaring into rounded hips, hips a man would anchor himself on while he thrust inside her. Shapely thighs that would clutch a man tight as he jerked in pleasure within her velvet heat.

Again and again, until he forgot what or who he was.

Such heat rolled over his skin that Luca's fingers dug into her soft flesh.

With a protesting moan, she stilled her mouth on his. The tips of their noses collided and a soft sigh left her. Hot breath kissed his hungry lips. Then she moved that mouth again. Testing and trying. This way and that. Halting thoughtfully and then hurrying along urgently when she liked the fit.

Brown eyes met his. And the world stilled. Time and space narrowed to this minute, this space around them. Never breaking his gaze, she slanted her head and dragged a kiss from one corner of his mouth to the other.

She took control of the kiss like she did everything else.

And Luca let her take over. Let the scent and taste of her fill every hungry crevice. Let her imprint herself on him.

Flames of fire raced along his veins when she licked the seam of his lips and probed for entry. Desperate, Luca opened his mouth under hers. The throaty sound of her gasp shivered down his spine. Never had he been waiting like this for pleasure. Never had he been the recipient.

Suppressing every instinct to take over the reins of the kiss—he'd never waited to be pleasured—he let her seduce him. She obliged, stroking the inside of his mouth with bold flicks, teasing and incinerating. Took his mouth with a carnality that left him shaking to the very marrow.

Christo, he'd never been so aroused by just a kiss.

The sound of footsteps behind them brought Sophia back to earth with a thud.

Her mouth stung with the taste of Luca, her body

thrumming with unsatisfied desire. The crisp hair on his wrists teased her palms.

But she felt anything but exultant. She wanted to cry. She wanted to ask him to take her to his bedroom, turn off the lights and—no, not his bedroom. Not the place where he'd probably made love to a horde of lovers, each more stunning and thin and wispier than the next. Maybe they could slip away into that veranda, hide under the moonlight and he could kiss her a little more.

She could pretend that he'd never broken her heart and that he wanted her just as much as she did him.

Because when Luca kissed her, Sophia was always carried off to some faraway land. A land where she could be strong enough to be weak, where she could let someone care for her, where she didn't worry about her family, where she was not mocked for who she was.

Where a man like Luca didn't have to be induced into seducing a woman like her...

She hid her face in his chest. His heartbeat thundered against her cheek. He was warm and male, both exciting and comforting, something she hadn't realized until this moment she missed.

Sophia couldn't dredge up anger for that kiss. Toward him or herself.

His fingers wandered up and down her hips, questing and caressing. "I'd rather we kissed again, but I keep my word." Deep and hoarse, his voice pinged over her heated skin. "So tell me, why do you wish to..."

Suddenly, a hand on her shoulder pulled her from his arms, turned her around.

"Tina, *non!*" she heard Luca shout dimly.

Sophia didn't see it coming. Someone slapped her. Hard.

Her head went back, pain radiating up her jaw and through her ear. Tears blurred her vision and she blinked to clear them away. Pulling in a shuddering breath, she looked up.

Valentina—Luca's sister and Kairos's wife, stood before her, her lithe, willowy body shaking with rage. Her entire face was mobile with emotion, turning her into a volatile beauty. "You...*you tart*!"

Sophia raised a brow, refusing to show her dismay. "Tart, really?"

Her composure seemed to only rile the younger woman more. "You're determined to go through all the men in my family, aren't you? First Kairos, and now Luca? And to think I felt sorry for you when Leandro broke your engagement."

"Basta, Tina!" Luca again. His arm around Sophia's shoulders, he was a wall of lean strength against her. A dark scowl framed his features, his fingers rubbing against her arm in unconscious comfort.

Against every rational warning, Sophia felt her body leaning into his.

"You know the rumors about Kairos and her?" Tina screeched, her eyes filling with tears.

"If there's truth to them, confront your husband, Tina."

"Fall into her clutches, then. Maybe she will leave my husband alone." Her black gaze raked over Sophia in a sneer. "Although I do not see the appeal."

Valentina left with the same fierceness as she had come in. Like a storm, leaving a minefield of awkward silence behind.

Sophia untangled herself from Luca's side and ran her fingers tentatively over her cheek. She thought she might be a little sick but it could be because of how much dessert she'd eaten in her anxiety tonight after the strict diet of the last two weeks.

Luca pulled her to him; she tried to swat him away.

He won in the fight for possession of her. She swallowed hard. Fingers on her chin, he examined her cheek. "I apologize. She had no right to behave like that." His mouth became a hard line. All the charm, the wicked laughter, was gone.

She waited for the inevitable question about her and Kairos, but it never came. But then, the one thing Luca had never been was a hypocrite.

"Marriage to Kairos is not good for her."

She frowned but he didn't elaborate. "Kairos can be hard to—" he raised a brow and she realized she'd jumped to her supposed lover's defense "—understand."

"You feel sorry for her?" he said, amazement in his eyes.

Sophia shrugged. Despite the sting in her cheek and the burn in her stomach at the comment on her looks, something inside Sophia recoiled at the vulnerability in Valentina's eyes. A palette of emotions for Kairos, who was as hard-hearted as hell, to see. And everything was acted upon, too...

No man was worth that self-doubt, that haunting sense of inadequacy, Sophia wanted to tell Valentina.

Swift anger rose through her at Kairos; he was supposed to be her friend. Couldn't he have reassured Valentina instead of using Sophia to keep his own wife at a distance?

"It's obvious that what I suggested is a disastrous idea." She chanced a glance at Luca, greedy to the last second. She'd make sure it was another decade before she saw him again. Something in her clenched tight. "Forget what I suggested."

Without waiting for his answer, Sophia turned and walked away.

And in that moment she hated all men.

Antonio, for planting that horrible idea in her head, for using her desperation to promote his own agenda.

Kairos, for using their friendship as a barrier against his own wife.

Salvatore, for never giving her a chance in the company, even though he called her his daughter.

And the man behind her, more than anyone else, for kissing her like he meant it. Now and ten years ago. For making her want him so much, for making her weak and foolish, for making her imagine, even for a second, that she was all the things she could never be.

CHAPTER THREE

LUCA SPENT THAT Monday morning with Huang from the design team of Conti Luxury Goods, studying the prototype for new heels that would be released the coming spring.

Huang and he had worked together for almost ten years now, since Leandro had convinced Luca to take a small part in Conti Luxury Goods. Luca interacted only with Huang, and Huang worked with the rest of the design team.

He picked up a royal blue pump, tracing the aerodynamic sole with his fingers. The success of these pieces didn't worry him. As always, anything he designed, from pumps to handbags, became instantly covetous among the fanatically fashionable.

Seeing something raw and shapeless transform into something so pleasing, that was success to him. But this particular design run had come to fruition and he felt the loss of it keenly. It had been quite a challenge—the design of the new heel. Now the production team would take over.

Familiar restlessness slithered through his veins. What to work on next? Sophia's outrageous proposal from Friday night winked at him.

Dio, but that had challenge and fun and all kinds of things written into it. She hated him—had every right to, but she was still attracted to him. When his looks tripped Sophia into that kind of a kiss, he couldn't quite hate them. It should have been one of a hundred kisses, she one of numerous, interchangeable faces he filled his life with and yet, the taste of her lips lingered, the passion with which she had taken him lingered, filling him with a restless craving for more.

Since he had no intention of following that up with Sophia, he needed a woman. To forget her and her kisses and that he had no place in her life. *Soon.*

He was at the door when Huang said, "You're not going to wait?"

"For what?"

"You don't even know, do you? Your brother—" Huang's smile dimmed for the rift between Leandro and him, the first in their life, was fodder for office gossip "—is at the board meeting today. The one that's going on now."

"Well, he's the CEO of CLG, Huang." His mind ran over the next few days. He couldn't disappear without checking on Tina first.

"There are rumors that he's making a big announcement today."

Luca stilled.

His brother claimed to have changed, that he regretted ruthlessly arranging Tina's marriage to Kairos, pulling such deception over their sister, even if he intended it for her own good. But Leandro did nothing without reason. Needing to control everyone and everything around him was an itch in his brother's blood.

A lot of fates depended on Leandro's decision. Including Salvatore's. And Sophia's.

Her problems are not yours.

No warning could curb his thoughts, though. The poor state of the Rossi finances was common knowledge now. What would be her next move? Who would she propose marriage to next?

Curiosity was wildfire in his gut, eating away at that

restlessness that never deserted him. Her expression when she had walked away, defeated yet resolute, stayed with him.

If nothing, it would be amusing to see what Sophia would do next. So Luca waited, for Sophia was a breath of fresh air, cold and yet invigorating, in his predestined life.

Leandro was stepping down as the CEO of the CLG Board.

Two hours and a million thoughts later, Luca still hadn't recovered from the shock. For years Leandro's life had been CLG. Kairos, his brother-in-law, would be the front-runner for CEO.

What use would his sister, Tina, then be to the ruthlessly ambitious Kairos once he had that?

His thoughts in a tangle, Luca walked past the alarmed secretary and pushed the door open to his brother's office.

Kairos was in Leandro's office, his hands on Sophia's shoulders.

Jealousy twisted Luca's gut, his blood singing with that same possessive fury again. *Dio*, only Sophia reduced him to this. Willing control over his emotions, he stayed by the door. The question he'd refused to ask, because he'd believed that Sophia was above such disgusting behavior as him, even after Tina's accusations gnawed at him now.

How well did Sophia know him?

Sophia's quick shake to Kairos's whisper, the intimacy their very stance betrayed…suggested something more than an affair, something far more dangerous.

He couldn't be the only man in the world who realized Sophia's worth, the only man who wanted to claim her in every way. Did Kairos want more, too?

Even if they weren't having an affair, it was clear Sophia had something with Kairos that Tina could never reach.

He'd hated this match between Tina and Kairos from the beginning, but seeing the stars in his sister's eyes, he had stayed out of it. Even now, every instinct in him wanted to let Kairos have the CEO position he'd pursued with such cunning and ruthlessness, to let their marriage reach that destructive conclusion.

Only the tears he'd seen in Tina's eyes at that party stayed his hand now.

It had been Leandro who had brought Tina to live with them after their mother's death but it was Luca who'd made her laugh. Luca who'd gained her trust first; Luca she laughed with over all these years.

With her smile and generous heart, Tina loved Luca unconditionally, provided as much an anchor in his life as Leandro had.

Smarting at the direction of his thoughts, Luca ran a hand through his hair.

If there was a chance that Tina's marriage to Kairos could be saved, he had to take it. He had to trust in Leandro's belief that Kairos was the right man for Tina.

And to give Tina a running chance, he'd take away what stood between his sister and Kairos—the CEO position of CLG and Sophia Rossi. Luca's seat on the board, which he'd have to claim for the first time in his life, would see to the first.

The second...

The solution that appeared released a panic in his gut, as if a noose were tightening around his neck.

Of all the women in the world, Sophia was the last woman he should be contemplating marriage to. She had proved to be dangerous to his peace of mind even as a chubby, composed nineteen-year-old. Now she was a force to be reckoned with.

"Can we borrow...*your office, Kairos*?" Luca interrupted the sweetly nauseating scene. "Sophia and I have something important to discuss."

"I won't let you bully Sophia."

"How about you show that concern for my sister? Your wife, remember?" Luca retorted.

Another squeeze of Sophia's shoulders and Kairos left.

"That looked like a very cozy scene, very tender," Luca said, leaning against the closed door, batting away at the ugly emotion festering in his gut. "I gather he knows what Tina did."

He saw her spine stiffen, making her look like an angry crow in her black dress. "I didn't tell him. And I came by to tell him that he should clear this misunderstanding with Valentina."

As always, the black linen was unadorned with the skirt falling demurely past her knees, high necked and severely cut. Yet the very cut and the way it enfolded all of her emphasized the very voluptuousness of the woman's curves. If her intentions were to cover up that exquisitely luscious body with those painfully severe dresses, then she was an abysmal failure.

The only thing her horribly dowdy dresses showed was her rejection of style and fashion. Of her femininity. That she found herself not worthy enough of even trying.

He wanted to tear the ugly fabric off her and dress her in slithery silks, discover that satiny soft skin that he'd tasted once thoroughly, make her—

"Luca?"

Christo, two minutes in the same room and he could imagine only one scenario. The easy way she unmanned his control made Luca's tone uncharacteristically harsh and bitter. "How did he receive *your mutually beneficial proposal*? Should I be flattered that you asked me first?"

Disgustingly shameful words, he realized the moment he spoke.

She stilled, dismay pouring out of her entire frame. That she was hurt by his callous remark, that she could be pushed to some reaction by him, any reaction, elated Luca. *He was truly a twisted devil.*

"No," she said, boldly meeting his eyes, only the shadows in her own betraying her emotions, "you're the only one I've proposed marriage to. And before you ask another disgustingly hypocritical question, no, I've not propositioned Kairos into some sort of illicit affair, either.

"I do not sleep with married men. Much less a close married friend. Much less a man who already asked me to marry him and I refused."

Shock stole coherence from Luca. Suddenly, he saw it.

Ruthlessly ambitious, Kairos had first wanted Sophia and Rossi Leather. When she'd refused, he'd set his sights on Tina and the Conti Board instead, with Leandro's blessing.

And now his dear brother-in-law probably wanted to eat his cake, too…

Dio, now he couldn't undo knowing that Tina's marriage was in trouble.

Sophia hitched her handbag over her shoulder, knuckles white, and glanced at her watch. "If you'll excuse me, I have several other men I have to proposition, blackmail, extort so that I can save my family's livelihood. If you've had enough fun at my expense, I'd like to get started."

"I want to talk about your proposal."

Her hands stilled on her desk. "No." Fury bristled from her. "I used to think you still possessed some notion of decency. But no. You are every horrible thing I thought of you all these years."

"I'm serious, Sophia."

Something shone in her eyes. He'd never met a woman who worked as hard as Sophia did, one who dusted herself off even after being denied every opportunity she deserved.

Such strength, such endurance and yet he knew, like no one else did, that she was vulnerable, too. Was it any wonder she fascinated him?

Sophia stared at Luca, trying to gauge his mood. Trying to banish the taste of him from her mouth.

Even as she knew that she had a better chance of forgetting how to breathe. For a week, she'd lain flushed and restless in her bed, touching her lips, as if she could invoke that feeling again.

Ran a hand over her breasts and down low, where she'd been already damp. Just imagining his fingers down there, his mouth on her heavy breasts, she'd been aching all night. Reaching for something only he could give and she could never ever want again.

Today, he was wearing a V-necked gray sweater and black jeans. With a bristly beard and dark shadows beneath his eyes, he looked exactly the man he was—a recklessly gorgeous playboy with a long night behind him.

"Sophia?"

She came to with a startle, her cheeks on fire. He was serious? He wanted to hear her proposal? "I've heard that Leandro and you are on the outs now?"

"Si." One long finger traced the edge of the desk, and Sophia could tell this was something that bothered him—this rift with his brother.

"With Leandro stepping down, your vote could become the deciding factor on a lot of things."

"Like whether Rossi Leather should be cut for pieces and distributed among everyone."

She nodded, hiding her shock. For a self-indulgent, indolent playboy, Luca grasped the situation far too quickly. "You enjoy the extravagant lifestyle being a Conti affords you. I mean, you're used to those custom designed Armani suits, that flat in downtown Milan, that Maserati and all those women, yes?" she said spitefully, knowing full well that Luca could be a pauper and women would still strip for him in the middle of a birthday party.

He sighed, even as deep amusement glinted in his eyes. "You know I do. I dread losing any of it. I didn't realize Leandro was serious about letting it all go to hell."

"If you give me the required rights, I will do everything Leandro has done for you all these years. Represent you on the board and take care of your interests in CLG. You won't have to lift a finger."

"I see you've used your superior knowledge of my likes and tastes to reel me in." If there was any justice in the world, her glare should have turned him into dust.

"What do you get in return?"

"If we marry, my stepfather could be convinced to bring Rossi's under the umbrella of CLG. He's been resisting it because he thinks his legacy would be swallowed up."

"*Dio*, controlling old men and their obsession with their legacies. So this agenda is not driven by Kairos, then."

"What?"

He shrugged. "You have to admit it's a good theory. Kairos decides you'll marry me, can have me by the balls and consequently, has my vote in his bid to be CEO."

"That is too ruthless even for him. Not forgetting the obvious flaw in the plan that I, of all women, could have your ba—" She gasped; it was like there was her own personal furnace inside her, and the rogue grinned as she cleared her throat. "Could have you under my control, in any manner."

"I could never marry a woman who lacks in feminine wiles."

She gritted her teeth. He had to pick the most uncomfortable aspect of that. "Another fantastic reason for why it's a crazy idea."

He gave her a considering look. "If you have such faith in that bastard Kairos, then why not accept his help?"

"Luca, what is your problem with Kairos?"

"He's too hungry for power. Which means he'll do anything in his hunt for it."

"Yes, how infinitely atrocious that Kairos is so ambitious when he could be chasing woman after woman in eternal pursuit of pleasure."

"Why isn't he helping you with Rossi's?"

"He offered but I don't like his solution. Everyone, including Kairos, has an agenda for Rossi Leather without considering what's actually best for the company or my family. And the problems we have aren't going to be solved by a simple influx of cash. Salvatore will bring us back here into this same situation in a year again. No one can help us."

Not even Antonio.

The minute she didn't toe the line—which would probably include some impossible task like domesticating the devil in front of her—Antonio would tighten the screws on her. Threaten their company or withdraw his support.

"The only way to ensure we don't fall into this hole again," she said, with a mounting sense of defeat, "is if I take the reins myself."

"You think Leandro would have recognized how smart and efficient you are and given you the reins. That's why you were so eager to marry him."

"He always struck me as a fair, principled man."

Her unshakeable trust, the admiration in Leandro's implacable nature, rubbed Luca raw.

He had never bemoaned the fact that only he, and not Leandro, had inherited every despicable thing from their father—his good looks, his brilliance and maybe his madness. But in that moment he envied his brother the freedom to be his own man, the right to his own mind that made Sophia admire him so much.

"You would have married him, shared his bed?" Fury threaded his tone, which shocked her as much as him. "After the history we have?"

Color mounted her cheeks. "Rossi's needs a complete rehaul, five years to build it to a stable position again. Leandro would have given me that chance."

Her stepfather's damned company... It always came back to that. "I've no doubt that you will do it in three. You'll make Rossi's better than it has ever been."

Shock rooted Sophia to the floor, a faint whooshing in her ears making her dizzy. She ran a shaking hand over her brow. "What?"

"*Dio*, you sang this same song even a decade ago. You went into raptures, *non, you almost climaxed* with anticipation every time you talked about your plans for your Rossi Leather. Extension, branching away from leather production completely, focusing on accessory design... Just do it already, Sophia."

He stared at her, brows raised in question while Sophia processed those words slowly. Dear God, he remembered all of her naive, hopeful, detailed plans for Rossi's.

Heat pricked her eyes. Her head hurt as if under some great liquid weight; even her nose felt thick. Or rough. Or something very close to tears.

Did he know what a gift he gave her?

He didn't give the compliment grudgingly like Kairos,

who recognized talent and hunted it with a ruthless will. He didn't give the compliment insidiously, as if her intellect and smart business sense were odd, distorting it into some sort of stain on her femininity. As if somehow they minimized her as a woman.

He didn't give it to placate her, like her mother. Even her mother, she knew, wished Sophia was different. Wished *Sophia made it easy on herself*; wished *Sophia didn't feel like she had to prove herself in a man's world*.

Wished *Sophia wasn't still fighting, even after all these years*.

No, Luca stated it as a matter of fact. With the same tone as if to say: people need oxygen to live.

Given the chance, Sophia Rossi could make Rossi's better than it has ever been before.

Simply that.

Just that.

Joy bloomed from her chest, spreading like warm honey through every cell, stretching her mouth into a wide smile.

He came to stand before her, and for once, Sophia couldn't step back. It seemed as if he had thoroughly bypassed all her defense mechanisms. "Sophia?"

"Hmmm?"

"You have a blank look in your eyes, and I'm not sure you've breathed in the last ten seconds. Also...you're smiling at me like I'm your favorite person in the world. *Dio*, you're not dying, are you?" He tilted her chin up, raked her face over with that searing gaze. "Now that I think about it, you look like you've lost weight and there are dark shadows under your eyes."

Her hands drifted to her hips and his gaze followed it eagerly. She pulled them up as if burned. The scent of him stroked over her senses. Just a little dip at her waist and her breasts would graze his chest. Her legs would tangle with his. And then she could—

"This is not some pathetic, last-minute attempt to have some good sex before you die, is it?" Something glittered in his gaze as he gently ran a finger over her cheek. "Because, *cara mia*, we don't have to marry for that. All you have to do is ask and I will *gladly* show you how fun it is on this side."

When was the last time she'd had fun? "I'm not dying."

"As much as that would solve a lot of problems for me, that is good to know. Now, I will give you three months of marriage."

Sophia couldn't believe he was agreeing to a proposal she'd made in sheer desperation. He seemed to decide as easily as he'd decide which party to go to. *Or which woman to take home on a given night.* Worse, she couldn't believe the way every cell in her leaped at the chance to be near him. Three months as his wife... *Lord*, it was both her salvation *and* utter ruin. "Why are you helping?"

"One, I want to throw a small hitch in my brother-in-law's plans. Two, I hate working, as you neatly pointed out."

Her heart sank to the floor. "You're doing this to drive a wedge between Kairos and me? I told you I'm not sleeping with him."

"A little distance wouldn't hurt, then. Especially if it is provided by me. Leandro has washed his hands of me. I'll have to claim my seat on the board. And like you said, who better than my own wife to watch out for my interests and work in my stead? We both get what we want."

"What is it that you're promising exactly?"

"You can't turn Rossi's around in three months but it's a start in digging it out of that hole, *si*?" He tucked an errant curl behind her cheek, a wicked smile on his mouth.

"I want to give you what you want, Sophia. And a couple of things you are too stubborn to ask for."

Her cheeks heated up. If it beat any faster, her heart was going to burst out of her chest. Her gaze lowered to his mouth, cinders lighting up her blood. *Don't. Ask. Don't—*

"Your arrogance in yourself is breathtaking."

"Arrogance, *bella mia*? I state fact. You know where you're going to end up."

Memories and sensations rushed through her—rough breaths, the slide of hot, damp skin like velvet over hers, pain giving way to incredible pleasure…every other sense amplified in the darkness that she'd insisted on…

Heat poured through her, like lava spewing out. Her skin felt tight, parched, her pulse ringing through her. "No…I don't want to sleep with you ever again."

"Who mentioned anything about sleep? Just don't fall in love with me," he added with a grin.

"I'm not a naive idiot anymore," Sophia replied, confident that she'd avoid that trap.

Luca was irresistible but she was walking into this with her eyes wide open.

Love wasn't for her; he'd helped her see that firsthand. She'd hated the loss of control over her own happiness, over her mood, over her sense of self-worth. In a moment Luca had stripped her of everything.

She despised the hollow feeling it had left in her gut. The haunting ache that she lacked something. She never wanted to be that vulnerable ever again.

He reached the door, turned the handle and looked back at her. "Do you have protection?"

He couldn't mean what she thought he did. *No way.* "Like a bodyguard?"

He grinned and Sophia wanted to wipe that grin off his pretty face with her bare hands. "No, like a contraceptive."

"That's none of your…" He moved so fast and so smoothly that Sophia blinked. The heat from his body was a tantalizing caress on her skin, beckoning her closer. She answered only to stop him from coming closer. "Yes, fine. I'm on the pill. Not that it's relevant to you."

He pushed a tendril of hair away from her temple. That stubborn lock that never stayed back. "Good." His warm breath raised the little hairs on her neck.

Knowing that he was saying it to shock her didn't stop a pulse of throbbing need between her legs. It took every ounce of her energy not to press her thighs close. She needed something distasteful, something to snap herself out of that sensual web he weaved… "You…I… You've had numerous lovers. I won't just—"

The glittering hunger in his eyes told her she'd already betrayed herself by talking as though she was considering it. *Damn!* "I'm clean."

Like a dream, feverish and hot and full of some elusive subtext, he left.

Sophia stared at the door for a long time, her knees shaking. Covering her face with her hands, she sank back against the desk.

Luca Conti was going to marry her. Of all the men in the world, that unpredictable, recklessly indulgent playboy was giving her the chance no one else would. It was going to tangle up everything with everyone horribly. Three months of her life would change the course of the rest of her life. Even after his reckless cruelty ten years ago, she was still affected by him.

But Sophia could only obsess over one thing.

That, for three months, she could kiss him all she wanted.

CHAPTER FOUR

LUCA HAD KNOWN rejection from his mother when he'd been seven. He'd suffered debilitating headaches, insomnia and worse before he hit puberty.

The first time he'd had sex, he had been seventeen, with a woman a decade older. He hadn't really wanted the sex; he'd wanted to be held by the woman, to be less lonely for one night. Messed up as he'd been, he'd still realized what he'd done.

He'd whored himself—his looks, his charm, his body, for a bit of affection.

One didn't need a degree in psychiatry to realize that.

When Leandro had finally discovered him—his brother had always come after him no matter the time of the day, no matter how devious Luca tried to be—sitting on the floor of the hotel room with his head in his hands, and looked at him with nothing but understanding and patience and that all-consuming love that his brother used to justify arranging his siblings' lives, Luca had thrown up all over the floor. And promised himself never again.

Never again would he sink that low.

Never again would he succumb to that cavernous craving within.

Never again would he be without control.

For the most part, he was sure he'd succeeded.

Instead of fighting the sudden bouts of insomnia and crazy energy, he poured himself into everything and anything he could get his hands on. He studied like a madman, inhaling and conquering every subject he touched. He'd become a human sponge.

Leandro would sigh and smile when Luca said he wanted to try something new.

Arts and history. Mathematics and astronomy. He'd dabbled in all of them, but moved on, nothing calming the restlessness within. Only music—the relentless, endless chords churning in his head released onto paper, played until he achieved every single note—could soothe it.

It was both his release and his curse. He'd fashioned a wooden doll for Tina after she'd come to live with them, and realized he loved creating things, designing things, too. So he'd started working with Lin Huang, the creative head of Conti Luxury Goods' design department.

Through the years he'd achieved a kind of balance, a normal—for him. He wrote music for hours on end when in that grip, worked at CLG and other projects of his own, surviving on an hour or more of sleep for days. Then he had those carefree days where he got drunk, partied, took endless women to his bed. And had uproarious fun at the expense of others.

Fortunately for him, he'd discovered he liked sex, just for itself. That he could enjoy it without whoring himself for something else. He'd slipped up only once from the happy path he was forging for himself.

Ten years ago, with Sophia. She'd been the first real thing in his life and he had let himself be carried away.

Sophia was the only one who'd ever made him forget himself, who had shredded his control so effortlessly.

For all his reputation as a self-indulgent playboy, control was tantamount to his peace of mind. It was something Leandro and he had rigorously worked on in those initial months after their mother had left. He'd spent hours on the mat mastering several martial arts disciplines.

He had an example from his father's life. He knew that like everything else he'd inherited from him, he could carry a speck of that madness—that devious, manipulative, cruel streak, too.

Control was everything to him.

Stepping out of the shower, Luca walked to the mirror and rubbed it to clear the steam. Hands on the marble sink, he stared at himself.

He looked past the compelling perfection of his features—a face he'd hated for so long—past the now bonedeep mask he showed the world. He had never lied to himself. Self-delusion would have been a welcome friend in all those miserable years.

He was doing this because of Sophia.

He was doing this because he wanted these three months with her.

He wanted to be near her, inside her. He wanted to unravel all the fiery passion she kept locked away.

He wanted to free her from the cage she put herself in; a cage, he was sure, he'd driven her into building.

But this time Sophia knew the score, knew what he was incapable of. She wasn't an innocent who mistook attraction, pure lust for anything else. This was not a marriage like his parents'.

Sophia wasn't some innocent, painfully naive young girl Antonio had handpicked like some sacrificial offering to his father's madness, to further the Conti legacy like his mother had been.

Sophia would never let herself be intimidated or drowned in Luca's personality.

The panic in him calming, Luca breathed out. Excitement filled his veins now.

For the first and only time in his life, the self-indulgent, profligate playboy he'd made himself to be was going to take what he truly wanted. And revel in it.

That he would set Sophia up for the rest of her life and do his part to protect Tina's marriage, *that* was the bonus.

Meet me @ Palazzo Reale Monday 10AM.
Don't wear black. J

The texts came on Saturday night at seven, a whole week after Luca had cornered Sophia at CLG offices. They also sent her soup down the wrong pipe at the dinner table.

Heart pounding, half choking, Sophia had escaped her family's curiosity.

She'd spent the week on tenterhooks. Wondered if she'd imagined the whole episode, if she'd somehow deluded herself into believing that the Conti Devil had proposed marriage.

When she saw Antonio come up toward Rossi's offices, she'd mumbled something to her team and skipped out like a thief.

Her reply—Why?—had gone unanswered. Which meant she'd spent half the night pacing her bedroom, and the rest of it thrashing in her bed.

Monday morning she stood on the steps of the centuries-old building, trying to ignore the curious looks from people coming and going.

She ran a nervous hand over her dress, her only non-black slightly dressy dress. It was a sort of muddy light brown made of the softest linen. Over it, she wore a cream cashmere cardigan to ward off the slightly chilly November air.

With cap sleeves, the dress had been an impulse purchase months ago. It boasted a false buttoned-up short bodice, then flared out into a wide skirt from high above her waist.

The saleswoman had assured Sophia it made her look tall and graceful.

A quick glance in her mirror this morning told Sophia she looked neither tall nor graceful. Nothing could create the illusion when she was two inches over five.

But the thing that had made her groan was that the dress, which had fitted neatly, now sort of hung on her. Like a tent. She'd slipped her feet into five-inch purple leather Conti pumps, throwing caution to the wind.

So what if she felt like her legs would fall off later?

Whipping her unruly hair into a French plait and adding a dab of peach lip gloss, she'd been ready. Her gut twisted into a thousand knots, she had guzzled down two cups of coffee and munched her protein bar on the way over.

Minutes ticked by. Quarter past ten flew by. A couple of old men walked past her, up the steps, and she had a suspicion they were friends of Salvatore's.

Before they could catch her eye, she turned away and checked her phone. She walked up and down the steps, went back into the hall, got a bottle of water then walked back out. And all the while she waited, a sense of déjà vu came upon her.

She'd been waiting, just like this, ten years ago, too. In his bedroom, in his bed. In her underwear, albeit the sheet pulled up to her chin.

Waited for Luca, to tell him that she was in love with him.

He hadn't shown up. Marco Sorcelini had, instead, with a lascivious smirk on his face and his cell phone in hand. Before Sophia could make sense of what was happening, he'd clicked a picture of her. Told her to put her clothes on and go home…

Because Luca Conti had won the bet.

He had seduced Sophia the Shrew, made her fall in love with him and walked away. *Why else would any man touch a woman like Sophia*, Marco had added, *who was neither beautiful nor docile and far too smart for her own good?*

She'd thrown the sheet away, launched at Marco and punched his nose. She'd lived for months in terror that that photo of her would be plastered all over everyone's cell phone. That her humiliation wouldn't be limited to Luca and his cronies.

It hadn't.

The most nightmarish day of her life and it was on repeat again. This time it was her entire family's future that she had trusted him with.

Forty minutes past ten. Frustration and fury scraped Sophia's nerves. Stupid, so stupid, to trust his word. To believe that he'd really want to help her. When everything she'd ever known of him said Luca didn't give a damn about anyone.

Just as she walked down the steps, a great beast of a bike came to a shuddering stop, right in front of her.

Black leather jacket, wraparound shades and a killer, megawatt smile that was like a shot of adrenaline straight to her heart. A small crowd of onlookers whispered behind her.

With sleek grace, Luca pulled his tall form off the bike and handed it off to a valet. Dark shadows, even worse than usual, bracketed his eyes. He looked gaunt, the curve of his mouth almost obscenely lush against the sharp angles of his face.

His jet-black hair gleamed with wetness. He looked like hell and yet, utterly, breath-stealingly gorgeous. The world wasn't a fair place.

He covered the few steps between them, looked her up

and down, leisurely, thoroughly. Took the fabric of her glove between his fingers, frowned and then sighed. A twinkle shone in his eyes as it moved over her hair and her face. "That dress is not only ghastly but loose. And that color is not an improvement on black.

"You have to do better in this department if we want the world to believe we're utterly in love. I do not need extra incentive to tear your clothes off you."

Her fingers clenched tight on her phone, Sophia counted to ten. He wasn't going to reduce her to a screaming shrew in front of the whole city. "You're late. By fifty-five minutes. I…" She gritted her jaw so tight, she was going to need dental surgery. "And you look like hell. I texted you and called you, like fifteen million times. You don't reply—"

"I overslept."

"You overslept?"

"I didn't get to bed until the early morning. And I didn't want to show up here for you all dirty and unshaved."

"You couldn't lay off partying for one night?"

"This whole thing made me nervous."

Her tirade halted on Sophia's lips. Of course he was nervous. Getting married was probably akin to being tortured for him. "Why didn't you just reply?"

"I left my phone somewhere." His long fingers were shackles on her arms. "You're shaking." He scowled. Used to that lazy, amused glance, it made him look dangerous, ferocious. "You thought I wasn't coming."

She braced herself against the concern in his tone. "I was expecting a media crew or at least those society pages social media punks to capture me standing there. Another joke. Only this time, on a much grander scale.*Conti Devil Jilts Sophia the Stupid Idiot… Again!*"

Eyes closed, he pinched the bridge of his nose. A

shadow of strain gave his usually laughing features a haunting look. "That is harsh. I never—"

"You've got to be kidding me. Was there a bet about who could seduce me ten years ago?"

"Si."

"Did you take part in it?"

"Si."

"Did you mean to disappear to Paris with your—" no, she wouldn't call some faceless, innocent girl vindictive names "—*new lover* knowing that I was—" a shudder went through her and she hated how all her strength disappeared when it came to that moment "—in your bed, naked and waiting?" Fresh out of virginity and hopelessly in love… she'd been a besotted idiot.

"Si."

"As long as we're clear, then," she added casually, when she felt like glass with tiny cracks inching around however much she put plasters over it. Somehow, she needed to channel this bitterness, this humiliation, when she was melting for one of his smiles. Because she did.

She melted. She thawed. She burned when it came to this man. She always would, apparently.

A hundred shadows drifted in his usually empty gaze. A vein beat in his temple. He opened his mouth then closed it. Wounded hesitation suited him to perfection like everything else.

Even now, she realized with a sinking awareness of her own foolishness, she waited. As if there could be some other fantastic explanation for the cruel trick he'd played on her.

She sighed and held up her phone. "A text would have sufficed to say you'd changed your mind."

He pulled her wrist up and looked at the dial of her watch. "We're marrying in fifteen minutes."

"What?" Astonishment made her voice screechy. "I... you never told me we were marrying *today*. This morning."

"Why do you think I asked you to come?"

"To submit our documents. I brought my papers."

"All taken care of by a friend."

"The mayor's sister, I assume?"

His gaze flared and she looked away. Damn it, if she didn't keep her pride in this thing between them, she'd have nothing left. Betraying that she knew of each and every woman he'd *dated* over the last decade definitely didn't leave her much.

She turned around and looked at the building with new eyes. "Do you have any contracts for me to sign?"

"Like what?"

"Like a prenuptial, Luca." When she'd have turned, he stalled her with his hands on her shoulders. She heard him take a deep breath behind her. His exhale coated her neck. His body didn't touch her but lured her with unspoken promises.

Now his nose rubbed from her temple to her hair, his fingers leaving scorching trails wherever they touched. "What scent is that? It haunts me sometimes."

"Honeysuckle," she whispered hoarsely, even as she warned herself this was his default. Flirting and seducing was in Luca's genes. "A small American company makes it and I buy it online." She was babbling, the only way to keep her sanity.

"It blends perfectly with your skin." His breath whispered over her cheek. "I can't wait to discover if you smell like that all over."

Liquid heat claimed Sophia, the very fabric of her dress scraping everywhere it touched. She took deep breaths, trying to not sink into his hard body.

He smelled of leather and musk, of quintessential male.

Pleasure and pain, all tangled up in her head. Freedom and captivity, one inseparable from the other. He made her so aware of things she'd forced herself to ignore. Of the thump of her heart, the thrum of her skin, the sudden heaviness in her breasts, the slow, pulling pulse in her sex. Of being a woman who denied herself so many things in the name of being strong. If she'd had a boyfriend, if she'd satisfied her body's demands, maybe she wouldn't have been this vulnerable to him.

Sophia Conti, expert in self-delusion. "A pity you won't," she offered finally, a pathetic sop to a protest. She cleared her throat, as if she could chase away the desperate need. "Please tell me you talked to your lawyer."

"Non."

"Christ, you can't approach this like you do everything else. You should make me sign a contract that what is yours will stay yours."

"I thought you thought me worthless."

"I'm sure just your stock in CLG is worth a lot."

Faint tension emanated from him, his roving hands clenched tight on her shoulders. "I don't care about that stock. Or the company or the legacy."

Something in his tone, a vein of disgust, alerted Sophia. It sounded so discordant, so jarring, for she'd never heard him speak in that tone before. This didn't sound like not caring. It was active loathing that hinted at a depth of feeling she didn't think him capable of.

"It's a legacy, Luca. It roots you to this place. How can you...*hate* it?"

She felt his shrug rather than saw it. "Is that why you want to head Rossi's? Don't let the idea of belonging become more important than everything else."

Faint alarm tripped along Sophia's nerves. *Was that her*

real intention beneath wanting to save her family? Was it an utterly selfish desire to belong?

"Keep your hands to yourself. You're distracting me," she burst out.

The man's hands were forever roaming and roving over her. Even when she was bristling with anger. He touched as if it was as natural as breathing. Sometimes, it was affectionate, sometimes, it was provoking. But always, as if he needed the physical connection.

It was one of the things she'd loved then—being touched by him.

He laughed and continued touching her.

"This is serious, Luca. When we…separate, I don't want any accusations."

"Do you intend to take me to the cleaners, Sophia?"

"It would serve you right if I did."

"There's nothing you could do that would make me end this in a bad way, *cara mia*. Except if you fell in love with me and made a nuisance of yourself."

She laughed. A brittle, fake sound. "That is an impossibility right there."

"Then we're good, *si*? I'm aware that you're placing a huge amount of trust in me. I'm doing the same."

She had no reply to that. In her wildest nightmares, she wouldn't have imagined Luca Conti of all men coming to her rescue.

One hand landed on her shoulder. A finger stroked her nape, between her knot and the edge of her cardigan. Back and forth, up and down, until all of her being focused on that spot. "This is romantic, *si*? Us eloping like this."

She snorted. "No one who knows me would believe I'd elope."

Now the finger moved, snuck under the seam of her dress and traced her shoulder blades. "*Si*, but then I corrupted you with my kisses and my infinite charm and my dazzling good looks. I stole away every bit of your famed common sense, enthralled you. Sounds perfect when you think about it."

She flushed and looked down at herself, at the horrible dress. Would she have dressed differently if she had known? Not that she had anything in her closet that was remotely better or dressy enough for a bride.

No, this was right. Their wedding wasn't a romantic affair. It wasn't even one of those advantageous society arrangements that seemed to abound around her. It had a shelf life of three months, if that.

Her spine rigid from holding herself so tight, she blew a breath. Turned around. "Let's get married."

He smiled then, and the golden sunlight illuminated that gorgeous face. Her breath caught. He hooked his arm through hers and walked up the steps. When she wobbled, one corded arm came around her waist. She felt him look down and followed it.

When he met her gaze, there was such genuine laughter etched in his face that she smiled back. "What?"

"I'm going to take a pair of scissors and rip up all those black trousers you usually wear. You're not hiding those legs again. Not if I have anything to say about it."

They were married fifteen minutes later, in a huge cathedral-like room. Sunlight gleamed through high, soaring windows, dusting everything with a golden glow. Every time she moved, the princess-cut diamond, set in platinum, caught the rays piercing it over and over.

That he'd remembered the rings—for him and her— still shocked her.

Even the impersonal civil ceremony with no personal

vows couldn't seem to dim the momentousness of the occasion.

Sophia couldn't meet Luca's eyes throughout the ceremony. Or anyone else's. Didn't want to see a mockingly wicked smile as if this was just another of his antics, another joke, just another day.

Much as she tried to not attach significance to the day, she'd forever remember it. At least, as her only wedding day.

So the images she had of that half hour were of ancient but stylish furniture, a seventeenth-century tapestry covering one huge wall, luxurious chandeliers, brocade-covered chairs and golden-framed mirrors reflecting back Luca and her every which way she looked—she short and dowdy in her ugly dress, which she promised herself she was going to burn the moment it came off her, and Luca, looking gorgeous and a little roguish in a white shirt and black jeans that gave the best view of his tight butt.

It was a place steeped in history and for someone who'd never been able to afford sentimentality, the hall impressed Sophia. Three months later, or a year later, or even a decade later, this hall would be here, a building that had stood witness to their strange wedding.

Her wedding...to the one man she shouldn't even come near.

The clerk asked for fifteen Euros for the banns license, which Luca didn't have. "My wife is responsible for all matters financial," the rogue added with a glint in his eyes.

The wedding felt both surreal and strangely kooky. As if they were co-conspirators in a reckless game. While the truth was that she was burning all her bridges by trusting Luca.

Her family was going to be excited for all the wrong reasons. Kairos was probably never going to talk to her ever again. Society was going to laugh at her. Even she didn't believe that a man like Luca could fall in love with a woman like her. Why should they?

Suddenly, she couldn't even breathe, the enormity of what she'd done pressing upon her. She was trusting the one man who'd broken the very thing into a thousand pieces with his recklessness.

As if tuned into every doubt coursing through her, Luca wrapped an arm around her. "Trust yourself, Sophia. You made the right decision, for you."

Two of Luca's friends—a woman who worked in the Piazza del Duomo and the mayor's sister, two of his exes, *of course*—stood witness as they signed the marriage license. Neither woman, at least openly, exhibited their shock that the Conti playboy, the man who'd been called a god for his looks, was marrying the short, snarky, shrewish Sophia.

And soon, she became Sophia Conti. A solemn expression on his face, Luca pulled her close and kissed her cheek. Not her mouth, surprisingly, for a man who'd said he was eager to get her into bed.

A tender, almost affectionate caress that brought a lump to her throat.

Waving his friends off, they walked out into the sunshine. It was a gorgeous day for November.

"Let's go," he said then, pointing to his bike.

"No way am I climbing that beast in this dress."

"No way am I leaving my new bride here. Hop on, *cara mia*. I want to get to the Conti offices before they disperse for lunch. I hear they have a board meeting today."

"You want to walk in there and—" she swallowed audibly "—announce what we did?"

"You sound as if we did something naughty. And why

not? I want to see the expressions on my Nonno's face. And Kairos's. And Leandro's."

Sophia wanted to see none of those people. She wanted to go home and come to terms with the emotions bursting through her before she faced anyone else. Once she processed them, she wanted to build a neat little cupboard in her mind and shove them all in there and slam the door.

"Is it necessary to upset them?"

"Stop chickening out, Sophia. You need to stop being scared of them." Which was exactly what she was doing. But for altogether different reasons.

Facing society as the Conti Devil's wife was going to be an exercise in humiliation and agony and a host of other excruciating things. But coward, she was not. With some difficulty, for she didn't want to flash him a glimpse of her underwear, she got on the bike.

With her awareness of the man and an active imagination, she didn't want to straddle anything when he was so close. The leather was supple against the tender skin of her thighs, both indecent and exciting, thanks to her libido.

"*Mio Dio!* Was that black lace and garters?" he asked the moment she settled on the scandalously wide seat.

He sounded hoarse and rough.

"You peeked? You actually peeked?" Outraged, she hit him on the shoulder, got off the bike and sputtered like a woman incapable of forming a coherent sentence. "You... you're the very devil."

He turned to the side, offering her his sharp profile. "You don't think your horribly closed-off dresses work, do you, Sophia?"

Throat dry, it took her a few seconds to speak. "What?"

"You have the lushest curves I've ever seen on a woman, *bella*. Those dresses, all they do is tempt and tease. Didn't you ever wonder why all those idiots made that bet about you ten years ago?"

All those idiots... He talked so glibly as if he hadn't been a part of it. The man seemed to have a selective memory along with a face that would tempt a saint.

And she had never been a saint.

"Because I beat them all in every test we took. Because I proved again and again that I was better than them at everything. And I didn't think they were charming princes like the rest of society did. They—" she swallowed tightly, for she'd never understood why he'd taken part in it "—wanted to see me humiliated."

That whole episode, along with being viewed as prize cattle that he could exchange for an advantageous marriage by Salvatore, everything that was tender in her, had taken a beating.

Before she'd a chance to understand her femininity, it had been crushed. So she had locked it, and any other vulnerabilities, away and continued on.

"All that is true, yes. But they were attracted to you. They thought you were the hottest girl around. They all wanted to be the ones who tamed you."

"Wild animals are tamed," she said in a tight whisper that hurt her throat.

"You can't change the world, Sophia. Men will be men—childish, arrogant and insecure. Any time we see a woman we don't understand, we call her names. All you do by hating the world is make yourself miserable."

"So I should lie down and let them beat me into what they think I should be." Because her mother, Salvatore, Antonio, Kairos, that was what they all wanted to do. They all wanted her to fit into the roles they had for her.

"No, *cara*. You fight, like you always do. You live. You

count your wins. You glory in what makes you stand out and you rub their noses in it."

She smiled, finding the idea intriguing, at least in theory. "And what would these wins be?"

"Convincing the most beautiful man in Italy, *probably Europe*, to marry you, should count as a win, *si*?"

Sophia burst out laughing. He possessed an uncanny knack to make her laugh, at the world and even herself. Like a ray of sunshine in a gloomy, dank cave.

But beneath her laughter, shock persisted, an uncomfortable knot in the pit of her stomach. Every moment she spent with Luca, he tossed her assumptions of him upside down.

He saw and understood far more than the world thought he did.

Even back then, even as he'd seduced her as part of that horrible bet, not once had he tried to minimize her to exaggerate his masculinity. Not once had he called her intelligence and ambition weird. Not once had he told her to be happy with her lot.

His betrayal in the end had colored everything of that time but Sophia didn't remember a time when she'd been so easy with herself.

"You are beautiful, *cara mia*. Enough to make stupid boys do a cruel thing to get close to you."

Was that why he'd taken part in that bet, too? Hadn't he known he didn't need it? She'd been putty in his hands from the moment he'd smiled at her.

She offered a wan smile, far too rattled. "You can make the earth believe it's the sky if you put yourself up to it, Luca. I'm not falling for you."

He sighed, that dramatic, larger-than-life gesture. "Oh, you will, *cara mia*. And you'll love every minute of your descent."

Hands snug around his waist, she hung on for dear life as he took off.

In two seconds flat, wind whipped at the knot of her hair. Her dress rode up to her thighs, and her breasts were crushed against his tensile back.

But for the moment Sophia found she didn't really mind being plastered to him. In fact, she decided to enjoy it.

She decided to call being plastered to the sexiest man she'd ever meet a win.

CHAPTER FIVE

A WWF SMACKDOWN would have had less dramatic effect than when Luca, arm in arm with Sophia, rushed past an aggrieved and bamboozled set of assistants and personal secretaries, and into the conference room on the tenth floor of the Conti offices.

"I thought we should share the good news with everyone in here first."

His grandfather Antonio rose to the bait instantly. His gaze moved from Luca's face to Sophia and then to the way their bodies were flushed together at their sides. A nerve began vibrating in his temple. "What have you done now?"

"Sophia and I got married an hour ago."

"If this is one of your shameless jokes—"

Luca cut off Antonio's building tirade by throwing their license on the table.

Ten pairs of eyes went to the license, scanned it and then returned to him and Sophia.

All ten faces, two assistants and eight board members, including Antonio and Kairos, looked at him as if he had crossed that final line into insanity.

Only his brother, Leandro, didn't exhibit any signs of the panic Luca saw in the rest. But it didn't mean Luca's announcement didn't rattle Leandro. With his autocratic control of his emotions, Leandro wouldn't betray anything until he'd decided on the best course.

Luca decided it was time to make the second, thoroughly satisfactory announcement. "Since my dutiful brother has decided to abandon me and his duties toward the board, I have decided that it is time I claimed my seat on the board and directed its decisions. After all, as someone very cleverly pointed out, it is my fortune, too. And where would my lifestyle be if I didn't have the Conti legacy to live off? I have to protect my assets, push the company in the direction I want it to go." He looked pointedly at Kairos, leaving no doubt as to his intentions.

Also, thwarting all board members who'd done nothing to stop his father's escalating antics felt good. Why hadn't he thought of this before? Luca could see the fear and the shock in their faces. They were terrified that he wasn't joking, that he would repeat history. That he would be another Enzo, and that he would be left to run wild, unchecked.

Luca tapped his knuckles on the glass tabletop, letting the silence thicken with the horror of their thoughts.

Sophia next to him became stiff, as if a pole had been driven into her spine. With the pretense of pushing away at a nonexistent speck on his collar, she reached close and glared at him. "What's going on? They all—"

He stole the words from her in a quick kiss, unable to resist the temptation. He teased and taunted her honeyed mouth with soft strokes, waiting for her to let him in. She was his wife, and damn his romantic soul, he liked it.

He'd never realized what a beautiful, intimate thing that bond could be until he'd seen Leandro and Alex. That it was another thing he could never have—that connection that went beyond anything else. He'd acknowledged that a long time ago, still, his heart raced when he looked at the plain band on his finger.

Fingers on his shirt, Sophia stiffened and then slowly melted into the kiss. He licked her lower lip, an incessant clawing in his gut to own her.

She stilled, blushed and then glared at him again. Her breath was a warm caress against his lips. "You couldn't have done this anywhere else?"

He grinned. "*Non*. I want them all to see I worship at your feet."

She rolled her eyes and he tucked her close against his side.

Leandro sighed. It was that same half indulgent, half disciplinary sound his brother had made countless times when Luca had been up to something new. Leandro hated pretending about Luca. But he had proven countless times that only Luca's well-being mattered.

Amusement flickered in his brother's gaze instead of the fury Luca had expected. Luca grinned, his heart feeling light for the first time in months.

Falling in love with Alex had changed his brother.

"You barely know anything about the business or CLG. And you hate dealing with...*people*, remember?" Next to him, Luca felt Sophia tense, her gaze swinging between him and his brother.

"I said I wanted to take an active role. Not that I would actually do any of the work."

A sort of a cross between relief and fear settled on the members' faces. One of them recovered enough to say, "What do you suggest?"

"My wife, Sophia Conti, from this day will have complete authority to make decisions on my behalf. The lawyers are preparing paperwork even as we speak. Come on, *cara mia*."

When Sophia, wooden and unmoving, only stared at him, he winked at her. Hand on the curve of her waist, he pushed her to the end of the table toward an empty chair. The members of the board watched like it was a movie.

Luca pulled the chair back, seated Sophia and then

stood behind her. "Sophia has seven years of experience working at Rossi Leather. She has an MBA and specializes in risk management and forecasting business trends and marketing. For all legal purposes, she now owns fifteen percent of the Conti stock."

A ripple of shock spread across the room and for once in his life, Luca felt a sense of rightness.

He had known her area of expertise.

He hadn't told her he was giving her complete authority over his stock.

That hadn't been part of their deal. She'd never even imagined...

Eight men—the most powerful in Milanese society—looked at her as if to figure out how she had persuaded/manipulated the Conti Devil into this.

Damn it, did he really not care what happened to the company? *Or did he trust her judgment and her that much?*

That thought sent her heart thumping against her rib cage.

Sophia somehow managed to smile and nod and accept the congratulations that came her way. Kairos, without looking at her, walked out the minute the meeting was concluded.

She'd understood one thing in the show her new husband had put on.

Luca hated, *no*, despised, his grandfather. The depth of that emotion from Luca, who seemed to fairly breeze through life with no concern and with nothing but surface involvement with everyone, had rattled her.

While Luca's small exchange with Leandro had been civil, too, the bond between them was anything but. There was love between them.

After the depth of emotions she'd seen play out on his

face in the conference room, Sophia wasn't sure she really knew the Conti Devil.

Her gut said one thing while her history with him, quite the opposite.

She had just started looking for him when Luca appeared in the carpeted corridor and pulled her into a small, private lounge that was the size of her bedroom at home.

Cream leather and cream walls greeted her, the quiet luxury of the room markedly different from the business-oriented layout of the rest of the building. Afternoon light poured through the high windows, touching the space with a golden intimacy.

The most surprising thing about the room, though, was a piano that stood in the corner.

And in the middle of all that light, stood Luca, looking like a dark angel in his black jeans and white shirt with buttons undone to his chest. Dark olive skin gleamed like burnished metal, beckoning her touch. The leather jacket was gone.

The devil had intentions. And not good ones, for her mental health. Her body, however, had very different ideas for it was thrumming like an engine ready to take off.

Sophia rubbed her hands on her hips, had to swallow the butterflies in her throat before she could speak. "What is this place?"

"My brother's private lounge."

"It is soundproofed, isn't it?"

"Si." He raised a finger and shook it. "Don't ask me why."

Sophia stole a glance at the door as he closed it behind him. "You have key card access?"

"Si. Why is that so surprising?"

"I thought maybe this was the first time you came into the building."

He shook his head from side to side, making a thick lock of hair fall on his forehead. "No, I've been known to crash here, once in a while. My brother used to be a very hard taskmaster years ago. He's worked for the company since he was sixteen or seventeen. He refused to leave me alone at home."

"Where were your parents?" She'd vaguely heard of a scandal involving their father, Enzo Conti.

"Absent." The shrug that accompanied it seemed far too practiced to be real.

"So, wait, Leandro had this...room built for you?"

"Si."

She looked around the room again, noting the dark, floor-to-ceiling bookshelves. At first glance, the subjects were varied from art to space to the leather industry in Italy. "Wow, all this to just keep you out of trouble?"

"My brother takes his responsibilities very seriously."

"Why do you hate them all so much?"

A shadow flitted over his face and Sophia knew she'd hit the nail on the head. "Will you not move from the door?"

Evasion. If it didn't work, he'd smile at her. Or touch her. Or kiss her. She was beginning to see the pattern. She pushed off the door and casually strolled toward the bookshelves. None of the books were for amateur readers and looked quite worn. *Who did all these books belong to?*

"I thought it was all a joke to you. I still think a part of it is. You're like Puck in *A Midsummer Night's Dream*."

"A good-looking Puck?"

She ignored his little quip. "You do your little thing and stand back to watch the explosion. But what happened in that boardroom was more than that." She turned around to see him standing close. Instantly, she felt the zing in her blood. The hungry clamor to touch him. The simple need to look at him, study him, to her heart's content. "You let them think you were going to join the board and for all of three minutes, that pack of gray wolves looked terrified. It was kind of funny."

He raised a brow. "Gray wolves?"

She shrugged.

"Why gray wolves?"

"They whiff out their prey's weakness from a considerable distance. They stalk and hunt it until it gives up out of sheer exhaustion. I have seen them all turn on Salvatore these last few months, from the minute things began to get worse, ready to tear *Rossi's* out and keep the good parts. Except Leandro, and Kairos, for his own reasons. Your grandfather leads that pack."

"So the wolves scared you, then?"

Sophia shivered. "Yes. But then I reminded myself that they need me just as much as I need them at this point."

A sense of coiled tightness emanated from him. And Sophia knew instinctually that he was shocked that she'd figured him out. "Why do they need you?"

"To corral you. To keep you amused and away from them." Her fingers shook as she rubbed her temple. Nothing, she was beginning to realize, was simple with Luca. And she'd hitched her already limp pony to his ride.

He touched her then. A mere brush of his fingers over her jaw. Sophia let the bookcase dig into her back, anything to keep her grounded in reality. "Have I ever told you how much I love that clever brain of yours, *cara mia*?"

Warmth fluttered through her stomach. "No. And you are probably the only one."

"I do." Something like pride glittered in his eyes. "And to show my appreciation for it, I'm going to kiss that lush mouth of yours."

She raised a brow. "First, tell me what that was about."

"Is it only me that finds this bossiness of yours hot?"

Another flicker of warmth. Another pocket of heat. "Luca…"

"They had the particular pleasure of seeing my father go off the rails. Now they look at me and wonder if I will do the same."

"Why you?"

"Because I'm the mirror image of him, a carbon copy. The man embezzled from his own company, used his power to prey on women and generally blazed a destructive path through every life he touched. He almost brought CLG to its knees and only then Antonio interfered. He brought Leandro into the company, and together, they ousted him in two years." There was no intonation to that statement. Yet the very bald way he said it sent a shiver through Sophia.

"What happened to him? Your father?"

"He died in jail." A vicious gleam, a dark fire in his eyes that transformed his face. To that of a disconcertingly cruel stranger. "So Antonio waits and watches, as he's been doing for years, to see if I will self-destruct like that, too. He tries to do a course adjust every few years."

Which was why he'd stalked and cornered Sophia. After Luca's latest debacle with a minister's wife, Antonio had been desperate.

But how could anyone think Luca would turn out like his father?

She couldn't imagine Luca ever preying on anyone's weakness. Couldn't imagine Luca destroying anyone's life with such malicious…

What do you call what he did to you ten years ago? the rational part of her whispered. *What he does every day with his life? How much do you really know him?* "You—"

"I think we have had enough talk about bloodthirsty wolves."

Trying to calm her ratcheting heartbeat, Sophia focused her gaze everywhere else but him. "Why are we here?"

"To have a celebratory drink, why else?" He made a show of glancing at his watch, as if he hadn't timed all this with precision. "We have been successfully married for a whole morning."

That was when Sophia noticed the ice bucket with a champagne bottle and next to the bucket, in a cardboard box with a little bow that looked very familiar and dear to her heart, chocolate truffles.

He was seducing her; another warning from that increasingly annoying voice.

She groaned, her mouth already watering as she imagined the dark, rich taste on her mouth. Other disturbing sensations floated beneath. She had told him once that she would sell her soul for truffles.

Countless women he'd seduced and countless little nothings they would have whispered in his ears, flushed from the good sex he gave...did he remember all those details? she wanted to ask. "Keep those away from me, Luca. They are the very devil for my diet."

His mouth pursed tight, as if he was trying to stop himself from bursting into laughter. Which in turn animated the rest of his face.

Mouthwatering chocolate, knee-melting Luca and she— locked behind a closed door.

Ignoring her plea, he tugged her toward him and raised a truffle to her mouth. "A wedding like ours, that sets at least some things to right, deserves a little celebration, *si*?"

Caught in the startlingly deep conviction in his words, his gaze intent on her mouth, Sophia licked her lips.

He groaned then, a deep, husky sound that pinged

through her, leaving pockets of heat all over. "Open up, *cara mia.*"

The taste of that melting chocolate exploded on her tongue. A moan she couldn't stop escaped her throat, while his fingers lingered on her lips. Pressed at the soft cushion of her lower lip.

His gaze was hot, hungry. His mouth even hotter as he bent and swiped at her lower lip. A jolt of pleasure traveled through her, so acute that Sophia jerked.

Sinewed arms came around her, pulling her closer. The muscles in his arms clenched under her questing fingers. Air became short in supply. And what was there was coated with the scent of him. She felt dizzy, like she was high. On him.

She licked her lips again.

He bent and dug his teeth into her lower lip. And then stroked the nip with his tongue. Liquid heat rushed between Sophia's legs. His fingers tightened over her hips. "You lick your lips like that, I will think it a call to action."

She tried to wiggle out of his hold. Only managing to press herself tighter against him. "I'm not doing it on purpose."

"I know."

His chest pushed against her breasts. Muscle and sinew, he was rock hard everywhere she touched. What the hell did the man do to have a body like that? With his lazy lifestyle, he should have had a paunch. At least a small belly. Not this washboard abdomen that she wanted to touch and lick and scrape with her teeth.

But she didn't want to let go of him. Not just yet, she promised herself. She didn't want to give up this intimacy with him. This easy familiarity that they were slipping into. The laughter they shared. The way he made her see things about herself she didn't know. She hadn't realized how deprived she'd been of this kind of companionship, how monotonous her life had become.

Maybe there were other advantages to this short marriage of theirs. The zing in her blood, the ache between her thighs, begged her to consider them. She traced the shadows under his eyes, something she'd always wanted to do. "Do you not sleep at all?"

He held her wrist and pressed his face into her hand. Leaned into her touch as if he needed it. Breath whispering like a whistle, Sophia traced the sharp angles of his face. The pad of her forefinger reached his mouth. That mouth, God, that mouth… She had such hot dreams about it.

With no warning, he turned his head, opened his mouth and closed it over her finger. And then sucked it. A hungry, stringent pulse began at her sex, in tune with the pulls of his mouth.

Her skin felt too tight to hold her. The silk of her panties was wet. Rubbed against her inner thighs as she shifted restlessly.

He released her finger. Sophia clenched her thighs closed instinctually, needing friction there.

A dark flush dusted his cheekbones. He knew, oh, God, he knew. He knew where she was burning to be touched.

"I'm an insomniac."

It took her several long seconds to realize he was answering her question.

He was an insomniac? "How bad is it?"

"I sleep a few hours every few days."

"That's it? I need at least eight hours every day to feel remotely human. Doesn't that have side effects?"

"It does. But I have learned to live with them."

It made him more three dimensional, more…human. As strange as that sounded. "What do you do, then? In all that time?"

Fingers busily shifted the collar of her dress. His mouth landed on the skin he bared. His tongue licked that juncture, sending hot shafts of pleasure down her spine. "Do you taste like silk all over, Sophia?"

"Yes," she said, completely lost in the magic he wove. She tried to recall some warning, some common sense as to why she shouldn't be in his arms, pressed up snugly against him. With him sucking on random parts of her.

Zilch. Nada. Nothing came up.

Then the diamond on her ring finger glinted, a twinkling ray of common sense. She ordered her body to stiffen, to move away, but it had different ideas. "We can't be doing this. We can't... If you gave me that power over your stock thinking that will make me grateful, thinking I'll happily—"

"Spread your legs and take me inside you?" He was the one who pulled back. "You really think I'd have to pay for sex? I'm not sure who it reflects badly on that you think that, you or me. Or have you truly become as cynical as they call you?"

He castigated her so softly and yet Sophia felt his words like tiny pricks. "Then why?"

In response, he dipped his mouth and took hers again. This kiss was not an invitation or a tease. It was full-on assault, demanding surrender. Almost brutally efficient in the way he slowly but surely made her into a mass of shuddering sensation.

She'd made him angry, Sophia realized beneath the avalanche of sensations. His tongue laved the interior of her mouth, while his hands moved up and down her body, inciting her into a frenzy.

Expert strokes, here and there, perfect pressure, a master of seduction at work. A routine.

His heart wasn't in it. He was seducing her with technique and experience. He was proving a point. She could be a tall, blonde model for all that it mattered to him.

The difference, even as heat drenched her, sent bile up her throat.

"No, Luca, please." She sank her hands into his hair and tugged his face down. "That was moronic. What I said," she finally whispered, her hands molding and tracing the line of his shoulders. "I...have never been able to believe that someone like you could want someone like me."

She didn't want to mention the bet again. It was in the past. But she saw his understanding of it, saw those same shutters come down.

He sighed and instantly gentled. A devil so easily calmed with honesty? A man whose feelings could hurt under that almost impenetrable mask he wore? She wasn't so sure anymore that she knew him.

Across her temple, then over her nose, and then her jaw, he placed soft kisses. "I kiss you because you're thoroughly kissable, Sophia. I kiss you because I can't bear the thought of those lush lips not quivering under mine, of that stout will not surrendering to me. I kiss you because I want to hear that sigh you release when you realize this fire between us is too hot to fight. I kiss you for that moment when your shoulders lose that stiff line, when you melt into willing softness. I kiss you for that moment when you make that little growly sound in the back of your throat, as though you've just realized that you've been a passive spectator. I kiss you because then you take over the kiss, you forget why you should resist me and you devour me as if I was your favorite dessert in the world."

He whispered the last words against her mouth. As if he was infusing her very blood with those tender words.

She sighed.

Then she groaned.

Then she kissed him back with a ravenous hunger. All things he'd predicted. He knew her so well, even in this... It was a faint warning at the back of her mind that dissolved under the influx of such delirious pleasure.

His lush mouth delivered on the fantasies it promised. Hard and soft, sometimes masculine demand, sometimes a tender entreaty.

Vining her arms around his nape, she stretched to reach more of him. He was right; she hated being a spectator. One hard thigh pushed in between her legs, but didn't quite hit the spot.

When she shifted, one hand landed on her thigh, pushed up her dress and then pulled her leg up and around his buttocks.

His thigh moved even farther between her legs. And up. Right against the hungry core of her.

Shamelessly, Sophia clenched her thighs and then moved on his leg, back and forth. Up and down. Pleasure spiraled through her pelvis, building to an unbearable rhythm.

Teeth banged, tongues sucked. Clasping his jaw with her hands, she held him for her delectation. Then she dug her teeth into that carnal lower lip, hard, and sucked it into her mouth.

A growl rumbled from his chest. A wild beat danced in her blood as she realized something had changed between them. Tension radiated from his lean frame. His fingers became more urgent, his mouth harder and hotter.

Playtime was over.

His fingers crawled into her hair, tugged at the clip she'd used to pull it back into a tight knot. The clatter of the clip against the wall where he threw it was a bang in the hoarse silence. Fingers pulled and plumped her hair until it fell in unruly waves around her face.

She forgot what she'd meant to ask him. She forgot what had disconcerted her so much about the scene in the conference room. She forgot why she shouldn't kiss him like this. Only sensation mattered. Only the heat building inside her mattered.

He moved his thigh away and she whimpered. She'd melt into a puddle if he didn't hold her up. Her mouth was stinging, her blood singing; Sophia was so aroused she was ready to beg him to finish it.

He lifted her leg again, pushing away at the ugly dress. Up and up. Until the lace of her garters was visible and then a strip of her thighs. "Sophia." He was panting against her cheek. "This is where you put a stop to it if you don't want to be bent over that table and have me thrusting inside you in three seconds."

Reality came crashing with that crudely worded statement. He'd put it like that on purpose. She growled, a demand and a plea twisted in that animal sound. He laughed, took her mouth with his again.

She jerked away from him, stumbled on jelly-like legs and then reached for him again to steady herself. "No," she said, running a hand over her mouth.

All she wanted was to cry. Her mind felt soaked in desire, frustration. "God, I came looking for you because I wanted to talk." His pupils were dilated, his chest still falling and rising. But he didn't look the least bit put out for being denied the same satisfaction. "I didn't mean to hump you like a dog in heat. You're not angry?"

"I'm in considerable pain, yes…" He sighed "I'm not angry. I know you'd like to believe the worst about me but I do have a little self-control."

"Oh, is there anything I can do to—"

"You can fix your dress and stop offering to help. Next time you offer, I'll ask you to go down on your knees."

O went her mouth again. An instant image fluttered through her brain. Did he ask it of all his lovers? Did they do it because they didn't want to lose his interest?

Personally, Sophia had always thought the act a little subjugating, undignified and maybe even a little painful to the participating woman's mouth. "Do you ask it of all your lovers or—"

"Stop talking, Sophia," he growled again.

Sophia dashed into the attached bathroom. She splashed water over her heated cheeks. His fingers had built her hair into a cloud around her face. She looked soft and feminine and like a woman who lost her mind after two kisses.

Damn it, she had the most important meeting of her life in a few minutes and here she was, climbing all over Luca. He was like her craving for that chocolate truffle. A bad habit she thought she'd beat only to succumb again and again.

He'd suggested she fall. And she was falling gloriously. She thought herself above all those women who threw themselves at him. How bitchily righteous she'd been... If anything, she was even more foolish because she'd already had a taste of him ten years ago.

She'd thought herself beautiful, special to have attracted his attention. And it had been nothing but a bet. "Maybe deprivation will build a little character," she said, coming out of the bathroom.

Could she sound any more naively hopeful, any more sanctimoniously righteous? She couldn't, *absolutely* couldn't care if he satisfied himself with another woman that night.

He was scowling. "We're both consenting adults and have been joined in the holiest of bonds in front of God and man just this morning. You're making us both walk back out like horny dogs. You have enough character, don't you think?"

He sounded so pained, so disgruntled, that Sophia burst out laughing.

It was easy, far too easy, to be mesmerized by Luca's easy charm. As long as she remembered that there was nothing of substance beneath. "I scheduled a meeting with you and Leandro in an hour."

"Your plans for Rossi Leather are ready for Leandro?"

She nodded, barely bracing herself against the admiration in his eyes. "I want to run them by you and Leandro first before I present them to Salvatore. That way, we're all in the loop."

How was it that with of all the men she'd dealt with— CEOs and ruthless businessmen and millionaires—it was this wastrel playboy that was never intimidated by her? Who only showed respect for her accomplishments and her ambition.

Could that easy confidence come from just his looks? Or was there more to Luca than met the eye?

He uncorked the champagne bottle and poured it into two flutes. Handing her one, he clinked his against hers. The bubbles kissed her throat on the way down. She looked up to find his gaze on her. Rattled by the line of her thoughts, she said nothing.

They talked of a varied range of topics, sometimes agreeing and more than once, getting into a heated argument. Only when her watch pinged did Sophia realize how invigorating and informative their discussion had been.

And how enjoyable.

Throughout the meeting with Leandro and Luca, all Sophia could think of was how jarringly discordant, how disconcertingly different this side of Luca was from the man she'd despised for so long.

CHAPTER SIX

THE LAST THING Sophia wanted, after the events of the last week, was a party.

A party thrown specially in honor of Luca and her.

A party to which every member of the high society of Milan was invited, including men who'd known of her humiliation ten years ago.

A party thrown by her in-laws, the Conti family, which was a minefield of dysfunction—her family seemed so normal even with her differences with Salvatore—she couldn't imagine navigating without setting off an explosion.

The last she'd seen of Luca had been outside the Conti building, six days ago. He'd called a taxi for her after her meeting with Leandro and him and then driven off. The invite for the party came later that night, in the form of a phone call from Leandro's wife, Alexis, her new sister-in-law.

When she'd moaned about attending, Salvatore had warned her that she couldn't alienate her husband's family. *Her new family*, in fact.

To which, she had, quite forcefully and uncharacteristically, asked him if he was that happy to be rid of her. Only silence had remained then. Full of guilt and shame, Sophia had apologized to him and left.

She'd never confronted Salvatore like that. There had never been any need. Since he had married her mother, he'd been kindness itself to her. He'd paid for her to go to University, given her a job at Rossi Leather, provided her with everything she could have ever asked for.

The only thing he didn't give her was his trust when it came to business matters. Could she blame him when it was a one-hundred-and-sixty-year-old legacy that he wanted to protect for her brothers? Maybe asking for him to take such a big risk on her, when she'd never really excelled at the things he wanted of her, was too much?

Maybe things would have been different if she'd been born a Rossi.

At least, she had done the right thing in marrying Luca. Salvatore was delighted that finally he had a connection to the venerable Contis.

Sophia had come to Villa de Conti straight from work that evening, and had been shown into Luca's suite by a smiling Alexis. Aware that she'd wanted to chat, Sophia had claimed a headache and rushed in for a bath.

After her shower, Sophia put on a silk wrapper and stepped out into the bedroom. Her impulse purchases lay in chic, expensive bags on the bed, having left a hole the size of a crater in her bank account. Designer heels lay in another box.

The glittering bags mocked her. She flopped to the bed, feeling foolish now for splurging—when the devil hadn't even answered her texts. *Again*. Was he going to show up tonight?

She'd just rubbed lotion in and put her underwear on when the door opened quite rudely. Cursing, Sophia grabbed her towel just as Valentina, of all people, came into view.

Spine rigid, Sophia preempted the tall beauty, who looked stunning in a long black evening dress. "I'm far too nervous already, so please, Valentina, no theatrics right now."

The younger woman had the grace to look ashamed. "I came to apologize, Sophia." When Sophia remained stubbornly silent, Valentina changed tack. "My brother sent me to see if you wanted help."

"Thank Leandro, but I'm good."

"*Non*, Luca sent me."

The towel slipped from Sophia's hands. "Luca is here? Downstairs?" Her breath ballooned up in her chest.

"*Si.*"

He hadn't deserted her. Just for this evening, Sophia needed him by her side. After tonight, after getting through facing the society that she'd never belonged in, she wouldn't need him again.

"You thought he would not come?"

Curiosity filled Valentina's question. The last thing Sophia wanted was the Contis or anyone else for that matter, to know how little familiarity she had with Luca's lifestyle. "I'm nervous because I know everyone's eyes will be on me and I don't handle attention well."

Valentina's gaze swept over her almost clinically, assessing, and Sophia tugged the towel toward her. "You are hot, Sophia, why do you hide it?"

The question was so matter of fact that Sophia forgot that she was supposed to be angry with Valentina. "Did he ask you to be kind to me?"

"*Non*, I'm not being kind. He did tell me to stop being bitchy to you." The woman didn't mince her words and Sophia was beginning to like her. "You have breasts I would kill for." To punctuate it, she looked pointedly at Sophia's breasts, contained dangerously in a pink bra and then at her own relatively smaller ones, which wasn't saying much because everyone had smaller breasts than Sophia's.

And then Valentina sighed.

Sophia half groaned, half choked.

"I developed very late and even then, they were like apples. Yours are more like..." Sophia wanted to crawl under the bed sheets. "Small melons."

"Please, Tina...stop!" Sophia rubbed her fingers over her forehead, shook her head and then let the laugh building in her chest escape. Tears filled her eyes, her nose, she was sure, was running and her throat and lungs burned. "Oh, how we torture ourselves...I've always been so jealous of your model-like figure, your style and grace. You're like a gazelle, whereas I...waddle like a penguin. Your sense of fashion is...just wow."

Warmth entered Valentina's eyes, transforming her entire visage. "Sense of style and fashion can be...acquired, *si*? But not curves. Unless I go for those silicone implants. But I don't think Kairos will like artificial boobs and there is already too much he..." Stricken black eyes shied away from Sophia's. "I know now that Kairos and you are just friends."

"You confronted Kairos?"

"*Si*. He was angry that I struck you. *But*... I had no business acting like a bitch to you. Not when the problem is between us." Misery radiated from her. "Will you forgive me, Sophia?"

Sophia smiled. "If you help me, yes. Since you're a fashionista who Milan looks up to, can you advise me? I bought three dresses. I don't want them to see a wobbly penguin paired with a strutting peacock. I want to look back on tonight and not cringe." There were far too many cringe-worthy episodes already in her life.

Valentina burst out laughing. "My brother is a peacock?"

Sophia nodded. With a brisk efficiency, Valentina vetoed all three dresses in two minutes flat.

"The saleswoman assured me that they are the height of—"

"*Si*, but she followed your direction to cover up every inch of skin. What is in the last bag?"

"That one…I picked that one. But it's going straight back to the shop. I don't know what I was thinking."

Valentina floated through the room, picked up the last bag on the bed. The knee-length turquoise silk slithered out in a silken whisper. "This dress is perfect."

Alarm rattled through Sophia. "That was a foolish purchase. It is strapless and too snug and my *melons* will surely pop out and then—"

"What are you so scared of, Sophia? That people will realize you're beautiful under the hideous clothes you wear?"

"Hey! They're not hideous and—"

"Fine, look like a penguin, then. There will be at least three women downstairs who have, at some time, been linked with Luca."

Sophia gasped. "Oh…you play dirty."

No way was she going to be shown up by Luca's willowy exes. Tonight might be a farce, but *she* was going to be the heroine of the farce.

A thousand butterflies flying in her stomach, she let Tina do her hair, even her makeup. When Tina pronounced her ready, she faced the floor-length mirror. Her breath halted in her throat.

The low cut of the bodice showed the upper curves of her breasts. Simple beadwork on the bodice caught the light with every breath she took. The hem of the dress kissed her knees just so, baring her legs. She turned her foot and looked at her legs. She did have sexy legs.

The woman in her, the part she tried to hide and ignore

and forget, preened that she looked good in it. Nothing was going to make her tall, elegant or graceful but that was okay. She would continue her diets, grumble about never being svelte but she would also enjoy what she was. No more hiding, as if she was ashamed of herself.

Rub their noses in it...

Her hair, air dried during her chat with Tina, fell in dark waves, softening the strong planes of her face.

Bright red lipstick, brighter than Tina's, made her mouth look scandalously seductive. Like her red lips could somehow balance the rest of her features that she'd told herself were far too stubborn for a woman. "This is too red. It will make everyone look at my mouth—"

"You married the Conti Devil. Of course they will look at you. Why not give them something gorgeous?" She looked Sophia up and down with a strange glitter. "How like my artistic brother to see what you so carefully hide, to see what no one else could."

A cold shiver snaked up Sophia's spine. "Luca is artistic?"

It was Tina's turn to look surprised. "Luca is a lot of things that I can't even keep track of. He works for CLG only to please Leandro. He has a personal..." She threw Sophia a startled glance. "Leandro even calls him our very own mad genius. Apparently, Luca's musical talents have no comparison."

"In a fond, useless sort of way, right?" Sophia asked, her heart thundering in her ears. "He lives off his brother and his family's fortune and dabbles in music, surrounds himself in beautiful things, that kind of artist?"

Her nose high up in the air, Valentina flayed her with her gaze. "That indulgent playboy thing he does—that's only one side of him. Your marriage to Luca, I know that it's an agreement for a few months. That he lets you use him in them. But still you should know that—"

"I'm not using him as much as we're using each other," Sophia interrupted, in prickly defense. Of course, the devil would try to come off as her savior in his account of their deal.

"Luca is not all he seems, Sophia."

Luca works at CLG, just to please Leandro.

Luca is artistic.

Luca was turning out to be more complex than any man she knew.

Sophia halted on the top of the stairs, trying to corral the panic spearing her belly. She tried to let very little in life unsettle her—in that way, she and Luca were alike, although with him, she supposed it was easier, more his natural state.

At least, that's what she'd assumed.

Even taking a couple of deep breaths didn't calm the furor in her veins. She couldn't get a grip on why it mattered this much.

All she knew was that she needed him to be what she and the entire world though him to be. A wastrel, a playboy. A man who cared for nothing and no one.

She appeared at the top of the curving marble staircase like a beautiful thought from his mind come to life. Luca felt a pressure on his chest, as if there was weight there, making it harder to pull a breath. He'd known, and guessed, she would be a revelation.

Oh, but what a revelation she was…

He heard the stunned whispers behind him, like a gathering wave rushing toward the shore.

The gasps, the *bellissimas*, the frantic reassessment of a woman they had all been duped into not seeing. Joy sang through his veins. The same he felt when he finished a piece of music or when he manipulated stock numbers into a pattern, into making sense. Like seeing a piece of art, unfinished and raw, come to life.

His joy in her was possessive and primitive. Suddenly, he didn't want anyone else to see her like this. He didn't want the whole world to see and covet this beautiful creature.

She was his, at least for now. He wasn't arrogant enough to think he'd created her but he'd discovered her, hadn't he? He alone had seen what Sophia was beneath that prickly nature and tough attitude. And tonight, she was a true reflection of the woman beneath—soft and yet formidably beautiful.

He wanted to pick her up, throw her over his shoulder, carry her away to his studio and lock the world away. He wanted to bury himself deep in her, until neither of them could breathe, until he was rid of this obsession with her. Until her mind, body and spirit, they were all only his.

He'd never chased a woman before. They all came to him. That he was chasing a woman who was determined to not be caught by him was perfect irony.

The bold, sensual lines of her body were a feast. The upper curves of her breasts swelled over the strapless bodice, beckoning to be savored. The silk followed the dip of her waist and the flare of her hips, lovingly touching everything he wanted to.

Their eyes met and the world floated away.

Her brown gaze raked over his face, lingering, assessing, almost frantic in its search. A clamor began in his veins as he stood at the foot of the steps and she took each step down.

Shards of light from the crystal chandelier caught at the

white beads on her dress. And glinting brown eyes. They didn't look average or dull right then.

They glinted with a fierce intention.

She looked at him as if…she wanted to peel off all the layers he covered himself in and reach inside the core of him. A shiver traveled down his spine.

As though she'd somehow bypassed the surface sheen of him—his looks, his charm. As though she hungered to know more.

But he couldn't reveal himself to her. He couldn't show the dirty truth of his birth, couldn't show her the devouring hunger for something more than he was allowed to have. Only then would this work. And he was so lust-riddled for her that Luca would have taken even a morsel of Sophia.

By the time she reached the last step, he'd calmed himself down. His practiced smile curved his mouth.

She raised a well-defined brow, all haughty arrogance.

He imagined that was how she commanded her team at work. One raised brow and one blistering remark from Sophia would probably send the staunchest soul scrambling to do her bidding. She wielded it with the same skill now, he thought, as if to start the evening with swords drawn.

All it made him want to do was kiss that brow. And probably her temple. Then that stubborn bridge of her nose. That lush, carnal mouth. Then he would bite, none too gently, on that defiant chin.

A line of fire swept along his nerves at the delicious path he could trace down her glorious skin. Very soon, he promised himself. Very soon he'd have her all rumpled and flushed beneath him, screaming his name. Only he would unravel all that strength she wore like armor. Only he would know the soft, vulnerable woman beneath.

He could have had her that day at the CLG offices but

he didn't want to see her regrets later. He wanted Sophia present and pleasantly ravished when he was through with her. "You look biteable, *cara mia*."

She looked startled at the compliment, looked away then back at him. Had he done this to her? Luca wondered for the millionth time. Had he shattered her confidence so badly?

"Nothing to say, Sophia?" he prompted softly.

"You disappeared for six days, three hours after we were married." Accusation punctured every word. "Even for the short-term agreement that our marriage is—" She bent toward him, her voice lowered to a husky whisper, for she was flushed with awareness. "You can't just rush me into a taxi and walk away. I ate a ton of chocolate and probably gained three pounds in three days. Do you know how many questions I've faced just from my family alone? Salvatore is desperate for your plans for Rossi's."

"But they are your plans."

"Yes, but he doesn't know that." She slowed down her words as if he was a bit slow in the head. Luca had never had so much fun just talking to a woman. "I told him Leandro and you are finalizing them. Damn it, Luca, there has to be some accountability even in this sham. We didn't even talk about where we'd live."

Her whisper caressed his jaw; the honeysuckle scent of her wafted over his nostrils, tightening every muscle and sinew. Acres of glowing skin taunted him. He shrugged, struggling to get a grip on the desire riding him. Hard. "I've never been a husband before, so you have to forgive me. I will check in with you every night at eight. *Si?*"

She sighed, and that made her glorious breasts rise and fall. "Wonderful. Now I feel like your parole officer."

"Will you put me in handcuffs if I violate my conditions, then?" he offered and saw her swallow visibly. "I could not give up control like that for any other woman, *bella*."

Desire shone in her enlarged pupils, a song sung by her hurried breaths. She licked her lower lip, took it in between her teeth, flushed and then pursed it into a thin line. As if she could hide her mouth.

Three hundred people waited for them and he was painfully hard.

Dio, when had lust ever taken control of him like this? Six days and nights he'd spent cooped up in his studio, and he'd still not gotten it under control.

He didn't like needing her so much. He didn't trust himself in this state for he'd never been in such before. He intended to ravish her out of her senses, not lose his own.

"If anyone asks," she said, coming to stand by him, "and by that I mean my mother, we aren't doing a honeymoon because I'm super busy. And you, too."

A tiny sneer curled her mouth every time she talked about his "work." Or lack of it, to be precise. It made him want to pull that snobby upper lip into his mouth and suck on it. He would do it, too.

He was going to need a little notepad to jot down all the numerous things he wanted to do to her. Suddenly, three months felt like a very short time in which to indulge his darkest fantasies with her, to drive her from his blood, once and for all. Especially because the woman was an obvious workaholic.

Urgency laced with his desire now and he ran a brave finger down her jaw. She swatted him away, like he was a fly. "You want her to believe this is a love match."

"Of course I do."

He nodded. "It'll probably break her heart to see her daughter doesn't have a romantic bone in her body."

She rolled her eyes. "Her daughter can't afford a romantic bone. Anyway, we steal all kinds of time during the day to see each other and get up to all kinds of…"

He raised his brows and waggled them. Warmth tinted her cheeks, the brown of her eyes gleaming bronze. Oh, she wanted him, all right.

"Afternoon sex—how delightfully imaginative, Sophia."

"I had to say something when she burst into my bedroom and demanded to know why I wasn't with my beloved husband on my wedding night."

"Why do you live with your parents? Doesn't that curb your nightly…activities?"

"I don't have any nightly…" She clamped her mouth tight, her face flushed. "I…work a lot of late nights and I like to keep track of what's going on with Sal and the company… It's just easier that way."

Again, a pang stole through Luca. Had he so thoroughly crushed her heart that she had no romantic notions left like any other woman?

"I do regret not spending our wedding night with you. Did you wait for me to spirit you away?"

She flushed and it lit a fire inside him. "You're absolutely cuckoo. I can't stay with my parents anymore. Not if I want to have some peace to work in the evenings."

"So move into Villa de Conti. Into my room. Alex and Leandro don't stay here all the time. Neither will I distract you, except when I feel like it. But—"

She hissed. The woman hissed at him. "Where were you? And why do you never answer a single call or a text?"

Luca raised a brow. No one ever asked him where he went and when he came back. Not even Leandro, after he had reassured himself that Luca wasn't going to self-destruct. The novelty of it was amusing and a little disconcerting.

"Here and there," he said, tucking her arm through his. "I can take society only in small doses." Which was more truth than he'd ever confided in anyone. "After the drama in the conference room that day, I needed time to recoup."

"Time to recoup?" she repeated, but with more consideration and less belligerent disbelief this time. Like she was thinking far too much again.

Dio, the woman really needed less thinking, worrying and planning and more ravishing in her life. A good thing he was so committed to it.

"*Si*. But now I'm ready to be your adoring husband." He smiled then and brought her to the huge ballroom.

He frowned as the music filtered through him.

A string quartet was playing. There was dynamics, articulation, wonderful fluctuation to the tempo but no soul to the music, no risk-taking except perfectly executed sharps and flats.

The lifelessness of it jarred through his head. A near compulsion ran in his veins to either yell for the music to stop or to stalk out of the room.

"Luca?" Sophia prompted.

Neither option was feasible, though.

Pasting on his megawatt smile—the one that had once driven a tempestuous young woman to avow love to him in the midst of her own engagement party—Luca turned to her. "Yes, *bella mia*?"

Light brown eyes studied him like he was a fly under a microscope.

Not the effect he intended in that perceptive face. Not even that endearing snort or roll of her eyes. "The music, you don't like it?"

Pure panic bolted through Luca for a second. As if every facade he had built over the years was being ripped away, leaving him utterly stripped of his armor. To face who he was, what he was capable of, in front of the whole world and see the horror he'd seen in his mother's eyes. He couldn't bear that look in Sophia's eyes. "Do you know what is happening with Kairos and Tina?"

"No," she said with an arched look that told him she saw through the ploy. It was becoming harder to pretend with her. Like his mask was slowly but surely cracking, giving her glimpses of him. "We spoke briefly, though."

She offered that tidbit reluctantly as if Kairos needed her protection. From Luca. She gave so much of herself to just a friend. "What did your friend say?" he asked casually, swallowing away the jealousy her friendship with another man aroused.

"That he'll be waiting to offer his support as a friend *when you leave me in pieces*, to quote him. I think Tina is causing major ripples in his life."

The goodwill he heard in her tone for his sister warmed Luca's heart. It confirmed his growing belief that Sophia had only ever wanted Kairos's friendship. "Why do you assume that?"

"Because he said 'We should have never gone near those *Contis*' in a pained voice before he hung up."

Luca laughed. "Good for Tina," he whispered in Sophia's ear and pulled her onto the dance floor.

CHAPTER SEVEN

TONIGHT, SOPHIA DECIDED, as she tried to not search the huge ballroom for Luca like a desperate, clingy wife, she could be a deer. Never a gazelle or a swan, but at least not a penguin—and unlike the last Conti party she attended, this time she was not a skunk.

She also, quite uncharacteristically, decided to put away all the things Valentina had said about Luca into her newly commissioned cupboard in her head. Tonight she wouldn't worry, plan, obsess, hide or hate. Tonight she would take a leaf out of her playboy husband's color-ful book and enjoy herself. She'd dance, drink and flirt with Luca, even. Maybe.

It was without doubt the best evening of Sophia's life. Suddenly, it seemed, all of society, the same people that had always looked on her with begrudgingly given kind-ness wanted to talk to her, invited her to posh luncheons and generally wanted to figure out how she'd corralled the Conti Devil.

Even knowing that Luca had been with half the women there, Sophia met a few women whom she'd love to get to know more. It was as if by lowering her own walls, she could see the others clearer, too.

And with a haunting clarity, she realized how right Luca was. She'd always been different in this strata of soci-ety, which in turn had made her defensive. Thirteen, un-polished but streetwise, she hadn't trusted that Salvatore wouldn't change his mind about keeping her; she'd decided from the first moment that she didn't belong there. Instead of risking rejection, she'd built a wall between her true self and everyone else. And then that episode of the bet had given her even more reason to hate them all. A shield, she realized now.

She danced with Luca, who was, of course, a graceful, slick dancer, then with Leandro, who to her surprise, told her she was welcome to come to him for any matter regarding the CLG board. Almost as if he'd been warned by his brother to not offend her.

Kairos was away on a business trip, thankfully.

Then there was Antonio, whom she'd avoided all evening. Sheer cowardice? Yes, but Sophia didn't want him to ruin her perfect evening.

Luca heard the snick of the door behind him and sighed. He'd come into Leandro's study, looking for the legal papers he'd asked Leandro's lawyer to draw up.

Without turning, he knew who it was. He'd been waiting for this confrontation all week. Dreading it. Loathing it.

For his grandfather was quite adept at turning Luca back into that needy, emotional boy he'd been during those hard years. Unable to manage his headaches and his restlessness, unable to sleep.

Cowardly as it had been, hiding out in his studio for a week had an added advantage to it. Antonio never ventured there. For one thing, Leandro had decreed long ago that it was Luca's space—sacred and safe and inviolate. For another, the studio was evidence that Luca had inherited more than just his father's good looks.

Antonio preferred to believe the Contis were invulnerable to anything from simple mood swings to brilliance-induced madness. Even after Enzo's life proved otherwise.

"You cannot give Sophia power over CLG stock or your seat on the board."

"I already have," Luca retorted. So there was at least no pretension to niceties to be had. He grinned; riling up Antonio was a task he'd enjoyed immensely even as an innocent child. "You have hounded us for years to marry. You even picked her as the perfect Conti bride. For the first time in my life, I agree with you. Sophia is perfection."

"You do this now only to mess with all of us."

Trust Antonio to know Luca as well as he did. "Sophia is my wife and has my best interests at heart."

Antonio scowled.

The thought that riled Antonio more than Sophia sitting on the board was a bastard, self-made man like Kairos taking his place at the head.

"Let her be your proxy. That controlling stock of Contis should lie within the family members."

Luca shook his head. "This fixation you have about the glorious Contis needs to be contained, *Nonno*. Haven't you done enough damage in the name of it?"

His grandfather flinched, backed a step as if Luca would attack him physically. Provoked as he'd been, Luca had never done that.

"All I ever did was to make sure your father didn't ruin our family name."

His head jerking up, Luca watched, stunned. Antonio had never offered a defense before. "You knew your son better than anyone. You hushed up so many little things he'd been doing all his life. You should have seen what he was becoming. You should have protected her…" He turned away, breathing roughly, mustering his emotions under control.

"You accept Sophia or you don't." He shrugged. "I've no problem cutting you out of my life, unlike your dutiful grandson Leandro. But she will continue on the Conti board even if I have to legally give her all my stock."

Rage filled Antonio's eyes. "She…married you because I suggested it."

"What the hell are you talking about?"

"Your affairs, your reckless disregard for our name… I was desperate. So I went to her. I thought she was the one woman who could handle you. I offered her a fortune if she brought you to the altar."

Luca smiled easily, more amused than affronted by Antonio's revelation.

Sophia had never hidden the fact that she'd do anything for her family. *Dio*, he knew with a faintly increasing alarm that half his attraction to her was based on that. It was her beauty, inside and out, that enthralled him.

He wanted Sophia untouched by the dirt in his family, away from the unrelenting grasp for power, the manipulations.

He wanted her to be only his, in his moments of light, separate from the dark, self-loathing part of him. But he'd not only brought her into it, he'd made her two powerful enemies already—Kairos and Antonio.

"You give her even a single share of Conti stock and I assure you, you will never see any of it back ever again. She might not be Salvatore's blood but she is as grasping as he is."

Luca couldn't care less, if he tried, about what Sophia would take from him. "Go to hell, *Nonno*. And say hi to your son while you're there."

"I did not offer her up, your mother, like a sacrificial lamb to him, knowing what he was." Luca stopped at the door, knuckles tightening on the knob. Antonio, for the first time in his life, sounded old. Frail. "He married her in secret, just like you did Sophia. He could be even more charming than you, when it pleased him. He claimed he was in love and I allowed it. I thought she would bring balance to his life…calm him. He was happy enough for a while. Your mother… *She married him*, Luca, of her own free will."

It had just struck eleven when Sophia realized she hadn't seen Luca's prowling gait in the ballroom for over an hour. The party was in full swing, champagne was flowing, couples still dancing.

Now she wondered if he'd disappeared. Again.

Apparently, Luca was like a mirage, present for as long as it took to entice and lure. Only to disappear the second you got close.

She had drunk three glasses of champagne with Valentina and her friends. Imagining the calories in three drinks, she'd delicately munched on glazed carrots and fruit from the scrumptious buffet.

The result was that she was mildly buzzed. She walked the perimeter of the huge ballroom, smiling and nodding at people she didn't even know. A woman pointed through the corridor with a perfectly manicured finger and a malicious smile.

Sophia's buzz evaporated as if someone had siphoned off the alcohol from her brain. Strains of husky laughter, of the female variety, greeted her from one open door. Luca's deep tones followed the husky laughter.

Ice slithered through her veins, rooting her there.

Run, run, run. Her brain issued flight responses as if the threat was fatal.

One breath and then another, Sophia forced herself to concentrate on just that. No, it was only her pride that chafed, she reminded herself. It was only sheer disbelief at the man's utter lack of decency. Her heart was stout and uninvolved.

They had no claim on each other, true. He hadn't promised her fidelity, this time or the last. But he wasn't going to show her up as a fool again.

One evening, *Dear Lord*, one evening was all he'd given her and already…he was smarting at the reins? She hadn't even demanded much of him.

She marched into the room, somehow managing to not fall on her face in four-inch heels.

The room was another lounge offering a view of Lake Como. It seemed there was an endless quantity of those at Villa de Conti but not enough distance from his family for Luca. Another fact she'd gleaned tonight. He'd happily offered her a place here because he never was here.

Was there anyone or anything Luca didn't need escape from?

A piano was the focal point of the room and on the bench, with his fingers desultorily playing with the ivory keys, was Luca. A stylish, contemporary chandelier threw patches of light onto his sharp profile.

The notes, though played slowly and haltingly, made up a haunting tune that plucked at Sophia's nerves. At some heretofore unknown place that had become arid from neglect.

A stick-thin blonde sat on his left on the bench, her silk-clad thigh flush against his, leaning over him to reach the keys. Which, from Sophia's angle, clearly showed her lemon-sized boobs—*thank you, Valentina, for that*—rubbing against his upper arm.

Luca stilled, all sleek and wiry strength, but Sophia didn't wait to see if it was in anticipation or in defense. *She'd had enough!*

Refusing to give in to the urge to run and grab the

blonde by her hair, which would give credence to her reputation as a shrew, she walked, sedately, toward the couple so seemingly immersed in each other that they didn't notice her.

"Please take your paws off my husband," she said with a sweet smile that hurt her cheeks. "Also, get out of our house."

The blonde had the grace to look ashamed at being caught out. Sophia fisted her hands, fighting the urge for violence. If *lemon-boobs* so much as smiled at Luca, she was going to lose it.

But the woman, perhaps sensing that Sophia meant business, stood up, slid out with a sort of gliding grace—*another damn swan*—and left the room.

Sophia counted to ten, went to the door, closed it and then leaned against it. Wrenching herself under control. Seeing the stick-thin woman sidling up to Luca… It ripped away her own self-delusions. Her pathetic reassurances.

God, when had she begun lying to herself?

When had she started believing that she was the Sophia that the world saw? How had she believed she could resist this man?

How had she convinced herself that she could take him on and come out unscathed at the end of these three months?

After his talk with Antonio—somehow, his grandfather managed to sink under Luca's skin every time, like an eternal monument to the darker aspect of his life—Luca had felt an overwhelming need to disappear. Antonio had known what his revelation, about Enzo falling in love with his mother, would do to Luca.

Caustic fear had beat a tattoo in his head that he was

like Enzo in this, too, that he was beginning to buy into his own pretense that all he wanted was fun with Sophia.

Had his father married his mother with the best intentions? Had he meant to keep his promise to love her and cherish her? Had he thought he was in control just as Luca thought he was with Sophia?

Had he been aware that he'd become a monster toward the woman he'd loved and yet hadn't been able to stop?

Rattled by Antonio's revelation, he hadn't gone back into the ballroom. To her.

He had not followed the blonde, nor touched her. But he'd been sorely tempted. Here was the way to delineate from the path his father had taken, the only way, it seemed, to retain control of this farce that was already pulling him under…so destructively simple—to touch the nameless woman, to sink into her inviting body and prove to himself that his defenses were intact.

That he was intact.

Only he had looked at the woman and bile had risen in his throat.

Would the ghost of his father haunt him here, too? Was it not enough he'd passed Luca his looks and his madness? Would he now drive him into humiliating Sophia?

Even for a farce, she would never forgive him. And that was one thing Luca couldn't bear.

He faced himself every night in the mirror and only self-loathing remained. He was never alone in his head; he was never alone when he looked in the mirror.

So he'd stopped looking and lived as best as he could. But if Sophia looked at him like that…*non!*

So he stayed. A little weak. A little undone. And a little ragged in his hunger for her. He wanted to be inside her. He wanted to learn everything there was to know about her. In that wanting, Luca realized there was no one else.

No one drove his actions, not stupid bets from which he thought he would protect her; no one whispered in his ears that this, too, was already set. Nothing but pure, scorching desire motivated him. No ghosts of mad fathers or distraught mothers. Nothing but Luca and his desire for her.

He was alone in wanting Sophia, like he wasn't in anything else.

She stood there, plastered against the door. Stubborn chin tilted high in challenge. Luscious breasts fell and rose as she battered at her temper, beating it into submission.

She would not win tonight, not against him, not against her own nature. She was his. The only question was how much she would make him chase her.

But it made sense, that she was different in this, too. That she demanded to be chased, demanded to be won over.

He wanted nothing less for his wife, anyway. Half turned away from piano, he raised a brow. "That was quite impressive. Alex would have nothing on you if you decide to be mistress of the manor, or the estate in this case."

He wasn't grinning, which was strange in itself. She'd have thought he'd love seeing her struggle with her temper. Second, there was an almost somber quality to his expression.

"You couldn't contain yourself for one evening?"

"So the claws are out?"

"Claws are all I have." Damn it, how could she be feeling this sense of betrayal? Had she not truly changed where it mattered?

No, she had. She'd grown a shell to keep the world out while hiding away herself. Even convinced herself that she didn't need or want anything or anyone.

Until this moment.

And she was truly seeing him this time, now that her

own naïveté was gone. Now that she didn't have to hide from herself. "No pretty feathers like your...*numerous friends*. Did you—"

"I have quite the craving for claws, *cara mia*, when they are yours. So stop threatening and start using them."

It was said in a voice taut with challenge. Not mocking or teasing. Shadows moved in his eyes where there had been nothing but insouciance before.

Sophia felt like she'd locked herself in with a predator. Gone was the easy, charming Luca that she could handle, if not admire. This man who looked at her with darkly hungry eyes was not he. He seemed edgier, less controlled. More real.

Back down, a voice whispered. *Back down and walk away.*

Sophia smothered that voice and shoved it out of her head. No force on earth could make her leave the room now. Not now, when maybe, there was a chance she could understand why she was so drawn to him. Why this... madness claimed her so easily when it was Luca Conti.

"I'm a novelty to you right now. But you can't help it, can you?" She couldn't let him bespell her with such words. "You attract women like you were honey and they bees. It's probably coded into your DNA—"

"She. Followed. Me." His nostrils flared. A pulse flickered in his sculpted jaw. Dark fire leaped in his eyes, a lethal warning. "It's a little disconcerting how much the idea of a quick screw with another faceless woman holds no appeal right now."

A sense of coiled danger radiated from him and the woman in her, instead of being terrified, wanted to court that danger. Wanted to sink under his skin and burrow there. Wanted to leave a mark on him this time, like he'd done on her.

Like a moth called toward a column of fire, she went to him. She straddled the bench, uncaring that it pulled the dress to her thighs. That it signaled so many things that she hadn't even realized she was ready for.

The air around them thickened. The party outside melted away. Slowly he moved closer. The masculine scent of him filled her lungs.

"You didn't discourage her. You didn't push her away. You sat there and let her paw you. You didn't act like a man who wants another."

Something gleamed in his eyes, a sudden, violent energy radiating from his frame. His hands curled around her nape and pressed none too gently. The rough scrape of his fingers against her tender skin zinged through her entire body like an electric charge. He dipped his head, and licked the rim of her ear. Arching her back, Sophia closed her eyes.

Deft fingers pulled away her chandelier earrings. Teeth nipped at her earlobe. A surge of liquid desire went straight to the place between her thighs.

Lights and stars behind her eyelids.

The soft tinkle of the earrings as they hit the marble floor threw her a rope toward sanity.

The devil was distracting her and how well. For now, his tongue was licking inside her ear. "You want a claim on me yet you refuse to even wade in?"

"If you're going to make a fool of me again, look into my eyes and admit it."

Her scalp tingled as long fingers sank into her hair and tugged hard. Exposing the curve of her throat to his mouth. Hot and open, he breathed the words against her skin. "You'll not make me feel guilty for something I haven't done."

His fingers were over her bare shoulders now. Stroking

back and forth, up and down, reaching lower and lower over her neckline. Her nipples puckered when he almost touched one on the downward trajectory.

He didn't.

She gritted her jaw hard to keep from crying out. From begging. She was sure that was what he wanted of her. Utter surrender. "Then why can't you just say 'I wasn't going to touch her'?"

She was desperate for him to say he had no intention. But he didn't. Because Luca never lied. The thought of his mouth on that blonde let out a feral anger in Sophia.

"Why set the rules for a game you're too cowardly to play?"

"It's not enough they chase you day in, day out? You can't let one go even when you're not interested?" His hands stilled.

Why couldn't he, for one evening, be hers and hers alone? "Is your self-worth that low? Is it their adulation you crave?"

His arms returned to his sides, abandoning her aroused flesh. He stood up from the bench and walked away. Panic bloomed in her stomach. "I think I've had enough of this drama, this marriage business, for one day."

Denigration, disinterest; it was a slap to her face. Carefully orchestrated to hurt her, to push her away.

There had been such amusement in his eyes that day at the board meeting. But underneath it, Sophia had also felt something else. And when she'd asked him about it, he'd distracted her.

It had definitely short-circuited her brain and stopped her from pestering him. But she now saw it all clearly.

Like an expert writer, he'd controlled the narrative at the board meeting—from their open shock and fear that he might start taking part in the Conti board politics, to suspense for his own shockingly deep reasons, and then, finally, to relief that it would be Sophia who would take his place.

Presented without that convoluted act, they wouldn't have tolerated her presence in their midst, much less welcomed her opinion. But by presenting her as an alternative to him and the mischief he could wreak, he'd forced them to accept her.

Luca was not without control.

Luca was control. He walked it like a tightrope. Every breath, every smile, every word, every gesture, it was all done with a purpose.

"You control what everyone thinks about you." *But why?*

CHAPTER EIGHT

HE GROWLED FROM across the room. This horrible noise that came from his throat, as if he were a ferocious but wounded animal and she the hunter.

She got off the bench and moved toward him.

"Your affairs are always splashed about. There's always some drama at some big party where you behave abominably. The only time one of your affairs wasn't splashed about was with me."

Now his hands were fisted by his sides.

Somehow, that disgusting bet had never reached anyone's ears. Of course, she saw the knowledge of it in those friends of his over the years, taunting and offensive, but no one had actually dared say a word about it to her face. Or spread it around that the chubby geek, Sophia Rossi, had fallen for the devilish Luca Conti.

"Will you give me sainthood now for *not* making a public spectacle of you, Sophia? Are you that desperate to justify this?" The sneer in his voice struck her like a stinging slap.

She bucked against his tone. But she didn't break and run away as he intended. She reached for him and leaned her forehead against his back.

Warmth from his skin radiated through his shirt. Hands shaking, she pulled his shirt out of his trousers. She sank them under it, frantic in her search for bare skin.

Skin like hot velvet, the muscles bunching under her

touch. She moved her questing hands around to his abdomen. Up and down, like he'd done with her. Ropes of lean muscles. And his heart thundering like a ram under her palm.

He was a study in stillness, in tension, in rejection. Every inch of him was locked tight. Another push and he would lash back at her, would break her.

But how could she back down now?

She'd always thought of his looks as the gateway to his arrogance, to his indulgent lifestyle, but now she wondered if they weren't just a mask, hiding so much more than they revealed. Every woman was blinded by his smile; every man wanted to have that natural, effortless charm he possessed; everyone willingly bought into the role he played.

She'd bought it, too, all these years. "You...you perform, Luca. For Antonio, for Leandro, for Tina, for the entire world. You have created this specter of you and you use it to keep everyone at a distance."

He turned and Sophia braced herself for his attack. She was learning him now, learning when there was a hint of the real Luca and when it was the abhorred playboy.

Something changed in his face, then. An infinitesimal tightening of those razor-sharp cheekbones. A thinning of those lush lips. A glitter in those eyes that were always quick with a smile and a comeback, usually laden with sexual innuendo.

He seemed to see straight through to the heart of her—the fears and desires, everything she kept locked away to get through hard life. "You want to have sex with me. Desperately. You crave it and yet, you can't give in to the inevitable. So you look for some redeeming quality in me.

"I shall never be the man for you, Sophia. So, if you are not going to screw me, at least stop pretending."

She blinked, dazed by how much he saw. How accurate he was.

Both of them were right. Both of them saw far too much of the other that no one else saw. And both of them were far too gone to back out now.

He was hers in that moment, Sophia knew. Against his own better judgment perhaps. And the fighter in her reveled in this victory, in wrenching a part of him away that no other possessed.

He could have been with a million women but it didn't matter. Not anymore. She had a piece of him no one else had.

She vined her arms around his waist. Tension thrummed in every line and sinew of his body. His fingers gripped her wrists tight enough to leave marks, intent on pushing her away. And she was the one who calmed now; she was the stronger one in this moment.

"What do you want, Sophia?"

She let her body slowly mold itself against his. "I want you to make love to me, Luca."

His thigh shoved in between her legs, his hands on her hips, pulling her tight and flush against him. He was long and hard and unbearably good against her throbbing sex. The jolt of heat that went through her was instantaneous, all-consuming.

Their eyes met and held. No challenges were issued. No deals were made. There was nothing but will and heat and the desire to burn together.

The neckline of her dress was tugged and pulled, her nipples left knotted and needy. Fingers busied themselves with the zipper at her side now. Breath was fire in her throat. Fever in her blood. The ripping sound of the zipper scraped against her nerves. Cool air touched her breasts and she gasped. Still no fingers where she needed them.

"Interesting." Hoarse voice. Clipped words through a gritted jaw. Muscles under her fingers clenched. Lean body pressing against her suddenly became tense. "No bra."

"Backless dress." Cool as a cucumber she sounded, while she was incinerating on the inside. A breeze touched her skin and she shivered.

"You are like hot silk. I'm going to lick every inch of you."

She closed her eyes and heard him shed his shirt.

Long fingers on her back—gentle, kneading, almost possessive as they pressed her toward him.

Breasts flattened against skin, hot and velvet-soft stretched taut over tight muscles. Nipples rasped.

Hands in her hair held her like that, their torsos flushed tight against each other. His shaft lengthened and hardened against her belly. Her sex clenched and released, hungry for his hard weight. Their breaths rattled in the silence. He took her mouth then.

Soft and slow, his kisses were like honey spreading through her limbs. Roaming hands touched her everywhere, restless and urgent, belying his tender kisses. "Sophia?"

"Hmmm?"

"I should very much like to be inside you now, *cara mia*."

Only now did she focus again on the people a little distance away. Music and laughter. She stilled at the prospect, her pulse in her throat. "Here? Now? They are all… right there."

Fingers tightened in her hair. "Now, Sophia."

It was his way or not. He did this to her on purpose. Pushed her into this corner where she realized how desperately she wanted him. Pushed her past her own boundaries into new territory. Like she had done with him.

He expected her to back off. He expected her to shrivel and hide and ask for the cloak of a bedroom and the dark night.

"Yes," she whispered, pressing little kisses to his chest. Flicking her tongue out, she licked the flat nipple and tugged it between her teeth. She pressed a trail upward to his throat and then closed her lips over his skin. "Here, now."

She felt the shudder in him then. And it was another small victory.

When he turned her, she went. Her will was not her own now. Her body was his to do with as he wanted. "Look at us, *bella mia*," he whispered at her ear.

Sophia looked. They stood in front of a gilt-framed mirror, below which stood an antique writing desk. Two chandeliers cast enough light to illuminate every inch of the huge room.

Light and dark, soft and hard, he lean and wiry and she…voluptuous and flushed, they were different in every way. Skin pulled taut against those sharp features, he was a study in male need.

But she was…she was the one who looked utterly erotic.

No rouge could make her cheeks that pink. Her pupils were large, almost black. Her mouth was swollen, unashamedly wide and seductive. The pulse at her neck throbbed as if someone had pulled at it like a string.

The turquoise silk hung around her hips, baring her breasts. Her nipples were plump, distended and meeting his gaze in the mirror, Sophia felt like she was scorched to the very core of her.

"What do you see, Sophia?"

She closed her eyes, her breath coming in short puffs. "I look indecent. Like everything I want is written all over my face."

"I see a woman whose curves and valleys are as complex as her mind. I see a warrior, a seductress, and I see a woman who hides her heart from even herself."

His words were just as powerful as his caresses. His fingers moved restlessly over her flesh, stopping here and there, pressing and kneading, but never staying. Learning and pressing all over—the rim of her ear, the line of her spine, the demarcation from her waist to her flaring hips, the crease of her thigh, the fold of her elbow...

There were so many other places crying for touch but he didn't touch her there. Her dress slithered to the ground and she stood in just her wispy lace panties. Then those were pushed down, too.

Sophia barely processed it when he turned her and then lifted her onto the table, as easily as if she were a china doll. The wood surface was cold against her bare buttocks as was the wall at her back. Yet, she was burning up all over.

Eyes wide, she watched as he kicked off his leather shoes and socks and then those trousers and black boxer shorts.

He hardly gave her a breath to savor the tall, darkly gorgeous form of his before he stood between her legs. Rock-hard thighs pushed her own wide, baring the heart of her to his wicked gaze. He took her hand in his, kissed the underside of her wrist and he pushed her palm against the heat of her.

Sophia jerked at her own touch.

"Are you wet for me, Sophia?"

Brown eyes widened into molten pools in her face, she looked so innocent.

So pure. So hot. So perfect.

The equation between them was changing and morphing, and all because he had oh so cleverly thought he could control himself. So full of himself, he'd forgotten Sophia was an explosive variable… Joke was on him. Rarely had anyone ever surprised him like Sophia did.

She saw far too much. She didn't tread lightly even in this; she marched in, banners raised, breaking walls down, determined to reach the part he hid from everyone.

It should have sent him running. Instead, here he was.

He was alone, always, where it mattered. It was the only way he could live. But that she saw him, even such a small part, in this moment, he didn't feel alone.

He felt a connection. He felt like someone knew the true him. He was weak enough to want to hold on to that for a little longer. Human enough to want to protect this. Just a little longer, he promised himself. No lasting damage this time, he'd make sure. Only pleasure for him and her.

"What?" she said, all spikes and thorns.

"Take your lovely fingers and dip them into your—"

She kissed him then and swallowed his filthily provocative words. Hard and fast, desperate and a little fierce, until he was deluged in sensation. "If my fingers would do just as well as yours, I wouldn't be here, now, would I?"

Acres of glowing skin, pouty, lush breasts, plump nipples begging to be sucked into his mouth, soft belly and a cloud of brown curls hiding the velvet heat of her. Wide eyes sparkling with desire and curiosity and possession. Such an irresistible combination of strength and vulnerability. So strict even with herself.

She was the most real thing Luca had ever seen.

His lovely Sophia. His lioness, his warrior, *simply his* in this moment.

He wanted to stay in that moment forever. But it could not last. Whatever it was that tugged at them relentlessly could not last. Because he was Luca Conti.

So he did what he did best. He reduced this moment of excruciating intimacy to nothing but animalistic sex. Into nothing but raw heat and primal possession.

"Is it not enough that I'm here, now, Luca?" she finally murmured. Her breath was stuttering. The pulse at her neck throbbed.

"No, I want more, I want everything, Sophia," he whispered, and felt her name move through him like a powerful invocation. "Tell me, did you touch yourself the night of our wedding?"

"Yes," she answered tightly.

"Did you finish?"

"No. It wasn't… I've never before…"

He bent and pressed his mouth to the upper curve of one breast. Her nipple rasped against his chest, taunting him. He gripped the table until his knuckles turned white, his erection pulling up tight against his abdomen.

But there was a keening pleasure in the need riding him hard.

Every inch of him felt alive. Every inch of him felt like a pulse. Denial, even for a few moments, was an alien concept for him. He had so very little, so he reveled in what he could have. He glutted himself on it.

Sexual gratification, once he'd stopped whoring it out for other things he'd needed desperately, was the most uncomplicated thing in his life. But now anticipation was like a drug, heightening every sense, a fever in his blood.

He opened his mouth and sucked on the tender skin. Hard. She was salt and desire and delicious on his tongue.

Nails digging into his shoulders, she convulsed against him. Not pulling away but pushing into his touch. So he did it harder. Her moan reverberated around them. "Touch yourself and tell me if you're already swollen. Take the edge off."

"No." Defiant chin lifted. Demand sparkled in her eyes. And a challenge. His erection lay stretched up against his belly now, engorged and ready. She moved her hands down the slopes of his shoulders to his chest. A pink nail scraped against his nipple. A finger traced the line between his pectorals.

He waited on a knife's edge, his breath bellowing through his throat.

Featherlight and fluttery, her touch made him ache. Everywhere in his body. He felt like that cavernous hungry thing that was his mind had taken over his body now. All he was was desire. As if answering his unspoken request, she touched his painfully thick erection.

No tentativeness, no hesitation, as she wrapped her fingers around the hard length and pumped him, up and down. He thrust into the circle of her elegant fingers and growled. Covered her fingers with his own and showed her how to do it.

"I'm a very fast learner," the sexy minx whispered as she stroked him just the way he liked it. Hands on the wall on either side of her, head bowed down, Luca closed his eyes and let the pleasure wash over him.

Honeysuckle and something of Sophia filled every breath of his. "In your mouth now, Sophia," he demanded roughly.

She would back off now. She hated being told what to do, didn't she? She hated anything that she thought made her weaker or exposed or vulnerable. And of all the people in the world, she'd never bow or bend to his commands—

He tensed as he felt the tentative slide of her tongue over the head.

Dio in cielo, she looked up at him, a wicked smile in her eyes and then her wide mouth closed over the tip of his shaft. His head went back; his vision blurred as he slid into the warm crevice of her mouth.

"Like that?" she whispered when she slid him out, her pink mouth wet, her nudity a luscious invitation.

Challenge and entreaty. Siren and slave. Desire and defiance. He had never seen a sight, heard a sound, more beautiful than her. For the first time in his life, he had no saucy retort, no way to reduce this into simple carnality. How when only Sophia and her wicked mouth would do?

She flicked her silky tongue over the slit and repeated her question. He saw stars, and sky and pleasure so blinding that he couldn't breathe. His hands sank into her hair, holding her in place. He had meant to disarm her; he had meant to somehow bring the chains of this thing between them back into his control.

Instead, he felt unmanned. Distilled to his essence, stripped of his armor.

Sweat dampened his skin as she continued her little ministrations with an eagerness and efficiency that pushed him closer to the edge. There was a fever in his muscles and he found it was he that was shaking now. Coming inside her mouth would be heaven but more than that, he wanted to be inside her, he wanted to see her face when he finished, he needed to drive her to this same…bewildered, out-of-control state she drove him to. He needed to be one with the incredible woman that was cajoling, stealing, wrenching away parts of him.

He pulled her up in a hurry of need, never having felt this sense of urgency, this potent urge to feel and revel. Pressed his mouth to one softly rounded shoulder before thrusting his thigh between hers. Against his muscular, hair-roughened thigh, she was like satin silk, a sweet haven.

"Luca?" she whispered, her eyes impossibly round in her face. The innocent but curious interest in it pounded in his veins.

Dio, was there nothing about the woman he could hold against her? Even in this, she shed her inhibitions, willing to go wherever he took her.

He delved his fingers into her folds to test her readiness. Pink spilled into her cheeks, a spectrum of browns in her eyes. She was slickly wet against his fingers. He stroked the swollen bud there and she jerked into his touch, demanding more. Twisting her chin, he kissed her plump mouth. "First, I need you like this, *cara mia*," he offered, before he took himself in hand and pushed into her wet sheath from behind.

The tight fit of her flesh stroked every nerve in him, a flare of heat pooling at his groin.

Her gasp, throaty and husky, tore at his nerves. Desire and lust, need and something more, everything roped together, all independent flames merging together and setting him on fire.

He met Sophia's eyes in the mirror and Luca believed everything in his life—every ugly thing he'd lived through—was all worth it, if it had brought him to this woman in this moment.

Sophia scrambled to keep a millionth of the wits she possessed, for she didn't want to miss a single moment of being possessed by Luca. She wanted every sense open, for she felt like she was turned inside out, every secret, every fantasy, exposed. In this position, she didn't know where she ended and where he began.

He had made it good ten years ago; even her virginal body huddled under the covers on his bed, had known it. Even as she had refused to let him turn the lights on, look at her in daylight. He'd handled her with tender caresses, reverent touches. However ugly his motives, he'd made seeking and giving pleasure a beautiful celebration, made her body feel like an instrument of pleasure instead of a source of shame.

But this was different. She was not an awkward girl who didn't know what to do with her suddenly voluptuous curves or the sudden, unwelcome, indecent attention from the same boys who despised her guts. She was not ashamed or confused by the demands or the reactions of her body.

Now she was Sophia Conti, the devil's wife, and it had already changed her. For better or worse, she had no idea but it was irrevocable. She owned him in this moment and she owned her sexuality.

Instead of distaste, as her expectations had been about this experience, she felt like she was an extension of him. Or he of her. Instead of shying away, she boldly raised her gaze and met his in the mirror.

Smoothly contoured shoulders framed her slender ones. Dark olive skin, stretched tightly over sinew provided an enticing contrast against her skin. Nostrils flaring, plump mouth pursed in passion, he was magnificent. And so was she, the perfect female counterpart to his masculinity.

Dark fingers moved from her hips, across her rib cage to cup and lift her breasts. He rubbed the turgid peak lightly, then moved to the other one. But even the gossamer touch was too much when she held his hard heat inside her. She clenched her inner muscles, the need primal, instinctual.

He pressed his forehead against her shoulder, a guttural growl coming from the depths of him. He didn't withdraw, but rotated his hips and again, Sophia clenched around him.

Sensation spiraled, inch by inch, until Sophia felt even the jerk of his hot breath against her skin like a stinging caress. They stayed like that, learning each other and testing all the different ways they could move against and with each other, their bodies in perfect harmony, the tension building to an unbearable pitch.

Sophia was afraid she would fragment into a million little pieces if she didn't climax soon. She held on to his forearms and pressed herself against his chest. "Luca?"

He licked the pulse beating frantically at her neck and spoke against her skin. *"Si, cara mia?"*

She arched her spine and pushed back into him, until he was more deeply embedded within her. Voluptuous pleasure suffused her at the hard length lodged inside her. Head over her shoulder, she looked back at him, half-delirious with need. "I'm dying here, Luca."

A quick stroke of his fingers at her clit made her groan wildly. "All you have to do is ask, *bella*."

She panted, struggling to form a thought. "Please, Luca…don't make me wait anymore. I need you. I need this like I've needed nothing in my life before."

Long fingers gripping her hips with such deliciously tight pressure, he pulled out of her. All the way before thrusting back into her again.

Sophia arched her back, threw her head against his chest.

Her breath came in soft little pants, her channel still trying to accommodate his large size. Every inch of her sex quivered at his stark possession. At the unbelievable pleasure pulsing up her spine. Her thighs shook under her, her knuckles white where she gripped the table.

There was no technique, no experienced caresses. This was raw, real. And so damn good that she thought she'd implode from the inside.

A palm on her lower back pushed her down and she bent, malleable and willing. Like heated clay in his hands, his to do with as he wished. Another hand quested toward her breast, plumping and molding.

Her entire body was like a bow for him. Long fingers pulled expertly at her nipple before moving down, down to tug at the sensitive, swollen bud at her sex again.

He thrust in again, his fingers and his hard length applying counterpoint pressure over her throbbing flesh to his rough, upward thrusts. Pleasure screwed through her pelvis again, nearly cleaving her in half. Sophia sobbed, screamed.

"*Dio*, Sophia," he whispered, before withdrawing and pushing in again.

The intimate slap of their flesh, the slick slide of their sweat-dampened skin, there was nothing civilized or romantic about what he did to her. He was not the experienced lover whose technique and skill in lovemaking was rhapsodized about in silkily whispered innuendoes. He was not the masterful seducer.

With her he was desperate, his thrusts erratic, raw, his need nothing orchestrated. With her, he was just a man who was as desperate for her as she was for him. He took her, savage and uncompromisingly male, and Sophia reveled in it as she climaxed in a wild explosion of pleasure. Fingers roughly holding her down, Luca thrust in a long stroke and then he was convulsing against her, a rapid stream of filthy Italian words filling her ears.

Sophia smiled and decided they were the sweetest words she'd ever heard.

CHAPTER NINE

"MALEDIZIONE, SOPHIA! Stay away from Antonio."

Sophia stilled as Luca, for the first time since she'd known him, raised his voice. He stormed into her brand-new but mostly bare office on the floor newly given over to displaced Rossi staff in the CLG offices in the heart of Milan's business district.

"I have kept every promise I made. What more could you want from that manipulative old bastard?"

Her newly appointed assistant, Margie—Sophia had never had an assistant or an office or even a stapler of her own before—stood staring at Luca, her mouth open wide enough to catch any stray butterflies. The woman had to be fifty and yet, like clockwork, a faint gleam of interest appeared in her eyes and she abruptly straightened out her shoulders, sucked her tummy in and thrust out her meager breasts clad in a thick wool sweater.

Bemused, Sophia turned to Luca. Who was completely unaware of anyone but her in the room. Like nothing but Sophia in the entire world had any consequence to him whatsoever. Whether meetings or parties, whether they were surrounded by a hundred guests curious about their marriage, or just at an intimate dinner with the Rossis— they hadn't socialized much with his family after the party, as if he wanted to keep her separate from them—Luca had the addictive habit of zeroing all his focus on her.

A woman couldn't be blamed for getting used to being

looked at like that. For misunderstanding fiery lust for intimacy, camaraderie for affection. For starting to believe in her own fairy tale that she could tie the charming, incredibly insatiable Luca Conti to herself.

Thick hair disheveled, sporting a stubbly beard along with the constant blue shadows, and dressed in a rumpled white Polo T-shirt and blue jeans, her husband looked like a thwarted grizzly bear. An utterly sexy and thoroughly disreputable version.

Her husband; she was calling him that far too frequently, even if in her head. She was becoming possessive, and she had no idea how to stop.

She sighed, waiting for the stinging awareness that took over her body every time he was near to lapse into a bearable pulse.

Luca, she'd come to learn in four weeks of their all-too-real-feeling marriage, was given to bouts of intense restlessness, which usually signaled that he was going to retreat, from which he emerged a day or two later and then followed furious social activity.

The restlessness wasn't violent or physical as she had learned the night she had found him sitting at the veranda, staring into the pitch-black of the night. It was in his eyes, in the detached, distant way he looked at everything around him, in the long walks he took around the estate as if his energy was boundless. In the warning that radiated from him to be left alone when he was in such a state.

But when he emerged from it, it was as if he hadn't been absent for hours.

She'd hurried back from work one afternoon to Villa de Conti, intensely relieved to see his bike and marched straight into the shower. A wicked glint in his eyes as he watched her, water caressing his hard body. "Please tell me, *bella*, that you came home for an afternoon quickie."

"This is not funny," she'd said then, fighting off his nimble fingers. He'd still somehow shed her of her linen jacket, leaving her in her stretchy camisole.

"Luca, this is serious."

His knuckles traced her nipples, tight and wet against the fabric. "I have a new appreciation for your starchy suits, *cara*. I feel like a kid unwrapping a present every single time I undress you. Only I know the treasure that is beneath."

"We can get help." Her hair plastered to her scalp and her mascara ran down her cheeks. For once, Sophia didn't give a damn how she looked. "I did some research and there are all kinds of new research to beat a drug addiction." It was the only thing that made sense.

To which he had replied that he didn't do drugs, kissed her and then proceeded to show her how *she* could calm him down. He had taken her then, against the wall, under the onslaught of water, with swift, desperate, hard thrusts, his mouth buried in her neck while she had halfheartedly and nearing climax, objected that this was the opposite of calming.

She had no idea what calmed that restless look in his eyes or why he needed to escape.

For a lazy playboy, the patterns of his days and nights were utterly demonic. Her mind reeled at the highs and the lows, at the chaotic clamor that seemed to be his life. She couldn't imagine surviving the erratic quality of his days and nights, the lack of structure… How could he get anything done?

He doesn't do anything, remember? a voice whispered. The shrew, as she had taken to calling that voice, the one she'd developed to distance herself from anything she sensed might make her weak.

But he hadn't once left her hanging.

He'd given her every bit of his attention in numerous meetings she'd had with Leandro and him to reinvent the Rossi brand as a subsidiary of CLG. First she had had to sell Leandro that Rossi was still a household name, prove that it had upped manufacturing standards in the last five years, a project she'd overseen personally. Then she'd shown him sales numbers proving that when it came to belts, men's wallets and other niche leather goods, Rossi was still beating CLG.

"And here I thought you were taking my brother on a ride," Leandro had said drily, pinning her with his implacable gaze.

Once Leandro had come on board, she had taken on Salvatore.

Which had needed a show of support from the Conti brothers—even Sophia had been impressed by the complementary strengths of the brothers, one silent but reeking of power and the other charming but persuasive. An agreement that CLG signed saying it would never do away with the Rossi name *and* endless business proposals, finally convinced Salvatore.

Though he'd grumbled when she'd suggested discontinuing any Rossi products that competed directly against CLG and instead develop a range of more complementary products. Luca had managed to convince Sal in a matter of minutes that Rossi's had sunk because it could never compete with CLG and yet kept trying to, a point she'd been trying to make for several years now.

An official press release said CLG was investing in Rossi's to make their renowned clutches, belts and other accessories, redesigned to meet the luxury standards of CLG and enter the market again.

Sophia had been appointed as the director of overseeing the first production line from design to marketing. An appointment that hadn't filled Sal with confidence until Luca had winked at him and said, "Good to keep someone from your side in there, Salvatore. You can't trust my brother or Antonio completely."

When she'd thanked him with a kiss on his cheek, he'd grinned wickedly. "I love this whole man behind the woman concept with you, *bella*. Although I like being above and under you, too."

Leandro had watched them with something like shock in those gray eyes.

She'd hidden her face in his chest, her throat dangerously close to tears, and pretended to find his lascivious comment obnoxious. He'd warded off the emotional moment with humor. As always. But Sophia didn't believe that Luca was shallow anymore.

The truth was that he was weaving himself into every part of her life, into her very being. All too frequently now, Sophia wondered what she would do when he was gone from her life.

Who would she cry to about Salvatore? About the entire species of men? Who would make her laugh? Who would drive her to the edge of ecstasy? Who would hold her in bed as if she were the most precious thing in the world?

She ran a hand over her stomach, as if she could calm the panic. "Hello, Luca. Do you like my new office?"

He pushed a hand through his hair and walked around, his long, sinuous body overpowering the space immediately. Then he turned to her with a frown. "You should have one with a nicer view. Not the one looking at the back alley."

Smarting at his dismissal, Sophia said, "I don't care about the office so much, Luca. Salvatore has agreed to let me pitch the idea for—"

"You should care, Sophia. As long as you act like you

deserve only this much, that's all you get. All these years, you have let Salvatore box you into a position that you were overqualified for. You—"

"I was learning the business, every part of it."

"What is your excuse now? Why are you still pussyfooting around him?"

"Too many things have changed in the past few months. He needs—"

"He needs to hear you say that this is your company as much as it is his. That you're the best thing that's happened to it in the last decade. Have you decided to neatly play in the boundaries you set for yourself, afraid that if you push, he might tell you you're not his daughter after all? Have you decided that is all you could have, Sophia?"

It felt like the ground was melting away from under her feet. Like something she hadn't even seen was ripped open for everyone to see.

Like she was standing naked in the midst of a crowd, her worst nightmare, all her toughness, her strength, her pride, mere illusions. She was that little girl again, desperately pretending that she was not scared at the prospect of leaving the only home she knew. Her throat felt raw. "You don't know what you're talking about."

He reached her then and the tenderness with which he clasped her jaw was enough to break her. She should hate him, this man who saw past everything, but she couldn't. "What will you do when I'm done with you? How will you convince Sal of anything then?"

All Sophia heard in that little outburst was *when I'm done with you*. Her entire world felt colorless, lifeless, in that sentence. "I haven't thought that far ahead."

"Then you aren't much of a planner, are you?"

"Wow, is this how you are when you don't sleep for a few days?"

He ran a hand through his hair in a rough, restless gesture. "No, I'm like this because I found out that you're making secret deals with Antonio. Again."

"*Again?* What do you mean?"

"I know he's the one who put you up to marrying me."

"He told you?"

"*Si.* So tell me what are you doing meeting with him in secret in the middle of the night? Alex saw you."

"So she told on me?"

"She thought I should know that my wife is continuing negotiations with my wily grandfather, *si.* Alex despises Antonio as much as I do."

Sophia knew there was a guilty flush climbing up her cheeks. "I just… I told him to stop bullying Salvatore, and every one else, that's all. He and his gray wolf pack."

The sinuous lines of Luca's face became still. "You did?"

"Yes. It's high time someone stood up to him. He plays with everyone—Kairos, you, me, Tina. Only Leandro seems to escape his clutches. I might have gone a little overboard, I was so angry about it."

"How overboard?"

"I told him if he wasn't careful, I would send him and his pack out of the board with their tails tucked between their legs."

But Sophia had approached Antonio only to ask about Luca, for she knew Leandro could never be induced to talk about his brother. The bond between the Conti brothers, as she'd guessed, was inviolate, for all they were diametrically opposite in temperament.

What haunted Luca? Was it a medical condition? Why weren't the Contis, with all their bloody wealth, doing something to help him?

With each passing day, she felt as if she'd go mad if she

didn't understand what drove Luca. It felt like an invisible wall was already pushing her away from him.

For a man who gave every outward proof of despising Luca, Antonio hadn't betrayed a single thing. Only stared at her as if she was an apparition that had appeared out of thin air. Beyond frustrated, Sophia had vented the anger, the fear that was slowly consuming her from within.

She took Luca's hand in hers, the long, elegant fingers as familiar as her own now. She'd never known this intimacy, this sort of connection with another person, in her life. Not even her mother. Somehow, Luca had become a part of her own makeup. "I would never whisper about Valentina to another soul."

"He told you about Tina?"

He sounded so disquietingly furious that the words poured out of Sophia. "I would never betray your family in that way. I would never ever pull the rug like that from anyone, much less Tina. I know what it feels like to not have a name. To not know where you belong. You believe me, don't you, Luca?"

Luca stared at Sophia, the wistfulness in her tone calming the anger inside. His grandfather really needed to keep his mouth shut. Sensing the wariness in her tense stance, he pulled her into his arms. "You fight so ferociously for Salvatore, I forget you're not even his, Sophia. Tell me more about you."

"There's not much to tell. My English father died before he could marry my mother. She became the village pariah when she found out she was pregnant. She moved to Milan to find a job and to raise me. For a long while, we struggled to make ends meet. She wasn't really suited for any kind of job. So she cleaned houses. Big, posh houses, and I tagged along whenever I could."

"It made you determined to succeed."

"Yes. I wanted to go to college, I wanted a career. Luckily for me, I did well at school. I never ever wanted to have just a glass of milk for dinner. Can you blame my fixation with cakes and pastries? Diets are torture for me, to deny myself food when we didn't have much for so long, my body revolts at the very idea."

He buried his nose in her hair, tenderness enveloping him. "Then why do you?"

"It's okay, I'm coming to realize that I'll never be stick-thin, anyway."

"You're a fighter, *cara mia*. It lights you from the inside out."

"That's what good-looking people say to the ugly ones," she retorted instantly.

They burst out laughing. She hid her face in his chest. It felt as if his lungs would burn if he even tried to contain this.

Dio, what was he going to do with this woman? She made him laugh like no one did. She cast such bright light onto everything she touched. She made him so protective of her, as if that was his only reason in the world.

She made him ache and want with a fierceness he had never known. And the days were dwindling down slowly but surely. Like sand in an hourglass. There was nothing he could do contain it. He had let her see more of him than anyone else.

Every moment he spent with her, he was living an entire lifetime in it.

Everything was becoming twisted, twined together so messily that he wasn't able to keep it separate. Different compartments for different activities, different emotions used in different places, some never to be indulged in; that was his life. There was order in his chaos.

And he didn't know how to stop it. How to harden himself against her. How to remind himself that he could not have her for more than a few weeks.

"When I was thirteen, Mom met Salvatore. He fell in love with her. I wasn't sure he'd want her with me tagging along. So I…" Her voice wavered here and suddenly, a pushing pressure came upon Luca's chest.

He stroked the tight line of her mouth. "What did you do, Sophia?"

"I decided to remove myself from the equation. I packed a bag with two pairs of clothes, took enough money for bus fare, packed two sandwiches and a banana—more than I should have, I know, but I didn't know when I would be able to eat again and I knew Sal would take care of my mom, so I ran away."

Luca's throat felt raw, imagining a barely grown girl disappearing like that. "*Christo*, Sophia! What were you thinking?"

"She needed him more than I did. I couldn't bear to see her like that anymore, shriveling to nothingness, working all hours just to get me through school."

Thirteen, she'd been only thirteen. And so brave. He didn't mistake for a second that it hadn't cost her. That it hadn't left a mark on her. That it hadn't changed her in ways even she couldn't see.

Seeing the best or worst of yourself at such a young age, it set a precedent. Now she thought it was up to her to solve her loved ones' problems.

How could Salvatore not see how precious her loyalty was? For the first time in his life, Luca offered what he always took. What he craved like he did air. Comfort, touch, companionship. That she'd revealed a part of herself, a part he was sure no one knew, made him feel as if he had gained a treasure.

Hooking his hands on her hips, he pulled her into his lap on the settee. She jerked first, as if to reject the embrace. "Sometimes, I dream the bus left with me in it."

"You're here, *tesoro*. In my arms."

Something fierce rose inside Luca. He would ensure she never had to do something like this, he promised himself, that she'd never have to sacrifice her happiness for the sake of her family. He'd look out for her.

Her thighs bracketed his as he enfolded her within his arms. He nuzzled her hair, needing to touch her as much as she needed it. Settled as she was snugly against him, it wasn't lust that she invoked in that moment. But something far more tender, and rooting.

"What happened then, *cara*?"

She inhaled noisily. "They both came after me. Mom said she didn't want a man who didn't accept me, too. Salvatore went on his knees in front of me, I mean, can you imagine the scene? Rough, abrasive Salvatore being gentle… He looked me in the eye and told me he was my father from that day. He's always been kind to me."

Luca's respect for the man rose. "Except when he arranged your marriage."

"He's traditional. He thinks women, including his shrewish daughter, need to be protected. I was ready to marry whoever he pointed at. Only the man he picked found out that I'd given up the prize to you and refused to marry me. At least, he never told Sal why." Uncertainty threaded through her tone, her soft body tense in his arms. "It was you, wasn't it? You warned them all."

Suddenly, it felt like the most important thing in the world to Luca that Sophia didn't think him cruel and heartless. Or shallow. Or a useless waste of space. Or a man who was incapable of caring. All the things he'd made himself to be became an unbearable burden when it came to her.

"If I had known what Marco intended, I'd never have sent him there. I…"

That she burrowed into his arms instead of withdrawing, his breath seesawed through him. She felt like warmth and generosity, strength and softness, the woman placed in the universe, it seemed, to balance him.

Forehead tucked into his neck, she hid her face, but the quiver in her words was still there. "Why did you take part in that bet? I can't just believe you could knowingly take part in someone's humiliation. At least, tell me it was that dumb need to prove yourself among them. Tell me I was incidental, Luca and not the—"

"Hush…*cara mia*, it was nothing like that. Believe me, I…I never meant to hurt you." When she became stiff in his arms, he forced her to meet his eyes. For once in his wretched life, to show the truth, instead of hiding behind shadows. "When I heard about the bet, I was furious. But there was no way to dissuade that lot. So I joined in. Only to protect you from their stupid ploys. Instead, I got involved with you. Those weeks we spent together… It was incredible.

"But I was barely a decent man, Sophia, much less worthy of you. I had to end it. So I told them I had won the bet. Marco was supposed to see you, and then walk out quietly. But that scoundrel humiliated you. You were never supposed to know about the bet.

"When I found out what he did, I smashed his cell phone. Warned them I didn't want to hear your name again on their lips. I knew you would be cursing me to hell, which was for the best."

CHAPTER TEN

FOR A FEW SECONDS Sophia felt dazed.

He'd meant to protect her. Knowing that he'd fallen for that indescribable pull between them, she felt light. As if the invisible boulder of shame and humiliation and self-doubt she'd been carrying around her neck for a decade had been lifted away.

It didn't matter that he'd ended their relationship like that. It didn't matter that he'd run away with a lover, in an effort to sever whatever they had shared.

It only mattered that those weeks had been special to him, too.

"I did for a long time," Sophia replied. Had a woman ever been so happy to find out the real reason of why she'd been dumped? But then their whole relationship was strange. "I cursed you, and for a really crazy period there, I even considered having some voodoo done on you. You know, have your manhood shriveled or some such."

"Manhood?" he said, the word full of mockery.

She could feel her cheeks burn but for the life of her she couldn't say the *p* word. "Fine. Your instrument of pleasure."

He laughed. She loved making him laugh. It was quickly becoming the most favorite thing about herself. Second in that quickly growing list were her previously hated breasts. Anything that could fuel those dark fantasies he kept whispering in her ear proudly earned that place. "Your mighty sword? Your shaft of delight?"

Tears rolled down his cheeks and he pulled her on top of him until she was straddling him. "Say it, Sophia."

"I don't want to."

"You prude."

Her chest hurt for the laughter bursting through her. "I'm a liberated woman who has no qualms about her sexual needs. Now, go back to the house, pretty yourself up and be ready to satisfy me when I come home tonight. See?"

"You're going to pay for it."

"I'm not a prude."

"Then say it."

"Luca, that word is so clinical and dull for the fantastic, mind-blowing things you do with it. I will not call the most awesome thing in the world that horrible name."

The most debauched man on the face of the earth blushed then. His nostrils flared, his mobile mouth pursed and there was such delight in his eyes.

Sophia giggled.

He hugged her then. Tightly and like she were precious cargo. "You, *cara mia*, are going to be the death of me."

His hands reached for her shoulders again and Sophia exhaled in shuddering relief. Suddenly, she couldn't imagine going another minute without his hands on her. With urgency that was part desperation and part fear, she kissed his mouth.

"Just stay away from Antonio. And Kairos and Leandro, too, for good measure. I don't trust any of them."

"Not even your own brother, Luca?"

"Leandro will not harm you, true, but he's the master of manipulation. I don't want to take a chance."

She traced the bridge of his nose with a finger, warmth

settling in all the neglected pieces of her soul. "You're doing that thing, Luca. That thing that I love you for not doing."

Luca was sure his heart had stopped for a second. "What is it?"

"Other than what you're doing now?" the minx whispered saucily against his mouth.

He laughed. "What is the other thing, then?"

"You never used to tell me what I could or should do. You only used to say *get on with it, cara mia*. Now you are like the rest of them. You want to change me."

If there was ever a warning put so perfectly, Luca didn't know what it could be. He was becoming someone else with Sophia. He had had so many lovers and he'd never been possessive of anyone.

And yet, with Sophia, the urge to protect, to possess, was primal.

He knew why, too. She made him like himself. Gave him a different definition. Beyond what he'd been predetermined by genes and history.

He saw someone else when he looked in the mirror these days. He saw the man Sophia saw. The man who evoked that slow but saucy smile when her gaze flicked to him across the boardroom, the soft flush that dusted her cheeks when he passed by and made sure he touched her amidst a crowd, the man who gave her that flushed and well-loved look when she came, the man she'd held tight when she was finally on her way to saving Rossi's from sure ruin.

The man she looked at with such fierce protectiveness when she thought he didn't know. The man she kissed when she thought he was finally asleep after seeing him walk around like a ghost. Just for her peace of mind, he'd pretended a couple of times, stayed with her until the worry for him cleared from her brow.

It was addictive, exhilarating, how she made him think of himself.

"I would never change you, Sophia. But Antonio has a habit of ruining things. And I won't always be here to shield you from him or his pack."

That was what had bothered him since Alex had told him. In his reckless need to have her, he'd made her a lot of enemies and robbed her of her one true friend.

"Then why not tell him that my advisory capacity for your stock is only temporary?"

Because he didn't mean for it to be. The idea took root, digging deep.

"Luca…"

"Now for the real reason I came here," he said, filling his hands with her breasts.

She laughed, her eyes wide, her breath already erratic. A voluptuous Venus. "Margie—"

"Margie cleverly disappeared."

"Luca…this is my first week working with members of CLG, in a new office. Your brother, your grandfather, they all work here… We can't just…"

"The question is…do you want me, *cara mia*?"

"Yes. I'm a little ashamed that I always want to say yes, Luca. It's setting a bad precedent between us, isn't it?"

"There's nothing to be ashamed about, *tesoro*. We… Our bodies were made for this…" He snuck his hands under her blouse and reached the hard tip. Lifting one lush breast, he took the nipple in his mouth through the silk of her blouse. He bit on the distended tip and suckled.

A moan fell from her throat. She muttered something filthy. He'd never been so hard and so amused at the same time.

Luca pulled her skirt up, thanked the man who invented

thongs and touched her between her legs. She was utterly ready for him.

He pushed his fingers up and down the crease of her folds, played with the swollen little bud there, keenly aware of every hiss of her breath, of every shift in her body.

"Oh, Lord…" Tiny shivers shook her frame. He buried his face in one shoulder and tasted the salt of her. Sweat made her skin soft and damp.

"I wish you would say my name. It is *my* fingers deep inside you." He hooked his fingers and swirled them in tune with his words.

She rewarded him with a groan that sent a flare of heat over every inch of him. His erection pushed against his trousers. "Oh…you…*arrogant, conceited*… Luca…I need…"

He took the tender skin between his teeth and suckled while he penetrated her lush heat with two fingers. She convulsed against him, pushing her wetness against his fingers. "What do you need, *cara mia*?"

"You. Inside me. Now."

Lifting her up, he unzipped his trousers and freed himself.

Cheeks flushed, irises dilated, wide mouth bee-stung, she took him inside her. Luca felt a deeply primal satisfaction as he glided deep into her invitingly slick heat. Like a glove, her flesh closed around him and his head went back with a groan.

Her hands in his hair, Sophia stared at him with a startling intensity.

For a few seconds, they stayed like that, unmoving, gazing into each other's eyes. Just reveling in the beauty of the moment, the raw intimacy of it.

He didn't shy away from it. Neither did she. And Luca

knew it was getting out of hand. This was not merely good sex. This was not even just fantastic sex.

This was Sophia and he creating something special, something he'd never known before. The sum of them becoming more than their individual selves.

She kissed him tenderly, as if she was aware of what the moment meant, too. As if she, too, was shaken by the wild beauty, the palpable magic of it.

And then because they were so desperate for each other, because they were greedy for what they could give each other, she moved over him.

That first slide of friction was unbearably good.

"Rotate your hips on the way down," he ordered hoarsely.

"Your wish, *my master*, is my command." Hands tight on his shoulders, she did as he said. The movement rubbed her breasts against his neck and chest, rubbed him against the slick folds of her.

"Oh, Luca..."

Loosely holding her hips, Luca let her set the pace. "I know, *cara mia*." Measly words for the fever spiraling in their blood.

Confident now, she moved faster.

Tense and fluid, demanding and supplicant. Her moans became keener, louder, signaling she was getting closer to the edge. When she arched her back on her way down, he took her mouth with his, swallowing away her cry. Not to mollify her, but because he didn't want anyone else to hear how she sounded in the throes of falling apart.

She was his, her cries, her moans, her sensual demands and her husky whimpers, *all his*.

He thrust up, fast and hard, as her muscles milked him. Climax beat at him in relentless waves, a fire breathing through his veins. Sated and in good terms with himself and the world, he wondered why in hell their marriage had to be temporary.

What was the harm in continuing like this?

They both knew what the score was. Maybe this was his chance at companionship. He was so tired of waking up with women he had no intention of knowing. Never standing still. Even if she only knew a fraction of him, it was still more than anyone else did.

He pushed damp hair away from her forehead and pressed his lips to her temple. She snuggled against him, and Luca, for the first time in his place, felt completely at peace with himself.

CHAPTER ELEVEN

Sophia woke up with a start, something sinuously haunting seemed to have lodged in her veins, and peered at the unfamiliar surroundings. This was not the high, luxurious bed that she had taken to falling into in exhaustion the past month. The walls were not the pale cream, the drapes not the sunny yellow that Luca pulled away a couple of times, calling her a lazy cat. No great Conti wealth peered down from paintings on walls.

This was not the bedroom in Villa de Conti where Luca had joined her at all hours of the night in the past month— once it had been 3:00 a.m. and she wasn't sure who was more shocked, she, to see him emerge buck naked and dripping wet from the shower, or he, to see her sneak into the bedroom with her laptop and a sliver of red velvet cake from his niece Izzie's birthday party.

What had followed had been a crazy night of cake, champagne, a wet Luca and the bed.

Here, the walls were bare and the general impression of the room was utter chaos. The bed on which she lay was the only surface not covered in books and loose paper. Realization came slowly to her sore, sated body—this was Luca's studio. The only familiar thing here was the unmistakable scent that their bodies created together—the scent of sex and sweat and raw intimacy.

When she hadn't seen Luca in a week, nor heard a word, she'd invaded Leandro's office, demanding to know where

Luca was. With each passing day that she hadn't seen him, a frenzy of fear and worry had built inside her.

Kairos had been defeated in his pursuit to be CEO of CLG, leaving the position empty, and wouldn't even talk to her. Rossi's financial future looked better than it had in a decade. And Luca had thoroughly ravished her, his eagerness and passion chasing away her own inhibitions, not that she'd need much persuading once she'd seen past his facade.

Now that all his goals had been achieved, was he done with their marriage? The memory of how easily he'd walked away last time—whatever the reason—wouldn't leave her alone.

This time, she wanted him to say to it to her face.

She wanted closure if he was ending this. But more than that, she had enough of the game he played with the world. She wanted to face the real Luca. She wanted the truth of him, a part of him that no one else knew before she let him finish this.

Grudgingly, and with warnings, Leandro had driven her to the high-rise building that was only a few miles from the Conti offices. He'd accompanied her to the door.

If Luca had been shocked to see her standing on the threshold of his apparently inviolate space, he'd hidden it quite thoroughly. Naked torso and blue jeans molded to hard thighs, he'd sent her heart thudding. Dark hair all kinds of rumpled and a gaunt, introspective set to his features that she'd come to recognize as a need for solitude, he looked utterly delectable.

Arms folded, Leandro waited and watched them, a faint tension emanating from him. He didn't know what Luca was going to do. With her, she'd realized with a sliver of alarm running up her spine.

But even the thought that Luca could harm her was ludicrous. Strip her armor and distill her to the core of her, yes. Hurt her with reckless or cruel intent, no. She was as sure as the wild beat of her heart in her chest, like the flutter of a trapped bird.

"Hello, Bluebeard," she'd tossed at Luca then with a manufactured sauciness, and ducked under his arm, refusing to give him a chance to turn her away.

She didn't care that he hadn't even sent her one of his teasing, quirky texts in a week. That he didn't want her infiltrating whatever it was that he guarded so fiercely. She didn't care that in a matter of weeks he wouldn't want her in his life.

Already, there were warning signs. At least once every day, he reminded her the days were counting down, a calculating look in his eyes. Afraid that that one question would start a conversation she was in no way prepared for, she'd evaded him. She didn't care that slowly her heart, her emotions, her very soul, were slipping away from her. That she had lost all rationality about this thing between them. That for the first time in her life, it wasn't her career or her family's future keeping her up at night.

That had been at seven in the evening. He'd closed the door and turned to look at her, a devouring light in his eyes. Slowly relief gave way to other uncomfortable emotions—awkwardness and anxiety. They stood there staring at each other, both aware that a line had been crossed.

She didn't say, *you didn't call in six days.*

He didn't say, *you're acting like a clingy wife.*

When he reached her and cupped her jaw, she'd almost wept with relief. "You look exhausted."

She'd leaned into his touch, too far gone to even think of hiding her need for him. "Didn't sleep much the last few days. I don't know how you do this all the time."

His fingers covered her nape; his nose rubbed against her jaw. "How did your proposal go?"

She smiled against his shoulder, the familiar scent of sweat and soap and skin anchoring her. "It went very well." Nuzzling into his skin, feeling the thud of his heart under her hands, only then did the clamor in her blood calm. "With you on my side, I can even achieve world domination."

"Bene."

He'd picked her up then, as if she weighed nothing, and declared they'd go to bed. For sleep, first, and then other things that they both were in desperate need of, he'd declared throatily against her hair.

The scrape of her skin against the soft cotton told her she was still utterly naked. Instinctively, she pulled the duvet up toward her chin and turned to her side.

The pillow didn't even bear an indentation—he hadn't slept at all. Whereas she'd been thoroughly wiped out. Like a possessed man, he'd driven her to the edge again and again. He'd always been playful before, even when he'd made her do the wickedest things.

Laughter colored everything they did. Even when they were hungrily going at each other like rabbits. He said the funniest things and found her no-nonsense outlook humorous. Except tonight.

A price, he'd said, scratching his stubble against the tender skin of her inner thigh, when she'd begged him to stop. She had to pay a price for coming to Bluebeard's lair. And even with his wicked mouth at the core of her, and her throat raw from screaming his name, Sophia realized she'd already paid a price.

A crisp breeze flew in and she shivered, the last remnants of sleep chased away. Her eyes adjusted to the darkness punctured by the moonlight through the floor-to-ceiling glass doors. Wrapping the sheet around her, she walked to them and peered through.

It was pitch-black, the darkest time of the night, just before dawn.

She went into the bathroom, washed her face. Sneaking into his closet, she found a dress shirt and pulled it on over her underwear.

That was when she heard it.

The strains of music. That same tune he'd played haltingly, almost lazily, that night of the party. *It* had woken her.

Heart beating a thousand times faster, she went, her entire being tugged as if by a rope. Just as she reached the door and pushed it open, the music stopped.

No, no, no.

Like a wisp of smoke she'd been chasing for hours in some deep, dark forest but forever lost now. Only an echo of it lingered, in the very stillness of the air, in the loud thud of her heart.

"Play it again," she demanded, leaning against the wall, her voice loud and uneven.

Skin stretched taut to stiffness over muscle, his bare back was a map to his mood. His hands still on the keys, he didn't turn around. "I didn't realize you were awake."

Sophia walked a couple more steps into the room and halted. An urgency was building in her, as if she was at a crossroads that would change her life. "You gave it your best shot to wear me out, I know. What did you think to do once I fell asleep? Smuggle me out of here? Drug me and take me back?" For the life of her she couldn't keep the accusation out of her tone. "Even you, with your unending energy and libido, can't keep me in that room forever."

He turned and leveled a look at her over his shoulder. "You're developing a sense for drama."

"Dramas and masks are your forte."

He raised a brow then. Masculine arrogance dripped from the lazy gesture. Her breath held, Sophia waited, for he could rip her apart in that moment. It was the same look he'd worn when she'd said he thrived on control. He would have decimated her then, too, but Sophia had backed off. Stalled him by offering herself up.

Only a few steps between them but it could have been an oceans-wide chasm. A stranger looked back at her. Not the one who laughed with her. Not the one who'd moved inside her like he was an extension of her own body.

She stayed at the door, afraid of breaking whatever tenuous thing had built between them. Afraid that if she walked out the door tonight, it was all over.

"Please… Only once. I…would give anything you ask of me to hear it once."

Something akin to shock flashed in his eyes.

She forced herself to smile, to act as if her heart wasn't rearing to leap out of her chest. As if she weren't standing over some abyss, ready to fall in. Fear and hope twisted into a rope in her belly.

"I…have never played for anyone. Not even Leandro and Tina."

"I don't give a damn. I want to hear it."

He didn't blink at her outburst. He didn't reply. He just turned back to the piano. Silence reigned for so long that Sophia was sure she had lost.

But then long fingers moved on the keys. The tension melted from his shoulders and back. He became fluid, an extension of the instrument. He forgot her, Sophia realized. There was no one but him and the tune that flew from his fingers.

Slow, haunting, full of a soul-deep pain. It continued like that, sneaking insidiously into every pore, every cell, until Sophia felt the haunting desperation as her own. It was gut-wrenching, visceral, with a swirling motif turning back on itself again and again, as if it couldn't free itself of its tethers. As if it was choking but still couldn't escape.

Until a different note emerged and almost disappeared. She tensed, wondering if she was imagining it. If it was her own audacious hope that she was hearing in the music.

But that note emerged again, like the crest of a wave, like the brilliance of light in a darkened corner. Again and again, until the haunting pain was slowly being washed away by the tremulous hope. The tempo picked up, now the notes of pain and fear being lost among the high notes. It rose and rose until nothing but hope remained. Even that hope was tentative, fragile, a jaggedly painful life but still it glittered.

The high note held and held until it soared like a bird in the sky, stretching every nerve in her tight.

Sophia sank to the floor, her body shuddering at an avalanche of emotions she couldn't even name. Her knees and hands shook, tears running a blistering path over her cheeks.

She felt transformed, like she herself had risen from the ashes, painfully new but full of hope. The beauty of the composition was an ache in her throat. For several minutes—or was it aeons?—she stayed there on the floor, her heart too full to feel anything.

Slowly, her heartbeat returned to normal and the contrast of the silence that descended was deafening. Like the silence a storm left after its destruction.

Luca stayed at the piano. She'd never seen him so remote, so distant, almost as if he stood at the edge of civilization instead of being the charming lover pursued in droves by women.

She pushed herself to her feet. Today she would heed

his unspoken warning for she felt like a leaf that could be blown away by the wind. She couldn't laugh if he told some slick joke. She couldn't bear it if he became that... that travesty of an indulgent playboy when that astonishing beauty, that incredible music, resided in him.

For once, she didn't feel victorious for being right. She felt nauseous and furious and frayed at the edges.

"What did you think of it, Sophia?"

His question stilled her hand on the door. She looked at the dark oak, unwilling to face him. How could he contain so much inside himself? How had he bared a part of him but ripped away something of her?

"It was...interesting," she replied. There was no word that could do justice to that piece of music. All she knew was that she needed to get away from him before she did something stupid like bawl over him...or rage at him with her fists. Was this what came out of those periods of restlessness, those times that he disappeared?

It was like that piece of music had broken open the cupboard in her head and all she could see, feel, were messy emotions roiling in and out of her. She was spoiling for a fight, a down and dirty match. She felt a huge wave of emotion building inside her, battering at her to burst out.

"Interesting?" he said, and she heard a sliver of laughter in that single word. "I think that's the first diplomatic thing I've ever heard you say."

She turned and faced him.

He looked like the same Luca who'd mocked her three hours ago. The same one who had fed her strawberries and cream while she'd worked on her laptop, the same one who'd brought her pots of tea and pastries when she'd worked into dawn. The same man who had licked and stroked her to ecstasy as if it were the one and only reason he was put on the planet.

But he wasn't the same.

She didn't know him at all.

Slowly, she realized what he was telling her. What his slick smile was about—an invitation to join him in the parody he carried out every day. Nausea welled up inside her.

"Whose composition is it?" she asked, giving him a chance, giving him a warning of her own. "It sounds… classical."

He smiled then. And instead of charm, she saw condescension. Instead of genuine amusement, she saw smugly bored arrogance. Instead of miles of charm and insouciant wit and reckless antics, she saw pain and utter anguish and a thin flicker of hope. Instead of a man who went through life in pursuit of reckless pleasure, she saw a brooding, dark stranger.

Like she was at a reproduction of Dr. Jekyll and Mr. Hyde.

"Do you know classical music, then?"

Look at them, holding a conversation as if they were on a first date. Thrusting and deflecting as if there wasn't a storm gathering around them.

She shrugged, preparing herself for the fight. He knew nothing of her if he thought she would back down now. "There were a few months there after my mom and Sal married where he thought I required a little polish. It was a bleak time. There was a piano teacher, ballet classes and even an art teacher. Penguin me and ballet, can you imagine?"

"If you call yourself a penguin one more time, I shall spank you."

"I also now see why Tina was so amused when I called you a peacock."

"What am I, then?"

"A panther."

"Why?"

"Its spots are in plain sight under that black coat. It is more vulnerable than any other jungle cat for, however much it tries, it can't blend in like the other ones. It automatically stands out."

He stood like a statue, with his hands behind him. The man she had thought couldn't be still in any way, the man she'd thought lacked any depth. What a laugh he must have had all this time...

"But we were talking about music, weren't we? I practiced for hours and hours, determined to be the perfect little princess to please Sal. Even though my strength lay in numbers. Mr. Cavalli said I was brilliant with technique, but I played without soul. That for me it was just a means to an end." How right old Mr. Cavalli had been.

Music, music like Luca played, just was. It defied paltry human parameters. It defied night and day; it defied constriction or boundaries. It defied definition of any sort.

"Like a piece of flaky, buttery pastry, he'd say, only without the warm, sugary goodness in the middle. It was such a good metaphor, I was completely horrified and quit. So, yeah...I do know a bit about music."

And before she could regulate the words, they shot out. Like pieces of jagged rocks shattering the carefully constructed glass wall around him. "It's yours, isn't it, Luca? You wrote that piece."

CHAPTER TWELVE

THEY'D HAD SO LITTLE time left. A handful of moments. Of laughter and making love. Of late-night feasts and frantic early-morning sex. He was going to pack so many things into that time. He was going to persuade her the best way he knew to extend the duration of their marriage.

To however long it would take for them to get each other out of their systems.

Now they had nothing.

It was over.

Luca felt a strange kind of relief on one side. That it was all over. The end of things was something he was infinitely familiar and comfortable with.

Hiding in plain sight had never been harder than it was with Sophia. She clawed and ripped, cajoled and kissed her way to the core of him. The rational part of him that reminded him whose son he was and how he had come to be took a beating at her hands.

You are Luca Conti, it shouted in an eternally tireless voice, forever reminding him what he should and shouldn't have. It grounded him. It balanced him.

Then there was the second half. The part that he had never made peace with. The part that craved and gobbled up everything and anything, that demystified the most complex puzzles for him in a matter of seconds.

He'd always thought of it as a yawning blackness, forever hungry.

There was beauty in it; there was intellect in it. And above all, it just was.

And it was that part that was thrashing, wild with grief, already mourning the loss of this woman. The woman who above everyone else had seen and identified it. The woman who promised friendship, companionship, acceptance with her words and demands.

But Luca had a lifetime of practice suppressing this part of him. Or at least ignoring it just enough. Pretending that it didn't exist had only pushed him even more toward the edge. Like Antonio had done with his father.

So instead, he had compartmentalized it. Like a wild dog that was fed just enough from time to time to keep it compliant, to keep it tethered.

He felt Sophia's hand on his flesh and realized how cold he was. Or maybe that was grief, too.

"Luca?"

Turning toward her fully, he answered her. "It is my own. I finished it this last week. Which is why I didn't call you."

Her beautifully intelligent eyes flared then steadied. "A week?"

"*Si.*"

"You don't sleep or stop until you finish it."

He shrugged.

Now the truth lay between them, a dark specter.

He could see that she hadn't expected him to agree. She had guessed it but there had been a small hope that it might not be true. That he was the waste of space she thought him rather than...*whatever freak of nature* he was. It was the same realization he had seen in his mama's eyes for years before she'd left.

The tremulous hope that his last episode of restlessness and headaches and the furiously written music was all just a one off. And the crushing sense of defeat as she realized that he was just like his father. Not just in form but in his mind, too.

As if that wasn't unbearable enough for her.

With Sophia, however, that bucking lasted only a few seconds. He saw, with a strangely detached fascination, the moment she faced the disconcerting truth and accepted it. Her shoulders squared. Stubborn chin lifted, ready to march into battle.

He laughed then. And because he was so weak, and because he had trapped himself without a way out, he hauled her toward him and kissed her. He, the creative genius with an IQ off the charts, he had thought himself so clever. He would seduce her, he would steal a part of her and then go on his merry way. Or he would take and take of her but give nothing of his own self.

What an arrogant fool he was...

At the back of his mind, furious panic was setting in. Like a gathering wave of blackness that would rip him apart. It sent his heart thudding so loud that he could feel it in his throat.

His lips on Sophia's became more demanding, rough, desperate. He wanted to sink under her skin and never emerge. He wanted to drown in her forever. He'd barely breathed the pure, shining wonder that was she before she pushed him away. Wiped her mouth with the back of her hand.

"Is my touch already that distasteful, *cara mia*?" he retorted, unable to keep the ugly jeer out of his tone. Unable to not slide a little into the quagmire of self-pity.

This was what happened when he forgot who and what he was. *Dio*, he became a wounded, raving dog. And if she didn't leave soon, he would take a chunk out of her.

"What?" She glared at him first. Then her eyes lost that

glazed look, her mouth became a purse of displeasure and then she shook her head at him. "You kiss me and I lose all rationality, all common sense. I will not let you sex me up and send me on my way again, with a pat and an orgasm."

Something in him calmed at the matter-of-fact tone. As long as she didn't loathe him, he could still keep his dignity even as he ended the one meaningful relationship of his life. He sighed, folded his hands and leaned against the wall. He would last through this, too. He always did. "Sophia, you are making a big—"

"You cheated me, again. You—"

He laughed. "Even you couldn't rise above making this about you, could you?"

She flushed. "I was just warming up. Your entire life is a lie."

A shaft of anger pierced him and he welcomed it. He never lost his temper, as a rule. There was enough unpredictability in his head and he ruled the rest of it with a tight leash. Trust Sophia to provoke that, too. "My life is what I need it to be."

"And why is that? This is not the dark ages to fear... talent, *no...talent* is such a lukewarm word, isn't it?" Her entire body bristled with the force of her words. "To fear such beauty, such...genius, whatever else it is accompanied by. You can't just...throw it away like this. My God, what is your brother thinking?"

His faith in her wavered then, at the strange light in her eyes. "My brother thinks I have enough problems to deal with without pursuing fame and recognition."

"Fame and recognition, Luca? That's not what I mean. There is such beauty in your music, such pain and hope..." Tears filled her eyes and swept down. "I...I just wish... Looking at you, at the perfect foil your looks and your charm provide you, I can hardly believe it.

"Until I close my eyes and that music moves through me. Then I open my eyes and I see you. All of you."

The sight of Sophia's tears unmanned him like nothing else.

"Why have you made your life into such a travesty? How can you bear to contain all that and breeze through life as if you were nothing? You have made a joke out of a gift—"

It came at him then, fraying the edges of his temper. Anger and self-loathing and utter helplessness. He stepped away from her. It was the helplessness that flayed him. Always. And he knew Sophia wouldn't stop until he laid himself bare in front of her. Until he stood there in all his utterly powerless nakedness. Until he satisfied her, too, that this was all he could be.

"I've never had a choice to be anything else. I do not believe it is a gift."

He saw her blanch then. "The headaches and the insomnia... I'm sure they make it very hard. But you said yourself—"

"You're not listening, Sophia. My father was like this but violent. Antonio neither helped him nor controlled him, with the fear of the Conti name being dragged through mud. Enzo ran wild, buried those headaches in alcohol and drugs. He became abusive. And when my mother told him she was leaving him, he...lost it. He..." His voice broke here, and Luca felt like he was a jagged rock, full of painful edges, never changing. "He forced himself on her. And you know what she had as a result? Me, in his image, every which way."

There it was, his shame. The very cause of his existence. A mass of ugliness shrieking in the room with them.

Acid burned through his throat. He wanted to sink to his knees and cry as he'd done the day he'd found out. He wanted to throw himself into her arms as he'd done once with his brother. He wanted to…take Sophia and bury himself in her sweetness; he wanted to escape in her arms one more time.

But he would not give in to any of those urges.

To not rail at something he could not change, to not become what his father had, that was in his hands. It was his choice to make.

So he stood there, bending and bucking at the fresh grief that tore through him with vicious claws, but refusing to break. For it had been years since he had felt the loss of the freedom to be anything else. But she made the grief and the loss fresh tonight.

Sophia made everything hurt again, ravage him. Everything was excruciatingly raw again.

Her face had lost all its color; tears filled her eyes and overflowed. Luca held her gaze, locked away his own. Crying had ever only made his headaches worse and all his pain was reflected in her clear gaze, anyway.

She didn't utter platitudes. She just stood there unflinching, absorbing everything he threw at her. As if his pain was hers. As if she would stand and fight for him, too. As if he, too, had been accepted into that band of people she loved and protected so fiercely… He had never wanted to belong to someone as desperately as he did then. Never wanted to put himself in another's hands so much.

He never wanted to believe that he could have loved so much.

He weakened then. Almost broke. Until he started speaking again, until he reminded himself. "He was a monster to her. And every time she looked at me, *Mama* broke inside a little. And then I started having these bouts of restlessness, these…episodes. In the beginning, I was barely rational through them. They terrified her. *I terrified her.*

In the end, she walked out. So do not dare to tell me that it is a gift I should celebrate or rejoice. Or share with others. Do not presume to tell me how I should live my life."

He thought he was like his father. That wasn't just Antonio's fear.

It was Luca's, too.

But Luca, unlike half the thickheaded men she knew, was also extremely self-aware, was so much in touch with his emotions. He had to know he was nothing like his father. That he would never hurt anyone.

"Did you ever get violent like him?" she asked, still processing everything he'd told her. He looked remote, painfully alone. This was his cross to bear, she could see. This fear was the invisible wall she'd been throwing herself against.

He shook his head. "No. I… When I was too young to understand, Antonio thought I was just being a boy. But my brother, he understood it. He would never leave me alone, night or day through it. Headaches, or insomnia, or madly scribbling notes on paper, Leandro stayed with me like a shadow. He…helped me develop self-discipline, told me again and again that just because I was a genius that didn't mean he would be my servant. But he became more—he became mother and father and friend to me."

Sophia smiled and nodded, a little of the pressure in her chest relieving. She would kiss Leandro when she saw him next for what he had done for Luca. But there was also panic building inside her. A sense of cavernous loss and a chasm of distance between her and Luca that she couldn't cross. "Then you're nothing like him, are you?" She heard the crack in her tone then. The desperation.

But none of it touched him. "You're a foolish woman if you think I'm not. After everything I just told you."

Standing helplessly there, Sophia realized it then.

That he was like his father was not a fear. It had become his shield against more hurt. More rejection. It was his reason to separate himself from everyone, his reason to loathe himself.

What else could a mere boy do to protect himself against the violent image that he'd been brought into life through such a horrible act? Against a fate he couldn't change? And what torture to be always reminded of it, again and again, of the man who'd wreaked that destruction, to have no escape from it?

Something so beautiful, but tainted in ugliness. Much as she pitied his mother, Sophia was filled with a powerless rage. "She should have protected you. It was not your burden to bear."

For it was nothing but a burden. An unimaginable one. Every inch of her flinched when she imagined how trapped he must feel always. How much he must crave escape from himself…

"How can you blame her of all people?" He was blazingly furious now. But Sophia much preferred him like this instead of that cold smile he'd given her earlier. She preferred the wild, unruly part of him, the part she was sure he hated. "She was innocent in all this."

"So were you!" she yelled, fresh tears pouring out of her eyes. "She could've been stronger for you. She… It was not your fault. None of this is."

"I'm aware of that. You think I have been punishing myself all these years? Do you see the life I have lived?"

She wiped her cheeks and smiled. "No, and I think that is your greatest accomplishment, isn't it? Not that beautiful piece of music. Not whatever mysteries your genius mind can solve. Not the big joke you play on the whole world. You laugh through life, you strut through it, you don't make any apologies for the way you do it…" She was laughing a little and crying a little again. "You…*live it so gloriously, Luca.*"

Her chest constricted, every inch of her yearning to hold him to her, to mold him with her fingers. To feel that hard body against hers and tell him that he was loved. That he was the most glorious, wonderful man she'd ever met. That he'd filled her life with courage, and laughter and love these past months.

That he was better, more than any man she'd ever known.

Genius or not, Luca was generous, kind, magnificent. But now that she knew the reality of him, now that she had heard his music, there was no escape. Her fate was tied to his.

She had toppled into love and it was exactly as she had feared. Her knees were skinned, her body bruised, her heart already taking a beating. And after all her careful maneuvering through it, after being strong for so many years, he was going to rip apart the very fabric of her life.

For there was no light in her world without him. No laughter, no joy, no color. She was nothing but the drab, colorless, staid Sophia.

His poisonous hatred about his genius, his self-loathing, it all stood there like a dark, forbidding stone wall that she couldn't climb, much less conquer. An almost tangible thing rushing him away from her, blocking her. "You live this life you've been given, Luca. I can't help but admire that."

Something flashed in his face then—relief or peace—and she thought it might be a small chink in his armor. A tiny crack in that impenetrable wall. "Then we are in agreement, *si*? Because I thought we could make this a more permanent arrangement. With some ground conditions."

The offer was made with a tease, a lighthearted tone. But it was full of wretchedness, too. For he also knew what it meant if she hated the other part of him. If she agreed it was a shame to be hidden away because now she knew where it came from.

She could see it all in his face, she understood his complex mind so well. Not now, but eventually, he would hate her a little for what he was already doing, too.

She was damned if she did and damned if she didn't. Despair gave way to anger. How dare he decide their fate like this? Who had given him this right to govern her joy? "No, we're not in agreement. I will not hate, I *can't* hate something that is part of you. Like you do. I won't pretend. I can't look at you and not see all of you. The masks have come off—there's no going back, Luca."

"I didn't realize you have a love for such melodrama."

"Drama? You think I choose this any more than you choose to be what you are? I accept the part of you that flitted from woman to woman all these years because you thought that was the only kind of connection you could have. So I must accept this, too. Please, Luca." She reached for him then. "Don't you see I understand?"

He stiffened, his features haunted. Pain was a live thing in his eyes then. "You see me as broken now, and I can't stand it. I have never pitied myself and neither will you."

Her own fury rose, fueled by fear. Why wasn't he seeing what he meant to her? She wasn't the sentimental sort; she didn't know how to make big declarations. She didn't even understand half of the riotous emotions coursing through her right then. All she knew was this: they could not end that night, not over this. "Do not presume to tell me what I feel about you, then."

"I have given you everything I'm capable of, everything I have, Sophia."

"I have found that place, Luca, the place where I want to dwell. By your side. Just don't ask me to pretend like I don't know the true you now. I can't unsee you. I can't unhear that music…" But even as she said it, she knew nothing would change his mind.

His beliefs about himself were bone-deep, a disease that would steal him away from her. He would never accept himself. And he would never accept what she felt for him.

He had not left her with an illusion of her strength, either; he'd left her nowhere to hide. Reckless, he'd ripped it all from her and now she had nothing to fight him with.

Such powerlessness flew through Sophia's veins that she wanted to throw something at the wall. She wanted to beat her fists into something and feel the crunch of bones.

But she did nothing like that. Sensible as always, she realized the futility of a violent tantrum. There was nothing to do but wait and hope that he would let her in again. That years of deeply held self-belief might shift.

She reached him and laid her hands on his shoulders. Her fingers moved over the slopes of his neck, the jut of his collarbone, the warm, taut stretch of skin over muscle.

He didn't reject her touch. He didn't return it, either. The man who always, *always*, touched her as if he couldn't bear it otherwise, who had taught her what it was to touch and kiss and learn another, didn't touch her now.

Head bowed, he stood there like a statue, a warm, wonderful man who'd all but ripped a vital part of himself and kept it away.

She kissed first one cheek and then the other. Masculine and sweaty, the scent of him made her blood sing. The clench of his muscles as she wrapped her arms around his naked back… She was aware of every breath in him as if it were her own. Finally, she clasped his cheek and kissed his mouth. Poured every bit of her into that kiss. "If only

you would give me one chance—yourself, one chance—
Luca. Give this thing between us one chance…"

Sophia turned and left his studio. His world. And a huge
part of herself with him.

It took Sophia three weeks and a clip of Luca dancing with
a seminaked burlesque dancer in a night club in Paris—
circulated by Marco Sorcelini—to realize Luca wasn't
coming back.

When she'd discovered from Leandro that Luca had
left not just Milan, but Italy, the morning after that painful
night, something inside her had frozen. She had packed it
all away, told herself that he needed time to figure it out,
to stop running. After all, the fear that he could be like
his father, the ugly truth that he should have never had to
face, that isolated lifestyle he'd made into an art form, had
a decades-deep grip on him.

It had been his shield against more rejection, against
pain.

How could he let go of those beliefs just for her? How
could she expect him to, after knowing her for only a few
months?

Interestingly, it was a discussion prompted by her stepfather that had torn the blinders from her eyes.

Sophia had returned from work at almost eleven when
she'd seen Salvatore waiting for her in the study. Knowing that she couldn't indefinitely avoid her parents' concern, she'd joined him. She was exhausted, sleep-deprived
and she'd caught the first hint of the rumors about her record short marriage.

No one woman could keep the Conti Devil…
Conti Devil seeking new distractions…
Conti Devil flees Italy and his marriage…

Her cheeks hurt from the number of times she'd tried to keep her expression calm.

Salvatore offered her a glass of water and peered at her patiently while she finished it off. "Sophia, have you decided what you're going to do?"

"About what, Sal?"

His dark brows had gathered into a frown. "About your marriage. I think it is better for you and Rossi's if we see a lawyer immediately. Now, I have—"

Wretched fury burst out of Sophia. Her whole adult life, it was all she'd heard about—the Rossi Glory, the Rossi Legacy. "Is Rossi's all you care about?"

Salvatore blanched. "*Non.* I worry about you, too, Sophia. But after years, Rossi's is benefitting from the Conti family's influence and it is better to separate your marriage from the business as—"

"Christ, Sal! Rossi's is not thriving because of Leandro or Luca or the great CLG. But because of me! I'm the one who turned the company around. I'm the one who..." Shameful tears blocked her throat; Sophia looked away from him. But the tears had also released her fear.

She had had enough of lying down and taking what she was given. Tired of fighting for a place without actually demanding her due. Like a faithful dog happy with scraps.

That infuriatingly slick charmer had been right in this, too.

Looking thoroughly befuddled, Salvatore took her hand in his. "I have loved you like you were my own—"

The dam broken, Sophia snatched her hand away. Words were so easy. Staying behind lines, worrying about Sal's fears, justifying Luca's past as reason enough for his current cowardice... It was all so easy. "Do you truly, Sal? Then why not trust me with your great Rossi legacy? Why have you never considered me to be your successor? After all, I've worked damned hard to be here. I'm the best thing that's happened to the company in years."

And just like that, Sophia fought her own insecurities, ripped away the cocoon of self-delusion she'd built for herself. Even then, guilt about her family and her love for this abrasive but inherently kind man almost took her out at the knees. "I have only ever worked to make Rossi's whole again. It is my company as much as it is yours. But unless you see that, unless you give me the role I deserve, I quit, Sal. Tonight, now. Consider this my official resignation."

Sophia had barely turned around when Sal stopped her. Her tears ran down her cheeks, a testament to what the cruel Luca Conti had done to her again.

Hands on her shoulders, Sal lifted her chin, quite like he had done when she had been thirteen. Black eyes filled with regret and concern and a gruff sort of tenderness. "You will forgive an old man his old prejudices, *si*, Sophia? You are right. You are and have always been stronger than any son I hoped for. Rossi Leather and its future, they are all tied to you. You are its future, *bella*. Forgive me, *si*?"

When he pulled her into his warm embrace, Sophia broke down into shuddering sobs. She cried for herself and for Luca, wondered if he would ever come back.

That night, desperate for a little connection to him, Sophia packed a bag and went back to Villa de Conti at the stroke of midnight. If Leandro and Tina thought her a little mad, they didn't betray it by word or look. Her throat had filled with tears when they had silently stood in support while she wandered through Luca's room like a wraith.

He'd given her everything—a chance to save Rossi's, an opportunity to explore her potential, a new family that somehow seemed to love wholeheartedly despite their differences, and more important than anything else, her belief in herself.

What was she supposed to do with all the riches in the world when he wasn't there? What was pride when her heart itself was broken?

She lay awake in the bed she'd shared with Luca countless times and cried again. It was time to face another truth.

Her foolish belief to wait and hope that Luca would let her in again was nothing but sheer cowardice. The deep freeze that seemed to have settled around her heart ever since that night, her self-possession, her brittle calmness in the face of the rumors flying about Luca dumping her after three months of marriage was nothing but docile acceptance of his decision. A habit that was as embedded in her, it seemed, just as Luca's fear was.

Instead of fighting and scratching and kicking her way into his life, she hid beneath her fake strength. She had even started withdrawing from society, afraid of facing their pity, or scorn or both.

She'd done this the last time, too. Instead of confronting him, she'd quietly slipped back to her life, accepting his decision. Not this time.

Not when she knew that the kind of intimacy and connection and laughter that she and Luca had shared came once in a lifetime. Not when she knew they were made for each other. Not when there was so much love to be filled in both their lives if only…

If she had to break Luca to make him face himself, face Sophia and her love, she'd do it. If it was destruction he wanted, she would hand it to him. She would shatter every pretense he'd carried out, rip apart every lie he'd weaved around himself.

And maybe when there was an end to all the things he

clung to, an end to the farce, an end to life as he knew it, maybe then they could have a new beginning.

But one thing was sure: she wasn't giving up without a fight.

CHAPTER THIRTEEN

Two months later

LUCA WALKED INTO the high-ceilinged breakfast room of Villa de Conti and stilled. Shock rippled through the room, a tangible tension in the air. His family looked up at him—relief the more prevalent of emotions flitting across their faces.

"Where the hell were you?" Leandro shouted across the vast room, his legendary self-control absent. "*Dio*, Luca! You could've been be lying dead in some part of the world for all we knew."

"*Papa*, you're shouting and swearing," Luca's seven-year-old niece, Izzie, piped up.

Luca raised a brow at his brother. "If I die, you would hear."

"We know you're not dead." This was Tina. "You made sure we all knew what you were up to."

Something in her gaze caught Luca and for once in his life, he shied away from his little sister. Had he changed or she?

Izzie lifted her arms to him. "I missed you, *Zio*."

Here was another one of the female variety from whom he'd never been able to hide. He lifted her from the breakfast chair and buried his face in her sweet, strawberry-scented hair. Something loosened in his gut.

Small arms clutched his neck tightly. He pulled her tiny

hands from around his neck, kissed her cheek and put her back in her chair.

His sister-in-law, Alex, was next. Usually, Alex, who was slender and willowy, coming at him was like holding a bouquet of dainty summer flowers. Pleasant and leaving him with an utter sense of well-being, of deep, unwavering affection. Of the innate goodness of life.

Heavy with pregnancy, when she threw herself at him today, though, Luca wavered on his feet and smiled. Her grip was just as tight as her daughter's around his neck. "You worried the hell out of all of us. Are you well, Luca?"

A lump lodged in his throat and he nodded.

What a fool he'd been... He'd denied a part of himself for so many years. And in the process, denied himself so many good things, too. He kissed Alex's cheek soundly, knowing it irritated Leandro. "You still won't run away and marry me, *cara*?" He said it loudly and saw the scowl on his brother's face.

Alex pulled back from his arms, ran a shaking hand over his cheek and laughed. "Bigamy, I believe, is a crime in Italy, too, isn't it?"

And just like that, the pressure on his chest returned.

Dio, he felt like he walked around with a permanent boulder on his chest. Or he was developing some serious heart trouble. Personally, he preferred the second. At least he could get it treated.

But no such luck.

He was in the peak of his prime, a physically perfect specimen of mankind. Although, lately, he'd begun to loathe himself less for what was inside, too.

He kissed Tina's cheeks, leveled a cursory nod at Antonio and sat down.

The scent of coffee and pastries filled the air, the tinkle of coffee cups and cutlery discordant in the awkward silence. Izzie finished her milk and toast, hugged him again, sought reassurance that he wouldn't disappear again and left the room.

Luca waited, his breath pent up in his chest, his fingers not quite steady.

They were looking at him, and then shying away. He put his coffee cup down so hard that half the coffee sloshed over his fingers. "I haven't gone mad, so everybody can breathe easier." Only the frown on Antonio's face relaxed.

He had to give his dear old *Nonno* some points for constancy—always a little afraid for Luca.

Leandro shrugged. "I never thought you would."

All his brother had ever done was tell Luca that he had a choice to be like their father or not. But Sophia had showed him that the choice was not just to be different from his father. But he had the choice of accepting himself, too. Of being happy in his own skin.

"Destroy every chance at any happiness you could have, like I almost did? *Si*," Leandro continued. *"Fall into some kind of mad abyss and froth at the mouth? Non.*

"What Enzo did or was, what resides in you, that is not our legacy, Luca. What we do with our lives, is. Aren't you the one who told me that?"

His throat full of unshed tears, Luca nodded. And then he asked the question that had been tormenting him all the way through his trek through the markets in Marrakesh. Through the deserts of the Middle East and the cold winter of Prague.

Through endless parties and long lonely nights even in the midst of crowds. Because Sophia was right. His mask was off and he was tired of pretending that he was worthless. He was tired of acting as if what he had was enough.

For years he'd made an art form of running away from himself. But he couldn't run away from Sophia and his thoughts of her. He couldn't run away from the man she made him to be, the man she thought him to be.

"How is she?"

There, he was bare naked again. With no place to hide, no mask in place to retreat behind if it hurt. No shallow facade to reject before being rejected. It was not a feeling he was going to get used to anytime soon.

"Ask her when you see her."

"Why am I seeing her?" He wanted to, desperately. But for once in his life, he didn't know what he was going to say. All his charm, his quicksilver mind, nothing really helped when he lay awake for long hours wondering what he would say to her.

How he would beg.

"She's taking you to the cleaners," Leandro added with quite a relish.

It would serve you right if I took you to the cleaners.

The shock on Luca's face deepened his brother's smile. "Her exact words. She wants a huge divorce settlement."

Divorce? She was talking divorce? Had she decided he wasn't worth it, after all?

Luca's heart sank like a stone, leaving a gaping void in his chest. Had he self-destructed, then? Had he become that self-fulfilling prophecy? Had he lost the one woman who'd loved him despite the fact that he hadn't deserved it? And he couldn't blame it on what Enzo had passed on to him. No, this was all his doing.

Merda, was it all over already?

"I told you to give her my share of the Conti stock," he offered numbly. Suddenly, his world felt emptier than it had ever been before.

This blackness, this yawning stretch in front of him, this was what would break him. His love for Sophia, that was the only thing that would knock him out at the knees, he realized now. Not some pre-decided genetic sequence. Not a lack of control.

Living without Sophia's love, returning to the meaningless, empty tomb of his life, would send him to madness.

"To quote, 'It costs him nothing to give it away, that bloody stock.' She doesn't want it, Luca." When Luca glared at him, Leandro shrugged again. "Don't shoot the messenger. You left me here to deal with her and she is on a warpath. She wants your personal fortune, your studio, even your countless pianos. Apparently, everything you have ever hidden, everything you have ever made through your *genius*, she wants it. And your antics all over Europe with all those women, you have given her lawyers enough rope to hang you with."

Why say no to CLG stock when it would give her a seat on the most powerful board in Milan? When it would mean the culmination of all her dreams?

She had him utterly baffled, more than a little disconcerted, and he was supposed to be the genius. *Did she hate him so much, then?*

He hadn't left her any other choice when he had left Milan in the dark of night, when he'd made sure tales of his escapades had reached every big media outlet that had chased him. His cruelty haunted him now.

Dio, what had he done?

Leandro wasn't quite finished.

"She has discovered, *to her delight*, her words again, that you're a millionaire a hundred times over. 'Your dear brother is full of little secrets, isn't he?' Her lawyers are quoting 'emotional distress, spousal abuse and abandonment of marriage' as grounds for divorce. Even society's sympathy lies with her. Sophia Rossi is not only clever, she's extremely resourceful."

"What the hell do you mean *society*? This is between me and her."

"No, it's not. It is a scandal now, another Conti spectacle like the last one...like Enzo started. Alex and I can't step out without being hunted by the media. Sophia and Salvatore are talking about *your separation* to everyone who will listen. There was a featured article last week that hinted you were the mastermind behind the innovative waterproof sole technology we use in Conti pumps and those gravity-defying metallic stilettos that made us big globally."

"Huang?" Luca said. "She spoke to Huang."

Leandro nodded. "They are all speculating what you've been up to all these years to have made so much money. They are all questioning your behavior all these years, wondering if you're like Enzo. She made you a person of interest to every rabid newspaper, every network station. I...I can't control what they get their hands on, Luca."

Wave after wave of shock barreled at Luca. Now he understood the gravity in his brother's voice, the concern in those gray eyes.

If someone found out about his birth, if they knew that the same hungry cavern dwelled in his mind, too, the same fear and distaste he saw in Antonio's face would appear in everyone's...

He put his head in his hands, his breath sawing through his throat. Was this all just to hurt him as he had hurt her? Would she reveal the circumstances of his birth, too? Would she make the world think him a shame, as he'd thought of himself for so long? Would she—

"*She is outing me.* She's telling the world who I am," he said, his stomach clenched so hard he couldn't breathe.

Leandro finally leaned back in his chair. "I believe so. Nothing I could say would convince her otherwise."

Luca groaned, the sound coming from the depths of his soul. The groan morphed into laughter that made his lungs burn. He felt like he was caught by an eddy, tossed around this way and that. He laughed until there were tears in his eyes and he was shaking, shivering with relief, with the release of fear and so much love that he couldn't even breathe.

Hands on his temples, he ducked his head, waiting for the dizziness to abate. Tears poured down his cheeks, and he wiped them with shaking fingers.

With his breath returned the image of Sophia that had tormented him for months.

Sophia with her heart in her eyes, her body shaking violently as she kissed him and told him that she accepted all of him. That all he needed to do was give them a chance, a real one.

Sophia, who would not take defeat lying down. Sophia, who fought to the last breath for the people she loved. "Please tell me you did not threaten or manipulate my wife in any way?"

Something flashed in Leandro's gaze. Leandro seemed to have frozen as if he could not believe it. As if it was impossible that Luca had finally, irrevocably fallen in love. "She has also already turned around Rossi's stock. According to some of my sources—"

"Your sources?" Luca demanded. "You are having her watched? Guarding your company?"

"I was worried about her, Luca. So is Salvatore. She works like a demon, she… The news about you that has reached us, she…she has not been the same. Salvatore appointed her CEO of Rossi Leather.

"Her idea for a flagship design store in the midst of Milan's fashion district made the CLG board salivate. The store will display every new product line weeks before they actually hit the market. It will become the center of every designer event in the city. But she fought for her stepfather like a lioness, said it was her family's legacy and they finally voted to call it *Casa Rossi*. Ten designer brands, including Maserati, are going to be part of her inaugural event tomorrow night."

Despite fear beating a tattoo in his blood, Luca nodded. He had no idea if Sophia would take him back, but he meant to spend the rest of his life begging, hounding her, chasing her, generally turning her life upside down. Like she had done with him. If he had to spend the rest of it on his knees, naked and shivering, he would do it.

If he had to spend the next hundred years waiting for her forgiveness and her love, he'd do it happily.

"I have never met a woman quite so ferocious," Tina added with no little pride in her voice.

Ferocious and funny and far too softhearted, the woman he'd fallen in love with was too good for him. "You take her side over your gorgeous brother's?" Luca threw at Tina.

"Since I have discovered that my brother is a donkey's behind, *si*." Tina waited for Leandro to stop laughing, a serious light in her eyes. "Since she has done me the favor of telling me the truth. Since she's the only one who treats me as a grown-up woman and not a commodity to be protected or controlled. Or used as a bargaining chip in blackmail."

Instantly, all humor evaporated from the air. Tension rippled across his shoulders and he saw the same in Leandro's face. Anguish danced in his brother's face and for his sake, Luca hoped Tina would forgive Leandro.

She threw the last words viciously at Antonio, her voice breaking. Antonio, whom Tina had loved so unconditionally, had the grace to look ashamed.

"What truth?" Luca finally managed to say. It seemed

Sophia had left no stone unturned in opening their family's vault of secrets.

"That I am not a Conti. That my father was a poor chauffeur *Mama* fell in love with after she left you and Leandro. That my older brother, the Conti Saint, set up my marriage to Kairos because he thought I would fall apart if the truth ever came out and a powerful, handsome husband could make up for it. That my second brother, the Conti Devil, married her to keep my power-hungry husband from breaking my heart. I think I prefer your way, Luca. If I had to choose between one of you manipulating my life as if it were a chess board."

"Tina, *tesoro*, I'm so—"

Tears rolled down Tina's cheeks as she cut off Leandro. "I'm not angry, Leandro. At least not anymore, now that I have had time to recover from the shock. All you and Luca have ever done is love me, *si*? You could have hated me for *Mama*'s abandoning of you. You could have left me to my own fate when she died. I am your sister and nothing could change that. But I look at Sophia, I look at the state of my marriage, and I realize what a naive fool I am. I am leaving Kairos. And Milan." *She was leaving them both.*

Luca reached her the same time Leandro did. He held her tight while she sobbed. Luca had never been more proud of his little sister.

Fear danced in Leandro's eyes, and Luca shook his head in warning. His brother's job for years had been to protect Luca and Tina. But it was Tina's life now.

Luca kissed her cheek while Leandro compulsively said, "Where are you going? Will you stay with friends? You will tell us if you need help, *si*?"

Tina laughed at Leandro and hugged him tight. "I am an adult, Leandro. I can take care of myself. You're to stay out of this thing between Kairos and me. But *si*, I will keep in touch, although only if you tell me what state Sophia leaves Luca in when she's through with him."

A weight lifted from Luca's chest and he hoped Tina would find happiness in her new journey. He found himself frantically praying to a God he had only ever hated before.

"You're a genius, *si*?" she said to him, exaggerated doubt in her teasing tone.

Luca nodded.

"Then, *per piacere*, do not lose the most wonderful thing to ever happen to you."

Casa Rossi, the first major designer store of Rossi's after its reinvention and the lounge bar on Piazza San Fedele, glittered on its opening night. Creamy white carpet and sofas, with different designer pieces from every noted brand on the shelves, made the space an intimate, exclusive event.

Pink champagne flowed freely, designer-clad men and women walked around and talked and got noticed by people they wanted to be seen by. More than a few people had approached her. Sophia had no doubt it was more to feed their own curiosity than anything else.

Because she'd dragged the venerable Contis into an out-and-out war. She refused to let Luca hide. She had been terrified when Leandro had come to see her but refused to back down.

Already the list of people who wanted to be invited to the next event was growing exponentially according to her assistant. Sophia had quickly looked through and struck off some of the men who'd called her quite a range of names over the past few years.

She adjusted a buttery-soft white leather clutch, still amazed at the success of her idea. Where Conti Luxury Goods entered, the entire range of companies who had once turned away from Rossi's joined in. The gray wolves were all walking behind her now, like domesticated dogs, following the line of meat to Rossi's.

Luca would so totally get that, she realized with a laugh. She'd have to tell him and then they would make fun of… And just like that, the painful knot in her stomach returned.

Two months since that night. She'd been pitied, smirked at, laughed at, that she had thought herself good enough to take on the Conti Devil. She'd turned her very life into a circus, herself into a cheap act for him. To make their marriage, its failure and Luca the focus of every rabid gossip in Milan.

Already, so many things had come out about him. Luca had to face himself. Accept himself. Only then was there a chance for them…

Having given up even a pretense of pride, which was all she had these days after making such a thoroughly public and humiliating spectacle of herself, of manipulating everything to lure him out, she'd begged Tina to tell her if she'd heard anything from him.

Hysterical that their fates had reversed. Now Tina was the stronger one, the one who told Sophia her brother wasn't worth it while Sophia became a shadow of herself.

She lay awake at night, aching in mind and body, worked like a demon during the day…and it was taking its toll on her. This…faith in him, in her, in their love, the laughter they'd shared, it was burning out now.

What was she going to do if he never returned?

And then she heard it, the soft strains of music coming from the lounge bar beyond the foyer. It had a piano but she had actively looked away from it, for it had the power to send her to her knees now.

This was what he'd made of her. She, who had never been afraid of anything, was now scared of pianos, and music, bikes, the streets leading to the Piazza del Duomo, and couldn't look at chocolate truffles without breaking down into sobs.

Suddenly, a strange silence replaced the soft chatter. And in that silence came that music again, the point in that vicious circle where it was trapped. Sophia felt like she was living the song.

Heart in her throat, she walked to the lounge.

There he was. He sat at the piano, his head bowed, his fingers flying over it. White shirt and dark trousers, hair wet and gleaming, shoulders fluid. Soft pink light filled the room, casting flashes of light on him. Teasing and taunting her. Driving her utterly mad.

Sophia blinked.

It had to be one of her feverish dreams in which she heard that tune again and again, in which she saw him look at her with that hunger and desire, in which she felt his hands on her, holding her, touching her, driving her out of her own skin. In which she saw him poised over her wet sex, his expression one of utter reverence and wicked desire.

She could feel him between her legs now and she clutched her legs closed tighter.

Her heart thumped. Her breath stuttered. She felt feverish. Tears threatened to spill over. She leaned against the far wall and closed her eyes. She was so cold, exhausted. Like she was breaking apart again and again.

And then the tune rose to its pinnacle, hope and life twisting together.

"Stop, please," she yelled. It did.

A frisson went through her and then she felt him in front of her.

His warmth. The scent of his skin. The air charging around him.

Her eyes flicked open.

Dark shadows under jet-black eyes. Wide, wicked, sensually carved mouth. Blades of cheekbones. Perfectly symmetric planes of his face.

The most beautiful man she had ever seen.

The man she loved beyond bearing.

She extended her arm, fluttered her fingers over his cheek. Ran her thumb over the sweep of one cheekbone and then over the defined curve of his upper lip. Her fingers kept sliding away from his face, so violently was she shaking. She felt his fingers clamp her wrist and hold her hand there against him, leaning into his touch.

She felt the pulse in his neck against her hand, frantic and hurried.

She felt his breath on the back of her palm, frenzied and rough, as if he had run a great distance to find her, instead of prowling from one corner of the room to the other.

She felt him, all of him and she shuddered violently. Her heart slammed against her rib cage.

He *was* standing before her. He was finally here. He had returned.

Sophia drew her hand back and slapped him across the cheek. So hard that his sculpted jaw went back and shock jarred up her arm. The sound of it reverberated in the silence, propelling her out of her nightmarish state. "Leave me alone," she whispered, her voice on the verge of breaking.

He didn't move. Didn't utter a word.

Only gazed at her with glittering eyes. Even in the pink light, Sophia could see the mark she'd left on his cheek. Desperate, panicky, words came and fell away from her lips.

Please stay. Please want me. Please love me.
Please don't ever leave me like that again.

No, she wouldn't beg.

She made to push away from him but he moved faster. Trapped her against the wall, his arms bracketing her on either side. He said nothing, though, only stared at her, held her like that as if he was completely complacent in that position. As if he was content to hold her in place and gaze at her for eternity.

She kept her gaze at some far point in the distance. If she stared into those eyes, she would break permanently.

"Will you not look at me, Sophia?"

"I hate you. I...despise you. You...are exactly what I always thought you were," she spat at him, her dignity, her self-respect, everything in tatters. Her strength nothing but a shadow in the face of her love for him. "A heartless bastard who can see nothing past his own bloody genius, nothing past his own demons. You were partying with your... damn groupies while I...I..." And then she fell against him, hate and love inseparably twining into a rope, binding him to her. "If you kissed a single one of them, Luca, if you have even touched one with a long pole...I'll kill you with my bare hands." Only then did she raise her eyes. He had never lied to her, but this... She needed to see the answer for herself. "If you so much as... This is over. We are over."

"*Non, cara mia.* I couldn't even look at another woman. I...was a bastard. For those first couple of weeks, I wanted to make sure you hated me. Your words that night, they haunted me. They hurt me. They mocked me. I thought I would give you all the reasons in the world to hate me. I thought I would shake that resolve in your eyes, show you what I truly was.

"But, *Dio*, I couldn't go through with any of it. For the first time in my life, I realized what I had lost and that it had nothing to do with being my father's son. That it was

I that was ruining my life with my own actions. I promise, *cara*, I could not look at another woman but you."

Something small and tenuous built inside Sophia again. Hope had never terrified her like that. "I did hate you. But I couldn't shake off that faith in us. Is that what love is? This blind, illogical, irrational faith in the man who tears you apart so recklessly when all you've done is love him? I have no more, Luca. I'm done loving you."

He shuddered around her, like a flash of lightning in the sky. His lean body jerked and settled around her again. "You did all this to make me face myself. You would give up on me now?"

She felt his hands move through her hair, his nose buried in it, her name a mantra on his lips. He held her gently as she sobbed her heart out. Two months of tears, two months of fears…two months of staying strong for him. "Sometimes, I feel like you have taken everything from me. Like a bus carried me away from everything that I loved. Like I will never breathe properly again. Like I will never be free again.

"I hate being in love. So much. I… It hurts so much."

"Shh…*tesoro mio*. Shhh…please, Sophia. No more. I can't stand the sound of you crying." She heard the tension rise in him, too, heard the catch in his voice as if he, too, was breaking down.

He pushed away her hair from her forehead, wiped the remaining tears from her cheeks. Gently, oh, so tenderly. "I…ran so far, so fast, that night. But you…you were already a part of me. You… Everything was so colorless, Sophia. Even music could not soothe me. And then I saw myself. As you saw me. And I realized this life that has brought me to you, I could never hate it. *Ti amo, tesoro.* With every breath in me. Will you let me love you, Sophia?

Will you give me the chance to be the man you deserve? I swear, *cara mia*, I will never hurt you again."

Sophia threw her arms around his neck and held him tight. Breathed in the scent of him. He was solid and male around her. "Yes, please, Luca. Love me. Spend eternity with me." He breathed a sigh, relief maybe, and held her tightly back. She gave herself over to Luca's love. Her heart was his already.

EPILOGUE

Three years later

"I'VE BROUGHT SOMEONE to see you, Mrs. Conti."

Sophia whirled around at that voice so fast that her head spun, her heart climbed up into her throat. She had seen them only this morning before she left for work, but her heart still ran away from her at the sight of them.

It was only three weeks since she'd returned to work after a six month maternity leave. But she missed spending those lazy mornings in bed when Luca would bring their bawling bundle into their bedroom and all three of them would cuddle, play and sometimes just fall into exhausted sleep after a cranky night.

Luca stood at the door, with the baby basket in hand, wicked mouth curved wide in a smile.

Her assistant, Margie, was faster than Sophia in reaching the new arrivals. She took the precious bundle instantly away from his father and cooed over him, before Sophia had even managed to breathe normally. "You're lucky, Mrs. Conti," Margie said in between the baby gibberish she spouted to their seven-month-old son. "You've got the two most gorgeous men in Italy chained to you."

Sophia looked at her beaming son, gave him a cuddle and a quick kiss before Margie stole him away from her again. "I do, don't I?" Laughing, Sophia met Luca's gaze.

White shirt and blue jeans hugged her husband's lean figure. Blue, ever-present shadows under his eyes. Stubble on his jaw, because he wouldn't have found time this morning to shave. He looked thoroughly disreputable, for once, the very image of the crazy genius he was, and heartbreakingly gorgeous.

"You left without saying goodbye this morning."

Her heart still racing, Sophia sighed. "You looked dead to the world." She knew how little sleep he managed.

"Yes, but I don't like you leaving for the day without kissing me goodbye."

Reaching Luca, she threw her hands around him while he took her mouth in a fast, scorching kiss full of frantic hunger. The same desire flooded her limbs and all she wanted was to steal away with her man for an afternoon of pulse-pounding sex, like they hadn't indulged in a while. Her sensitive nipples peaked when he stroked inside her mouth with erotic expertise that to this day stole her breath. That made her want to be just this wanton creature who made the sexiest man rock hard, and forget all her other roles—daughter, aunt, CEO of a multinational company and even a mother.

Pulling back slowly, he sank his fingers into her hair. Eyes glittered full of wicked invitation. "Take the afternoon off," he said, mirroring her very thought.

Sophia kissed him and drew back quickly before he could ensnare her again. "Even if I did, what about your son? He gets crankiest before his afternoon nap, remember? Takes after his father, the devil."

"He's an angel. Just look at him."

Dark-eyed, dark-haired, with a charming toothless grin, Leo was a mirror image of his father. The look in Luca's eyes when he had held their son for the first time had almost crushed Sophia's heart.

There had been fear, and wonder and hope and so much love. He had lifted the squalling infant in his arms so tenderly, tears running down his cheeks. And then he'd met her gaze. "He looks like me," he'd said then, a sort of helplessness in his voice. As if it broke his heart a little, all over again. "*Dio*, Sophia, what if he…he is like me, too?"

Luca's scars had healed, but not vanished.

Sophia had been crying, too. But she had stayed strong for him. She'd clutched Luca's free hand with hers and squeezed tight. "Does it matter who he looks like when we love him so much? He's a piece of our hearts, isn't he?"

It had taken them only twenty-four hours, however, to realize their son, notwithstanding his cherubic looks, had the temper of the very devil. Within two days he'd reduced Sophia to hysteric tears and a dark fear that she couldn't even calm her own son.

Packing them into his Maserati, Luca had driven them around all night, lulling them both into frantic sleep. The next night it had begun all over again. Until Luca had started playing the piano.

Only those two things calmed Leo enough to sleep every night now.

The smallest disruption to his schedule, and Leo was known to scream at decibel levels that could rupture unsuspecting eardrums. A thing that seemed to endlessly amuse his two cousins, the perfect little girls they were. "Why couldn't I have a beautiful little doll like Izzie or Chiara?"

His arms around her, Luca nuzzled her neck. "You know what we could do if you want a girl, *cara mia*."

Sophia snorted. "No way. I haven't even lost half the weight I've gained. I wish men gained weight when their wives got pregnant. It's not fair that you…you continue looking like you do while I look like a baby elephant."

"Watch that mouth. That's my lovely wife you're talking about." He pressed a kiss to her temple, reverent and tender. "I love you just as you are, Sophia. I wouldn't change a single thing about you. I would change everything about my past, everything about myself, to prove it, if I could."

The regret and pain in his tone was like a lash against her skin.

He accepted her for everything she was, flaws and all those little eccentricities, and she loved him, too. That she'd hinted, even unknowingly, at denying him that same acceptance was anathema to her.

"Si," Sophia whispered urgently. A shiver went through her and he held her tighter. "I do. And I trust you, Luca."

Even to this day, she woke up sometimes in the middle of the night, saw him next to her on the bed, usually hogging all the sheets and pushing her to the edge of the bed in his need to hold her tight, and wondered at how much this gorgeous, beautiful man loved her.

And how deeply and how completely. The wonder in his eyes when he looked at Leo and her every day, it humbled her.

"Did you really want a girl, Sophia?"

Sophia locked her hands on top of his, settling into his arms. "Not really. Although I do worry sometimes."

"About what?"

"I think of the future, and I'm sure I'll dread mornings where I have to leave you two at home and walk away. I imagine coming home to a disaster zone."

"Are you saying I'm going to spoil our son?"

"I know you're going to spoil him rotten. And I'll have to be the strict one."

He nipped at her shoulder, his lowered voice a caress. "But you do strict so well, *bella mia*."

Melting on the floor of her office was not an option so Sophia snorted instead. "I see that you're not even saying no."

His hands tightened around her waist, pressing her into his front. The length of his erection was a brand against her back. Her mouth dried, a rush of wetness pooling at her sex.

Sophia caught the moan in her throat, thanking Margie for discreetly walking away with their son to her private sitting area.

In the short time she'd been back at work, Luca and Leo's visits to her workplace were already the highlight of the day for all the women in the office. Everyone wanted to hold her son, and everyone wanted to see Luca—the infamous playboy turned devoted husband and doting, stay-at-home dad—tease, taunt and make their strict boss blush. Or so Margie had told her when Sophia had asked why there was always a rush on their floor during lunchtime.

"I have asked Alex if she'd watch Leo tonight," he said now, swiping that clever tongue over the very spot he had dug his teeth into at the crook of her neck. "She said yes. She also said she was surprised that it had taken us this long to ask her. She *also, also* said she would be keeping tabs, that the minute she hears that Leo's sleeping better, she expects us to take Izzie and Chiara. Even if we have to rip away the little one from my brother's hands."

Sophia laughed. Leandro was so protective of the girls that it took all of Alex's energy to ensure they had the freedom that little girls needed to run around and express themselves.

On the opposite end of the spectrum was her husband,

who praised their little boy for his perfect aim when he threw his bowl of mashed peas across the room like it was a soccer ball. Luca had converted a whole room in his studio into a kid-safe playroom for Leo, who even as a seven-month-old challenged himself into how destructive he could get each day.

"The whole night? Is he ready for it, do you think?"

His fingers laced with hers, he held her tightly. "He is. Are you?"

It was both alarming and a little guilt-inducing to see how easily Luca had taken to fatherhood. He loved doing everything from morning to night without a single complaint. His energy, it seemed, was boundless.

He had watched Leo the whole night for weeks, only bringing him to Sophia for feeding. While Sophia had struggled, Luca had decided it was the perfect cure for his insomnia.

"I know that right now, you know more about his habits than I do, but I thought maybe—"

"Shhh, *bella*. Didn't we talk about this? You've got nothing to feel guilty about. I love looking after him. I love bringing him to visit you here. I love seeing the glow you get when you work your ass off and you make a win in this world. This is our family, Sophia. Our life. This is what works for us. You've worked so hard to get here and it's not like I'm ever going to work a nine-to-five job."

"Yes, but I'm worried that you're not getting any time to yourself. And that you'll probably resent me sometime in the future, or think I'm not—"

"I love you. All of you. The woman who bawled like a baby when she held our son the first time, the woman who told her stepfather, in an uncompromising tone, that she and only she, could run Rossi's the best, the woman who resurrected Rossi's from its broken state, the woman who fought for me like a lioness, the woman who cries every time I play the piano.

"And that woman, that is who I fell in love with. That is who made me see a future full of love. Don't you dare change on me now, *cara mia*.

"I'm aware every minute of every day that I have this happiness, this love, this family with you and Leo because you're who you are. I adore you, *cara mia*, more every day."

Tears pricked at Sophia's eyes, a lump in her throat blocking any words from coming out. Even if she was capable of them with her heart swelling in her chest. She turned and buried her face in his chest.

God, she loved him more and more each day, too. And sometimes, the depth of that love, the power it gave him over her, the possibility of her entire life falling apart at his hands...it choked her, too. That fear was becoming less frequent, though.

When Luca loved, as she'd learned in the last three years, it was with such unerring devotion, it was with such absolute giving, that it filled her with awe.

She squeezed him for all she was worth. "Okay, you and your son have to get out of here if I'm going to take the afternoon off."

Desire glinted in his eyes. *"Si?"*

"Yes, but not for what you're thinking."

"What, then?"

"Shopping," she whispered against his mouth. She stroked her tongue into his mouth and pressed herself against him. His erection was a long, hard length against her belly. Darts of desire shot straight down to her pelvis. "I need new lingerie. Lots of red and black lace, I'm thinking, and those stilettos that I hear are new in the market."

He groaned and leaned his forehead against hers. He was breathing hard as if he'd run a mile. "I guess I should shave, then."

She ran a hand over his jaw, loving the bristly texture against her palm. "No, no shave," she whispered at his ear. Laughing, he hugged her one more time and Sophia thought life couldn't get any better.

* * * * *

In case you missed it, book one in
the LEGENDARY CONTI BROTHERS *duet*
THE SURPRISE CONTI CHILD
is available now!

Uncover the wealthy Di Sione family's
sensational secrets in brand-new eight book series
THE BILLIONAIRE'S LEGACY *beginning with*
DI SIONE'S INNOCENT CONQUEST
by Carol Marinelli
Also available this month